The Secundus Papyrus

Albert Noyer

THE SECUNDUS PAPYRUS

The Toby Press

The Toby Press
First Edition 2003

The Toby Press LLC
POB 8531, New Milford, CT. 06676-8531, USA
& POB 2455, London WIA 5WY, England
www.tobypress.com

ISBN I 59264 034 6, *paperback*

A CIP catalogue record for this title
is available from the British Library

Typeset in Garamond by Jerusalem Typesetting

Printed and bound in the United States by
Thomson-Shore Inc., Michigan

With special thanks to the writing group:

Jennifer, Melody, Mary, Frank, Russell
and
Leslie S.B. MacCoull Ph.D.
Society for Coptic Archeology (North America)

Fallite fallentes: ex magna parte profanum
sunt genus: In laqueos quos posuere, cadant.

Deceive the deceivers;
they are mostly an unrighteous sort.

Let them fall into the snare they have made.

Ovid, *Ars Amatoria*

Getorius Asterius	Surgeon at Ravenna, son of Treverius and Blandina
Arcadia Valeriana Asteria	Wife of Getorius, training with him to be a medica
Flavius Placidus Valentinian III*	Emperor of the Western Roman Empire
Licinia Eudoxia*	Valentinian's wife, Empress
Galla Placidia*	Mother of the emperor, daughter of Theodosius I
Theokritos of Athens	Palace Library Master
Feletheus	Assistant to Theokritos
Brenos of Slana	Abbot of the Abbey of Culdees at Autessiodurum
Fiachra	Secretary to Brenos
Sigisvult	Architect of the mausoleum of Galla Placidia
Surrus Renatus	Archdeacon of Ravenna
Flavius Aetius	Supreme Commander of the Western Roman Army
Publius Maximin†	Wealthy senator at Ravenna
Prisca Maximina	Wife of Publius Maximin
David ben Zadok	Rabbi of the Judean community at Classis
Nathaniel	Rabbinic student of ben Zadok
Charadric	Guard at the palace, friendly to Getorius
"Smyrna"	Gallican League's secret contact at Ravenna

* Real people recorded in history
† The character Publius Maximin was based on the real person Petronius Maximus but as his role in the novel was largely fictionalized, his name was changed.

GLOSSARY OF PLACES MENTIONED

GERMANY
Mogontiacum—Mainz Treveri—Trier

FRANCE
Aballo—Avallon Forum Julii—Fréjus
Arelate—Arles Genevris—Genévre
Autessiodurum—Auxerre Lugdunum—Lyon
Cabillonium—Chalons-sur-Saone Massilia—Marseilles
Cularo—Grenoble Narbo—Narbonne
Flavia Aeudorum—Autun
Culdees—"Friends of God" fictional monastery at Autessiodurum

ITALY
Albinganum—Albegna Florentia—Florence
Augusta Taurinorum—Turin Forum Livii—Forli
Caesena—Cesena Genua—Genoa
Classis—Classe Mediolanum—Milan
Faventia—Faenza Ravenna—Ravenna
(Somewhat fictionalized)

HIBERNIA (Ireland)
Clonard—in County Meath
Slana—Slaine

RIVERS
Arar—Saone Rhenus—Rhine
Bedesis—Montone Rhodanus—Rhone
Icauna—Yonne Sinnenus—Shannon
Padus—Po

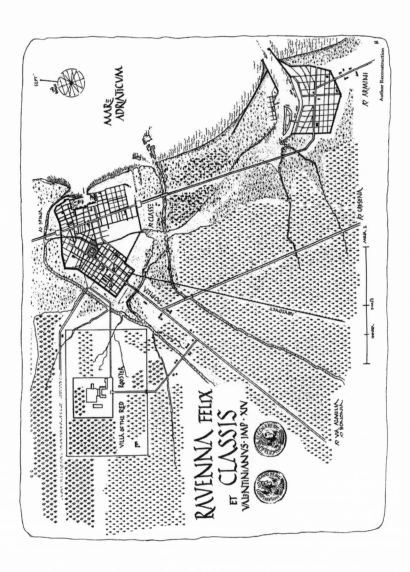

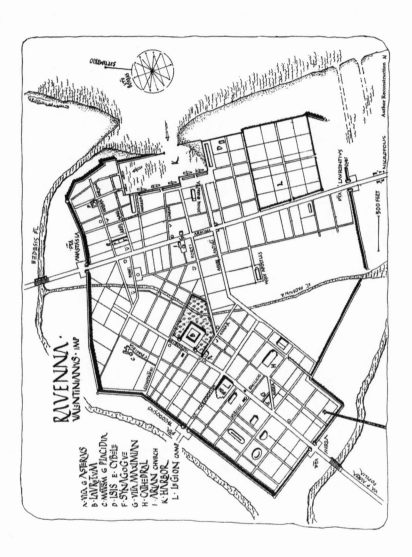

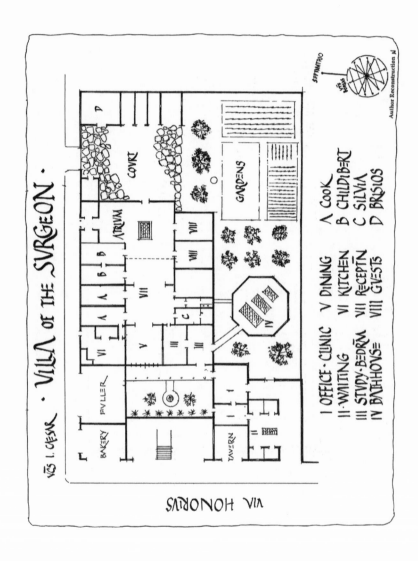

VIA HONORVS · VILLA of the SVRGEON · VŌS I. CÆSAR

BAKERY · PVLLER · TAVERN · ATRIVM · COVRT · GARDENS · SEPVLTVRO · Author Reconstruction N

I OFFICE·CLINIC   V DINING   A COOK
II·WAITING   VI KITCHEN B CHILDIBERT
III STVDY-BEDRM   VII RECEPTN C SILVIA
IV BATHHOVSE   VIII GVESTS D BRISIOS

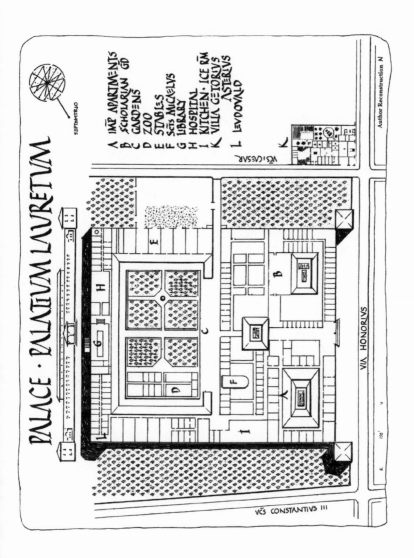

Ravenna

Chapter one

Emperor Valentinian III halted his horse to take in a deep breath of the chill November air, pungent with the scent of evergreen resin and the musty odor of decomposing leaves. A less pleasant fishy smell, from marshes on the nearby Adriatic seacoast, also filtered into the earthy fragrance of the pine forest.

The emperor grinned at a jay that scolded his intrusion from the top of a dead tree. It was good to be hunting in the forest outside the imperial capital of Ravenna with only his two bodyguards, Optila and Thraustila, even if it was only for a few hours. Inside the palace, he, Flavius Placidus Valentinianus, the Augustus of the Western Roman Empire, still had to endure the endless nagging of his mother, Galla Placidia.

"'Placidus, you *must* take more interest in the government,'" he mimicked in a falsetto voice to the jay. "'You spend too much time, Placidus, with your filthy Hun guards.' 'You should pay more attention, Placidus, to Licinia and your baby daughter.'"

Licinia Eudoxia…pregnant again. Valentinian frowned at the thought of his young wife. He had been married to his cousin for two-and-a-half years, and half that time she had been pregnant, or

3

sullen at having had to leave the Eastern capital of Constantinople. Marriage had been exciting at first, but now it was boring. *Thank a lucky zodiac moon sign that Heraclius can always find me any number of slave girls who are willing to do anything for a bronze coin they can stash away toward buying their freedom.*

The jay called again, a harsh warning this time, but Optila, nearby, had already seen the boar.

"There, August-us," the guard whispered in Hunnic-accented Latin. "In clump of sumac to right."

Valentinian squinted in the direction of the fire-orange bushes. The boar stood rigidly still, with only a glimpse of its angry red eyes and breath vapor visible. Snorting, the animal tried to assess the danger from the intruders. Valentinian slowly brought up his bow and let a feathered shaft fly. A sharp squeal of pain betrayed that the beast had been hit, yet rather than charging, it turned and shambled off into the forest's dark-green shadows.

"*Caco!*" Valentinian spat out. "Shit!" He clucked his horse forward into the sumac, ducking his head low to avoid being bruised by the tangle of branches, trying to keep the boar in sight. Optila, with Thraustila behind, followed to help track the wounded beast.

As Valentinian deftly guided his mount between the pines, he heard a splash of water ahead—the boar had crossed a stream that flowed eastward into the tidal swamps of the sea.

"Zeus, let the furcing beast go," he muttered, reining in his horse at the waterway.

The two Huns halted a short distance away. Thraustila unstoppered a calfskin bag to share gulps of wine with his companion.

While his mount guzzled from the stream, Valentinian picked gobs of pinesap off his leather vest and brooded. Between his wife, his mother, and army commander Flavius Aetius, life was becoming increasingly unpleasant inside the Lauretum Palace. Eudoxia was merely bad-tempered, but Galla Placidia had gotten more critical—of practically every piss he took. *Mother resents giving up her hold on me now that I'm twenty and married. Well, she'll have to furcing well live with it. Aetius, secure at being big shot Supreme Commander of the*

Western Roman Army, still treats me like a child. His strutting around reminds me of those two ostriches that the African galley master just brought in for my palace zoo.

After the Vandals captured Carthage in October, Valentinian, as Emperor newly freed of Galla Placidia's regency, had had to sit in on endless emergency meetings with his ministers. Something about African grain no longer being available and the threat of bread shortages spawning riots in Ravenna. Aetius even worried that the city of Rome itself was in reach of the barbarians, by way of Sicily, because the Arian sect bishop on the island had promised to shelter his fellow believers.

Aetius again. *After he drove that barbarian, Theodoric, from Narbo in Gaul, then came back to Ravenna, the Senate appointed him Consul for the second time. Yet the bastard never came to report to me, his emperor. He resents the fact that he has to deal with me now, not mother. The only person I can trust is my eunuch steward, Heraclius.*

Valentinian spat and glanced around. He was in a small clearing. Although he often hunted in the vast forest outside Ravenna called *Pini,* the Pines, and knew the stream, he had not been to this particular location before. Trotting his horse along the left bank of the waterway, the emperor noticed a hut a few paces downstream, half-hidden among the evergreens. He surmised that it was a woodcutter's shelter and reined his mount toward the hovel. There might be smoked pork, wine, and bread stashed away inside.

Optila and Thraustila each took a final, gurgling swig from the wineskin, wiped mouths on sleeves, then clucked their horses forward after him.

At the bank opposite the hut, Valentinian's mount shied, almost throwing him to the ground. He regained control then looked down to see what had frightened the animal.

"Wh...what the...?" he stammered at the unexpected sight.

A man's body bobbed stiffly in the icy stream, his arms out-stretched in a cruciform stance. He was naked except for a cloth that swaddled his genitals. Both feet were pressed against a small rock dam in the current, which kept the thin, white body bizarrely jerking in place.

Valentinian recognized the man's tonsured head and pale features. "It's that Hibernian monk who comes to the palace library," he scoffed. "I heard that the fool does this kind of penance…staying in the water until he can't stand the cold any longer."

Optila laughed, then dismounted and knelt beside the stream to take a closer look. The monk's eyes were open in a sightless stare.

"Shave-head in trance, August-us," he called out. "I wake him up." The Hun poked at the monk's midsection with the end of his bow, but the body only continued its grotesque bobbing motion. After a sharper jab at the torso, Optila looked up, his grin of amusement replaced by a puzzled look. "It not trance, August-us. Shave-head dead!"

"Dead? Then that stupid monk's done his last penance." Valentinian made the customary sign, small crosses against forehead and heart, more from superstition that piety. "The shock of being in that icy water must have killed him."

"Who was he, August-us?"

"Named Behen, Behan, something like that," Valentinian replied with a shrug. "Came here from someplace in Gaul."

"August-us Val-tin," Thraustila called out, "order palace healer to come see body. Don't want to be blamed for this."

"You won't be blamed," Valentinian assured him, "but Antioches is too old. He'd probably die before getting out this far."

"Young healer on Via Cae-sar healed my knife wound," Optila recalled. "Send him."

Valentinian hesitated. Perhaps his two bodyguards had the right idea about bringing out a surgeon to see the body. Peter Chrysologos, the Bishop of Ravenna, would surely be informed of the hermit's death. And after his mother found out, Galla Placidia would pester him about details. Better that a surgeon confirms the Hibernian had accidentally drowned. That would end the affair.

The jay returned and settled on a branch to clean its beak against a branch. Valentinian eyed the crested, blue-gray bird, reminded of why he had come to hunt in the Pines.

"Optila, you bring that surgeon here in the morning," he ordered, reining his horse away from the stream and its grisly occupant. "Let's flush out another furcing boar. Right now I've got a real taste for wild pig meat at supper tonight."

Chapter two

Arcadia looked at the thin white corpse of the monk lying on the rough boards of the hut's table, and then turned to her husband. "Getorius, why did the judicial magistrate ask *you* to come out and examine Behan?"

"Antioches is too old—restricts his practice to the palace," he replied in a curt tone. Getorius set his instrument case down hard on the seat of the only chair in the room, muttering, "The real question is why you came out here with me."

"I heard that, Husband. I'm training with you to be a medica, remember?"

"Right, but you don't need to see this, Arcadia," he said more gently. "A drowning victim isn't a pretty sight."

"I told you before we married that I wanted to study medicine," she reminded him, her greenish eyes meeting his blue ones. "It didn't seem to bother you then. Let's just examine the poor man."

"August-us sent messenger to abbot of Shave-head at Autess-odurum," Optila volunteered, standing at a distance from the body.

"Autessiodurum? I think that's in central Gaul." Getorius

frowned. "Even with luck it should take, what, over thirty days for someone to come this far in winter? It'll be close to the feast of the Nativity by then."

"What will happen if Behan's abbot doesn't authorize burial here?" Arcadia asked. "Does Bishop Chrysologos have jurisdiction over the body?"

"I don't know, but it's a good thing the weather's turned colder. Optila, look around outside for anything that belonged to the monk. I thought I heard a rooster crowing."

Getorius turned back to his task. "Let's start. Bring my medical case over here."

Arcadia paid no attention to his brusque tone. Examining the body of a fellow human was always unsettling, and he was already annoyed with her for insisting on coming along.

While she held open the leather box, Getorius studied his array of bronze probes, tweezers, clamps, and surgical knives. He indicated an instrument in the top row of the kidskin-lined case, "The long probe. I'm not exactly sure of what to look for here. The holy man must have surely died from exposure. His body is as white as Germania's snows."

"And as cold." Arcadia noted the monk's glassy stare. "At least shut his eyes."

Getorius grunted and closed his fingers over the dead man's eyelids, then began an examination of his head. The sunken cheeks were shadowed by beard stubble, which was studded with bare scar spots. A few splotches reddened the pale skin, and scabby lesions crusted the shaved portion of his ear-to-ear tonsure.

"When did Behan die?" Getorius abruptly asked his wife.

"When?" Arcadia gritted her teeth and lifted the right arm to test its flexibility. It was somewhat rigid, but she knew the monk's emaciated condition and the cold water would have retarded rigor mortis. Her estimate was a hesitant question, "Since...since about the last night hour of the day before yesterday?"

"Possibly. It's still dark then, so Behan began his last penance before sunup."

"Poor man,"—Arcadia touched the pale skin stretched over the monk's prominent rib cage—"so thin."

"Probably lived mostly on bread, with fish now and then. Not exactly banquet fare."

When her husband scraped at small red spots on the dead man's forearm, Arcadia bent down for a closer look, then blurted out, "He had the pox!"

"Ah…*cara,* these are old insect or mosquito bites," Getorius corrected with an indulgent smile. "We're near offshore marshes, remember?"

"Sorry," Arcadia mumbled and plucking self-consciously at her hairnet, resolved to be more observant next time before voicing a diagnosis.

Getorius traced his fingers over the skin, pausing at white scars where Behan had been injured and healed, and wondering if some of the wounds had been self-inflicted as penances. He touched a reddish welt around the neck, then used the probe to examine inside the monk's mouth. Arcadia turned away to keep from gagging and looked around the hovel.

The walls were constructed out of upright pine poles interwoven with thick willow branches that had been chinked with sandy mud. Daylight showed through the coating in several places where it had crumbled and fallen away. Three rough boards on the dirt floor partly covered with a gray blanket, and a rounded wooden block, served as Behan's bed and pillow. Yellowish evergreen needles lay strewn on the bare earth around it.

Arcadia stepped around a circle of rocks framing a pit in the center of the floor. The depression was filled with cold ashes and partially burned sticks. An iron kettle hung over the pit from a chain attached to a pole rafter. *The monk's kitchen.* When she noticed a clothes chest that was carved with beautifully intricate Celtic patterns, she thought it an incongruous vanity for someone who had renounced worldly goods. In contrast, Behan's simple eating utensils lay on top—a wooden trencher and spoon, an iron knife, and a brass cup stained with a green patina.

The sturdiest article of furniture was a slant-top writing desk with a storage cabinet beneath. It stood by one of the walls, to the left of a window covered by a parchment skin that admitted light but kept out the cold. Examining the items on the desktop, Arcadia saw pots of ink, a box of quill and reed pens, and an erasing knife arranged toward the left edge. Next to them a smooth river stone kept three rolled-up manuscripts from sliding down. Above the desk, a shelf sagged under the weight of several books.

Behan's belongings certainly reflect the reported passion that Hibernian monks have for writing and literature, she thought.

Glancing from the bookshelf to the narrow door through which Optila had brought the body, Arcadia saw a short rawhide strap, with knots tied on the ends, hanging next to the frame. It made her recall the bruise on the dead man's neck.

"Getorius," she called out, examining the strap, "there's a thong here that looks like it might match the welt on Behan's throat. Could he have been strangled?"

"By whom, and for what reason? No, Behan obviously drowned." He beckoned to her with the probe. "As long as you *are* here, do you want to examine him as part of your training?"

"I…I suppose so."

"What were those books you were looking at?"

"See for yourself," she said, taking the probe with fingers increasingly stiff from cold.

Getorius watched her begin searching gingerly around the dead man's head, then turned away to examine the books.

Jerome's recent translation of the Testaments propped up smaller volumes. Getorius skimmed past a codex by Bishop Eusebius, an account of early Christianity up to the time of Constantine, and several pamphlets, then took down a parchment-bound booklet. Its title page was written in a language and alphabet style he had not seen before, but from the Latin subtitle, REGULAE ABBATIS CIAL-LANI, Getorius surmised it was a list of rules formulated by Abbot Ciallanus, who had recently brought Hibernian monasticism to northeastern Gaul.

Getorius brought the volume to Arcadia. "Do you recognize this writing?"

She glanced at the page. "It's probably Celtic. Behan did come from Hibernia."

"Celtic. Interesting. I didn't think it was being written much any more."

"He is...was Hibernian, so it's logical Behan would write in his native language."

Getorius grunted agreement, put the book back, then unrolled and studied the three manuscripts on the desk. "One of these is in Latin," he called to Arcadia, "but the other two also seem to be Celtic. Hmm, they have three-word groupings and phrases...like short verses. I'm taking these back with us until someone from Behan's order claims them. His belongings too. Bandits will clean this place out of anything we leave behind."

Arcadia stepped back, moved the instrument case, and sat down on the chair, trembling slightly. "I...I think I'm finished."

Getorius came behind her, kissed his wife's hair, and began to knead her neck muscles. "Does this help relax you, *cara?*"

"Mmm, nicely," she murmured.

"Sorry I was a little curt with you earlier. What did you find out about Behan?"

"Well, that long scar on his right leg was from a nasty gash. Probably by an ax while he was cutting wood. It fits with the fact that he was left handed."

"Good, you noticed." Getorius gave her neck an affectionate squeeze.

"He has slightly larger muscles in that arm," she continued, "and the palm has thicker calluses. Also by the position of his desk and writing instruments next to that window."

"Very good, Arcadia. Anything else?"

She stopped his hand and turned around. "He *did* have the pox at one time."

"Yes—pock marks on his face and chest. What about that welt on his neck? You still think he was strangled?"

"With that strap. It's obvious to me."

"A holy man of God murdered?" Getorius sounded skeptical. "I can't see that anything's been stolen…not that he had much anyone would want. Even that clothes chest probably contains only a spare cloak and tunic. His books are the only real things of value."

"All right! His heart stopped pumping because he drowned. Galen wrote…"

Getorius interrupted his wife: "Galen never dissected a human body!"

"Surgeon, neither have you," Arcadia retorted softly, realizing it was a point of contention with her husband. "Yet, you also think the heart works like a pump."

"Fine," he conceded, "Galen did recognize it as a pumping organ, but he thought it circulated pneuma, some kind of invisible animating spirit. Ridiculous!"

Although Galen had been dead for almost three centuries, Arcadia knew Getorius became vexed whenever he discussed the ancient physician whose ideas still dominated medicine. She decided to return to her conclusions about the dead monk.

"Behan wasn't old. *Can* we determine exactly how he died?"

"I might be able to diagnose things like that more accurately if the bishop would let me dissect the body of one of those beggars who die every day."

"Optila thinks Behan drowned."

"So do I." Getorius agreed. "Let's find out. Use that speculum to keep his mouth open."

"This one?"

"No, the smaller one."

Arcadia winced as she inserted the bronze dilator into the dead man's jaws, and then helped her husband turn the body and ease Behan's head over the table edge. Mucus dribbled to the floor. When Getorius pushed hard on the monk's back, a gush of water and phlegm spurted from the open mouth. Arcadia fought again to keep from retching.

"The Hun was correct about drowning," Getorius concluded.

"Behan may have fallen into a trance and not been aware of what was happening. Let's get him faceup again."

After the monk's body was again lying faceup on the table, Getorius took the rough blanket off the bed and laid it over the corpse. "I'll have a wicker cage made. The body can be put inside, then put back into the stream so cold water will preserve it until the bishop hears from Behan's monastery." He glanced around at the room's furnishings. "Call the Hun inside. We'll carry some things back with us."

"Just a moment." Arcadia went to the doorframe and disentangled the strap, then compared its width with the bruise on Behan's neck. "The welt *does* match the strap, Getorius."

"Would a murderer bother to come back inside and replace it on the door?"

"Behan could have been strangled here, then his body put in the stream."

"Why go to all that trouble? And, as I said, there's no motive."

"None that we know of," Arcadia retorted. "*You* get Optila. *I'll* carry the books out to the cart."

Stubborn female. "Fine, we'll take only the books, desk, and clothes chest." Getorius gathered up the three manuscripts, wondering if Theokritos at the palace library could translate them.

❦

After helping load the two-wheeled cart and propping the hut's door shut against wolves, Getorius sat next to his wife on the chest, in front of the desk. Arcadia had put on a full-length beige wool tunic and shawl against the cold. After pulling an elk-skin pelt over their knees, she leaned against the desk's back. The five-mile journey back to Ravenna would be an uncomfortable one.

Arcadia glanced up at the cobalt November sky that played host to a brilliant sun. *At least the afternoon has warmed up a bit.* She took a deep breath of the keen odor of pines to dispel the rancid taste of the monk's hut that was still lodged in her throat, then snuggled against Getorius' shoulder.

Optila guided the mare as it pulled the jostling cart along the rough path Behan would have used to reach the Via Popilia, a stone-paved road that led north to Ravenna. Getorius was silent until the cart turned off the lane and slid into the ruts of the Popilia.

"I'd seen Behan in the library a few times, when I'd gone to read medical texts," he recalled. "He's been here about two years, yet I don't know a thing about him."

"Perhaps Theokritos does."

"I'll ask him." Getorius slipped an arm around his wife. "You've been quiet since we left the hut. Are you thinking of Behan?"

"Partly. I was also remembering the story of how you came to Ravenna."

"That's an old scenario, but it does read like one of Plautus' dramas."

"Except the plot is so implausible that it would be hooted out of the theater." Arcadia sat up and kissed her husband's cheek. "Still, tell me about it again, Getorius. It was a tragedy, yet it eventually brought us together."

"Nicias told me the story. He was the legion surgeon at Mogontiacum and knew my parents."

"Treverius and Blandina."

"Yes. I was four years old when Burgondi warriors attacked the city. They were both killed in the bloodbath to make a usurper, Jovinus, emperor, but Nicias and some men from the garrison managed to escape and take me with them. They wanted to get to Ravenna."

"But, after that unhappy beginning, Fortuna certainly cast dice favorable to Nicias and you."

He nodded. "And that's the unbelievable part that would give Plautus trouble. Nicias happening to meet Galla Placidia while she was on her way to Gaul, and her brother at Ravenna being the Emperor Honorius. She gave Nicias her ring and an introduction to him."

"And Placidia remembered Nicias when she returned to Ravenna..." Arcadia reached for her husband's hand. "Fortune... God...someone was looking out for you."

Getorius blew on her cold fingers. "And for Nicias. Placidia made him palace surgeon." Remembering, he looked away at the lengthening shadows of the evergreen forest that hemmed the road, then added softly, "He was the only father I really knew."

"Nicias took care of you and trained you to be a surgeon."

"I'm grateful, and now *cara,* I'm training you to be a medica. Despite the archdeacon's opposition."

"Surrus Renatus thinks wives should only manage their husband's households. Did you know there's a woman presbytera at the Arian sect church in town?"

"A woman?"

"I think her name is Thecla."

"Well, Arians *are* also considered heretics."

Arcadia pushed his arm in mock annoyance. "You mean that I'm one by not following a woman's tradition and wanting to be a physician?"

"You'll be a good one, *cara.*"

"Yes I will. And," she jested, "after you're made palace physician, I'll take over our clinic."

"Being surgeon to the Augustus and his family could be a deadly honor. Anyone who serves inside Lauretum Palace is undoubtedly caught up in court politics."

As the Via Popilia neared Ravenna, the pine forest gradually gave way to patches of farmland. On either side, marshes lay as flat as Behan's table. After the road passed under one arch of the aqueduct that supplied the city from the Apennine springs, skeletal poplars and the green-black spears of cypress trees began to line ditches bordered by the peculiar yellowish earth that had been reclaimed from swampland. Dormant gray vines tied to high trellis supports and distant, tile-roofed white farm buildings gave occasional relief to the monotonous landscape.

The Via Popilia crossed a small river, then, about a half mile before reaching the city walls, the road angled sharply to the northeast. As the cart careened into new ruts on the roadway, Arcadia tightened her grasp on Getorius. When Optila half-turned to see if his load and passengers were safe, the flattish profile of his Hun ancestry was evident.

As the cart approached the bridge over the southern arm

of the Bedesis River, which went on to encircle Ravenna to the north, cultivated land gave way to marshes once again. Earlier that morning the glittering expanses had been shrouded in autumn fog, but under the late afternoon sun the smooth surfaces sparkled like dancing pearls. Beyond the bridge, the Porta Aurea was bathed in warm sunlight, momentarily living up to its name, "The Golden Gate." The portal gave access to the ancient quarter of the city, the Oppidum, and dated back some four hundred years, to the time of the Emperor Claudius.

Massive round brick towers flanked the Aurea's twin marble entranceways. Slouching sentries, eating chunks of roast pork impaled on their daggers, waved Optila through. A beggar on crutches hobbled forward, saw the Hun driver, muttered something, and walked back to the shadow of the portal.

Inside the wall, Arcadia saw the familiar roofline of the Basilica Ursiana and the square end-towers of Lauretum Palace. To the far right, a cluster of masts marked the port quadrant of the city, where merchant galleys could moor in a protected harbor, after being rowed in from the Adriatic Sea. Getorius wondered what was happening at the old naval base of Classis, two miles to the south. With the new Vandal threat at Carthage, hopefully war galleys would be under construction, or older ones refitted. He frowned when he thought of the legion camp on the Via Armini, where Ravenna's garrison was billeted. There never seemed to be much training activity there, or on the adjacent Campus Martius.

"Flavius Aetius can't seem to get the men to train properly," he muttered aloud.

"What, Getorius?"

"Our barbarian mercenaries. They're the butt of every tavern jest," he complained.

"But the Augustus had to open enlistment to Goths, didn't he?" Arcadia probed.

"Ever since Theodosius ordered it, yes, but it was a decision of desperation. Officers still train the men to fight in a line, behind shields. No room to maneuver against an enemy like...like Huns, who attack as suddenly as Jupiter's thunderbolts."

Arcadia gestured toward Optila with her head, but the driver gave no indication that he had heard the remark. "Husband," she asked, "how did you get to be such an expert in military tactics?"

"I don't read only medical texts, you know."

Fragrant smells of baking bread, food frying in olive oil or lard, and roasting meat and fish, were heavy on the late afternoon air. The rays of the setting sun tinted the brick and stucco buildings a pale vermilion, even lending a temporary splendor to the damaged temple of Apollo, closed now for half a century. Further on, the shadowed front of the Basilica of Hercules acted as a backdrop for a colossal statue of the demigod. He stooped on one knee, supporting a hemisphere on his shoulders whose flat top surface was a solar and lunar hour dial.

Stalls in the new market square on the north side of the Via Theodosius were almost empty of customers; only a few slaves still bought bread and meat in the shops along a plaza colonnade. Subdued babble came from taverns, where patrons were eating supper. As they passed the public baths opposite the old forum, Getorius nudged his wife. The resident white-bearded philosopher was on the rostrum again, haranguing a scattering of idlers who were interested—or amused—enough to indulge him.

When Optila guided the mare onto the Via Honorius, a cold northeast wind buffeted the cart. Arcadia pulled up the elk skin, suddenly aware of how much her back ached and rump hurt. It would feel good to relax in the warm pool of her bathhouse.

Getorius's villa, "The House of the Surgeon," as it was commonly called, had been deeded to him by Nicias. It was located just south of Lauretum Palace, at the intersection of the Honorius with the Via Julius Caesar. The villa had a separate wing for the clinic where patients were treated. A side facing the Honorius was built into a second story whose lower level was divided into shops, including a fuller's cloth works and a bakery. The latter's bread aromas helped mask the unpleasant odors from the fuller, who used urine to set his dyes.

Nicias had designed the rooms to be ranged beyond the atrium, rather than around it. The villa's main entrance was located off the Caesar, near the carriage gate, where a side door led from a courtyard into the house. Beyond the stable and the quarters for Brisios, the gatekeeper and gardener, were a small apple orchard and plots where herbs were grown. A walled garden of trees, flowers, and a fountain at the west end of the house provided a cool haven from the summer heat.

The unique feature of the building was a separate bathhouse with the same sequence of tepid, hot, and cold baths as the public one. Arcadia looked forward to the water's comfort. After the unsettling experience of examining the monk's body and the long, bone-jarring ride, it would be good to relax with a long soak in the warm pool— and perhaps entice her husband into some slow love-making.

Optila reined in the mare for the turn into the Via Caesar. The gatekeeper, Brisios, had been watching for him and opened the courtyard portals. He grasped the horse's bridle as the cart rolled through the opening.

Getorius helped Arcadia down, gave Optila a gold *tremissis*, and watched the Hun walk across the street toward the palace barracks, before the gatekeeper closed the portals again.

"Brisios," he ordered, "store that desk and chest in the stable. We may have to keep them until someone arrives from Gaul. Take the books to my study."

"I will, Master."

"I'll take these three scrolls myself," Getorius told his wife, "but I'm too tired to do anything with them right now."

"I wonder if we've had patients today. Childibert will know."

The end of the atrium facing the villa's rooms was curtained off from the cold. Childibert, their Frankish house steward, had evidently heard them arrive. He pushed aside the drape and held up a letter.

"You must read now," he said in a Latin corrupted by his guttural Germanic accent.

"Who is it from, another creditor?" Getorius quipped, taking the white vellum note.

His question was answered when he turned it over and saw the flap sealed by a blue wax lump stamped with the signet of Galla Placidia. Underneath, Valentinian III had traced his monogram through a template. Arcadia glanced at the twin imperial signatures.

"Take the letter to our bedroom, Childibert," she ordered. "Good news or not, we're going to wait until morning to open it."

"What?" Getorius objected. "It…it's from the Augustus and his mother. We can't wait."

"Ask Silvia to bring towels to the bathhouse," Arcadia added, ignoring her husband's comment. "Tell her no one is to disturb us. We may eat something later on."

"Are you insane, woman?" Getorius persisted. "Placidia is my patroness. Her son is emperor."

Arcadia waited until Childibert was gone, then confronted Getorius. "I notice you didn't say '*they* are my patrons' and you're right. Galla Placidia, not her son, still runs the palace. *Patroness*? Were *you* made palace physician after Nicias died?"

"I was still young."

Arcadia turned away to open a clothes storage cupboard. "I'm changing into my night tunic. I need a soak in the tepidarium, Husband, and so do you."

⁂

When Silvia brought the towels to the bathhouse, she also lit three lamps and a silver censer that gave off aromatic smoke. Her eight-year-old son, Primus, carried in a pitcher of warm wine mulled with honey and mastic, spilling some as he poured two wide-mouthed cups too full.

Arcadia sighed. "That's fine, Primus. Leave the cups near the edge of the pool."

After the boy and his mother had gone, Arcadia dropped her tunic on the tiled floor, knelt to swallow a gulp of wine, and then slid into the warm water. Getorius followed her.

While he clung to the rim of the small pool, she massaged his shoulder muscles, then came around to sponge his face and touch at the gray hairs that interlaced with his black ones. She thought he looked tired, and rubbed at the creases in his forehead, wondering how much of his Celtic ancestry was reflected in his features.

Nicias had said that Getorius's father was born at Treveri, in northern Gaul, yet had not spoken much of his mother, other than saying that Blandina had also had Celtic ancestors. The name Getorius was a Latinized form of that of an ancient Treveri chieftain, Cingetorix, and a diminutive of Getorius' grandfather's name, Cingetorius.

Arcadia's ancestry was Roman, going back to Campania. Her father told her that adventurous forebears had emigrated from there to Ravenna, to serve in Augustus Caesar's new fleet. She wondered what a child of theirs would look like, and recalled that she had not inserted the acacia juice pessary she used as a contraceptive.

The tepid water was relaxing. Reaching for the wine, Arcadia took a sip and passed the spicy drink from her mouth to her husband's as she clung to him. When she felt him harden against her thigh, she brought her legs up around his waist and eased him inside herself. Eyes closed, holding onto his neck with both arms, she began a gentle thrusting motion that sent wavelets lapping over the pool's edge and soaked their tunics. Arcadia quickened her rhythm to match the rate of Getorius's breathing, then paused to let the pleasurable sensation ripple through her own body and isolate them from the world outside, to concentrate on the warm island their bodies had become.

After she began thrusting again her own quickened breathing matched her husband's. When she heard his sharp intake of breath and felt his body stiffen, she pushed harder until her own rush of pleasure melded with his. As her orgasm slowly subsided, Arcadia clung tightly to Getorius, keeping her eyes shut tight, to block out the world beyond the pool. There would be time enough in the morning for the sick patients who crowded into the clinic waiting rooms. For now she only wanted the safe world of the water and their joined bodies.

Lately, Arcadia had come to feel that Ravenna was like that, a city only seemingly secure behind its protective ring of walls and swamps. She feared that one day it would be jolted by the reality of barbarian—even internal—enemies, who could destroy a world that had been secure as recently as her father's childhood, less than fifty years earlier.

In a short time the warmth gave way to sleepiness. Arcadia let go, passed Getorius his wine to finish, and climbed out of the pool. As she helped him dry his back, her momentary tranquility was upset by thoughts of the dead hermit. Why *had* Behan come to the Western capital from the most remote edge of the world? At the same time she began to feel curious about his Celtic manuscripts. What might they say?

There was also the matter of Galla Placidia's letter. It would have to be dealt with in the morning, at breakfast, before the clinic opened.

Chapter three

Getorius felt nervous as he watched his wife slide a silver knife blade under Galla Placidia's wax seal and work it loose from the note's vellum flap. What might the Empress Mother and the Emperor want from him?

Despite the soak and brief lovemaking in the warmth of the pool, Getorius had not slept well. The dead monk and putting off reading the unexpected letter cluttered his mind, yet it was usually he, not his wife, who postponed facing things that could possibly be unpleasant.

"There, the seal's broken." Arcadia handed him the note.

After Getorius read a few lines, his frown of concern dissolved. "It's an invitation to the palace for a dinner," he said in a tone of mixed surprise and relief.

"Really? Let me see." Arcadia scanned the text. "It looks like an early style of writing. 'In honor of the Fourteenth Anniversary of the elevation of the Illustrious Flavius Placidius Valentinianus III to Augustus, and the Second of his Marriage to Licinia Eudoxia, Augusta.'"

"Why are we being invited?" Getorius asked.

"I have no idea, but the dinner is on the ides of November."

"The ides? The day hasn't been called that since the first Theodosius ordained a seven-day week."

"I think it's either the thirteenth or fifteenth of the month. And listen to this," Arcadia continued, "Placidia wants to pretend we're living in the days of our ancient Republic. She's asking us to dress accordingly."

"As Romans did four hundred years ago?"

"Presumably." Arcadia laughed at her first thought. "At least I won't have to compete with one of Placidia's elaborate silk tunics. We'll need to look at statues in the old senate house to get your toga right, but they don't portray women there. I'll have to have an idea of what to wear and how Silvia should do my hair."

"Will we lie down on couches to eat?" Getorius scoffed. "What is Placidia thinking?"

"Nostalgia, who knows? She lists the other guests, nine people in all, the way banquets were back then."

"Who are they?"

"Let me see…" Arcadia read a moment. "We should be flattered to be included. Besides the Augustus and Augusta, there'll be the archdeacon—"

"Surrus Renatus. We were talking about him yesterday."

"Also Flavius Aetius and Theokritos."

"Good. At least I'll be able to talk to the librarian."

"Placidia's architect, Sigisvult." Arcadia looked up. "We know him, he's been your patient."

"Perhaps he'll tell us about the mausoleum he just designed for her. Who else?'

"Just the two of us. That makes nine."

"Pelagia, Aetius' wife, isn't included?"

"Getorius," Arcadia reminded him, "you know Placidia doesn't like her because she's not Roman. Restricting the dinner to nine people is another excuse for the Gothic Queen not to invite Pelagia."

"Gothic Queen. I haven't heard that title used in a while." Getorius chuckled at the reference to Placidia's marriage to a Visigoth king, after she had been captured in Rome, twenty-nine years earlier. "Still, excuse or not, Arcadia, it's an insult to the commander. Again, why include us?"

"Placidia has her eye on you," she teased, reaching across the table to tousle his hair. "You'll be appointed palace surgeon yet."

"More likely, the Augustus has his eye on *you*," Getorius retorted, smoothing his hair back in place. "You know his reputation for womanizing…"

Silvia came in to ask if they wanted to have anything more for breakfast.

"Nothing." Arcadia glanced at her husband's empty plate. "You haven't eaten a thing, Getorius. Stay here, I'll see who's waiting at the clinic."

"I am a bit hungry now that I know the note wasn't bad news. If someone is there, take a urine sample and check for humor imbalances. I'll be in shortly."

After Arcadia left, he munched on some olives and looked through the glass-paned doors of the dining room. November's morning fog blurred the bare garden trees, but he could hear the splash of the fountain through the mist.

Arcadia's mention of Nicias yesterday had brought to the surface memories of the old surgeon to whom he owed everything. Fortune had indeed smiled on him at Mount Genevris, the pass through the Cottian Alps from Gaul to Italy, where they had met Galla Placidia and her husband Ataulf's Visigoth tribe who had happened to be crossing in the opposite direction. Placidia, from concern for Nicias and his four-year-old ward, had given him her signet ring as an introduction to her half-brother Honorius, the Western Roman Emperor at Ravenna.

Talk about good fortune. Now I'm being invited to dinner with the Gothic Queen. Getorius took up the invitation list again. Sigisvult had a background similar to his own. Placidia had brought him to Ravenna after Ataulf's murder and her subsequent ransom. She had fostered the youth into a local family, where he had trained as an architect, and she had recently entrusted him with the design for her family mausoleum.

When he came to the librarian's name Getorius muttered aloud,

"If I don't have patients this afternoon, I want to show Theokritos those manuscripts."

He liked—no, respected—the white-haired scholar who had been born in Athens. Greek was Theokritos' native language, but he was fluent in Latin and could translate enough words of Hebrew and Gothic to make sense of texts in those languages. Getorius felt fortunate that, because of his connection to Nicias, the library master allowed him to read the medical texts in the collection. It was annoying, though, that his assistant, Feletheus, always seemed to be spying on him from behind the storage racks.

Archdeacon Renatus. Getorius knew him from having treated his recurring fevers. The churchman had given a strange history when he had first come in. A Gaul, his full name was Surrus Martinus Renatios, born at Primulacium. The town was the site of a shrine to Blessed Martin, to which his mother had been on pilgrimage when she gave birth.

Having been raised on stories about the miracles of Martin, it was logical that Surrus adopt a middle name after the saint, and enter studies for the presbyterate. The bishop Latinized his surname to Renatus, which neatly corresponded with the verb "to be born again." His mother hoped—and Renatus had laughed when he mentioned it to Getorius—that he would be born again as a bishop in the growing Gallican Church. Instead, he had left his studies after attaining the rank of deacon.

When Renatus came to the new capital at Ravenna he had impressed the bishop, who made him archdeacon, an important church post that supervised the money and provisions given out to the poor of the city.

Getorius stood and wiped his fingers on a napkin, thinking that the sooner he finished with his patients, the quicker he could take the manuscripts to Theokritos. He passed along the garden portico to his clinic with the scroll case, half-wondering if Galla Placidia actually was interested in appointing him palace physician to replace the aging Antioches.

No one was in the examination room. Getorius went to his office, an area with a high ceiling and three clerestory windows in the north wall. Shelves underneath displayed the bones of animals that had been brought to him. Alongside the bleached skulls of a horse, a cow, two pigs, and several dogs and cats, were those of wilder species—boar, deer and bear. His prize skeleton was that of a Rhesus monkey that had died in the palace zoo.

Getorius' patients usually avoided looking at these reminders of their own mortality, and even more so at a collection of containers that held preserved organs. The glass jars were filled with liquids in which floated animal hearts, livers, and lungs, as well as several intestinal worms that had been purged from clients. Getorius had experimented with various substances that might preserve these tissues: a solution of wine and salt would keep hearts intact for up to a year, while a mixture of wine, honey and vinegar preserved stomachs and livers long enough to be dissected, although he had discovered that liver tissue tended to break down the quickest.

Before calling for Arcadia to bring in the first patient, Getorius put the manuscript case on his desk and went to look at the hog heart he had been dissecting. A fatty yellow mass surrounded the organ, a mass that was absent from the lean heart of a chicken next to it. Both animals were about the same age. What could cause the different conditions?

As he idly picked at the fat with a needle, Arcadia opened the door from the waiting rooms.

"Getorius? I thought I heard you come in. Ready?"

"What? Oh…yes. Who is the first patient?"

"Domina Felicitas Firma."

"Did you check her urine?"

Arcadia held up a glass flask. "It's cloudy. She's overly heavy, complains of being thirsty and tired all the time. There are ulcers on her legs."

"Good, you've completed half the diagnosis. Send the lady in. Did you ask her age?"

"Felicitas admits to forty-four. Her son is with her." Arcadia put the flask on the desk and eyed an iron stove in the corner. "It's cold in here. I'll have Primus light a fire."

After Getorius sat down, his wife brought in the woman and

her son. Felicitas shuffled to a chair. The man stood behind her, hold-ing a round basket. Felicitas looked ten years older than the age she had given, a tired-looking gray-haired matron in a soiled tunic, and shoes that were becoming unstitched. Even across the desk the smell of urine was strong. Her son was a gaunt Germanic type, Getorius noted, with unkempt blondish hair and a bushy moustache that needed trimming.

Getorius knew that beginning a conversation with a new patient was awkward. Most people would not come except out of desperation, so he tried to relax them before asking about health problems.

"Well, Domina, what seems to be the trouble?" he inquired cheerfully. "You're not too happy about our cold weather?"

"Mother doesn't want t'get up in the morning," the son com-plained. "Up all night pissin'…"

"Let her answer, please," Getorius interrupted. "You are?"

"Her son Fabius." He laid the basket on the desk. "This here's an eel for payment. Can y'help mother?"

"I'll try." Getorius glanced at Arcadia. "The eel will be fine. Now then, Domina, how long has this been going on?"

"Since…since a few months," Felicitas answered in a frightened voice. "I couldn't get up for Mass. Wet the bed…." Her voice trailed off in shame.

Getorius tried to reassure her. "Don't be embarrassed, that could be normal for your condition. What do you like to eat?"

"Take away her bread and honey and she'd die," her son inter-jected again.

"Fabius, please." *If I don't, she will be dead.* "So you like sweet things, Domina?"

Felicitas nodded and pulled up her ragged tunic hem to scratch a scab on her leg.

Getorius knew the symptoms—the excess release of urine and resulting abnormal thirst, sores on limbs, blurred vision. Death often came soon afterward.

Galen had written about the inability of the liver to synthesize and distribute certain foods, yet without knowing why this was so. Logic dictated that a body's excess should be treated with its opposite. This patient displayed an overbalance of sweet. It was not one of the four major body humors, Blood, Phlegm, Yellow or Black Bile, yet serious nonetheless. Her lethargy might indicate the presence of too much black bile. Getorius dipped a finger into the urine and tasted it. As he expected, it was slightly sweet.

"No more honey, Domina," he chided gently. "I'm going to prescribe a vinegar drink. It won't taste very good, but perhaps we can soon substitute wine. Not a sweetened one, though. My wife will rub your legs with a vinegar solution, and you must continue this at home. She will also give you a list of things to eat and those not to eat. Fabius, see that your mother follows my instructions."

"I'm not always there."

"Your father?"

"Dead ten years this Nativity," Felicitas lamented.

"Then a neighbor must help you." Getorius tried to be encouraging. "We must make you slim again, like Venus. Leeks, cucumbers, green beans…vegetables will do it."

"No pork?" she asked, squinting at him in disappointment.

"*Especially* no pork," he warned with mock severity. "I want you to be able to walk, no, *dance* around the church on the Feast of Palms."

"Felicitas, I'll take you into the clinic now," Arcadia said. "Your son can go back to the waiting rooms."

After his patient was gone, Getorius tasted her urine again. *Galen believed that food processed by the liver converted into* pneuma physikon*, an animating spirit transmitted to the body through a hollow network of nerves. I've seen organs other than the liver in animals I've dissected, but what in the name of Aesculapius are they all for?*

Galen had written that all the body's organs were perfect parts of a whole. Getorius also believed this, so it followed that these mysterious organs played a role of which he was totally ignorant. One of them must control Felicitas's imbalance. He felt his anger rise, stood up, and went to the row of jars and held one up.

"If the bishop would permit human dissection I could at least try to determine what function these organs played. His prohibition is endangering citizens' health."

Getorius turned when Primus came in carrying an armload of moss and kindling for the stove, an interruption that added to his frustration. He had only a short time while Arcadia treated Felicitas and then brought in the next patient, and he wanted to look over Behan's manuscripts.

"Hurry up with that stove," he ordered, handing Primus the flask of urine, "then take this out to the fuller's shop and take that basket to the kitchen."

Getorius went back to his desk and slid the scrolls from their case. He unrolled the one with Latin text that was penned in the elegant Celtic script.

"Father, the dawn watch has come," he read aloud. It continued:

> I living in them, You living in me, that our union may be complete. So will the world know that You sent me to them, and that You love them as You love Me.

"Sounds like a prayer of Christ for unity," he muttered, scanning the second verse.

> Father, the dawn watch has come. Give glory to your son. I pray for those who will believe in me that all may be one. I pray that they may be one in Us, that the world may believe that You sent me.

Getorius had begun reading the third of the verses when Arcadia returned.

"I let Felicitas out through the small courtyard. What have you there?" She came to look over his shoulder. "Behan's manuscripts. I might have guessed."

"Look at this third section. Read the others first, then tell me what you think."

He had realized that the last part was different. The meter of the third and fourth verses was shorter and the text of both was little more than half as long as the other two.

After reading, Arcadia looked up. "The last one sounds like a kind of prophecy."

"Good. That's what I thought."

Father, the dawn has now come, the hour when the proof of your love will finally be revealed. Proof that I love them, as You commanded me, is in the Testament of John. Let your Will, manifested at the Nativity, be fulfilled.

"The change is pretty obvious," Arcadia agreed, "but what does it mean?"

"That's what I want to ask Theokritos. Do I have another patient?"

"Varnifrid, a fisherman. He cut his hand at the thumb joint. It looks serious."

Getorius barely concealed his impatience. "So, send him in."

Varnifrid followed Arcadia into the office, cradling his left arm and a freshly caught mullet with the other hand. A clump of bloody moss was packed around the injured thumb. Fish scales glistened on the man's soiled vest and the smell of his trade came in with him. He eyed the room suspiciously, as might an animal put in a cage, but sat on the stool where Arcadia pointed.

"This mullet will be fine as payment." She smiled as she took the fish from him.

"Careless with a knife were we?" Getorius asked with sarcasm he regretted as soon as Arcadia glared at him.

"He speaks Gothic," she said. "I barely understood him, but you can see what happened."

"A Goth raiding mere fish? What wonders will we see next? Get that bloody packing off and put a bowl under his hand. I'll need to probe."

The wound was jagged, with shreds of flesh from a saw-toothed knife framing the cut. When Arcadia worked loose the clotted fibers that covered it, fresh blood oozed out. Getorius sponged it away and concentrated on assessing the damage to the tendons.

"Put a leather strap around his wrist and twist it," he ordered Arcadia. "Even if I can save the hand, he'll never use it again much, but I have to stop the bleeding before I can do anything."

Varnifrid grunted and tried to pull away. Getorius grasped his wrist. "*Lekeis*," he said, using the Gothic word for physician and pointing to himself, but the man only stared at him in fright. "This is ridiculous. Calm him down with a measure of eupatorium wine."

"I did. In the atrium."

"Then the sedative should be taking effect. Hold still, Verna…"

"Varnifrid."

"Yes."

Probing for tendon damage, Getorius recalled what Nicias had taught him about the basic procedure. Stop the bleeding and keep corrupted air away from the wound. Even so, more often than not, the flesh around such a laceration soon became dead and odorous. A spongy black bile replaced normal tissue. The swollen skin crackled to the touch, exuding a foul smell, and the patient developed a fever. Injured limbs usually had to be amputated at the nearest healthy joint, or an agonizing death would follow. He had noticed that dirty wounds, such as deep scrapes that bled little, were more prone to develop the bile excess.

"The Goth is fortunate in one respect," Getorius remarked. "Sea water kept this reasonably clean. No problem sewing skin back over the wound, but those tendons inside can't be joined together. He won't be moving that thumb again." He looked up at his wife. "Someday I intend to dissect a human hand, Arcadia, not just animal paws. I'll cut tendons and try to reconnect them…" He noticed Varnifrid's eyes beginning to glaze over. "The narcotic I gave you will make it hurt less when I sew your hand together," Getorius said, helping him to a cot. "This is quite deep, Arcadia. Prepare a dose of hyoscamus so he'll be asleep while I do the suturing."

"Do you want the alium ointment?"

"Garlic? Why not? He couldn't smell any worse."

34

"Getorius!"

"Sorry. Bring achillea as a poultice after I've closed the wound."

Arcadia noticed Varnifrid's regular breathing. "The eupatorium is taking effect."

"Hurry with the hyoscamus. And bring a gold needle...the medium silk thread."

While Varnifrid jerked reflexively in a drugged sleep, Getorius pulled his tanned skin over the cut and stitched the edges together. After the procedure, Arcadia dusted powdered achillea leaves over the sutures, then deftly tied a woolen strip around the hand, as Hippocrates had instructed in his treatise on the suitable form of bandages.

"Let him sleep," Getorius advised. "When he awakens give him ointment to put on the wound and try to make him understand that he must come back tomorrow." He straightened up, groaned, and stretched. "Who's still waiting?"

"A mother and child. The boy's feverish."

"Another phlegm imbalance. Could you treat him, Arcadia? Arctium root extract and cool baths at home."

"You can't wait to see Theokritos about those manuscripts, can you?"

"I can't shake the feeling that there's something mysterious about them. Perhaps even in that monk's death."

"Behan accidentally drowned, you said so yourself." Arcadia came to rub her husband's back a moment. "All right, go set your mind at ease. I'll treat the child."

❧

Getorius was familiar with the library wing of the Lauretum Palace, in the east sector of the rear second story. The windowed west side overlooked the garden, so copyists could glance out from time to time and relieve the strain on their eyes. These penmen were ranged along the wall at desks set beneath narrow windows whose openings were now sealed with alabaster slabs thin enough to admit light, yet keep out the cold. Manuscript illuminators, who worked with the copyists, inking in or painting designs to beautify pages, occupied three of the desks.

A reading area was set behind a curtain beyond the lattice bins and shelves, where most of the collection of Greek, Roman, Hebrew, and Christian texts were stored. Many of the scrolls and books had escaped barbarian raids, or been salvaged from the Alexandria library after its burning by the anti-pagan fanatic Theophilos, less than fifty years earlier. It was an outrage for which Theokritos had never forgiven his fellow Greek.

Theokritos had instituted his own index system for locating material, based on authors, rather than subject matter. The old librarian's memory, as clear as the crystals he used to enlarge words, could recall which author had written on a particular theme, and where it was stored. Even though labels on the manuscript ends helped identify their contents, Getorius found the system aggravating. A history of medicine by Artistotle's pupil Menon might be shelved next to a treatise on Manichaeism that was written in Syriac. With Arcadia's help Getorius had located all the medical texts and written their details on a diagram that indicated where they could be found.

As Getorius walked up the narrow stairway that led to the library, he passed a boy hurrying down. The child's face and arms were spotted with color, and he clutched his genitals through a smudged tunic. *One of the pigment grinding apprentices on his way to a latrine,* Getorius thought. He had seen the area where inks and colors were prepared, and the one for the final polishing and cutting of parchment skins after they were delivered from tanning shops. Workers in an adjacent room stored them as blank manuscript sheets, or bound the final lettered pages into books.

When Getorius reached the top of the stairs, a smell of fish glue coming from the bindery reminded him of his clients' payments. *Nothing but fish today!* His clinic had the pleasant scent of medicinal herbs. How could the library staff stand this nauseating odor day after day? He also heard the irritating rasp of marble slabs grinding the pigment material, a sound that always set his teeth in an involuntary imitative gnashing whenever he was in the reading area.

Feletheus had his worktable facing the stairs so he could scan visitors, but the assistant was not there. As Getorius entered the room, Lucius, the chief copyist, looked up from his desk and nodded a greeting. He was half way past the storage bins, on his way to Theokritos' office, when Feletheus' voice startled him from behind.

"Surgeon. You're here to consult a medical text?"

Getorius turned to the balding, sallow-looking man, who was about thirty years of age. The library assistant combed what hair he had to the front of his head, and the beginnings of a reddish beard fuzzed his cheeks. His eyes held either a suspicious squint, or a perpetually sad expression.

"*Salus*, Librarian, your health," Getorius greeted pleasantly. "I…"

"Is that a medical text, or have you brought me new material?" Feletheus interrupted, eyeing the manuscript case.

"Neither. I wish to see Theokritos."

"Ah. The Master, coincidentally, was about to send for you. Come."

After Feletheus pushed aside the curtain to Theokritos' office, Getorius saw the old librarian thumbing through a thick volume. His ruddy face was wreathed by a white beard and matching full head of hair, and his dark eyes had a nervous squint from years of poring over manuscripts and books. Dusty shelves had left him with a chronic cough. When the man turned around, Getorius noticed a gold medal hanging from his neck. The design depicted a serpent with its tail in its mouth, encircled by the Greek letters ΙΑΩ ΑΒΡΑΧΑΣ. *Abraxas…definitely not a Christian symbol!*

"Surgeon, you read my thoughts," Theokritos rasped, looking at him. "The last galley from Constantinople brought me books. One was this Latin translation of a treatise on gynecology by Soranus of Ephesos."

"There are midwives for that, sir. I'm never called on to assist at a birth."

"Then perhaps it would interest your *wife*," Theokritos countered. "I understand she trains with you."

Getorius flushed. "Thank you. Arcadia will be grateful."

Theokritos squinted at the leather case. "You have brought me a scroll?"

"Three, sir, to ask your help. Yesterday I examined the body of a holy man who died."

"Behan of Clonard. The"—Theokritos succumbed to a fit of coughing before continuing—"The monk read here often."

Getorius was not surprised that the librarian already knew about the death—there were few secrets kept from palace gossipers. He slid the parchments from their case. "These manuscripts were in his hut and I didn't want bandits to destroy them. Two are in Celtic."

"The language of the *barbaroi*."

Getorius ignored the implied slur about non-Greek barbarians and unrolled the sheets. "Sir, this one is in Latin."

"Perhaps a translation of the others? Feletheus can read the writing of the Keltoi for us in a moment." Theokritos scanned the Latin, then scoffed, "Even an acolyte could identify this paraphrase of verses in the Testament of the Apostle John."

"The last ones, too? They seemed different."

Theokritos read again. "Hmm…you're correct, Surgeon. Clumsy, but it seems to be a prophecy concerning the other two."

"I thought so."

"Such predictions are common, every cult has one. Feletheus, read the other scrolls."

After examining the writing, Feletheus admitted, "Master, I've not seen this alphabet style before." The assistant read silently a moment, then translated, "'The humble meditations of Behan, from Clonard Abbey. Know that the Eternal King, the Son of the Living God, speaks in threes. For this is the number of the Father, Son, and Holy Spirit.'"

"Hibernians are fond of spinning riddles involving a triad," Theokritos commented. "Words, numbers, verses and such. Please continue."

"'For one and two make three, just as three and four make Seven, the number of Completion.'"

"Of creation, I assume he means." Theokritos cleared his throat, spit into a cloth, then sneered, "A childish game."

"Truly, Master." Feletheus bent over the words and then continued,

> And Three…Blessed Jesus, Holy Mary, and the Saintly Joseph comprise the Unblemished Family.
> Three-sectioned Triangle, the Eternal Monogram of Three Persons in One.
> The Three of the enlightened Pythagoras…Beginning, Middle, End.
> Three astrologers who first saw the Blessed Child.
> Three days in the tomb.
> Heaven, Earth, under the Earth…

"Arkata!" Theokritos cried in Greek. "Enough! Great Zeus, the man tells us nothing with his riddles. These Hibernian monks are flooding into Gaul from their island, founding monasteries and trying to force Gallic bishops into adopting their liturgies. Get to the end of this ridiculous game."

Feletheus moved his index finger down to the last few lines.

> Know that the Nazarene was in the world, but not of its ways.
> Know this through the Testament in a book of John, to be revealed now, in our time.

He paused at the final six lines. "Master, another arrangement of threes."

> A book of John.
> A Testament.
> The Fulfillment.
>
> Faith, Hope, Love.
> The greatest is Love.
> Proof is hidden in a book of John.

When Feletheus finished reading Theokritos had already turned back to examine the gynecology volume. Getorius was disappointed in the librarian's lack of interest, but determined to ask about the interpretation of what he suspected was a prophecy.

"'To be revealed now, in our time.' Sir, what does that mean? Or, 'Hidden in *a* book of John? Shouldn't it be '*The* Book of John?'"

"Word games to pass the time," Theokritos snorted without looking up from Soranus. "These monks need a diversion from their penances and constant prayers."

Frustrated, Getorius snatched the scrolls from the worktable. He was rolling them up when he noticed a sketch at the bottom corner of the one with the prophecy. A few deft strokes in red ink depicted the outline of a cockerel. The symbol reminded him that he had heard a rooster crowing somewhere outside Behan's hut.

Why mention it to Theokritos and be ridiculed? He thought the verses prophetic, then dismissed them as a word game. If it was a prophecy, did the monk drown before he could proclaim it? *Getorius eased the scrolls into their case with an uneasy thought.* Was Behan strangled, as Arcadia thinks, so he couldn't predict an event that is to be revealed soon, 'in our time?' And why this emphasis on a dawn watch? Is that the significance of the rooster?

Getorius tucked the leather cylinder under his arm. "I'll give that volume by Soranus to my wife."

Theokritos nodded a reply and handed him the book. Feletheus held the curtain open, then followed Getorius out of the office.

"The master is preoccupied with a Gnostic Gospel of Thomas he received in the shipment from Constantinople," he said. "You saw his amulet."

"It's a Gnostic talisman?"

"Yes. I…ah…found the monk's word games intriguing, Surgeon, as I suspect you did."

"I found them a waste of my time," Getorius retorted, "and would have done better coming here to read either Galen or Hippocrates."

"What will you do with the manuscripts?"

"Keep them until someone from Behan's abbey comes to claim what I found in his hut."

"Let us talk of this again," Feletheus suggested.

"Fine, you know where my clinic is located." As Getorius started down the stairs the boy with the smudged tunic sidestepped around him, going back up to work. *At least he feels better. If Theokritos isn't interested, perhaps whoever comes from Autessiodurum can explain Behan's word games, and what this so-called prophecy signifies.*

Autessiodurum

Chapter four

Warinar, the courier who was sent from Ravenna to Autes-siodurum to report the death of Behan, arrived at the Abbey of Culdees before mid-November. A native of the area, he had been given more gold coins to make the dangerous journey than he could have earned in Ravenna all winter.

Brenos of Slana was abbot at Culdees. Germanus, the bishop who had appointed him, was a man after the abbot's ascetic heart, if not his humble background. Brenos had been born in Slana, a port hamlet on the island of Hibernia's eastern shore. The two main concerns of those who lived in its stone, thatch-roofed huts were catching enough fish to feed themselves, and coming back alive with them from the stormy seas.

The aristocratic Germanus had studied law in Rome. After the Senate appointed him governor of a province, he had administered it with model efficiency. This had prompted the then bishop to view him as good material for the growing Gallican Church. He had tonsured Germanus into the presbyterate with a ruse, then mollified his anger by telling of a vision in which God ordered that the governor would follow as the next bishop.

Germanus brought to his new Christianity the same discipline he had displayed as governor: he traded his splendid uniform for a homespun wool tunic and wore it over a goat hair shirt. For a bed, he spread coarse sacking on the ground and sprinkled ashes over the covering. At meals he refused to eat meat and most vegetables, rarely drank wine unless it was heavily watered, and abstained from salt as a seasoning. Germanus was seen chewing ashes as he cut into his supper barley loaf. As he ate, he sipped water from a wooden cup.

Brenos had met Germanus in Britain, where the bishop had gone to battle the heretic Pelagius, who was teaching denial of Original Sin and claiming that Adam would have died regardless of Eve's mischief in wanting to know the difference between good and evil. On the Feast of the Resurrection, three hundred and sixty-nine years after that holy event, Germanus used the military skills he had acquired previously as governor to defeat a Pict and Saxon horde. When his jubilant Briton army shouted "Alleluia!" the victory was so named.

Brenos, who had also come to dispute Pelagius, and to introduce Ciallanus' Hibernian form of monasticism to the island, was present at the Alleluia Victory. He took a liking to Germanus' asceticism but more importantly, saw the bishop as a conduit for preaching the rule of Ciallanus in Gaul. Brenos persuaded Germanus to build a monastery at Autessiodurum and to appoint him its abbot.

۲€

After word of a messenger from Ravenna was sent to Brenos's secretary, Fiachra, the monk, was surprised, then concerned. Sending a courier from the Western capital in winter meant news of extraordinary importance.

Walking down the path from the Collegium, a stone building that housed offices, monks' cells, a library, and a refectory, Fiachra saw an unarmed stranger inside the wooden palisade, warming himself around the guards' fire.

He greeted the shivering man. "God preserve you, messenger. What is your name?"

"Warinar of Aballo."

"Your journey in winter was either foolish, Warinar, or important," Fiachra probed.

Warinar unslung a waxed leather case. "The answer is in this, Brother, and for your holy abbot to decide."

"I am the abbot's secretary." Fiachra jingled a coin bag. "If news is hard, I soften it for him."

"How would I know an abbot's business?" Warinar countered, without taking his glance away from the small sack.

Fiachra eased out a shining coin. "Whisper it to 'Brother Silver.' I'll turn away."

Warinar snatched the money from the secretary's fingers. "Your monk Behan of Clonard drowned during one of his penances."

"Hard news indeed, messenger, but 'Brother Silver' thanks you. If you have no other place to sleep, you may stay in our hospice."

"A day or two, then. I've friends upriver."

"Ask for Brother Ailbe."

Behan dead on foreign earth, Fiachra thought, as he climbed the cobbled path back up to the Collegium. *Why did Brenos send him so far away in the first place?*

Fiachra knew some of Brenos' background since, like his abbot, he had been educated at the Hibernian Abbey of Clonard. Fiachra's ease at learning to write neatly formed letters had prompted that abbot to advise against ordination. Instead, two years ago, Fiachra had been assigned as secretary at the new Gaulish monastery of Culdees.

Three-fourths up the stony way, Fiachra paused to look over the monastery compound, and beyond, toward the valley of the Icauna River. He knew the rise of ground near the town walls was lower than Brenos wanted, but Germanus had already situated a chapel there. The abbot had ordered a log barricade built to surround the area, like the ones protecting Hibernian hill villages, lengthened the chapel nave, replaced a cluster of mud-and-wattle huts with stone dwellings, and erected the Collegium building.

Fiachra glanced at the nearby hospice. Pilgrims had started coming to venerate a bloodstained rock in the compound's Church of Saint Stephen. The stone was reportedly one of those that had killed the deacon, at Jerusalem, in the early days of the Church. Germanus believed the relic was genuine, and Fiachra had never heard Brenos voice a contrary opinion.

Ciallanus's Rule called for self-sufficiency, so the flattest area of the compound was given over to forage crops, gardens and animal pens. The monks divided their day into periods announced by a tolling of the chapel bell—hours of prayer, study, work and sleep. Sleep had the lowest priority, being constantly interrupted by calls to prayer. On the Lord's Day, the bronze clapper summoned citizens to Mass, where they heard about Christ and the monastery's harsh rules. Once curiosity had prompted their first attendance, Fiachra noted that few came back.

The day was cold but almost windless, with a winter sun in a cornflower-blue sky moving toward its seasonal nadir. Fiachra squinted at fallow fields sparkling in their clean tunics of white snow. Some were crossed by neat rows of gray vineyard canes. He momentarily imagined them as phalanxes of legionaries ready for the battle trumpet to sound, then corrected his vision to that of dormant Christians awaiting the greening life of Ciallanus' discipline. Brenos preached that Gaul was a vineyard which the Nazarene wanted harvested. Unruly people, like vines run amuck, needed frequent pruning, and Hibernians were the ones chosen, albeit relatively recently, to be His laborers.

Fiachra continued up the slope and into the Collegium. He stood listening at the door of Brenos' office for a moment, and then gave the three quick raps that identified his presence.

"Enter Fiachra," the abbot called out.

When the secretary crossed to the desk, Brenos was reading a letter. Fiachra observed his gaunt face while he waited. The brown eyes under thick, dark brows were extraordinarily intelligent, and the man might have been considered handsome were it not for the unflattering ear-to-ear tonsure shaved across his skull, that left a fringe of long hair growing at the back.

Brenos finally looked up. "This is Patricus's report from Hibernia. Have a lector read it at the evening meal."

Fiachra said nothing. He knew about the missionary who had studied at Germanus' school, then immediately been ordained a bishop and sent off to preach on the island of Hibernia—all because of a dream he claimed to have had. The monk listened in sullen silence as his abbot read aloud.

> I, Patricus, am one born out of time like the Blessed Paul, yet by the will of God ordained shepherd to convert a pagan flock, and sent to reveal to them the good news of their salvation.

"What arrogance!" Fiachra blurted out, his face flushed with resentment. "The man dares compare himself to the Apostle? And he calls himself Patricus now? His Celtic name of Padraic isn't good enough for him?"

"*Caritas*, Brother Fiachra, be charitable," Brenos gently admonished, realizing his secretary was venting a measure of envy that would have to be disciplined. "The name was given him by our patron Germanus, when he elevated him to the episcopacy. Let me continue. 'It is my joy to report the success of my earlier efforts in converting the followers of the chieftain Eirinn, although not without great humiliation to me. The pagans ridicule my tonsure, which I accept as a sign of the Nazarene's humiliation on being mocked with a thorn coronet. *Tailcenn* they call me, in our language 'Baldhead,' amid much laughter. Yet they are in awe of my bishop's vestments and crozier. The staff was left me, you will recall, on the island of…I have forgotten the name…in the Tyrrhenian Sea, by the Nazarene himself.'"

"*By the Nazarene?*" Fiachra burst out again. "Th…the insolence of the man! Even Paul never claimed—"

"Fiachra, Fiachra," Brenos admonished with a shushing motion of his finger. "Are you harboring envy in your soul?"

"Pardon, my Abbot," he mumbled, bending his head low. "I will do an extended penance on the stone cross, to atone for my pride."

"We'll talk of it later." Brenos gave him a thin smile. "Listening to the rest of this letter may be penance enough. 'I am opposed in my work by the druid priests who keep their countrymen in the darkness of error. Two of them attempted, by magic, to conceal my preaching in a mantle of darkness. I had gone to a wood called Focluit in answer to a dream about King Amalgaid and his seven sons. As I

49

was teaching about the Blessed Trinity, the druids caused a sudden darkness to appear.'"

"A lowland fog," Fiachra muttered. "I've seen it creep along the Sinnenus valley like a gray cat mousing in a barn."

Brenos ignored him and continued reading, "'To dispel it, I struck a stone with the tip of my crozier and the ground began to burn.'"

"A spark into a dry peat bog," Fiachra scoffed.

"It divided itself into twelve fires, one for each of the Holy Apostles. Lo! The darkness fled and with it the perfidious druids. The priests could not even evoke their god, Crom Cruach, because I had thrown down the idol on the Plain of Magh Slecht five years earlier—"

Fiachra suddenly gave a sharp, guttural cry, then pulled his coarse robe over his head and lay face down on the stone floor, naked except for a swaddled loincloth. "I cannot tolerate the man's boasting," he croaked, stretching his arms out as if on a cross. "Punish me, Abbot."

Brenos did not order him up. *It might be better to let him lie in that pose until he begins to shiver.* He looked at the thin body, whose pale skin was speckled with brownish moles and traces of old insect bites, and was pleased that Fiachra did not cultivate lice colonies, as did several other monks. Brenos had cautioned against penances that sapped strength, even while practicing them himself during the week that commemorated the Passion of the Nazarene.

The abbot noticed his secretary's body convulse slightly, and found it hard to understand how some monks could be sexually attracted to each other. Hibernian bishops were wise in permitting marriage among their presbyters, to forestall homoerotic liaisons. At the same time he realized that, in the past, Celtic warriors had considered it honorable to be loved by men of the same social class. Women had given themselves freely to the bravest fighter, and children born of such unions were raised by the clan without stigma. The Roman Church had changed all that.

Patricus the Briton might be doing good work by planting the vineyard of faith in Hibernia, Brenos mused, but he was putting in fragile canes that were in danger of being uprooted by the druids he mentioned. Ciallanus, on the other hand, was a native of the island and knew its fickle people. With more sense than Patricus, he had come to Gaul to cultivate vines that had been planted centuries earlier.

The Gallic vineyard had borne fruit sevenfold in the early days, but was now in need of pruning. Wild shoots grew everywhere. Dead wood rotted on the vines. And the Nazarene had given the mandate: "Every branch in me not bearing fruit he takes away, and every one bearing fruit he prunes, that it may bear more fruit." Ciallanus was sending abbots and monks to Gaul, even as far as the eastern empire, to wield the pruning knife.

Brenos noticed Fiachra's skin pucker into minuscule bumps and another shiver convulse his body. He rose from his chair and bent down to touch the monk's shoulder.

"My brother, put off the cloak of envy and dress yourself in humility," he urged quietly. "Envy shoots others and injures itself. Rejoice in the success of Patricus." As Fiachra stood and adjusted his robes, Brenos went back to his desk. "But you came to see me about something in that dispatch case?"

Fiachra nodded, but knelt again. "Forgive me, Abbot. Hibernians are known for boasting, yet Padraic also accepted the yoke of humility."

"His boasting, like Paul's, is for the Nazarene."

"Assign me a penance then, as Paul gladly bore with fools for His sake."

"*Enough*, Fiachra," Brenos ordered, sternly this time. "We will speak of it in private confession. Now. What did the messenger bring?"

"Sad news from Ravenna. Our brother Behan of Clonard is dead."

"You opened the case?" Brenos frowned and reached for it to inspect the bishop's seal.

"Couriers gossip in the manner of old women."

"Indeed, Fiachra. Did he speak of the cause of our brother's death?"

"Drowned in a state of penitential grace. He died in the arms of the Nazarene."

"There will be a report from Bishop Chrysologos inside." Brenos snapped the seal and opened the cover. When he pulled out two parchments, he saw that one bore the bishop's signet, but opened a smaller sheet first, which was sealed with red wax showing the imprint of a rooster. "The cockerel is ready to crow," he read aloud.

"Cockerel? Crow?" Fiachra looked puzzled. "What does that mean, Abbot?"

Brenos ignored his question, thumbed off the bishop's seal, and read a moment. "Chrysologos is asking for permission to bury our brother. A surgeon has preserved the body for now, but fears warmer weather. What is the rule, Fiachra? May Behan be interred in Ravenna?"

"There is a precedent, Abbot. Fithal of Limercu lies in Constantine's basilica at Rome."

"Indeed?" A sly smile creased Brenos' gaunt features. "Then, Fiachra, I have thought of your penance. You will accompany me to Ravenna."

"Ravenna? But...but by spring the body will be—"

"Not in spring," Brenos said, cutting off the monk's objection. "We will go there now."

"In winter? Abbot, consider the dangers. Surely—"

"Surely, the courier just did so. Are we monks lesser men?"

Fiachra desperately looked for an excuse to avoid the hazardous journey. "But...but the holy season marking the Nazarene's birth will begin soon."

"All the better," Brenos replied. "We shall celebrate His nativity in the bishop's church at Ravenna. You may go about your duties now." The abbot watched Fiachra stride to the door in poorly concealed fury. "Courage, Brother. Perhaps at Ravenna we shall hear this cockerel crow."

After Fiachra was gone, Brenos went to the door and slid the locking bolt into its socket. "Indeed we shall hear it," he muttered, returning to his heavy desk. He felt along the edge of two thick planks that formed the top until he located a groove underneath. Sliding the edge molding aside revealed a compartment containing a square parchment envelope.

Brenos untied the leather thong securing it and took out several sheets of soft white vellum. The top sheet bore a drawing of a cockerel in red ink, with a title underneath.

THE GALLICAN LEAGUE

He touched the symbol, pleased again at his cleverness in thinking of it. At Clonard he had learned that the word *gallus* was Latin for both a rooster and the land of the Gauls. The Church used the bird as a symbol of vigilance. What more appropriate sign to identify his league of associates on the Continent?

"Little cockerel," Brenos murmured fondly, "your crowing will soon be heard throughout two empires. Even Ciallanus will be forced to listen."

Whoever had paid the courier to put the cryptic note in the dispatch case had done his work well, Brenos mused, but the report about Behan was disturbing. Who was this meddling surgeon who had taken it upon himself to preserve the body? Still, it was useless to blame him. Chrysologos was uninformed about monastic jurisdiction, and was merely extending the courtesy of an abbot's decision, yet why hadn't the bishop mentioned the prophecy? Surely, Behan had had time to preach it, reveal it.

Brenos' self-satisfaction overcame his doubt; the first phase of the League's two-year plan was a success. By now the final legacy of the Nazarene was well hidden by the person Behan had recruited in Ravenna. What code name had the monk given his accomplice? The abbot turned to the last page of the vellum.

"Smyrna," he read aloud. "Yes, Smyrna will have arranged to conceal the gold case, and for me to read the Gospel of John at the dawn Nativity Mass. There, to fulfill Behan's prophecy, the Last Will and Testament of the Nazarene will be revealed."

Brenos recalled the text of John from memory. "The Word became flesh and made his dwelling among us, and we have seen his glory: the glory of an only Son coming from the Father, filled with enduring love." After he finished reading, Brenos would hold up the Nazarene's Last Will and announce that, by God's grace, it had been in the safekeeping of Hibernians since the time of the Apostle Peter. Simultaneously, at concurrent Nativity services in Rome, Constantinople, Mediolanum, Antioch, Alexandria and Autessiodurum, League associates would have visions of the revelation. And he, Brenos of Slana, would be in Ravenna to verify the discovery for his Order. Confusion would result until Sixtus, the Bishop of Rome, called a council of theologians to determine the authenticity of the document, yet by the Feast of the Resurrection, in the spring, the Gallican League would be ratified as the Will's executors, by virtue of their centuries of guardianship.

Brenos fingered the second sheet. For a moment its purity and sensuous feel reminded him of the white flesh of a village girl who had tempted him in his youth, but then he forced himself to concentrate on the Celtic script, writing that flowed with the regularity and beauty of waves rolling onto Hibernia's shores. It was appropriate for a document that heralded the most important message since the Nazarene's ministry was written down and completed God's plan for mankind.

After His Resurrection, the Apostles had asked about the restoration of the Kingdom of Israel. The Nazarene had replied that it was not yet time for them to know the season the Father had fixed—an unmistakable indication that the Judean kingdom would be restored. After Peter the Apostle was released from prison by the angel, he told his friends he was leaving them. "With that he went out and journeyed to another place." What was not recorded was that the angel told Peter, in a dream, to take the Nazarene's Last Testament and embark for Hibernia, where it would be safe until the Father's time came for its revelation.

Brenos winced and rubbed his forehead. One of his recurring headaches had returned, but he continued his mental summary of the League's origin.

Peter too had realized things were going wrong, writing about the passions of the flesh warring with the soul, of slaves and servants who did not respect their masters, of women who were not submissive to their husbands, and flaunted expensive robes decorated with gold. Today, one need look no further than Faustina, the provincial governor's harlot, for proof of Peter's accusation.

The weak emperor's court at Ravenna was also a scandal. Men were said to wear their hair long, in the manner of females. Women commissioned silk robes the cost of which would feed a dormitory of the poor for a year. And a woman, Emperor Valentinian's mother, not the Emperor himself, truly ruled this corrupt Western empire. False teachings were everywhere, affecting forms of worship among Hibernian, Gallic, Roman and Eastern churches. The faithful milled about like confused sheep, unsure of their true shepherds.

Brenos' head ached with a dull pain, and he felt again the fullness that periodically pressured his loins. He would usually practice a penance after succumbing to the erotic urge, but thought that if he read the League charter the temptation might pass.

"The Declaration of the Associates of the Gallican League," he read softly, "the vigilant ones who were chosen to fulfill the things predicted by Jesus the Nazarene concerning the end of the world."

Brenos skimmed through the preamble. It pointed out that even as a child Jesus did not suffer fools. The infancy narratives of Thomas related how He struck dead a child who accidentally knocked Him over, then rendered blind the elders who reprimanded Him.

The League brothers might not yet be many, but they were not blind. Was Matthew not speaking to them when he wrote with apostolic authority that those of a humble nature would have the earth as their possession? The Brothers had taken on Ciallanus' sweet yoke of humility, obedience and poverty, as the clause stipulated:

CLAUSE I. We have sold our belongings and given the proceeds to the poor in exchange for earthly perfection and treasure in the New Jerusalem.

CLAUSE II. The Nazarene's prophet, Sextus Africanus, confirms in his *Chronographia* that the Final Coming, and the end of the world, will occur five hundred years after His first Coming. Four hundred and thirty-nine years have passed. VIGILAMINI! It is time to be vigilant!

CLAUSE III. Blessed John, in an ecstasy similar to ones we have experienced, was privileged with a revelation. He saw, in the right hand of One seated on the throne of the New Jerusalem, a scroll. No one was worthy to open the scroll and break its seven seals except Jesus the Nazarene.

> You are worthy to take the scroll
> and open its seals,
> because you were slaughtered. With your blood
> you ransomed men for God
> from every tribe and nation.
> And you made them to be a kingdom
> and priests to our God.
> And they are to rule as kings over the earth.

Brenos' head throbbed now. He skipped past the list of seals that revealed in turn war, famine, death, martyrdom, and the day of Jehovah's wrath. The Seventh Seal brought a short period of silence in Heaven, then the seven angels before the throne summoned hail, fire, mountains of flames, and seas of blood. Water was made bitter by the fall of the star Wermut, amid total darkness. A third of mankind was destroyed.

The abbot came to the core of the revelation as the Gallican League interpreted it, and whispered it aloud. "Then another angel came holding only a little scroll in his hand, that the mystery of Jehovah might be revealed. The scroll was bitter to the stomach, but as sweet as honey in the mouth. And the angel vowed that there would no longer be a delay, that the days of the opening of the scroll of the mystery of Jehovah, as he announced to his servants, would be fulfilled."

The pain in Brenos' head and the fullness in his loins were almost unbearable. He needed to begin the purge. His mouth was dry, but he forced himself to finish reading.

CLAUSE IV. Wherefore, the contents of the angel's scroll are to be revealed on the Feast of the Nativity. Each of the periods of the six sealed scrolls is of ten years' duration, and six times ten equals the sixty years remaining of Africanus' prediction of the final Tribulation.

Let him who has eyes to see and ears to hear, see and hear!

Brenos rasped the last line. His swollen member rubbed against the rough cloth of his tunic. Without rearranging its pages he shoved the manuscript back into the hidden compartment. He avoided looking at his erection as he took off his tunic and slipped into the short goat-hair vest that hung by the door. Had not the African bishop, Augustine, written that a man could not control his sexual appetite through the will, and that even in an honest celibate 'the diabolical excitement of the genitals' was uncontrollable?

Taking one of the fresh yew branches that a novice brought every morning, Brenos lay down on the blanket that covered a broad ledge under his high window. He struck at his shoulders and chest with the yew, then decreased the intensity of the whipping as he moved downward, with satanic urgency, to his stomach and swollen penis.

Ciallanus' rule utilized penance to punish sexual lapses. Married men not in the Order who confessed to fornication, or even to fantasizing about the act, were forbidden to lie with their wives for a designated period of time. Guilty monks were assigned strokes with a leather scourge and ordered to fast. The hunger, paradoxically, sometimes brought on the hallucinatory sexual monsters that had tormented Blessed Antony in the desert.

Brenos moaned at the exquisite pain and thought of the girls in Slana, daughters of Eve whose pale flesh and wheat-colored hair would have seduced the serpent in Paradise, not the opposite. As a child he had heard the muffled laughter of couples during their awkward trysts in boat storage sheds. He was barely fifteen when he had succumbed to his first—and last—temptation with a girl.

She was the daughter of a boat caulker, with skin as smooth and creamy as ewe's milk. When she had bent over to untie his trouser lacing, he had seen her breasts, small and pointed. Even her underarm sweat was as sweet as the presbyter's incense at Mass. After she hiked up her tunic to receive him, white thighs spread wide, golden delta glistening, he had climaxed the instant he touched her warm wetness—just as he did in the erotic dreams that came a few times a month. He had grabbed himself to stifle the outflow, but his seed had spilled onto the sailcloth beneath her.

She had laughed at him in a combination of anger and scorn, then smoothed down her tunic and flounced out of the shack. Shamed, he had hidden there until nightfall. In that dim space, the nest he had made for her on a coil of rope, so filled with anticipation, reverted to what it was—a dirty, tar-soaked hawser under a musty linen sail that was spotted with his wasted seed, and lit by a soiled window laced with cobwebs.

At the next Lord's Day service, Brenos felt that the presbyter somehow knew. He did not speak of the Nazarene's miracles, but of Paul's condemnation of fornication among the Corinthians. The fornicator had been handed over to Satan, for his flesh to be destroyed that his spirit might be saved. That afternoon, Brenos had left for the Abbey of Clonard, to save both his flesh and his spirit.

Brenos' rapid strokes of the yew branch slowed to gentle caresses, until pain and pleasure suddenly melded together. When the unstoppable pulsing spent itself, the smell of his seed, mingled with that of evergreen sap, renewed his feeling of guilt. But the headache was gone and he fell asleep.

⁊

After Brenos awoke, he bathed in water as cold as he could stand. At supper he took only bread and water, then left the refectory before the reading of Patricus' letter.

Monks going to evening Compline service found their abbot lying on the ground alongside the chapel, stretched out on the snowy stones of a penitential cross. He was chanting psalms.

"Judge me, O God. Why have you cast me off? Send out your light and truth. May these lead me. May they bring me to your holy mountain and to your great tabernacle.

"Why are you in despair, O my soul?"

58

None of the brothers wondered about the nature of Brenos' transgression. Every man has his own personal demon to exorcise.

ə€

In the morning, the abbot told Fiachra to order the courier to meet with him and plan the route by which he would guide them back to Ravenna.

Warinar protested. He had wanted to stay in the Autessiodurum area and spend his gold. He warned of winter storms and said he had no inclination to tempt Fortune again.

Brenos insisted, demanding he be shown Warinar's crude map. He said that if they only took one packhorse to carry supplies, and relied on his status as an abbot to claim hospitality from local officials, they would make good time. Going downriver on the Icauna River by barge, they would be in Lugdunum in seven days. There, Brenos would visit the shrine of the martyred Blandina. Perhaps prayers to the virgin slave girl, who had been torn apart by wild beasts in the amphitheater, would help him overcome the beast of lust in his own body.

Warinar continued his objections, pointing out that even if they made it that far safely, the road would become more difficult as it climbed the Alpine foothills to the Genevris Pass. Snowstorms might leave them stranded there, or on their descent into the valley of the Padus River.

Brenos dismissed the warnings, and convinced Warinar to cooperate through an offer of gold coins coupled with the threat of spiritual damnation if he did not.

They would be in Ravenna, the abbot told Fiachra, no later than December sixth, the beginning of the second week of Advent. Brenos did not tell his secretary that at that time there would be just eighteen days in which to reaffirm the prophecy, contact Smyrna, the Gallican League associate, and coordinate the discovery of the Nazarene's Last Testament at the Nativity Vigil.

Nor that, in just six weeks, the period of the Final Tribulation would begin.

Ravenna

Chapter five

Although Theokritos had shown no interest in the dead monk's prophecy—a fact Getorius thought strange for a scholar—Feletheus continued to be intrigued by the cryptic verses. He sent word to Getorius, asking him to bring the manuscripts the next time he was in the library, so he could study the text at leisure.

A few days later Getorius brought the case to Feletheus, then stayed to read Galen's treatise on the body's parts, particularly the section on the anatomy of hands, because of his recent treatment of the fisherman's injured thumb.

❧

It was almost dusk when Getorius came out of the palace and walked briskly toward his villa. Arcadia heard him enter through the atrium and waited by the drapes. She was annoyed at his recent irritability around patients, and his complaints that he did not have enough time to research medical texts, but had guessed he was preoccupied with Behan's parchments. He had gone to the library that afternoon, taking them with him, and had been away most of the day.

"Well, what did you and that Feletheus discover?" she asked

coolly. "A prediction about the end of the world, or the date of the General Resurrection? Should we even bother opening the clinic tomorrow?"

"Sorry I took so long, *cara,*" he apologized, pecking her cheek. "I was reading Galen."

"You didn't go there to read Galen."

"Did any more patients come in?" he questioned to dodge her rebuke.

"Not unless you count the boy with the broken arm."

"Broken arm? You should have sent for me. How did you—"

"I took care of him. Come and eat now. Agrica has supper ready."

The cook's first course was a thick barley soup flavored with smoked pig hocks, onion and dill, to which she added a slight sweet-sour taste with a sauce of honey, vinegar, and boiled grape juice spooned separately into the bowls.

Getorius ate in silence. Arcadia did not speak either, upset over her husband's neglect of patients and the fact that he was not sharing information with her. She finally decided to play on his sense of guilt.

"You cut me off before, but you took those manuscripts to Feletheus, didn't you?"

Getorius nodded and reached for a chunk of bread.

"Well? I presumed you discussed them?"

"Briefly," he replied, between mouthfuls.

"Oh, swallow that, Getorius," she snapped, "and talk to me! Theokritos dismissed the text as a word game. What makes you think his assistant will find any other meaning?"

"Feletheus isn't stupid and he's around Theokritos all day. He's probably read most of the books in the library."

"That doesn't answer my question. You used to complain that he was always spying on you."

"That has nothing to do with this matter."

"No, but your obsession with those manuscripts has made you unpleasant around patients."

Getorius pushed his bowl away and stood up. "Are you going to start again?"

"Where are you going? Ursina still has a leek and sausage dish to serve."

"I'll forego that and bathing, and go to bed early."

"As you wish, Surgeon."

After he disappeared in the direction of the bedroom, Arcadia told Ursina not to bother with the second course, and decided to read in her husband's study. She had become excited about the gynecology book Theokritos had lent her and read it every evening, having reached the section on preparing a woman for the birth of her child. Midwives knew this information, but she did not. Soranus gave detailed signs of imminent labor and the preparations that should be made for the infant's delivery.

After reading for an hour, Arcadia had Silvia arrange her hair in braids for the night, then slid into bed alongside her husband.

Getorius was asleep. It was painful to feel estranged from him over some manuscripts, and she resolved not to pester him about them any longer.

❧

In the gatehouse, Brisios was awakened by a determined pounding on the courtyard gate and the frantic barking of his dog, Nigello. He opened the portal a handspan and saw two men standing outside, vagrants, to judge by their clothes. One man supported the other. Brisios quieted the hound.

"What is it?" the gateman asked. "This household is asleep."

"My friend is sick," the man told him. "He's got t'see th'surgeon."

"Bring him back in the morning," Brisios replied curtly. "I'll not awaken the master now."

"He may not live that long. He's…"

"No! In the morning." Nigello began to bark again as Brisios struggled to shut the gate against the man's resistant shoulder.

Childibert came out through the courtyard entrance to the

villa. "I heard your dog barking," he said to Brisios in Frankish. "What is it?"

"Some beggar says his friend is sick. I told him to come back when it's light outside."

"Let them in," Childibert ordered. "It's not for you to decide what the master would do." Brisios did not conceal his disgust when he pulled open the gate and winced at the smell of stale wine and vomit on the men's clothing. "Take them to the clinic. I'll tell the master."

After he was awakened, Getorius was not pleased at the prospect of treating someone at that hour. He thought of telling Childibert to send them to the new hospital at the palace, but changed his mind.

"I'll come, but get Primus up. Have him light the brazier in the clinic."

By the light of a single lamp, Getorius tried to pull on a pair of trousers and tunic as quietly as possible, but Arcadia heard him as he splashed water on his face.

"What is it, Getorius?" she asked in a voice thick with sleep.

"Someone's ill. I'm going to take a look at him."

"Shall I come?"

"No, stay in bed. According to Childibert, it's just some vagrant. Probably needs stitching up after a brawl." When Getorius came into the clinic, he saw the sick man sitting on the examining table, coughing with a deep hacking that left him gagging and gasping for breath. Blobs of bloody sputum stained the floor tiles. He felt the man's face. *Feverish. His hot-cold balance is critically upset.*

"What's his name?" Getorius asked the man's companion.

"Marios. Can y'help him?"

"Where do you two live?"

"We got a space in th'boat sheds by th'harbor."

Marios began shuddering despite the beads of sweat standing out on his face. Getorius brought a blanket from a cabinet and put it around the man's shoulders, wincing at the stench permeating his tunic. "How long has he been like this? What's your name?

"Me? They call me 'Brevius' on th'docks. Y' see, I'm not very tall, and—"

"Your friend. Sick how long? Eight, nine days?"

"About. We been livin' under an overturned boat."

"Well, Brevius," Getorius warned, "your friend is very ill. A phlegm imbalance has tipped his fever to the critical stage. I'm afraid he may not last the night."

As if to confirm the diagnosis Marios began to cough uncontrollably, then fell sideways onto the table. Getorius barely caught the man before he hit the wood. The vagrant wheezed again in shallow gasps that brought a bloody froth to his lips, then lay still. Getorius felt his throat for a pulse and found none.

"I'm sorry, Brevius. Your friend is gone."

"Marios *dead?* I…I can't afford no funeral for him."

Getorius pulled the blanket out from under Marios and laid it over his body. "If you want, I'll see to it that he's put in the beggars' field—" Getorius was interrupted by Primus shuffling into the room with a sack of charcoal and lighted taper to service the grate. "Get out, boy, you're too late," he scolded, and turned back to Brevius. "Wait here a moment."

When Getorius returned, Brevius was at the opposite end of the room, as far away as he could get from his deceased friend.

"The dead can't harm you," Getorius said, rattling several coins in his hand. "As I said, I'll take care of the burial. Here are a few bronzes to reward your loyalty to Marios. If you wish, you can sleep in our bathhouse until morning."

Brevius mumbled awkward thanks as he counted the money, then licked his lips. "I…I'd best be gettin' back."

"As you wish." Getorius guessed that the temptation of an immediate pitcher of wine was greater than that of a warm place to sleep. "You can go out that door, it leads to the Via Honorius. No one will see you."

After Brevius was gone, Getorius straightened out Marios' body on the table, then took a pair of shears from the instrument cabinet. He was cutting away the dead man's fur vest when he heard movement and looked up. Arcadia stood in the doorway in her night tunic, barefoot, with only a shawl thrown around her shoulders.

"You're going to dissect him, aren't you?" she asked.

"You'll be cold, dressed like that," Getorius replied, evading her question and putting down the shears. "Let's go back to bed. We'll have patients in the morning."

⸎

Getorius had trouble falling asleep again. His mind was filled with conflict over the prospect of cutting into a human body. Even Aristotle thought that dissecting a cadaver was useless research, since the body's functions ceased after death. Nicias was the only surgeon he knew who had actually examined a person's inner organs. The city of Alexandria, where Nicias had studied, had allowed the practice then, but Christian fanatics had since taken over the city's administration and forbidden dissection under threat of closing the medical school.

Dissection was not a subject preached about by the bishop at Mass, but Getorius knew that the Church's opposition had to do with the expectation of a physical resurrection for the dead. According to the Apostle Paul, the event was long overdue. He had implied that it would take place during his lifetime, warning men who were married to act as if they were celibate. Mourners were to live as if there were nothing to grieve for. The joyful, he had written, need not rejoice in their good fortune, and buyers should be aware that they might not have an opportunity to use their purchases, nor the wealthy to spend their fortunes.

Getorius got up and poured himself a cup of watered wine. There were some who had not believed Paul. Skeptical Greek proselytes, who were still surrounded by sculptures of the ideal human form, scoffed, or questioned the nature of the resurrected dead. How were they to be raised? In what kind of body? Paul had struggled to explain his vision. The perishable clay of Adam's body would be raised to an imperishable one, the Apostle had reasoned. What had been seeded in humiliation would be harvested in glory. What had been conceived in a human body would be raised as a spiritual entity.

Church scholars assumed Paul meant that all body parts should

68

be intact, without exactly explaining what would happen to those who had lost limbs battling pagans or heretics in the name of Christianity. Willful mutilation was out of the question. Christ's reference to those who castrated themselves for the sake of the Kingdom was interpreted metaphorically as a rejection of sexual relations—except by a few grim-faced fanatics.

Getorius had gone back to bed but was still awake when he heard the first rooster crowing, well before dawn. He rose quietly, trying not to disturb Arcadia, but she heard him dressing in the semi-darkness of the bedroom.

She sat up. "If you're determined to dissect that corpse then I'm going to help you."

"No. Besides, aren't you annoyed with me?"

"I was, but this is more important to you...to our work...than an argument over those manuscripts."

"*Cara,*" he objected, "this is not work for a woman."

"Am I a woman, or a medica-in-training?"

"I'll not have you as an accomplice in this—"

"If you keep arguing with me this loudly," Arcadia hissed, "you'll awaken the servants and *everyone* will be an accomplice."

"It will be cold as the Boreal wind in the clinic," Getorius warned, still trying to dissuade his wife.

"I'll wear my fur jacket." Arcadia slid out of bed and helped him lace up his leather vest. "Meet you in the clinic after I've dressed."

❧

Getorius had finished cutting away the dead man's jacket and tunic, and was positioning two oil lamps near his head when Arcadia entered.

"Where will you start?" she asked, then puckered her nose. "Agh! Those clothes will have to be burned!"

"I'm going to check the cause of the phlegm imbalance that killed Marios."

"His name was Marios?"

"Yes. I'll drill into his skull, but it won't be pretty. Phlegm will pour out like...like dregs from a wine barrel." As Getorius ran a spatula through the dead man's tangled hair he noticed crab-like insects moving on the scalp. "Lice. Dust his head with arsenicum. Armpits and pubic areas, too, we don't want vermin on us."

As Arcadia treated the affected regions, she noted, "He was also hosting colonies of scabies mites."

"Poor fellow didn't have the few coppers needed to get into the public baths. Bring me the auger while I shave a section of scalp."

Getorius knew Galen had taught that the brain was a large gland whose function was to produce phlegm. He would drill an opening in the skull and allow excess mucus to drain out. Then he could remove a section of bone and try to locate an abnormality in the organ that might account for the imbalance. He had done such a procedure on a cat, but the animal had been healthy and nothing leaked out. It would be different with Marios.

Arcadia came back with the boring tool. While waiting for Getorius to finish shaving a patch of Marios's hair, she noticed a crust of dried mucus that had run from the man's nose, but it was no more than when he had been alive.

"Getorius, this is puzzling. Herodotus wrote that the brain has an outlet through the nostrils. Embalmers used the opening to remove the organ when preparing a body for mummification."

"I know what Herodotus wrote. Bring a bowl over here, I'm ready."

Arcadia brought the clay vessel and held it under the shaved area. Getorius centered the auger on the white skin, then paused. "What was your point about Herodotus?" he asked in a more gentle tone.

"If the brain produces phlegm, as Galen believed, wouldn't the excess have leaked out overnight through this man's nose?"

Getorius shrugged a gesture of ignorance in reply, and began a slow turning of the bronze drill. The sound of metal crunching through bone made Arcadia flinch, but she forced herself to watch. In moments her hands began to tremble.

"Hold that bowl in place, woman," Getorius snapped. "I can't do both."

She steadied the vessel. Getorius' breath steamed in the cold air of the room as he strained against the bone's resistance. When the auger bored through with a sudden thrust, he pulled back quickly, expecting a gush of mucus through the opening. Only a trickle of clear fluid dripped into the bowl.

"That's strange," he said, confused. "The man was snorting like a leviathan earlier, yet nothing came out."

"Could it have drained into his chest? You know how people spit up phlegm when they have an imbalance."

"Perhaps. I want to look at his lungs anyway." Getorius felt at the sternum and rib cage. "Undernourished. Sad, but it will make my work easier. Get me that monkey skeleton. The bone connections should be similar."

He expected to find a quantity of blood in the two spongy masses. Galen's observations with apes concluded that the blood pumped into lungs evaporated and was breathed out as a gas. Getorius had found no proof of this in his own animal dissections, yet conceded that humans might be different. Marios had in fact been spitting blood, an imbalance that could give credibility to Galen's theory.

Glancing at the room's high windows, Getorius saw a faint tint of blue coloring the panes. Dawn would come quickly, and with it the first patients. He could smell bread from the baker's shop on the corner, and hear Agrica clanking pans together to show that she was preparing breakfast for the household.

"Bolt the door," he ordered Arcadia, after she came in with the skeleton. "We don't need the cook coming in here to ask how we want our pan of eggs."

Taking up a piece of charred wood from the grate, Getorius eyed the monkey thorax bones. While Arcadia held a lamp, he traced a rectangle on the left side of Marios's chest, estimating the man to have been about thirty years old. His musculature and various scars on his body suggested that he might have worked as a stevedore at one time, but poor food and excessive drinking had wasted his body to the extent that he had not been able to counterbalance the humor imbalance that had made this his final illness.

Following the dark line, Getorius made an incision along the ridge of the sternum to open a flap of skin and gain access inside the rib cavity. The skin membrane proved to be tougher than that of an animal, which usually peeled away with its fur.

"Use that forceps to hold back the bluish membrane," he told Arcadia, then blurted out, "Look at the size of his rib cage! I can't cut through it with the instruments I have, I'd need a carpenter's saw and probably a chisel. The best I can do is peel the membrane back far enough to see as much of his lungs as possible."

After Getorius made further incisions along the lower rib line, Arcadia held back the skin. "That large organ must be his heart."

"Yes. I had no idea it would be that big, yet, according to Hippocrates, it's the center of man's intellect." He probed the lung mass. "It looks like a sponge soaked in bloody water. Christ, nothing evaporated! The man drowned in his own phlegm."

Getorius sensed acrid bile rising in his throat. Despite the chill air he was sweating.

His stomach felt sick, the way it once had after he ate spoiled oysters. Even the faint fragrance of bread was nauseating.

"Are you feeling ill?" Arcadia asked, noticing her husband's pale face.

"I…think this is all I can manage to do just now."

"You wanted to try repairing tendons in a hand."

"Another time. Get me a little wine. Nothing sweet…the local Venetia in the cabinet."

While Arcadia went to pour the vintage into a cup, Getorius covered Marios' body again. His hands felt cold and greasy. "Pour some wine here," he said, holding them over the bowl.

Arcadia held up the cup for him. "Take a sip first."

Getorius gulped a swallow, then rubbed hard to wash away bits of flesh with the wine she splashed on his hands. Afterward, he dried them on a towel, more vigorously than he needed to, in order to purge the clammy sensation.

"How do *you* feel?" he asked her.

"Probably just a little less queasy than you." Arcadia glanced toward the covered body. "What will you do now with the…with Marios?"

"Bury him, just as I promised."

"His body is mutilated, how will you get him out of here? Even vagrants are given a presbyter's final rites at the graveside."

"I could say he died of plague. Few presbyters would risk it, and no one would ask questions."

"Getorius, a lie, too?" Arcadia admonished softly.

"Right. Let me think." He reflected a moment, and then reached for her hand. "Send Brisios to the docks for a piece of sailcloth. We'll wrap Marios in that, a shroud, with just his face showing for the anointing. Then we'll get Presbyter Tranquillus from Holy Cross basilica. He won't see anything of the actual body."

"Good. Now try to get a little rest before your first patient. I don't imagine you'll be eating breakfast?"

"Ah…no. Tell Agrica that I'm not feeling well."

"Alright. And then I'm joining you in bed for a while."

❧

Getorius stared at the bedroom ceiling in the half-light and pondered on what he had discovered. There was no reservoir of phlegm in the dead man's skull, yet the fluid had unmistakably originated in his head. Where? Was there another cavity, perhaps above the nose, where phlegm was produced? Galen described it a result of the Cold-Moist imbalance that developed in people who had been exposed to too much cold. That had surely brought on the condition in Marios.

The man's lungs were sopping wet. Had the evaporation process Galen described gone wrong, or was the physician's basic theory flawed? Perhaps human lungs worked differently.

When Arcadia joined her husband on the bed, she reached over to touch his face. "I know what you're thinking, Getorius. You'll want to do this again, but you can't let it become another obsession."

"Pandora," he said, chuckling.

"Who? And why are you laughing?"

"Pandora," Getorius repeated. "If we ever speak of today again—of Marios—we'll use the name Pandora."

"The first perfect Roman woman."

"Greek, actually, and she couldn't contain her curiosity either."

"Like you." After a pause, Arcadia turned to him. "Getorius, one day I'd like to open a clinic just for women."

"What gave you that idea?"

"Soranus' book on gynecology. I'm sure many women don't come in for treatment just because you're a man."

"I can't help that. Besides, they can hire midwives."

"For births. I'm thinking of other illnesses."

Getorius raised himself on an elbow and kissed her forehead. "You're doing well in the clinic, Arcadia, but you need much more experience. Dissecting—Pandora—shows that I do too."

"I could hire the best midwives in town to—"

He shushed her with a finger against her lips. "We'll talk of it later. How many patients do you suppose we have?"

Arcadia eased herself off the bed, annoyed at his indifferent attitude. "I'll get them ready."

Getorius lay back again and closed his eyes. Although he had been clever to disguise the dissection by referring to it with the name of a girl in a Greek myth, if he talked about the dissection, he now recalled that curiosity had almost been the undoing of the first Pandora.

❦

The weather turned dank. Dark clouds scudded in from the northeast, bringing sleet and snow down from the Norican Alps, which blew across the broad valley of the Padus River and into Ravenna itself. Fountains were glazed over, forcing slaves to break through the ice in the mornings to draw water. If children enjoyed the novelty of licking the white fluff off evergreen branches, and sliding on icy streets, their parents cursed the slush and mud tracked into houses and shops. Glittering marshes around the city walls were crusted with a coating of ice well into the day. Work on the docks ceased as stevedores clustered around fires instead of unloading snowbound cargoes from the last galleys that had arrived.

Ancient medical writers, and some philosophers, agreed that the body's functions were controlled by warm, cold, dry and moist conditions. The abrupt change in the autumn climate, from warm and clear, to cold and wet, was proof. A larger number of patients came to Getorius for relief. At best, they suffered from an increase in phlegm imbalances that caused headaches, fevers and constantly runny noses. At worst, older people went home to die in cold rooms before the imbalance could be leveled again.

Marios' linen-wrapped body was hardly noticed among those of the many vagrants who died from exposure and were given a hasty burial in the paupers' cemetery near the Church of the Apostles.

❧

Feletheus returned the manuscripts without coming to a conclusion. Getorius decided that Theokritos's lack of interest stemmed from cynicism—he had said that all cults had their own prophets. The old forum philosopher had once ridiculed a prediction that the world would end in the five-hundredth year after Christ's birth. The date was still some six decades away, but other more recent predictions of deadlines for Armageddon had passed without incident. Bishop Chrysologos occasionally warned against consulting 'seers, wise women and self-styled prophets,' especially those who used a copy of the Testaments for divination.

Getorius started to believe that Behan's enigmatic 'prophecy,' announcing an imminent event of earthshaking consequence, was no more than the delusion of a lonely monk.

Chapter six

Arcadia was at the Lord's Day service when she caught a glimpse of Publius Maximin wearing a toga—a lingering prerogative of his senatorial rank—and suddenly remembered the invitation to Galla Placidia's dinner, which was only six days away. She felt the Senator was too important a man to approach for advice on clothing, so the next day she went to the senate house in the old forum with her seamstress, Veneranda, to look at statues of past emperors and civic officials.

"Have you made a toga before?" Arcadia asked Veneranda, once she had let her observe the complicated drapery folds on a statue of Caesar Augustus.

"No, Domina. Only senators wear them now. They're made by house slaves."

"Can you figure out how to drape the cloth?"

"I think so. I know it's semi-circular, probably two and a half cubits long and about half that width. I have a friend in Senator Maximin's household. She'll help me."

"Fine." Arcadia glanced around at the sculptures, all of men. "There are no females here. If we went out to the old Roman necropolis along the Via Armini, perhaps we could find a woman's figure on some tomb statuary."

Leaving the senate house, the two walked east along the Via Caesar to the Via Muri Antiqui, a street that followed the ancient walls that Honorius had ordered torn down after he made Ravenna the Western capital of the empire. They turned right at the Armini, an arrow-straight road that was a paved-over canal that had once connected the city with a branch of the Padus River, to the north. The Armini led to a naval base at Classis, some two miles south, then on to connect with the Via Aemilia along the Adriatic coast.

"Your friend is fortunate to be in the senator's house," Arcadia commented. "I understand Maximin is very wealthy."

"Fortunate?" Veneranda retorted in surprise. "She's a slave, Domina. I'm a freewoman."

Arcadia was immediately sorry she had initiated a conversation about unbridgeable social differences. "Perhaps your friend could buy her freedom," she suggested lamely.

"The senator doesn't need money. Bassa told me he once spent a quarter million gold coins in sponsoring his son's games at Rome."

"A quarter million *solidi*? Unbelievable." *Including fish and other foodstuffs that Getorius receives as payment, he barely earns one hundred* solidi *a year. That's about five times what a skilled artisan makes, but Senator Maximin probably spends that much on wine every week.*

Arcadia led the way along the sidewalk of the busy roadway, past three blocks of apartments and shops which gave way to the wooden palisade of the garrison camp that Getorius had criticized. It was true that the men were largely Goths. Roman field armies were in Gaul, under Flavius Aetius, fighting a revolt and trying to resolve differences between local tribes. The barbarians served under their own officers and had proven to be generally loyal, despite fears of rebellion—never far from a Roman official's mind.

At the new Laurence Gate, workers were completing the south wall by extending it to the sea. A short distance beyond the entrance, the burial vaults and monuments of the old pagan cemetery began to line the roadway. Many of the stones were toppled, or inundated by the encroaching marshes that surrounded Ravenna.

At the first cluster of tombs, on high ground, Veneranda brushed snow off weathered stones until she uncovered a sculpted figure dressed in an appropriate garment. The woman, who looked to be about Arcadia's age, wore a flowing tunic that had sleeves reaching to her elbow. It was belted into folds beneath her breasts, and more loosely at the waist. A rectangular palla, a shawl like the ones Arcadia already owned, covered the woman's head and wrapped around her throat.

"Veneranda, I like it," Arcadia said. "Will it be difficult to make?"

"A simple design, Domina. I can have a first fitting in two days."

"Wonderful. Now all I need to find is a hair style of the period."

❧

Since Getorius had been brought to Ravenna as an infant, he had no busts of ancestors, male or female, in his house. Arcadia's father, Petronius Valerianus, was at his villa near Rome for the winter, but she could still go to his house near the Theodosius Gate, to look at portrait sculptures of the women who had married or been born into the family over many generations. One of them was bound to have a hairdo from the republican era.

Only a small staff was retained in winter and the rooms were cold. Arcadia wandered along the garden portico, looking for an ancestral figure with a simple style that would not compete with the way the Gothic Queen might arrange her hair.

She found one at the beginning of the collection. For her stone portrait the unnamed woman had brushed her hair to each side, then woven small braids in the back. A thicker, central plait ran from her forehead, back over the top of the head, and down the back. It was a Germanic style that Arcadia surmised was a fashion novelty at the time. She decided to bring Silvia on the morning of the dinner, and let her work from the statue.

Even though she felt chilled, Arcadia lingered among the portraits, realizing again how fortunate she was that Getorius had agreed to let her study medicine with him. Like Archdeacon Renatus, most men assumed that women only wanted to marry and bear children, therefore few wives had the option of entering a profession. They might supervise a small industry from their homes, such as weaving, but were usually restricted to running the household, while their husbands were out conducting business affairs.

That had not been enough for Arcadia. Her mother had died giving birth to her. While her father had showed no outward resentment, he had left his daughter's upbringing to servants and a governess. Their benign neglect had made Arcadia independent—to some people, irritatingly rebellious—when it came to what was expected of a young Roman woman.

Being in her father's house brought back memories. As a child Arcadia had loved animals, always hoping to find an injured one that she could nurse back to health. She recalled once chasing away a cat that was toying with a young sparrow it had caught. The terrorized bird had a raw wound in its breast, and she had sponged it with olive oil in the hope that the injury would heal. But the sparrow had died in Arcadia's small, cupped hands, its beak open in a gasp as the fright-filled black eyes fluttered shut. She had buried it in the garden, inside her favorite olivewood box.

At age eleven Arcadia had watched from behind a drape while an aunt died in the agony of childbirth. Despite lavish oiling of the birth canal, midwives had been unable to extract the baby. Desperate, one of the women had summoned the physician Antioches. He had been forced to use iron hooks to remove the child, which had killed it, and afterward he had been unable to save the mother from hemorrhaging to death. Arcadia understood more of what had happened now. Soranus' book detailed the awful procedure that back then had sent her retching into a garden fountain.

When Arcadia was fifteen, her favorite uncle Gaius contracted a fever from unhealthy vapors rising out of the marshes. This time Nicias had come from the palace to treat him, and brought a handsome, dark-haired apprentice whom he was training. Getorius was nineteen. He had barely noticed Arcadia at first, but she had decided he was the man she would marry. Furthermore, Getorius would train her to become a medica, just as Nicias was preparing him to heal people, not animals.

Gaius took almost three weeks to recover. Getorius had come every evening to monitor his condition. On one of the nights he showed Arcadia a similar case of a man named Herophon, written up by Hippocrates in a study of epidemics. The patient's fever had broken on the seventeenth day, as had Gaius'. By then Getorius was feverishly in love with Arcadia. Four years later they were married, and he agreed to train her in his clinic.

Marriage may now be considered a holy symbol of the union of Christ and his people, but most of the restrictions on women remained. It was one of the areas where the Church challenged social tradition, yet even so, if Getorius mistreated her, it would be difficult for Arcadia to divorce him. She would have to accuse him either of murder, sorcery, or destroying tombs. Arcadia chuckled at the ridiculous thought.

Bishop Chrysologos was also concerned about the gender inequities in marriage, and had specified penances for men who breached their vow of fidelity. If Getorius abandoned her he could not be reconciled to the Sacraments for seven years. Should she catch him in an adulterous liaison with a married woman, it would take fifteen years before the bishop accepted him back. Fornication, on the other hand, merited only four years for his reconciliation.

Arcadia was sure that Getorius was faithful to her. After a final look at the sculpted hairstyle, she returned to her villa.

On the day before the dinner, Veneranda was making adjustments to the drape of Arcadia's stole when Childibert announced that Surrus Renatus had arrived to see Getorius.

"The Surgeon is in his office. Take the Archdeacon there," she ordered, puzzled at the unexpected visit. "Have Silvia bring mulled wine and cakes. I'll be along in a moment."

When Renatus was shown in, Getorius was staring at a mass

of fresh pig liver he was dissecting. He wiped his hands on a linen towel to greet the churchman.

"Archdeacon, a pleasure to see you. Not a recurrence of your fever?"

"No, I'm quite well." Renatus hosted a fleshy face under a scalp that was almost bald. Thin strands of hair were brushed to each side, to encourage them to merge with a thicker fringe at his ears. Sparse brows were set in a horizontal line, above small hazel eyes. A bulbous nose offset his thin line of mouth. "Quite well," he repeated.

"Then how may I be of service?"

"I, ah, stopped by to ask you about something. Someone, that is."

Getorius thought he seemed nervous. "If I can help—"

"Welcome, Archdeacon." Arcadia came in and extended her hand. "I saw your name on the Empress Mother's dinner invitation at Lauretum Palace."

"She indeed accorded me the honor, Domina Asteria."

"We've been having our clothes made for the occasion. What did a deacon wear during the Republic?"

With an indulgent smile, Renatus replied, "I'm afraid, Domina, that the Church was born too late to be part of those times."

"Of course, how silly of me to forget that Augustus Caesar was emperor at the time of Christ's birth." Arcadia indicated a wicker chair. "Please, Archdeacon, sit down."

Renatus sat and smoothed his long tunic over his knees. "I…I'll wear a dalmatic much like the one I have on now. Perhaps of slightly finer wool, in honor of the occasion. My ministry is to spend the Church's money on the poor, not myself."

Commendable, Arcadia thought, eyeing his white garment. A wide maroon stripe angled from the right side to mid-body, identifying him as a deacon, one church office below that of presbyter. She surmised that the gold thread edging the stripe identified his rank as Archdeacon's and as supervisor of the funds he had mentioned. His calfskin boots were wet. Renatus had evidently walked to the house and not been carried in a chair litter.

Silvia came in with the wine and cakes. The archdeacon took

one of the sweets with a delicate hand motion, but paused to look over at the pig liver on the desk.

"What is that organ?" he asked, his brow puckered in disgust. "It seems more fitting for a butcher's stall than a surgeon's office."

"Not at all, Archdeacon," Getorius told him. "This animal liver may help me understand an illness in a human patient."

"Surely *not*," Renatus scoffed. "God created animals according to their own kind. Only man is made in His likeness."

"My studies—not only mine, but those of Hippocrates, Herophilus, Galen, and even Aristotle—all show a connection between species," Getorius explained. "That liver is from a pig, but the location in its body is similar to that in a dog or cat. The function must be the same in all of them."

"But hardly so in someone made in God's image," Renatus insisted.

"All the more reason for the Bishop to allow dissection. Physicians could see what diseased organs look like."

"Disease is a punishment for one's transgressions," Renatus countered. "A cure can come from the laying on of a presbyter's consecrated hands, or the relic of holy persons."

"That's nonsense, Archdeacon."

Renatus reddened at being contradicted. "I've been told that snips of hair from a martyr's head, drunk in a cup of water, is an effective purgative to cast out evil."

"Another of those superstitions—"

"Getorius, don't bore us with your work," Arcadia interposed, to avoid an argument. "I'm sure the Archdeacon has another reason for his visit."

"Yes." Renatus settled back and took a sip of wine, seemingly relieved at her intervention. "Surgeon, I....ah...heard that you recently were sent to examine the body of a Hibernian monk who died."

"Behan?"

"That's the name. You brought his belongings here, did you not?"

"We didn't want bandits to make off with them," Arcadia said quickly.

"Of course, my child." Renatus reached over to pat her hand. "I'm not implying anything, but the monk's worldly goods *are* the property of Mother Church."

"Don't they belong to his Order?" Getorius asked, still annoyed over the churchman's nonsense about curing disease. "Someone from his abbey is coming to claim the body and arrange a funeral."

"Quite. How did the unfortunate man die?"

"Behan evidently drowned while in a penitential trance."

"In the Holy Spirit, then." Renatus finished the cake, took a sip of wine, and cleared his throat. "Did he…did this Behan have a ring on one of his fingers?"

"A ring?"

"Perhaps a signet of his Order?"

"No. I didn't notice a ring."

"There *was* a white circle around a finger," Arcadia said, "as if he had worn a ring. I didn't think to mention it at the time."

Renatus' straight brows rose in surprise. "You were there, Domina?"

"She insisted on going over my objections," Getorius answered for Arcadia. "My wife trains with me."

"I'd forgotten." Renatus' curt tone betrayed his disapproval. "Surgeon, what did you bring back that belonged to the monk?"

"The only things of value were his writing desk and clothes chest."

"Any books? Surely, they would be valuable."

"A Latin testament. The rules of his Order…a few pamphlets against heresies."

"Tell the Archdeacon about the manuscripts on Behan's desk," Arcadia said. "As a churchman he might have some idea about what they mean."

Getorius gave her a sidewise glance—he had not intended to mention the documents.

Renatus put down his wine cup and leaned forward. "Manuscripts? What manuscripts?"

"Three," Getorius admitted. "Two were written in Celtic.

According to Theokritos, they were only word games to pass the time."

"The librarian has seen these?"

"I asked him to translate them. I was curious."

"As was Eve in the Garden," Renatus reminded him. "I suspect Theokritos has been seduced by the Gnostic heresy, I've seen that Abraxas amulet he wears." Renatus suddenly stood up and ran a hand through his thinning hair. "These manuscripts. Nothing of importance, you say?"

"Evidently not," Getorius replied, unsure of the penance for lying to a churchman.

"Still, Bishop Chrysologos wishes Behan's things brought to the episcopal residence until he hears from his abbot. I'll send servants tomorrow to pick everything up."

"Fine, Archdeacon." Getorius stood up to guide him out.

Renatus paused at the door and asked as an afterthought, "Was there...ah...an animal sharing the monk's cell?"

"Animal?" Getorius chuckled. "Why would he have a pet?"

"Monks are reported to communicate with God though such creatures. It's often a wild creature...a fox or raven. Noah of course first sent a raven to see if the floodwaters had subsided. Behan kept a rooster, perhaps?"

"I didn't notice one, but the Augustus was there the day before. He and his guards discovered the body."

"Valentinian brought his two Huns with him?"

"They were hunting. I asked Optila to look around, but we didn't come back to Ravenna with any animals." Getorius took Renatus by the elbow, wondering why the man was so interested in a rooster. "Let me show you out, Archdeacon."

After her husband returned, Arcadia asked, "Why would Renatus come with questions about an obscure monk? Especially when he already seemed to know a lot about him."

"Renatus did seem agitated when he heard about the two manuscripts, but forgot to ask about the third, the Latin one. Come to think of it, he ended his questions abruptly."

"And what was that about a ring? And a cockerel?"

"I don't know." Getorius sat down again and took a gulp of wine. "Perhaps he just came to tell us about storing Behan's furniture and was curious about the death."

"Didn't you think you heard a rooster outside the hut...and asked Optila to look for it?"

"Arcadia, I could have been mistaken."

"You showed me the drawing of a cockerel on the Latin manuscript," she reminded him, "and now one is figuring in this mystery again."

"A symbol. You think that's important?"

"Remember when Sigisvult was explaining about symbols to us? He said a cock stands for watchfulness, vigilance."

"So?"

"*So*? Husband, if I recall the story of Peter's denial of Christ, the bird also stands for betrayal."

"In this case, betrayal of whom?" Getorius asked bluntly. His head was beginning to ache, the first sign of a possible hot-cold humor imbalance.

"You're the one who's been reading the manuscripts. You and that Feletheus."

"He agrees that the triad riddles are word exercises, but not about the meaning of the prophecy verses."

"With all the sick who have come into the clinic lately, I've forgotten," Arcadia admitted. "What is this alleged prophecy about?"

"That some momentous event will happen soon. The key is evidently in the writings of the Apostle John."

Arcadia took a sip of lukewarm wine, thought a moment, and then put down the cup.

"Getorius, a prophecy needs a prophet. That could have been Behan, but because he accidentally drowned he wasn't able to announce...proclaim it."

"That might explain why Renatus came," Getorius speculated. "He could have been looking for some kind of information he didn't have because of Behan's accident."

Or murder, Arcadia thought. "You think the Archdeacon is involved in…in whatever's going on?"

"Behan's death might have upset some plan." Getorius rubbed his temples. "I'm getting a headache with all this, and being invited to the Gothic Queen's dinner isn't helping."

"Let me…" Arcadia massaged his forehead. Her hand was cool and he held it there until she pulled away. "I'll get you a dose of spirea. As for the Gothic Queen, I prophesy that she'll make you palace surgeon yet."

⊱

It was raining when Archdeacon Renatus left the clinic. To avoid spoiling his shoes and tunic, he hailed a pair of carriers with a covered litter chair, for the distance back to the bishop's residence. At the Via Honorius he covered his mouth and nose at the smell of sewage coming into the conveyance on the wet air.

Renatus felt as gloomy as the buildings of Ravenna that lay drab and colorless under a gray November sky. He did not like mysteries. Events should be as well ordered as his account ledger, which recorded how donations to the poor were received and spent. Now, not only was something hidden going on, but whatever it was may have taken a wrong turn.

Renatus remembered Behan coming to see him in October, the month before his death. The ragged monk had implied that he would soon reveal a prophecy to Bishop Chrysologos about an event of earthshaking importance. It would take place in the near future, and affect the twin Roman empires. Behan had hinted that Renatus, as an archdeacon, would have a role in what was to follow.

He had wondered if the monk's Order was about to make an enormous bequest to the Ravenna diocese, then decided that was ridiculous. Behan was dirty, like the poor fed by deacons, and his stained robe smelled of sweat and wood smoke. The monk spoke Latin with a strong Celtic accent, yet he was clearly well educated. Before leaving, he had asked for sealing wax. After he had pressed his signet ring into the soft blue lump, the image of a rooster was imprinted.

87

This was the prophetic sign, Behan said, and the bishop, his presbyters, and deacons must be ready to recognize and respond to it.

As archdeacon, Behan had emphasized, Renatus would be contacted prior to the time of the prophecy's fulfillment. Curiously, he had not asked for alms, as was normal with everyone who came to deacons. That alone gave the man's enigmatic words some credibility, and yet the monk would surely have known that an archdeacon controlled vast sums. Behan might still have been intending to demand money after the prophesied event had come to pass.

Renatus chuckled softly as the litter bearers turned into the Via Basilicae. Christ had predicted that the poor would always be present, but he had failed to mention their cunning ways.

The archdeacon was suddenly thrown to one side of the small conveyance when the two men carrying it ducked under a porch overhang to avoid being drenched by the water that was gushing from the eaves. He brushed water off his cloak, recalling that Getorius had called the Celtic verses 'word games.' Prophecies were often hidden in cryptic phrases that needed interpretation. Who would give out the meaning, now that Behan was dead?

At the side entrance of the bishop's residence the carriers made a show of refusing payment, but Renatus insisted that each take one of Valentinian's bronze coins, which proclaimed him SALVS REIPVBLICAE, 'The Health of the Republic.' The amount was generous, so Renatus assumed their snickering was connected with the inscription.

Inside, the old porter took Renatus' damp cloak, then said, "Archdeacon, while you were away a boy brought a sealed note."

"Boy? From where?"

"He didn't say, Excellency. It's on your desk."

Renatus nodded. Once in his office, he saw that the note's vellum flap was secured with a lump of red wax. He angled the seal up to the dim light of the window and squinted at the impression. It was the strong image of a cockerel, much like the one Behan had made with his ring.

Renatus' hand trembled as he slipped a thumbnail under the wax and worked it loose.

Perhaps this note will clear up the mystery and tell me what I'm involved in. After he read the greeting, he bit his lip nervously, then mumbled, "Who in the name of salvation is Smyrna? And why does he want me to meet with him?"

Chapter seven

Getorius watched the ides of November dawn with a cold deluge that poured in translucent sheets onto the buildings and streets of Ravenna. Well before midmorning the downpour sloshing off the roof tiles had backed up some of the city's sewers. Marshes already swollen by the wet autumn could not contain the extra water, and a foul-smelling effluent was forced over curbs and into the narrow streets. The sour smell replaced the fragrance of baking bread and roasting meats that normally filled the morning air.

Only a few patients braved the wet weather to come to the clinic. Getorius was able to continue his animal dissections, still disappointed that he had felt unable to continue on the body of Marios, yet realizing that the risk, had he been discovered, could have had him and Arcadia exiled from the city—and even Italy itself.

He was about to leave the clinic for his midday meal when a free servant arrived from the villa of Publius Maximin. Tetricus said that the senator's aged mother was ill, and Maximin wanted Getorius to look in on her.

Getorius knew that Maximin was the wealthiest and most influential man in Ravenna. He had been treasurer of the City of Rome twice, as well as Prefect of the Province of Italy, public services that had merited him a statue in Rome. Valentinian had appointed him Consul six years ago. The senator was out of public office now, but reportedly petitioning the emperor for the title of Patrician. All Ravenna knew that he delighted in showing off his affluence by hosting lavish banquets; one reason, Getorius surmised, that Galla Placidia had not invited him to her presumably austere evening. Another reason might be that Valentinian was rumored to be enjoying periodic hospitality in the bed of Maximin's wife, Prisca. Placidia wanted people at her dinner that embodied the ideal she believed—or pretended to believe—existed at the time of the Roman Republic.

⋇

Irritated, and wondering why Maximin had not asked Antioches to come from the palace, Getorius hunched down in a leather cloak and straw hat borrowed from Brisios, as he followed Tetricus. The senator's villa was in the oldest quarter of Ravenna, the Oppidum, where many of the wealthy citizens lived. His residence occupied a triangle formed by the Via Aurea, Via Honorius, and Vicus Maximin, the latter narrow street named after his family. Retired legionaries, who had no desire to give up urban comforts to begin a rustic life farming the land they had been allotted, patrolled the area.

After the two men turned into the Aurea from the Honorius, they were challenged by a scarred veteran and his companion, a burly brute who may have had only one arm, but who looked capable of strangling a bear with his remaining hand alone.

"Where y'going?" one-arm asked.

"Senator Maximin summoned this surgeon," Tetricus replied. "I'm his servant."

"Never seen you before."

"I work inside the villa, but was entrusted with this errand."

"This is my medical case." Getorius held up the leather box slung over his shoulder, then reached into his belt purse and selected a silvered bronze *follis*. "When you're off duty, men, get yourselves some hot mulled wine."

One-arm's companion grinned and palmed the coin. "On your way, bone-cutter."

"Money, the universal gate-opener," Getorius muttered. "How far is Maximin's?"

"Not far, Surgeon."

"Good, perhaps I won't be spending all of my fee on bribes."

Tetricus turned in at the entrance to a sprawling villa that was set back from the street and surrounded by a wall. Its brickwork was in disrepair, and sections of stucco on the villa facade were crumbling. In a port city like Ravenna, Getorius surmised, young freemen found it easier to make their fortunes in trading or shipping than through an apprenticeship in the building trades.

While Tetricus rapped a bronze Gorgon head against its plate, Getorius shivered. Even though the cape and hat had kept his upper body reasonably dry, his boots and trouser bottoms were soaked. That would not help his humor imbalance. He wiped drops of water from his face, realizing that Maximin probably had called Antioches, but the old man would have refused to come out in weather that gave only marsh ducks a reason to rejoice.

After a locking bolt grated through its retainer, Maximin's porter opened the door.

"I brought the surgeon," Tetricus told him.

The man nodded and led the way through a vestibule into an atrium. Both areas were paved in a pattern of alternating green and white marble slabs, rather than the mosaic tiles usually found in private homes. Not even Lauretum Place boasted a marble entranceway. A loud splashing sound came from an overflowing atrium pool, where water cascading from the roof was spilling onto the floor. Three soaking-wet slaves were frantically sponging the overflow into buckets.

"Where's Senator Maximin?" Getorius asked the porter.

"Master is away. I will take you to his mother."

"Her name?"

"Domina Agatha Maximina."

At the end of a colonnaded porch surrounding the drenched garden, a folding door led into a fair-sized bedroom. Getorius found it overly warm and smelling of camphor. Agatha, a cadaver of a woman who looked as if she should have gone to meet her namesake Saint Agatha years ago, lay in bed. Another woman, presumably her slave, sat by an oil lamp, sewing. She stood up when Getorius entered.

"What seems to be the trouble, Domina?" he asked Agatha, pulling a folding stool to her bedside. "Your ailment?"

Agatha fixed him with watery blue eyes that were alert, despite her emaciated face. "Which one, Surgeon?" she asked wryly. "Haven't you heard that old age has a thousand illnesses?"

Getorius smiled. *Nothing wrong with her mind.* "Then we must treat the worst one first. Where do you hurt the most?"

"My spine. Fabia has now become my legs."

"Fabia? Your slave?"

Agatha gave a hoarse chuckle. "Oh, I've freed her, Surgeon. She's just waiting around for an inheritance from me."

Getorius looked toward the woman. "Turn your mistress on her side, facing the wall, so I can examine her back. Gently."

Agatha's cervical and thoracic vertebrae were curved in a hump-back. Her shoulder blades, lumbar vertebrae, and pelvic bones protruded in sharp lumps through the silk of her night tunic. She winced as Getorius felt along the skeletal ridge of spine. *Agatha implied she couldn't walk. Her vertebrae have deteriorated to the point that all I can hope to do is relieve her pain.* "Fabia. Put a pillow against the headboard. I'll help your mistress turn back around and sit up." He grasped Agatha's bony wrist and eased her into an upright position with his other hand.

Agatha's wrinkled face creased into a smile that still suggested it had once dazzled young men. "Surgeon, your hands are strong. Not like Antioches, who spills most of my medication."

"The palace physician is old."

"And my son...the Senator...sent me rather a handsome replacement."

"Domina, you tease me."

"Tease? When I was younger..." Her blue eyes misted as she glanced away. Agatha wiped an eye and turned back to Getorius. "Well? Can you help me walk again?"

"I...I'm afraid I can only alleviate your pain. Send Fabia to my clinic for an opion solution."

"Opion?" Agatha looked back at him. "The water of the river Lethe...to forget."

"I...I'm sorry."

"Am I also to forget that Dis Pater beckons from the opposite shore?"

"Father Death? I don't think you'll—"

"I'll miss not being in my garden," she went on. "Do you think Dis Pater has a garden?"

"Domina Agatha," Getorius said as an idea came to him, "a carpenter could build you a cushioned chair fitted with light wheels. Fabia could roll you into the garden...around the house. Perhaps even to the marketplace."

"You *are* clever, Surgeon. My son should have thought of that."

"Publius Maximin is concerned with governing," Getorius replied. Fabia slid a small gold coin from a leather bag toward him as he stood up. "The Senator left your fee, Surgeon."

"A *tremissis*? That's too much," he objected. "The pay of a laborer for an entire day."

"The Senator can afford it..." Agatha winced and shifted position. "My son is a conceited man. Did you know they erected his statue in the Forum of Trajan after his consulship?"

"I'd heard. You must be very proud of him."

"I was at one time, but ambition has changed Publius. The saying is that it's better to be first in a village than second in Rome. He wants to be first in both."

"To be Augustus?" *The prospect is arrogant, if not treasonable.* "Yes, well, send Fabia for the opion." Getorius grasped both of the old woman's hands. "I'll look in on you again."

"I'd like that...Getorius."

"My gateman knows a carpenter. Brisios will bring him."

Agatha closed her eyes and murmured, "Then I can ride in style to meet Dis Pater."

※

Getorius sloshed home twice as wet, sniffling, and in a humor as foul as the weather.

There was about an hour left before he had to dress in a ridiculous garment, go to a dinner attended by unfamiliar people, and be forced to listen to conversation about undoubtedly boring subjects. If that were not enough aggravation, the Augustus of the Western Roman Empire would probably try to seduce Arcadia. She would not succumb, of course, but depending on the degree of Valentinian's fascination with her, the emperor might decide there was one husband too many still lurking around.

He found his wife in the bedroom, where Silvia was helping her dress.

"You're soaking, Getorius," Arcadia observed. "Is it still raining out there?"

He gave an authentic but exaggerated sneeze as an answer.

"Go to the hot pool."

"I haven't time."

"Then have Brisios give you a quick rub-down. Silvia, bring him here," Arcadia ordered.

"What is Placidia thinking?" Getorius grumbled as he dried his hair with a towel. "Does she expect to raise the body of the Republic like Christ did that of Lazarus? Ancient Rome has had rigor mortis for over four hundred years."

"Perhaps she wants to bring a little morality back into the court."

"Morality." Getorius grunted and stripped off his wet clothes, then lay on the bed watching Arcadia examine her hairstyle in a silver hand mirror. "The whole affair makes me uncomfortable. If I recall Livius' history, the Republic began with the rape of a Roman woman, and ended with the rape of the Celts and then the Senate, by Julius Caesar."

"Why are you so upset?" Arcadia put down the mirror, sat on the bed and rubbed his back. "So my ancestors are Roman and yours are mostly Celtic. Are you blaming me?"

"No, no, of course not, *cara*. I just think this play acting is in bad taste…to say nothing of going out in this miserable weather when my phlegm humor is acting up." Getorius brought Arcadia's hand to his lips and nibbled her fingers. "What if we spent the evening in the bathhouse instead? You know—"

"You satyr!" Arcadia tousled his hair and pulled the blanket over him. "I hear Silvia coming back with Brisios. I know, the whole affair seems silly, and I'm not sure of Placidia's motive, but it might get you into the palace."

And you into her son's bed. Instead of voicing the thought, Getorius buried his face in his wife's *stola*. "You smell good. What's that new scent?"

"Something Silvia found in a Syrian importer's shop near the docks. Make that a short rub," she told Brisios, after he entered with a jug of oil. "Veneranda isn't here to help with the Surgeon's toga. I'll have to adjust it."

Brisios poured out a palm full of warm, scented oil and began to knead his master's shoulder and neck muscles.

"Tell me again, Arcadia, who's going to be there?" The pillow muffled Getorius's question.

"The archdeacon. Your librarian. Sigisvult."

"'Aetius the Wifeless.'"

"Yes. Of course, the Augustus and Augusta."

Getorius looked up from the pillow. "I don't want Valentinian sitting next to you."

"It's not up to you. Besides, I doubt if we'll be sitting. Placidia will have us reclining on couches like all my decadent Roman ancestors did."

"Even worse!" Getorius started up, almost knocking over the jug. "I won't have that lecher lying next to you."

"Thank you, Brisios," Arcadia said, flushing. "The Surgeon will have to dress now. Please could you bring the covered carriage to the courtyard."

"Where then, is that *furcing* toga?" Getorius snapped. "Sorry, *cara*. Some army slang I picked up."

"Silvia, bring the toga," Arcadia said quietly, ignoring her husband's outburst. From helping treat soldiers she knew the term derived from the furca, a two-pronged cross to which legionaries were tied as punishment. It had become a derogatory term for the men.

❧

By the time Arcadia draped the length of material around Getorius—to her satisfaction if not to his—and Brisios had the carriage ready, the drizzle had stopped. A reddish glow in the early afternoon sky silhouetted the remaining dark wisps of cloud that were scattering to the east. The rose color was reflected in water gurgling through the streets to sewers, or lying in miniature lakes that mimicked the marshes surrounding Ravenna's walls. A cool freshness was tempered by the pervading stench of sewage that overlaid the air.

The Via Caesar was an open cesspool when Brisios left the villa and drove the short distance to the Via Honorius. At the intersection, the market square had become a pink lake cluttered with floating baskets and barrels. Vendors on the north portico were sweeping the water away, and opening shops for a few customers who might come after the rain. Unfortunate slaves, who had drawn the short straw, picked their way over the raised stones across the Honorius to reach the market.

While Brisios waited for a line of wagons to pass, Arcadia glanced at her husband. Getorius was hunched in his toga, against one side of the carriage seat, with a sullen expression on his face. "I did a little research on the old ides," she said, to lighten his mood. "It was the only festival day in November."

"One too many."

"The aedile still schedules a drama in the theater. I heard it was *Aulularia,* by Plautus, although I imagine the performance was rained out."

"It's a wonder that Bishop Chrysologos allows them to go on at all."

"The play is about a gentle miser. People make fun of him because—"

"I know the story, Arcadia," Getorius interrupted. "I hear our esteemed archdeacon counts the number of those who attend the theater against the ones who go to the cathedral for Mass."

Arcadia ended the exchange when the carriage turned into the Honorius. "The palace is just ahead," she warned, "try to be pleasant. Remember that our hosts are the emperor, his wife, and his mother."

Getorius roused himself when the carriage pulled up to the entrance, and two of the tallest men he had seen, Hun or otherwise, came down the steps. "Look at the size of those brutes!" he exclaimed. "Aetius is trying to impress someone with his personal guards."

"Put a shield over your mouth," Arcadia hissed, "your babbling could get us exiled. Next, you'll be shouting about Pandora during dinner."

Her comment surprised him. Arcadia had not mentioned the dissection again, but it was obviously on her mind. "Just an observation. Everyone invited lives at the Lauretum, except us and Renatus."

"Shield it, husband."

"Relax, *cara*. These Huns probably know about enough Latin to order wine in a tavern."

"*Getorius!*"

His goading dissolved into a grin as he tripped over the folds of his toga stepping down from the carriage.

Inside, the hallway was lined with eight more Hunnic sentries. Each man was a duplicate of the next, except for the belted tunic he wore. The silk material had different patterns, with gold coins sewed on as decorations. The guards wore sable hats, dyed calfskin boots, and stood as rigidly as statues, holding their curved swords down, with the tips resting on the floor.

Getorius was impressed. *If we had enough men in our legions with half the Huns' discipline, there might be more hope for the empire, despite inept rulers like Valentinian.*

Galla Placidia had chosen a reception room on the left of the hallway as the intimate location for her dinner. Warm light from the open door reflected off the floor tiles, and a scent of incense was drifting into the hallway from the room. Voices of guests who had already arrived resonated in soft inflections.

When Getorius escorted Arcadia into the room, Placidia was

standing a short distance from the door, speaking to Sigisvult. Valentinian and his wife Eudoxia were reclining on one of the couches, nibbling at a variety of first-course delicacies. Theokritos bent his head close to that of Archdeacon Renatus, speaking in a hushed tone.

Aetius did not seem to have arrived yet.

Arcadia gasped audibly when she saw Placidia, stunned by the magnificence of the tunic she wore—a direct contrast to the request that her guests dress simply. "It doesn't seem possible that earthly hands could have created that material," she whispered to her husband. "It shimmers as if it comes from some celestial realm."

The purple silk body of Placidia's tunic was decorated by twin stripes of gold cloth, embroidered with a motif of roses down each band. Gold thread letters sewn onto a blue background on her left sleeve spelled the initials G P R G, for *Galla Placidia Regina Gothorum*, which proclaimed her rank as Queen of the Goths. Amazed as Arcadia was at the rich material, she was even more astonished at the ornamentation on Placidia's head. Her hair's crowning glory—literally—was a gold-filigree corona that rested lightly on it. Gold letters hung around the lower edge to spell out the queen's name, G A L L A P L A C I D I A. Above these, the openwork was set with three rows of alternating pearl and sapphire gems.

Placidia looked around, as if aware that Arcadia was staring at her. She excused herself to Sigisvult and came forward, fingering a gold medallion struck with her profile and the words SALVS REIPVBLICAE. As did her son's coins, the inscription equated her with the health of the republic.

"Surgeon," she said, smiling at Getorius. "I'm pleased that you came to Our dinner."

"Th…this is my wife Arcadia," he stammered, bowing because Placidia had used the formal pronoun in referring to herself.

"Welcome. My dear, We noticed you admiring Our crown. It was a wedding gift from Ataulf. We were Queen of the Goths at twenty-six." Placidia gave a throaty chuckle, then turned back to Getorius. "You knew Our physician, Nicias."

"Yes. He brought me here…Empress."

"Of course, Surgeon. Tell me the story again." In her request, Placidia dropped the pronoun.

While Placidia reminisced with Getorius about the old physician, Arcadia studied the woman. She guessed her to be about fifty years old. Graying hair lightly tinted with a henna rinse set off the gold in the coronet. It was common knowledge that, as a child, Placidia had been raised in the imperial palaces of Constantinople and Rome, although her father, Theodosius, had come from Hispania. He was an army commander when Gratian appointed him Augustus of the East, after the disastrous Roman defeat at Adrianople. Theodosius had been elected emperor and had redirected Roman military policy by allowing Goths to be unconditionally recruited into the army.

Galla Placidia was as convinced as her father that Romans and barbarian tribes on the frontiers of the empire must join together for mutual security. Ataulf, her Visigoth husband, had shared her vision, but his untimely assassination had raised others to leadership who were not as fascinated by the Roman way of life.

Arcadia was suddenly roused from her musing by Placidia's voice. "We'll begin dinner without Flavius Aetius. Your names are on a papyrus which states which couch you'll share. Surgeon, come with your wife and meet the Augustus and Augusta."

Valentinian grunted an acknowledgement, eyeing Arcadia as he slowly licked his fingers. Eudoxia managed one of the wan smiles she reserved for social inferiors.

Getorius was not pleased to find himself sharing a couch with Sigisvult and the absent Aetius, while Arcadia was placed between Placidia and Theokritos. The emperor, his wife, and Renatus were to their right. Still, at least Arcadia hadn't been placed next to the Augustus.

After the guests had variously slid, rolled, or tumbled onto the unfamiliar slanted beds, servants wearing short tunics and the floppy Phrygian caps of freemen brought in pitchers of sweetened wine. Others carried dishes of what Placidia imagined had been served at republican banquets. A slave announced the nature of each dish, all of which took advantage of Ravenna's location on the sea. Rissoles of minced squid and lobster seasoned with pepper and oregano were served with a sweet-sour prune sauce. Arcadia thought the subtle hint of cumin exactly right. The spice could easily dominate any dish, and usually did in tavern food, to cover the taste of spoiled meat. She took a portion of sausages made with pork and eggs, flavored with lovage and grilled in sea salt. A servant spooned over a mustard, oil, and vinegar sauce.

Getorius tried to catch his wife's eye when a mould in the shape of a sea turtle was uncovered, but she was turned away, talking to Theokritos. The silver mould was filled with bread soaked in wine, then layered with soft cheese, cucumbers, pine nuts, capers, and then baked. He found it excellent, even if the mint in the accompanying herb sauce was a bit strong.

During the meal, it became apparent why the librarian had been included among the guests when Placidia asked him to tell stories about the heroes of early Rome. She wanted the company to be reminded of the ordinary men and women who had sacrificed themselves for the health of the Roman state.

Theokritos quoted first from Polybius, a Greek historian who had emphasized that the sacred destiny of Rome was to become ruler of the world—a thin attempt to justify the conquest of Greece by the legions of Lucius Mummius.

"Enough of Hellas, move on Librarian," Placidia ordered. "Tell us of thwarted conspiracies."

Getorius knew the woman was aware of Theokritos' Athenian origin. Had he deliberately chosen to goad the Empress Mother?

"The consul Brutus, perhaps?" he asked.

Placidia waved a hand in agreement.

Valentinian quickly lost interest in the story, as did his wife. The emperor was on the point of dozing when Aetius arrived in a clatter of makeshift armor that was evidently intended to show him dressed as a legate in the legions of Julius Caesar, if not as the great commander himself. Aetius wore the legendary red cloak of Caesar over a tooled cuirass. His stocky legs, bare, and ruddy from the cold, showed beneath a kilt of leather straps that were studded with bronze nails.

Getorius suppressed a smile behind his napkin, and saw Arcadia look down in embarrassment.

Aetius removed his own helmet—he had not bothered to have a historical one found or made—and acknowledged Galla Placidia, then saluted Valentinian. The Augustus waved a sausage at him in return.

"We were speaking of the men of the Republic," Placidia said, as Aetius tried to maneuver into place next to Getorius without revealing what was under the kilt straps. "My library master, Theokritos, was going to tell us about Brutus."

The name had its desired effect. Aetius looked toward Placidia with a quizzical frown.

"Ah, not the Brutus who also wounded Caesar's pride when he stabbed him," she added innocently. "No. The Lucius Brutus who ordered the execution of his own sons, after they were accused of treason. Commander, you have sons by your Gothic wife, do you not?"

"Two, Empress. Carpilio and Gaudentius."

Placida fixed Aetius with a cold stare over the rim of her wine cup. "And would you order their deaths for Rome, as did our Brutus?"

"Empress, I once gave Carpilio to the Huns as a hostage for Rome," he replied, maintaining his composure. "The 'treason' of Brutus' sons was to want to restore a king who, actually, was to be subject to the Senate."

Getorius doubted that Valentinian had caught the irony in the comment. Caesar's successors, now emperors, had stripped senators of their republican powers.

Placidia, across from him, caught it. "Well said, Commander. Let us drink to the Senate and People of Rome."

After the toast, as a servant refilled Aetius's cup, Getorius introduced himself.

"Yes. I know of you, Surgeon," Aetius responded. "You've treated some of my men."

"Commander," Renatus called over, "your Hunnic guard. Are they Arian heretics?"

Aetius helped himself to a rissole before glancing up at him. "Archdeacon, as long as they're loyal, I don't interfere with my men's religion."

"But Arians are not loyal to the Roman Church," Renatus probed. "This woman…Thecla…is their presbytera, yet Christ ordained none of Eve's Daughters."

Getorius knew that early on women had officiated at the Eucharist, but steered the conversation back to the guards. "Archdeacon, when Honorius was emperor, his army commander Flavius Stilicho had similarly loyal Hunnic contingents."

"A novelty thirty years ago," Renatus countered. "Now they're thick as…as pond scum."

"An unpleasant metaphor, Archdeacon," Aetius commented.

"Where are our field armies?" Valentinian asked the commander, more interested now that conversation had turned to the military.

"Augustus, they are stationed between here and Mediolanum."

"Who's in charge, someone named Hunwulf?" Valentinian laughed at his joke about names of barbarian legion commanders.

Getorius noticed Aetius flush, recalling that the commander's wife had been excluded because of her Gothic origin. "With respect, Augustus," he ventured, "barbarians who were granted federate status have never reneged on their obligations to Rome."

"As long as the bribes keep coming," Renatus taunted. "How disturbing to have only a barbarian's oath between us and another ravaging of Rome, as happened a generation ago."

"Where I was one of the prizes," Placidia reminded him. "I convinced Ataulf that the benefits of *Romanitas* were in his barbarians' interests."

"Roman-ness?" Theokritos scoffed. "That's not for Gaiseric. He and his Vandals at Carthage have come full circle, so to speak."

"Full circle?" Valentinian echoed, looking puzzled.

"Your Excellency is aware that Carthage, capital of our African province, fell to the Vandals last month?"

"Librarian, don't be impertinent," Placidia warned. "Of course the Augustus knows."

"Now Gaiseric poses a threat to Lucania in southern Italy," Aetius added.

Valentinian cut a piece off a sausage and held it up on the point of his knife. "Then order the legions that are down there to bring me this Vandal's head...like this."

"Augustus, we have no legions there."

"Well where in Hades' name are they, Aetius? You're the furcing commander."

"Northern Gaul. The Danube frontier—"

"The navy!" Valentinian suddenly shouted, as if Neptune himself had inspired his thought. "Use our fleet. What do barbarians know about galleys?"

"Good point, Augustus," Aetius responded, to end a pointless conversation. All of Ravenna feared that Gaiseric had probably captured the African fleet and would soon learn how to use it.

"Goths may be loyal to Rome," Renatus commented, breaking a silence that followed, "but not to the Roman Church. They're heretics, plain and simple."

"We have no trouble with them in Ravenna," Sigisvult objected.

"Yes, Architect," Renatus scoffed, "they're good for *your* profession. Duplicate basilicas, two baptistries—"

"They keep to their quadrant near the harbor," Sigisvult broke in angrily.

"Then there are the Judeans," Renatus continued. "An entire colony of Hebrews here and at Classis. And cryptopagans...even a temple to Isis, an Egyptian idol. God only knows what other hidden cults there are." The archdeacon looked toward Theokritos for support. "What do you think, Librarian?"

"As well as faith, the Goths corrupt language," Theokritos grumbled. "Who still speaks of pay as salarium? Now it's Gothic midzo."

"Sir, don't you think we share a common language?" Arcadia asked, feeling competent to discuss linguistics, if not legions. "Some words are so similar. Latin *rex*, and Gothic *reiks* for 'king.'"

"A coincidence, young woman."

Arcadia fortified herself with a quick gulp of wine. "You don't think there's a common root, sir?"

"Certainly not with Greek, young woman," Theokritos replied. "And Latin has its own corrupt origins."

"But take the present month of November," Arcadia persisted, feeling a bit giddy. "Goths call it Naubaimar. Surely the similarity is more than a coincidence."

"They stole it from us, like the land we're obliged to give them under the new laws. Soon two-thirds of our words will also be Germanic...like those Frankish terms creeping in."

"Come now, Librarian," Sigisvult countered, "Franks are a tribe destined to disappear, just as did the Germanic ones that Tacitus mentioned. Isn't that so Commander?"

Aetius shrugged and swirled the wine in his cup. "I'm not so sure."

"Nor I," Placidia agreed.

Eudoxia used the following interval of silence to complain that the room was chilly.

"I'll tell Heraclius," Valentinian said looking around, "Where is that eunuch of mine?"

"Magnaric"—Placidia signaled to her steward—"Magnaric, speak to the furnace attendants, and have the second course brought in."

Servants appeared with platters of cheeses, salt fish, and lentils cooked with mussels. These were followed by wild duck braised in a turnip sauce, roast venison with aromatic date-spikenard gravy, and the carcass of a boar basted with caraway.

Watching Magnaric carve the wild pig evidently reminded Valentinian of the one he had wounded in The Pines. "The boar I probably killed on the day that monk drowned was bigger than this one," he boasted.

Eudoxia giggled. Placidia let the insensitive remark pass, only commenting, "A pity about the Hibernian, but at least he died in Christ."

"These Hibernians"—Renatus paused to accept a serving

of duck—"these hyperborean islanders are gaining a foothold in Gaul."

"Whereas," Aetius quipped, "no Roman legion secured even a *toehold* on their island."

"The bishop sent word to the dead monk's abbot," Renatus said, missing the connection.

"Who is he, Archdeacon?" Placidia asked.

"Brenos, at Autessiodurum. There's a monastery there that Germanus built, but Roman bishops hope it won't attract too many Gallic men."

"Why is that?"

"Empress Mother," Renatus explained, "Hibernians differ in some of their practices...private confession, rather than public, for example, a different date to commemorate the Lord's resurrection. They also favor married clergy, when Rome is rightly trying to suppress this practice."

Placidia changed back to Behan's death. "Surgeon, you examined the monk's body?"

"Yes. Behan was evidently practicing a rather severe form of penance."

"*I* found him in the stream," Valentinian boasted through a mouthful of venison.

"Optila calls monks Shave-heads."

Getorius ignored the crude remark. "Empress, the cold water proved too much for Behan. He drowned."

"There was a welt around his neck," Arcadia blurted out from her couch.

What? Getorius stopped cutting a chunk of boar. *Is Arcadia going to tell everyone she thinks Behan was murdered? She does get a little reckless after drinking.*

"Of course, there was," Renatus agreed in a smug tone. "Didn't you find a leather strap somewhere in his hut?"

"Why...y...yes," she stammered. "H...how did you know?"

Getorius paled. *Yes, how could he have known?*

"It's another penance these Hibernians practice," Renatus

explained. "They wrap a strap around their necks and tighten it until they lose consciousness. I'm told it induces some kind of vision or ecstasy."

"Archdeacon," Getorius asked, to save his wife from further embarrassment, "when is this Brenos to arrive?"

"I doubt the abbot will come himself. He'll send someone with burial authorization. Would he be able to take the body back to Gaul? I mean, its condition—"

"I think it's been cold enough to preserve it."

"Archdeacon," Sigisvult suggested, "perhaps one of the Egyptian priests you mentioned could embalm the body."

"That's a thought—"

"Enough talk of Behan's death," Placidia interposed, turning to Theokritos. "I understand there were documents brought to you from the holy man's cell. What were they?"

"Riddles in the triad style of Hibernians. A fantasized prophecy, I would say."

Valentinian, who had been staring at Arcadia since the meat courses were brought in, took up the unintended cue with a wink at her. "My astrologer predicted that Eros would favor me in November. So far he's been wrong, but it's only mid-month."

"The man's a fool," Placidia told her son, glaring at him. "Go on, Librarian. Tell us of this prophecy."

"It sounds like another one of the predictions so common these days. Yet some of the words are not in the correct form."

"I noticed that too," Getorius confirmed, "but wondered if Behan had been careless."

"Hardly," Renatus told him. "Discipline is a virtue with Hibernians. Librarian, give us an example of this aberration."

Theokritos stroked his white beard, reflecting for a moment. "The last verse reads, 'The testament of this is hidden in the book of John.'"

Renatus continued probing. "Testament of what?"

"The monk was referring to Christ's discourse on love at his agape meal, and suggesting that its fulfillment would be in our time."

"What are the improper forms you mentioned?"

"Scribes have begun to initialize—to increase the height of letters that begin a sentence or important title," Theokritos told the archdeacon. "'Testament' should be so indicated. And rather than, 'the book of John,' the term should be 'The Testament of John.'"

"The first way makes it sound like there's a document hidden in a book that includes John's Testament," Arcadia ventured.

"Perhaps." Theokritos pushed a chunk of fat to the side of his plate. "I admit I was intrigued enough to have Feletheus search through our Vulgate editions."

The old fox. Pretending not to care. "And?" Getorius queried.

"He found nothing."

"I'm sure there's nothing hidden in my copy of Jerome," Renatus said, "but I'll check the Bishopric library."

Placidia had been distracted by her son's attraction to Arcadia. "Again, what are we looking for, Librarian?"

"A forgery at best, Regina. In times of crisis, prophecies give hope to fools."

"But...but this could initiate a new heresy," Renatus sputtered, jabbing the air with his knife. "The bishop would want it exposed quickly, rather than having some wild-eyed hermit shouting nonsense from the public rostrum."

Placidia allowed the conversation to subside while servants refilled the platters. Getorius guessed that everyone felt as stiff as he did from lying down. Except for Aetius and the women, they were shifting position and holding their bodies up with one arm or another. Theokritos, especially, was having trouble finding a comfortable position.

Arcadia allowed herself to be served only small portions of food and refused more wine. It was an excellent vintage, possibly still from the vineyards of Latium in the hills around Rome, she thought, but the honey sweetening masked its rich body.

She had been watching Eudoxia, aware that the eighteen-year-old Augusta had been raised in the court at Constantinople. She had obviously been spoiled by her father, Theodosius II, the Eastern Augustus, yet had also been taught court protocol, in preparation for her role as the potential wife of an emperor. Arcadia could see that the woman was bored by the scholarly talk and annoyed at her husband's interest in a guest who was not even a member of a Patrician family.

Eudoxia glanced up at Arcadia, who signaled back with eye contact and a smile that she had no interest in being Valentinian's new mistress.

The servants had begun to remove the platters of uneaten food, when Eudoxia called over, "Mother Placidia. Perhaps I could show our…your…guests the holy relics my mother brought back from Palestina."

Placidia was evidently taken by surprise. She had been watching Heraclius, who had slipped into the room to stand by Valentinian's couch. Tavern gossip suggested that the eunuch steward had too much influence on the emperor, not only in feeding his fascination with astrology, but also arranging the sexual liaisons that were the unspoken scandal of the palace. Now her daughter-in-law had suddenly interfered with a surprise she had planned. Was Heraclius behind this, too, his entrance being a signal for Eudoxia?

Placidia disliked her daughter-in-law's mother. Athenaïs, the daughter of a Greek Sophist, had been well educated in the Hellenistic culture of Athens. While on a journey to Constantinople, Athenaïs had caught the eye of Theodosius' sister Pulcheria, who thought her suitable for marriage to an emperor. The marriage took place after she was baptized with the Greek Christian name, Eudocia. Within two years, the pagan philosopher's daughter had been raised to the imperial rank of Eastern Augusta.

Placidia knew about the relics. Eudocia had recently returned from a pilgrimage to the Holy Land, where the Bishop of Jerusalem had given her several mementos of the Apostles. The most spectacular of these was the chain with which Herod Antipas had shackled Peter, and from which he had been miraculously freed by an angel. Eudocia had shared the relics with her like-named daughter, intending to dedicate a basilica at Rome with the chains as a votive offering for her safe return.

"Relics?" After stalling by rearranging her crown, Placidia forced a smile. "All in good time, my dear. I want my architect to tell us about the progress he's made on my mausoleum. I'm dedicating it to Blessed Lawrence."

Sigisvult looked up, startled. "Of...of course, Regina. As you wish."

"Begin with the symbolism."

"The building will be an allegory of the cosmos," he explained. "Its exterior is unfaced brick, to represent our visible world. Inside, the space shines like Paradise itself, with mosaics that rival any in Constantinople. Gold and lapis tiles...vermilions that have never been seen on this side of the Adriatic—"

"Now for my surprise," Placidia called out. "We shall look at the building this evening. Now, before the sweet course."

"But Regina, it...it's dark outside," Sigisvult objected. "The work isn't totally complete."

"Architect, didn't you tell me niches for two of the sarcophagi are finished?" Placidia demanded in the tone of a woman not used to being contradicted. "And the mosaics of Christ as shepherd...the martyrdom of Lawrence? No, we *shall* go to my mausoleum."

"Augustus," Heraclius stage-whispered to Valentinian in his womanish voice, "Marcian warned against outdoor night adventures in November."

"Visiting tombs for sure." Valentinian tittered drunkenly, then called over, "Arcadia, you don't want to see some gloomy vault. I'll show you the imperial apartments instead."

"She's going with her husband," Placidia intervened. "You needn't come, Placidus."

"And I'm staying here, too," Eudoxia whined, now deprived of her opportunity to be the center of attention with her relics.

"And I, Regina, with your permission," Aetius said, sitting up on the couch.

"Yes...Pelagia, your Gothic woman, will want her bed warmed," Placidia sneered. "You command legions, Aetius, but how lacking in any sense of adventure you are. Leave Us."

Theokritos crawled stiffly off the couch. "I would like Feletheus to accompany me, Regina. He wants to put a mosaic in the library reading area."

"Very well. Magnaric, send a servant to fetch him. Have four others light torches."

Getorius rubbed his stiff legs and half-limped over to Arcadia. "Thank Aesclapius we have a chance to stretch," he muttered, "but I hope those street lakes have drained off."

She laughed. "Husband, wet feet are a small price to pay for the privilege of seeing the imperial mausoleum. Besides, you have no choice. The Gothic Queen commanded it."

Getorius bent close to her ear. "Did you notice Renatus probing to find out about the prophecy? It's almost as if he's learned more since yesterday and wants to confirm it."

"Or so the wine you drank made it appear." Arcadia took his arm. "Let's go, husband. The Gothic Queen is beckoning us."

Chapter eight

The new moon had risen during the first night watch; now its slim crescent was visible through a scattering of clouds and accompanied by a retinue of dim stars. Although the rain had stopped several hours earlier, few citizens were in the streets. Corner bonfires threw sparks and smoke into the chilly air, and washed an orange light over civic guards who huddled around the blazes to warm themselves.

Galla Placidia had chosen the northwest quadrant of Ravenna, the Adriana, for her Basilica of the Holy Cross and new mausoleum. The buildings were on high ground that had been enclosed by her son's rebuilt walls. Here, older buildings were being razed to make room for the villas of senators and court officials who had followed Emperor Honorius to Ravenna almost four decades ago, after he made the port city his Western capital.

Merchants newly rich from government contracts and goods imported through Constantinople were also commissioning elegant homes in the quarter.

By now the rainwater had run down toward the Oppidum area, so the cobbled streets leading to the mausoleum were fairly well drained. A smell of burning pitch was strong on the damp air as the torchbearers moved ahead of the small procession. Placidia had removed her crown, and covered her hair with the hood of a white woolen cloak.

Renatus, following a pace behind her, expressed concern. "Empress, you should be carried in a litter. This mud will ruin your slippers and the hem of your magnificent tunic."

"Archdeacon," she quipped, "I've survived both the barbarian occupation of Rome *and* a Visigoth husband, so I can surely walk the short distance to my tomb. I'll be carried there soon enough."

"You don't wish to be buried at Constantinople near your father?" Renatus asked, "or the Theodosian family tombs at Rome?"

"In these dangerous times, even dead I might not complete such a journey."

"Empress—"

"No, Archdeacon. This way I can rest in the sight of Blessed Lawrence, and as a part of my Basilica of the Holy Cross."

Sigisvult walked next to Renatus, ahead of his unwanted visitors, but said nothing.

Getorius and Arcadia, in the middle, could hear Theokritos behind them, complaining to Feletheus that the bottom of his toga was being soaked by puddles which the assistant had failed to point out.

A short distance along the Via Honorius the group passed under the Porta Asiana, all that remained of a gate in the old Augustan wall of the town's northern limit. The wooden bridge over the Little Padenna River remained, but the stream bed had been paved over and was now used as a sewer. A new avenue named after Placidia's second husband, Constantius III, also now deceased, had been laid parallel to the wall foundations. Half way along this street, the mausoleum was reached by a smaller intersecting way, already called Vicus Galla Placidia.

Sigisvult had moved ahead of Placidia, when the dark bulk of the basilica and its attached mausoleum loomed in the near distance. Several men whom he had hired to guard building materials were huddled around a bonfire. One of them looked up, then stepped forward to challenge the intruders, his spear held level.

"*Pax*, peace," Sigisvult said quickly. "Guard, I'm the architect. My friends want a look at the mausoleum."

The man grunted and lowered his weapon, but evidently recognized Placidia and managed an awkward salute. "*Ave*. Hail, Empr'ss."

Sigisvult pressed a silver half-*siliqua* into his hand as he whispered, "Don't let your companions know the Empress Mother is here. We won't be long."

"And tell him to stopper that wineskin," Getorius muttered, watching the exchange. "He already smells like a harbor tavern at dawn."

"There's the mausoleum!" Arcadia exclaimed, "Sigisvult, I can't wait to see the mosaics you described."

The small cruciform building was at the south end of the narthex, a covered porch leading into the Holy Cross Basilica. Even by the sparse torchlight the austerity Sigisvult had described was evident. Blind arcades were the only relief in the raw brick walls, but the recesses gave a unifying motive to the twelve intersecting surfaces. Above, a squat tower concealed the domed ceiling of the interior.

At the unlocked door inside the narthex, Sigisvult hurried Galla Placidia into her building. Getorius knew he had bribed the guard, yet it would only be a matter of time until the man boasted of having protected the emperor's mother from imaginary assassins, and other guards came to gawk at her.

The interior, which Getorius estimated to be about five paces wide and three times that long, smelled of damp mortar and fresh wood shavings, yet instead of the dank space he had expected, the building was warm from the heat of braziers left glowing to dry the mosaic grout. A slave was lying asleep on the floor, next to one of the iron grates. Sigisvult nudged the man awake with a foot and ordered him out. After the palace slaves had propped their torches in the scaffolding, he told them to wait outside.

As the group's eyes adjusted to the dim light, the glow of the colored mosaic decorations materialized from the gloom. Getorius grasped Arcadia's hand, gazing at the splendor of the entranceway mosaic, which depicted Christ as a benevolent shepherd.

"Exquisite," Placidia murmured in a voice hardly louder than her breathing. "Most exquisite, Sigisvult."

The depiction of Jesus as a beardless youth had more in common with the pagan god Apollo, than with ragged sheep herders in Judea. Christ wore a golden tunic decorated with two aquamarine stripes on the front, and the purple pallium of an Augustus lay across his lap. The Imperial Shepherd held a golden cross as a crook in his left hand, while he reached over to fondle the muzzle of the nearest sheep with the other. Five other animals watched.

"I am the caring shepherd," Renatus quoted, "and I know my sheep and my sheep know me."

Even the usually opinionated Theokritos was uncritical at viewing the blue and green colors, which sparkled with gold tiles that had been worked into Christ's robe and halo.

"Sigisvult"—Placidia broke the spell again—"you've more than repaid my faith in you through this work. Come to think of it, there are two of you here who owe their lives to me. Surgeon, we'll speak of my plans for you later. Now, Sigisvult, I want to see the niche where I'll be buried. You said the mosaic of Saint Lawrence was finished?"

"Yes, Empress. We need to remove the scaffold, but the work is complete. Here...in the transept opposite the entrance." The group followed Sigisvult past two arched recesses. "These are where the sarcophagi of Honorius and Constantius will be placed," he explained.

"My brother and my husband," Placidia commented softly. "Near me for eternity."

In a semi-circular space above her niche, the figure of Lawrence hovered in spiritual ecstasy, next to the fiery grill on which he had been martyred. A flicker of torchlight played on the alabaster pane of a center window.

"I don't know anything about Lawrence," Arcadia admitted. "Why did you include him, Sigisvult?"

"It was the Archdeacon's idea," Placidia answered. "What did you tell me, Renatus?"

"Lawrence became a deacon during the reign of Valerian. The emperor generally let Christians practice the Faith, but then everything seemed to go wrong for Rome. Persians, Germani, Goths…all attacked our frontiers at once."

"Not unlike today," Placidia remarked wryly. "Continue."

"The Augustus wanted to divert attention and blame someone. One of his advisers, a member of an Egyptian cult, brought his magicians. They persuaded the old emperor that his toleration of Christians had offended the Roman gods—"

"Which was strange," Theokritos interrupted, "since Denys of Alexandria wrote that the palace was almost like a church because so many Christians worked there."

"Again, why was Lawrence singled out?" Placidia asked.

"Sixtus the Second, namesake of our present pontiff, was in Peter's Chair. Valerian's treasury officials cast greedy eyes on the Church's money, goods that were intended for the poor. It was Lawrence's responsibility to distribute them, as now it is mine. The assassins ambushed Sixtus in a catacomb, murdered him and some of his presbyters."

Renatus pointed up to the iron grill. "Lawrence was tortured on that device to make him reveal the location of the treasure."

Dressed in a white toga, Lawrence held a golden cross and an open book in his hands. A pale blue celestial background was in peaceful contrast to the angry red flames beneath the grill.

"Lawrence is rising in glory," Sigisvult said, explaining the symbolism. "It took some doing to get the folds of the toga to express his spiritual state. The cross is an emblem of his martyrdom."

"The tradition holds," Renatus continued, "that when Lawrence was ordered to reveal the Church's treasure, he brought in sick and poor people. That cabinet alongside the saint displays the Testaments of Mark, Luke, Matthew and John. Lawrence said those writings were his other treasures, a record of the Savior's life."

Feletheus edged up to Theokritos. "Master," he whispered, "I've been studying the mosaic. There is a book of John shown in the cabinet."

"A Book of John?" Theokritos gave a half-laugh. "Ridiculous. It's an *ikon*, a picture. What could it conceal?"

"Just the same, if I might look more closely?"

"What are you two conspiring about?" Placidia demanded, frowning. "Don't you like the artwork, Librarian?"

"Indeed, it is exquisite, Regina," Theokritos replied, "as you said yourself. My assistant wishes to examine the tile work of the Testaments more closely."

"Would that be all right, Sigisvult?"

"Have him get on the scaffolding. It's not high, but the man must still be careful."

Feletheus climbed the framework with surprising agility. Once he was facing the tile book design, he ran his fingers along its edges, and then called down, "Master, I feel a space around the sides. As if the book could be removed."

"Pulled out?" Getorius asked.

"Yes."

"Impossible," Sigisvult scoffed. "The tesserae are less than a finger's thickness in depth."

"Will the book come out?" Theokritos asked, watching his assistant.

Feletheus tugged at the edges. "It…yes…it's moving."

The John mosaic was at the lower right, about on eye level with Feletheus. As he pulled harder the book shape began to move forward and allow him a better grip. "It's… slid…ing out," he grunted. "There's a space…behin…"

Feletheus never finished mouthing the word. The bolt from a small crossbow concealed in the opening caught him in the forehead with such force that it passed through his skull and shattered in the Imperial Shepherd opposite. The librarian's body swayed on the scaffold an instant, like a puppet whose strings are abruptly cut, then toppled off, spattering blood on Galla Placidia's white cloak as he fell to the floor with a sickening thump. The square of tiles dropped with him, narrowly missing Arcadia before shattering on the floor.

Placidia instinctively stepped back. Renatus was too stunned to even cross himself. Sigisvult braced a hand on a corner of the scaffold and vomited. Theokritos stood staring down at his mutilated assistant.

"Christ Jesus!" Getorius blurted. "What happened?" He bent

down over Feletheus' body. "H…he's dead…killed instantly," he whispered in a hoarse voice, then looked up at the opening where the tiles had been removed. Something glinted inside the lethal trap, next to the bow, as if a metallic object was stored there.

"Archdeacon, cover the poor man," Placidia ordered, removing her bloodstained cloak and handing it to Renatus. "Isn't there a prayer you can say? An anointing? Anything?"

Before Renatus could react, two members of Aetius' Hunnic guard appeared at the door, their swords drawn. Getorius' first thought was that the violent death was a signal for a palace takeover, and that the two Huns had been assigned to capture or kill the emperor's mother. He suspected that Flavius Aetius constantly had the fate of Stilicho in mind. Their positions were similar—Honorius' army commander had been betrayed and murdered—but a wary Aetius would undoubtedly act first.

While one of the Huns bent over the body, the other sheathed his sword and bowed to Placidia. "You are…not…hurt?" he asked in hesitant Latin.

"No. How is it that you came here?"

"The Commander sent us as…as shadows to your person."

Placida exhaled and color returned to her complexion. "We will commend you to Aetius." She searched her purse and gave each a gold coin. "Return to the palace."

As the Huns left, Sigisvult, still retching, followed them into the cold air. Getorius took the cloak from Renatus and covered the body of Feletheus.

"I saw something shining in that niche," Placidia said, "and I didn't want those Huns looking at it. Surgeon, get whatever is up there."

"I noticed it too, Regina." Getorius gathered up the folds of his bulky toga to climb the framework.

Arcadia looked around and spotted a long-handled grout spatula. "Keep your head down and poke around in the opening with this first," she advised, handing the tool up to her husband. "There may be some other trap you don't know about."

After ducking low, and pushing the spatula from side to side to move the bow, Getorius reached in and carefully pulled out a long tube. His fingers felt the raised designs on the surface before he saw them on the golden cylinder. When he handed the container down to Placidia, he heard an inner case slide forward a short distance.

Getorius clambered down and stood with the others as Placidia turned the case over in her hands. The gold was embossed with designs whose motifs were three-looped triskelion circles, and bands of spirals inlaid with red and blue enamel.

"Celtic work," Arcadia observed. "My father has a brooch in the style. This must be very old, some of the enameling is broken off."

"Surgeon, clear that table," Placidia ordered, indicating a bench where workers cut tiles for the mosaics. "I want to see what this holds that is worth a man's life."

Theokritos watched Placidia try to twist off the cover. "It will take a goldworker to open it, Regina."

"No, the fewer who know about this the better." She handed the tube to Getorius.

"Surgeon, operate on the lid and open it."

A golden disc which had been soldered on sealed the container's bottom, but the top was closed with an overlapping cap, also soldered around the edge. Getorius poked around among the tools he had pushed aside and selected a tile-cutting chisel. Arcadia held the cylinder, while he scraped the sharp edge along the seam until he had worked the cap free. He pulled it off and found the gold case reinforced by a heavier inner cylinder of copper.

"There's a leather tube inside," he told Placidia, handing her the container.

When she slid the smaller tube out, a sheet wrapped around it came loose.

"Bring that torch closer," she ordered Theokritos, unrolling the page to scan the writing. "This is gibberish. The provenance is yours, Librarian."

Theokritos took the sheet and held it near the light and felt the material. "Papyrus. Old, the ink has turned brown. The writing is Hebrew…no, Aramaic, with some interpolation of Greek words."

"What does that mean?" Placidia asked. "How old?"

"Aramaic was the language of Judea in the time of Christ."

"Four centuries ago," Arcadia remarked. "Are you able to read what it says?"

Theokritos squinted at the words a moment, then read, "I, Simeon bar Jonah, called Petros by the Nazarene, when in the courtyard of the Praetorium, received this from the centurion Gaius Salutus, a secret disciple."

"*Simon Peter?*" Getorius exclaimed. "The letter was written by Christ's disciple?"

Theokritos ignored the question to continue, "It is the Last Testament of the Christ, but the presence of a centurion speaking to me aroused the curiosity of those around the fire. Fearing for the document's safety, and mine, I thrice denied the Nazarene and fled.

"It came to pass as the Lord had prophesied. After I had presided over the Assembly for twenty-three years, I was instructed in a dream to embark on a boat and sail beyond the Pillars of Hercules. Yet it was the power of God that steered the boat. I sailed north for seven days and sighted no land, and then the boat directed itself to an island where no Roman legions had set foot, to the village of Corcaigh. There, by the grace of God, I built a chapel where I placed the Testament until, in God's own time, He will choose to reveal these things."

Stunned, no one reacted. Theokritos stared at the niche as he rolled up the letter.

Renatus was the first to speak. "Peter in Hibernia? Ridiculous. The Apostle died at Rome...was buried in the Vatican Hill necropolis."

"That is the tradition," Theokritos agreed, "but there is no real evidence, no body. And the man cannot be accounted for during those years."

"Peter's chains," Placidia countered. "The chains from his imprisonment have been found. Surely, Archdeacon..." Her voice trailed off in a plea for confirmation.

When Renatus did not reply, Arcadia said, "There must be another document. The testament of Christ the letter mentions."

Her comment revived Theokritos. He examined the leather

tube, which was brittle and no longer smelled of tanned hide, and exuded a musty odor. Its shrunken top easily slipped off, revealing a gold foil lining inside that protected another papyrus from the sides of the case. Easing the sheet out, Theokritos read a few lines, then staggered against the bench for support.

Getorius helped him onto a stool. When he took the manuscript from the librarian, Theokritos' hands felt as cold as had those of Marios' corpse.

"Can you read it, Surgeon?" Placidia asked in an anxious tone.

"I...I think so. The style is old, but it's Latin:

THE LAST LEGACY AND TESTAMENT

Of Jesus of Galilee, the Nazarene, Proclaimed Messiah,
The said Son of God and King of the Judeans
Dictated to L. Flav. Secundus
Secretary to PONTIVS PILATVS, Procurator of Judea
In the Imperium of Tiberius Caesar Augustus

AVG. XIX. COS. V. PP. PM.

The Procurator, having asked the accused, "What is Truth?" the Nazarene replied, "I am the truth, the light and the way. But from today the Son of Man shall be seated at the right hand of the power of God. For I am a king. For this was I born and for this have I come into the world.

"A new commandment I give ye: love one another even as I have loved ye. Love those who hate ye. Do good to those who would do ye harm.

"If ye love me ye will keep my commandments. He who keepeth my commandments, he it is who loveth me, and he who loveth me shall be loved of my Father, and I will love him and manifest myself to him. He who loveth me not keepeth not my word, and the word which ye hear is not mine, but the Father's who sent me. That the world may know that I love the Father, and as the Father gave me commandments, even so do I give them to you."

Getorius paused. The text was rambling, made up of well-known sayings of Jesus.

Yet if he actually had dictated the words to Pilate's secretary—presumably while the procurator was outside trying to convince the crowd that the accused was innocent—Getorius knew Christ would be delirious from his night's ordeal. Cold, and the thirst induced by loss of blood from whipping and thorn punctures, would be enough to send him into the kind of shock he had seen before in patients.

Getorius continued, his hands trembling and his throat too dry to read the words loudly:

"I give thee a prophecy. Many will come from the east and west in my name. They will be gathered together in a great Assembly under Simeon-Petros bar Jonah.

"And I give to Petros and his successors the keys of the kingdom of heaven, to bind or loose on earth, that it may be also bound or loosed in heaven. For I am a king and for this have I come into the world. Even now I could call down the Twelfth Legion of Angels to avenge me, but Father, thy will be done."

"This is tedious," Placidia broke in. "Archdeacon, is this another forgery like that letter of Pilate?"

"What…what is the bequest, Surgeon?" Renatus asked nervously. "Read on."

"Last night I washed the feet of my disciples and commanded them to love one another. Yet how can I command them to love and do good to their enemies if I do not likewise love my enemies and do good to them?

"My heart is sad that the Children of Abraham have not listened to my words. Even now they are outside crying for my blood and have not listened to my Father. Yet I will remember their sins no more, and what I bind in heaven will be bound on earth.

"I will fulfill the promise made to Abraham and his offspring.

"THEREFORE: I bequeath to the descendants of the Children of Abraham, the sons of Isaac and Jacob, the Hebrews who were brought out of captivity by Moses and given the first Covenant, to them I give all the seas, ports, lands, cities, and estates of the world, to be theirs until I come in Glory to sit at the right hand of the Father.

"THIS TESTAMENT and legacy shall be known only to Simeon-Petros and concealed by him until it be revealed in the fullness of my Father's time.

"My time is short, deliver this to him by Salutus. Petros has just entered the courtyard."

When Getorius looked up, his face was as white from shock as Lawrence's supernatural garment. "Th…this papyrus gives the Western and Eastern Empires t…to the people who live in our Judean quarter," he stammered. "Sixtus, the Bishop of Rome, Christ's successor, will have to honor it."

After an interval of silence, Placidia snarled, "No! This could be a forgery. I am binding you all by your oath to the Augustus, my son, not to reveal what you have just seen and heard. Theokritos. You will test the papyrus to determine its authenticity, and report only to me."

"That Hun guard saw the body," Arcadia pointed out.

"I doubt that he could identify Feletheus," Getorius said, "but he will report to Aetius that someone was killed here."

"I'll deal with Flavius Aetius," Placidia retorted. "Meanwhile, I remind you all of your oath. Librarian, you will begin your work tonight!"

Chapter nine

That night Getorius found sleep impossible. The image of Feletheus' shattered skull and his limp body toppling off the scaffold would have been enough to disturb his rest, but the improbable discovery of the two papyri was a major cause of anxiety. The implications of finding a last will of Jesus Christ, with a bequest that would totally upset the social order, kept him and Arcadia awake.

❦

Getorius' first sense of relief came from the fact that Placidia's oath of secrecy seemed to be holding. Two mornings later, at the Lord's Day service, Bishop Chrysologos did not mention Feletheus, nor was he included in the prayers for the deceased. And none of the catechumens, who had been dismissed before the Profession of Faith, were heard gossiping about the library assistant as they waited for the deacons to distribute shares of the altar offerings.

On leaving the Basilica Ursiana with Arcadia, Getorius was surprised when Publius Maximin stopped him.

"Surgeon," the senator said affably, with a glance at Arcadia, "I apologize for not being there when you looked in on my mother."

"Sir, it was a privilege to be asked."

Maximin smiled at Arcadia. "This beautiful lady is your wife?"

"Yes. Arcadia trains with me in medicine."

She extended a hand. "How are you, Senator?" Arcadia had always thought him almost painfully handsome, his gray-flecked hair too well groomed, and his clothes always the latest fashion. Today, he wore a tunic of soft wool decorated with the twin purple stripes of his senatorial rank, under an elliptically cut cloak. Calfskin boots dyed red, the prerogative of a senator, protected his feet.

"Medicine. I admire your courage, my dear," Maximin said, touching her sleeve. "Roman matrons are usually homebodies."

"Thank you. I prefer to feel more useful."

"Quite." He turned back to Getorius. "My payment for your services was adequate?"

"Patients usually pay me in fish or sausages. Yours was overly generous, sir."

"Good. I wonder if you'd mind going to my home again? Now, Agatha…Mother…is complaining about bed sores."

"I can apply a poultice to relieve them, Senator, but she won't get better."

"Have you something for her pain?"

"Stronger opion, but she'll be addicted."

"As long as Mother is comfortable. Could you go now? Unfortunately, I have an appointment and can't be there with you."

"Of course, sir."

"Splendid. My dear…" Maximin acknowledged Arcadia as if to leave, but asked, "I trust you both had a pleasant dinner with the Empress Mother?"

"Very," Getorius replied cautiously. *Is the senator probing?*

"I understand that you both were privileged to visit her new mausoleum."

"Y…yes." *How would he know that? Has he heard about the death, or the twin papyri?*

"A rare occasion," Maximin said without expanding the

conversation. "Surgeon, do tell my Mother I'll be home early this evening."

"I will, sir." Getorius watched him walk away, across the basilica's square. "Who could have told him that we went to the mausoleum, Arcadia?"

"Renatus? Theokritos, or perhaps one of Sigisvult's guards? The senator is probably no stranger to uncovering palace secrets."

"Undoubtedly not. I'll go to his mother and wash her rawness with a boric solution. Her servant can purchase a soft sheepskin for Agatha to lie on. That should help a bit."

"And I'd better get back and talk to Agrica about our noon meal. I've invited Sigisvult to eat with us."

"Good, we can talk about what happened. Find out what he knows about that hidden niche in the wall. I shouldn't be at the senator's very long."

⁂

Getorius found Agatha about the same. He told Fabia to buy the sheepskin and continue the boric washes. She could come to the clinic on the next day for the opion.

Walking home, Getorius looked forward to talking with Sigisvult. Perhaps he could help make some sense of the horrifying incident in the mausoleum. The architect had been too upset after the murder to talk—Getorius had sent over a mild nepenthes sedative for him—but he should be feeling better by now.

As Getorius crossed the Via Theodosius to his villa, he realized he had not seen Sigisvult at the Mass service that morning. Perhaps the man was still not well. When he entered the door from the Via Caesar, Arcadia hurried into the atrium to meet him.

"Getorius, I've been waiting for you. Sigisvult has been arrested."

"What?"

"He's being held in the palace."

Getorius slipped off his cloak. "I can't say I'm too surprised. I'm sure he had nothing to do with placing that case in the niche, but

127

the building's architect would be the first person suspected. Where is Sigisvult confined?"

"One of the Lauretum anterooms. Flavius Aetius insisted on a form of house arrest, not an underground cell."

"Then the commander does know what happened, but exactly how much?"

"Probably only about Feletheus. As you said, his Huns would have reported a death."

"Arcadia, I'm going to my study, have Silvia bring me a cup of wine. Can you come in and talk?"

"I can, since Sigisvult won't be here," she said. "I'll bring us both wine."

After his wife brought the wine and sat down, Getorius took a nervous gulp of his, then nursed the cup in his hand a long moment before looking up at her. "Arcadia, even though Theokritos is testing the papyri's authenticity, genuine or not, we have to consider the implications of having them released. And someone was going to do that very soon."

"What would have happened after the will was made public?" she asked.

"Most probably, Sixtus would convene a council of bishops, like the one called at Ephesus a few years ago over the Theotokos controversy about Mary's role in the Incarnation. This one would probably be held in Rome. If they decide the will is genuine, Sixtus, as Peter's...and Christ's...successor, is bound to fulfill its terms."

"It *has* to be a forgery, Getorius."

"I agree, but who are the forgers? What's their purpose? If..." Getorius abruptly slammed down his cup on a table next to his chair. "My God, Arcadia! The will papyrus must be connected to that prophecy Behan was going to announce. Hiding the documents in his flimsy hut would have been too risky. Poor weather, or a fire would have destroyed them."

"But Behan would have had to have accomplices to conceal it in the mausoleum," Arcadia reasoned.

"True, workers would have noticed a monk wandering around the site. And that niche had to be left in the brickwork...the trap set." Getorius took a gulp of wine. "This was well thought out. Even with the will a forgery, some factions would be eager to use it for their own purposes."

"Placidia could simply have the documents burned."

"Theokritos wouldn't allow it, and besides him, there are five other witnesses. We would all have to be, ah, silenced."

"Silenced by whom?" Arcadia asked, while realizing there was no ready answer. "Getorius, I imagine Sigisvult is depressed. He must think Placidia feels as if a loyal dog has suddenly turned on its owner. Why don't we go see him after we've eaten?"

"Good idea, Arcadia. We'll bring a pitcher of that Venetian wine."

"And I'll have Silvia pack some of our dinner for him."

☙

The wind had shifted after the rain and now manifested as a mild southwesterly breeze that tempered Ravenna's unseasonably cold autumn. All but the largest sheets of water had drained off, leaving small lakes that were wind-ruffled and sparkling under a sky of fluffy clouds that allowed the sun to shine through at irregular intervals.

It was a short walk to the palace. "Will we have trouble getting in to see Sigisvult?" Arcadia asked, after she saw sentries patrolling the entrance.

"I doubt it. If his detainment is just a formality, he'll be lightly guarded. Ah, good, one of the sentries is Charadric. I once treated him for a nasty knife wound."

"Charadric, how is your hand?" Getorius asked when he came up to the guard.

"Doing good." He showed a white scar on his palm. "I owe you, Surgeon."

"Nonsense, I'm pleased everything turned out well." Getorius slipped a silver coin into the man's hand. "Our friend Sigisvult is being held on a ridiculous charge. Do you think we could give him this food my wife brought?"

"The architect? He's in an anteroom down the hall. I'll take you there."

When Charadric went with them to point out Sigisvult's room, Getorius noticed that the Huns were no longer on duty. "Hopefully, these Goths are the best men the Ravenna garrison has to offer," he murmured to Arcadia.

"You said the other evening that they were generally loyal."

"To Aetius, anyway. The man has more contacts among barbarian tribes than anyone since Flavius Stilicho."

Sigisvult was in a small anteroom off the atrium hallway, across from where Galla Placidia had held her dinner. It had been furnished with a cot, a folding stool, and an army field table. Several books were scattered on the bed, where the architect was reading one by the light of a lamp. He looked up when the couple entered.

"Getorius…Arcadia. It…it's good of you to come."

"We brought you some dinner." Arcadia looked around for a place to put her basket.

"Let me move that game off the table."

Getorius looked at the animal-headed pieces on the checkered board. "Whom have you been playing Hounds and Jackals with?"

Sigisvult laughed as he placed the board on the floor. "My own personal bodyguard."

"No cheating while he's out of the room," Getorius jested.

"He said he was going to the latrine…more likely to cadge food from the kitchen. Again," Sigisvult added more seriously, "thanks for coming."

"How are you?" Arcadia asked.

"Innocent."

"We know that," Getorius agreed, "but whom do you think might be involved in this?"

Sigisvult sat back on the cot and leaned against the wall. "Miniscius, my construction master, must have known about that hidden niche."

"Has he been questioned?"

"It seems they can't find him."

"What?"

"Getorius, he's disappeared," Sigisvult said. "I…I've had time to think about what will happen when that document is made public.

Communities that accept it will be pitted against those that don't. It will make all other civil wars seem like…like playing that board game. And the impact on the Judeans will be devastating…literally."

"We thought the same thing," Arcadia told him, "and whoever forged the papyrus must realize that. Why would they want to cause such a civil crisis?"

Footsteps in the hall indicated that the guard was returning. Arcadia glanced out the door and was surprised to see Surrus Renatus walking alongside the man. The archdeacon carried a round ivory box and glass container with a gilt cover.

When he saw her, the churchman looked as startled as she. "I…I've brought Sigisvult the Holy Sacrament," he explained, flushing. "The bishop requested that I do so."

"It's a bit late in the day," Arcadia commented, without intending to be sarcastic.

"I've been distributing food with my deacons." Renatus brushed past her and saw Getorius. "I didn't expect either of you here, you must both leave. Sigisvult should receive the Sacrament in privacy."

"No, let them stay," Sigisvult told him. "I have nothing to confess—certainly nothing to do with what happened in that mausoleum."

"They may return afterward," Renatus insisted. "Guard, you must also go out."

"It's all right, Sigisvult," Getorius said. "We'll wait in the garden." While the guard went back toward the kitchen, Getorius took his wife's arm and led her past an atrium pool. It was filled to the brim with water that was an opaque gray from being stirred up by the deluge off the roof. Even the bronze wellhead over the storage cistern was full. Rain had washed the garden trees and plants free of dust, but had also encouraged a crop of weeds to sprout up in the damp soil between them. A few of the tropical palms had not survived the recent cold, and now their withered fronds hung limply in black, twisted shapes. At the low wall around the plantings Getorius helped Arcadia sit on the stone ledge.

Both sat in silence, until she said, "Getorius, we have to help Sigisvult establish his innocence."

"I've been thinking of that, too. Galla Placidia could order a trial, but the magistrate would learn about the papyri. She isn't ready to do that."

"Let's hope Theokritos can quickly prove the documents to be forgeries."

"He should, with his knowledge of old books and scroll materials in his library."

"Yes, he'll probably…" Arcadia cocked her head at a low, menacing growl that came from an area to her right. "What was that?"

Getorius laughed. "The Augustus keeps wild animals in his zoo at that end of the garden. Want to look at them?"

"Let's, if we're allowed."

Arcadia eased herself off the wall. Getorius took her hand and had started toward the zoo, when the sound of a glass breaking sounded from the hallway.

"That came from Sigisvult's room!" he cried, then turned and bolted toward the area.

When Getorius reached the anteroom, Renatus was standing outside the door, his face white as he supported himself on the jamb.

"God's hand! I saw the hand of the Lord," he babbled. "The judgment of the Almighty is revealed."

"What are you talking about?" Getorius looked past him and saw Sigisvult lying on the floor, his face a bluish color. Shards of the communion wine cup were scattered beside him. Getorius knelt and felt his throat. "There's no pulse. What happened here Archdeacon?"

"The Father judges no one, but has given all judgment to the Son," Renatus gibbered.

Arcadia sucked in a breath of horror when she came in and saw Sigisvult. "Getorius, what happened?"

"I'm trying to find out, but Renatus keeps prattling nonsense. Archdeacon, I asked you what happened."

"The Testament of John reveals it."

"Reveals what? Make sense, man. Tell me what took place. You were giving him the sacramental bread and wine?"

"The judgment of God—"

Getorius stood up in a flash of anger, scattering some of the glass fragments with his boot as he grabbed Renatus' shoulder. "Tell me how Sigisvult died!"

The archdeacon shook off his hand, pushed the books aside, and sat down on the cot, trembling. "I...I gave him the Body of the Lord. No. First we said a *Confiteor* together. After the architect drank the wine of Christ's blood, he looked at me, seeming at peace. Forgiven. But he suddenly gasped and went into a convulsion...dropped the glass and fell. I went to help him, but realized I had just witnessed the hand of God. He took Sigisvult, after he had become one with Him through the Sacrament."

"I'm a surgeon, not a theologian," Getorius said, controlling his anger. "Death is not caused by supernatural means." He continued, softening his tone, "Archdeacon, Sigisvult was a patient of mine. I want you to get permission from the Bishop for me to examine his body and see what caused his death."

"A dissection? Impossible. Besides, I told you. It was God's judgment. I witnessed it."

Charadric had evidently heard the commotion and it was he who came into the room, instead of Sigisvult's guard. He saw the body on the floor, had heard some of what Renatus had said, and decided he wanted no part in the way God settled scores. He turned to leave.

"Wait, Charadric." Getorius pulled him back, searched out a coin, and pressed a half-*siliqua* into his hand. "Tell your tribune that his prisoner is dead, but I want the body left here with nothing disturbed. Understand?"

"I...I'll tell Tribune Lucullus." Charadric half-saluted and hurried out.

"Renatus. Go to Bishop Chrysologos now, so I can begin an examination—short of dissection—as soon as possible. I can do it here. While you're gone, I'll get my medical case."

"Let me cover Sigisvult until we get back." Arcadia pulled a blanket off the cot and knelt to lay it over the architect's body.

Outside, Getorius took his wife by the elbow and strode toward their villa. "Judgment of God," he scoffed. "I need to find the physical reason that caused Sigisvult's death."

"Then don't walk so fast." Arcadia took a circle of broken glass out of her purse. "This may help you."

Getorius stopped to examine the round shard. "This is the bottom of the glass that held the wine. How did you get it?"

"From under the cot, where you kicked it when you grabbed Renatus."

"After you bent down to cover Sigisvult?"

"Yes. I've seen these before. Gold leaf images fused into a commemorative glass, but look at the design on this one."

"Peter and Paul, the two Apostles. Appropriate for a Communion cup I suppose."

"Look at their symbols, a sword for Paul and a cockerel for Peter. Martyrdom and betrayal."

"Another furcing rooster!"

Arcadia ignored his outburst. "Getorius, I'm admittedly only an apprentice medica, but I think Sigisvult was poisoned."

"That entered my mind too, but by the archdeacon, practically in our presence? Why would he do that?"

"Perhaps Renatus didn't know. Someone else may have prepared the wine for him...a presbyter, or one of his deacons."

"He did act totally distraught...almost incoherent."

"He didn't expect us to be there."

"And it was a coincidence that we were." Getorius ran his finger around the inside rim of the glass. It was still damp with dregs of wine. He smelled, then tasted the residue, and grimaced at the bitter taste. "Atropa...you're diagnosis was right. That explains the color of his face and the convulsions Renatus described. I won't have to look further than his esophagus for traces of poison."

❧

When the couple returned to Lauretum Palace, the Gothic guards had been replaced by Huns, who made it clear that neither one of them would be allowed inside the building.

"So much for examining Sigisvult's body," Getorius remarked

as he walked back down the stairs. "The guards' commander must have spoken to someone higher up."

"Flavius Aetius?" Arcadia suggested.

"Possibly. Or even the Gothic Queen."

Getorius had turned toward the clinic when Arcadia pulled him back by the arm. "Would workers be at the mausoleum on Sunendag...the Lord's Day?"

"Work has been suspended and the building placed under guard, but I doubt if they'd be on duty today."

"Let's go over there, Getorius."

He nodded agreement. "With Sigisvult dead, we should look around inside."

Immersed in trying to understand the architect's murder, the couple said nothing as they retraced the same route to the mausoleum they had taken on the deadly evening. The fields alongside the Vicus Galla Placidia were still muddy, and rain had halted construction on the new villas.

There were no guards at the point where they had been challenged the night before, only the damp ashes of the men's fire. Ahead, attached to the narthex of the Basilica of the Holy Cross, the mausoleum stood as a stark, octagonal entombment for present and future dead.

Arcadia abruptly stopped and grasped her husband's arm. "Getorius, that's two murders in as many days. Perhaps we shouldn't be here after all."

"*Cara,* it was your idea to come," Getorius pointed out. "We'll be fine."

"I'm reconsidering. This isn't our business."

"True. Someone from the judicial magistrate's office would be investigating if the Gothic Queen hadn't sworn us all to secrecy about the librarian's death. Still, I believed Sigisvult when he said he was innocent. I'd like to go back inside and look around."

"I guess you're right," she relented. "We owe him that at least."

They found the mausoleum unguarded; even its door was not locked. Getorius surmised that Tranquillus, the presbyter at the adjoining basilica, must be having dinner with Bishop Chrysologos in the Episcopal Palace.

Inside, the cruciform building was as it had been the evening when Placidia brought the group in, but now a soft light entering through eight high alabaster windows, revealed the splendor of the mosaics and a marble wainscoting that was installed as background for the sarcophagi.

Getorius saw that the niche was still open. The small weapon that had shot the deadly bolt had not been removed. He traced a trajectory with his eye across to the mosaic of the Imperial Shepherd. The missile had hit at lower left, gouging out green landscape tiles between three of the sheep. The shattered wooden shaft and its iron head still lay on the floor beneath.

"What shot the arrow?" Arcadia asked, following his gaze. "It had to be small."

"A kind of miniature catapult…the army's Scorpion is a larger version. Greeks invented the weapon, called it a *gastrophetes*."

"That would mean…'stomach-shooter?'"

"Right, Arcadia. The bow is a composite of ash, horn and sinew glued together. A large one is so hard to draw that the person cocks the device by centering it on his abdomen and pushing against the ground or a wall."

"How do you know all this, Husband?"

"I don't always read about medicine in the library. Heron of Alexandria describes the bow. A wound is devastating—witness poor Feletheus."

Arcadia glanced at a dark area on the floor. Sand had been sprinkled over the blood-stain, but it was still evident. She bent to rummage on the floor among the broken tile fragments that had made up the book design, then picked up one of the larger pieces and brought it to her husband.

"Getorius, look on the back. There's another rooster symbol."

He studied the design a moment. "This one could be an artisan's mark. The kind they press into bricks to identify the kiln."

"But it's drawn in red ink, not impressed."

"It does seem to match the one on the prophecy manuscript."

He tossed the fragment on the worktable in frustration. "I just wish I knew what was going on here. Why would Behan, or the conspirators, choose this place to hide the documents?"

"You said the monk's hut was too risky, and an unfinished mausoleum wouldn't get any visitors. Perhaps if that workmaster Sigisvult mentioned is found…" Arcadia slipped the tile fragment into her purse. "Would Theokritos be in the library today?"

"Probably, it's almost his home. Why?"

"I'd like to show him the tile, but how can we see him when we've been barred from the palace?"

"There is a stairway outside, at the back," Getorius recalled. "Theokritos had it built in case of a fire, but I've never used it."

"How would we get inside the palace grounds? The laurel grove?"

"Let me think. Wait, there's a gap in the wall where the Padenna River runs out from the garden. Are you willing to get your feet wet?"

"Let's go, husband. We don't know what the forgers will do once they realize the will has been discovered."

The couple slipped under the iron grill at the stream opening, then threaded their way through the laurel trees to the rear of the palace. The wooden stairway was unguarded. At the top, the door into the library was slightly open. As soon as Arcadia entered she smelled smoke that had an herbal odor, like field grass burning.

"Something's on fire!" she cried.

Getorius had also noticed the smell. Running ahead of her, past storage bins and into Theokritos's office, he saw the librarian intent on watching two scraps of papyrus burn in a clay dish.

"Theokritos!" he shouted. "What are you doing? That document is priceless!"

Getorius beat the flames out with a bare hand, shattering one of the dishes and scattering ashes on the table.

"Surgeon, tend to your patients," Theokritos snapped, pushing him back. "That was part of a blank papyrus sheet from a manuscript by Lucius Annaeus Seneca. He wrote in Egypt around the time of the Galilean. I wanted to compare the nature of the ashes with those of a section I had cut from the Secundus Papyrus."

"The what?" Getorius asked, cradling his reddened palm in the other hand.

"I've named our mystery document after Pilate's secretary, Lucius Flavius Secundus…"

Arcadia came into the room. She saw the smoking papyrus scrap and scattered ashes around the broken dish and her husband holding his hand, and guessed what had happened. "Let me see, Getorius. Are you badly burned?"

"It's nothing. Theokritos was testing papyrus similar to the one we found."

"Go find a water pitcher and soak your hand in cold water."

After Getorius left, Theokritos muttered, "Impetuous fool. What did he think I was doing? Look over here, young woman." The librarian indicated a row of small dishes that held ashes or scraps of papyrus immersed in various liquids. "These are soaking in vinegar. Those two are in a solution of vitriol." He held up a vellum sheet on which he had recorded the contents of each plate. "This will detail my conclusions."

"You're comparing the composition of the manuscript fibers we found and those of a similar age."

"Greek manuscripts from the Palestina area, to be exact. You have more sense than that husband of yours. I'm also comparing the weave of the plant in manufacture…its color, texture, brittleness, and so on. The two papyri are comparable, finely made. Alexandria had the best quality papyrus back then."

"Clever—"

"Of course the Seneca manuscript has been here in Ravenna for some time, while…I'm calling what was found the 'Secundus Papyrus,' as I told the Surgeon…while that papyrus was presumably in the Hyperborean damp for over four centuries. Fortunately, the case was well sealed. There are stains on some of the fibers, from when the leather case was new, but someone put that gold foil lining in at a later time to protect the contents."

"So the case had been opened?"

"At some point."

Getorius returned with a wet cloth around his hand and mumbled an apology.

"I realize what you must have thought, Surgeon," Theokritos said in a kinder tone, "but I'm trying to establish the age of the papyri. If they're recent, there's no need to go on."

"What about the writing?" Arcadia asked.

"Its style is from the time of the Galilean. I've compared it with the Seneca."

Still on the defensive, Getorius countered, "Any skilled scribe could copy the hand."

Arcadia gritted her teeth, but Theokritos seemed to feel no offense. "True, Surgeon. That's why the material itself is of more importance."

"The ink is brownish," she noted.

"It is its nature to change, young woman. Look at the Seneca, the color is quite similar."

"Did you discover anything else about the papyri?" Getorius asked.

"A few signs of mold, as might be expected. But all in all it has been mirac…it has been remarkably well preserved."

Getorius noted that the librarian fell just short of saying, "miraculously well preserved."

"Theokritos," he apologized, "I'm sorry for my rashness. It's been an upsetting afternoon. Have you heard that Sigisvult is dead?"

"Dead? I understood he was being held under guard here in Lauretum."

"He was. We were visiting him when Renatus came in with consecrated bread and wine."

Theokritos fingered his Abraxas medal. "Go on, Surgeon. What happened?"

"We weren't in the room, but Sigisvult died after drinking the Sacramental wine. The archdeacon called it the judgment of God."

"Superstitious fool."

"Yes. I believe Sigisvult was poisoned."

"Murdered?" Theokritos dropped the medal as his complexion

blanched to the same colorlessness as his hair. "Now it seems we have one witness less to the discovery."

"A witness? I hadn't thought of Sigisvult's death in that light," Getorius admitted, "yet it makes sense…in a frightening way."

"Senator Maximin knows we were in the mausoleum," Arcadia said.

"He told you that?"

"After Mass. It seemed like a casual question about our dinner with Galla Placidia."

"Thanks to the man's wealth, he knows this entire palace as I do its library. His gold buys information." Theokritos snorted and probed at the papyrus scrap in the vitriol.

"Sir," Arcadia asked, indicating the rolled documents at the top of the desk, "are those the manuscripts we found at Behan's?"

"They are."

"Do you know any more about them?"

"Young woman"—Theokritos waved an impatient hand toward his experiments—"my concern is what I have in front of me now."

"May I look at the Latin text? My husband thinks your…your Secundus Papyrus is linked to Behan's prophecy."

Theokritos gave a shrug of permission. Arcadia unrolled the manuscript, then pulled Getorius aside. "The rooster drawing on this looks like the one on the broken tile."

"Broken tile?" Theokritos asked, looking up. "Rooster?"

"Sir"—Arcadia took the fragment from her purse—"we found this in the mausoleum, part of the Book of John mosaic your assistant pointed out."

"I thought it might be an artisan's mark," Getorius added, "but someone is using a cockerel as an identifying symbol." When Theokritos did not comment further, Getorius asked, "Will you let me know if you discover anything?"

"That, Surgeon, will be for the Regina's ears only."

Getorius took Arcadia's arm. "Let's go home. There's nothing more to learn here."

❧

Two days later, on November seventeenth, Childibert told Getorius that a body had been hauled out of the harbor near its silted south end, and identified as that of Miniscius. A magistrate ruled that Sigisvult's workmaster had probably slipped and fallen off an icy dock early in the morning, while inspecting a cargo of building materials.

No further inquiry was conducted.

Lugdunum

Chapter ten

Brenos of Slana left the Abbey of Culdees at Autessiodurum on the seventeenth day of the Celtic month of Samon. The
abbot rode on horseback, along with his secretary Fiachra, the guide
Warinar, and only one packhorse to haul minimal supplies for the
journey to Ravenna.

❦

Four days travel beyond his monastery, in the gloom of a late afternoon, Brenos sat huddled in the prow of a Roman patrol galley that
slid downstream along the current of the Arar River. The bearskin
coat he wore glistened white, coated with sleet granules that drove
in from the northeast. After the tribune in charge of the crew, Liscus,
had said that Lugdunum would soon appear in the distance, Brenos
wanted to be first to sight the old capital of the Three Gauls.

He glanced back at Fiachra, hunched with Warinar over a
charcoal fire glowing in a brazier under the galley's sternpost. Blowing on his hands to warm them, his secretary still looked sullen over
having to make the winter voyage. Warinar, too, had sulked on the
road. The guide wanted to stay at Autessiodurum, and had warned

about the dangers of a winter journey, but the offer of a silver *siliqua* for each day of travel had proven irresistible. Brenos had made sure the man did not take advantage of the generous terms to extend the time of the journey by promising him the bonus of a gold *solidus* if they arrived at the Western capital within three weeks.

The abbot pulled the bearskin collar higher around the hood of his cloak. Although the clear weather had turned nasty abruptly, things had gone well since departing from the abbey. The Via Cabellono along the left bank of the Icauna River was paved and the country-side relatively flat. Brenos had counted on his church rank of abbot to receive food and shelter along the way. The monastic discipline practiced at Culdees had served him well; the horses had made almost thirty miles the first day, before early darkness came on.

That first night the abbot had found them shelter in a walled farmhouse. At dawn he had shaken his companions awake. Shortly after a breakfast of bread, cheese, and raisins, the trio was once more on the road.

The second day's halt had been in the fortified hill town of Flavia Aeduorum. Brenos had gawked at the magnificent four-portal gate, at the stone bridge leading across a river to the citadel, and at the walls Augustus Caesar had built for the Aedui, who were long-time Gallic allies of Rome. Cavarillus, the bishop, had found housing for the travelers with a wealthy merchant. Both men had donated a gold piece to help the abbot defray his expenses. The nervous city prefect had scrawled a hasty petition for the abbot to give to Emperor Valentinian at Ravenna, pleading for a hundred field army legionaries to supplement what Frankish mercenaries he had been able to hire.

By the afternoon of November twentieth the three men had reached Cabillonum on the Arar River, in a mounting snowstorm. As a market center for shipping goods into northern and western Gaul, the river port housed naval garrison that patrolled that stretch of the Arar. Brenos had shown his abbot's ring to Tribune Liscus, the base commander, who was about to board a patrol galley that would tow a barge of lumber and wine casks downstream to Lugdunum.

Brenos bribed the officer to be taken along with the cargo. The four horses were led onto the transport barge and tethered among the beams and barrels. Two crewmen stayed aboard with the animals.

The sailors talked among themselves while erecting a leather canopy in the patrol galley's center as protection against the weather. Brenos understood enough of their regional Celtic dialect—Gallo-Roman descendants of the Aedui—to gather that renegade warriors from the Germanic Burgondi made regular raids on river communities. He had already seen burned and abandoned villas on the riverbanks standing as mute testimony to the barbarians' incursions.

Feeling a gust of wind, the abbot glanced out at the muddy, swift-flowing river, whose surface was rapidly being coated with a slush of icy sleet. The crew had mentioned that the normally sluggish Arar was swollen by fall rains, and was now flowing more rapidly to its conjunction with the Rhodanus River at Lugdunum. Brenos had smugly attributed that fact to an act of Divine Providence for his own benefit, yet inexplicably the snow squall was metamorphosing into a full-scale winter storm, blustering down out of Gothiscandza.

The abbot slipped a hand under his coat and felt at the bulge beneath his tunic. The case strapped next to his body containing the Gallican League Charter was reassuring. Even though the waxed leather cylinder had started to rub a raw wound in his side, that was a small enough discomfort for bringing the work of the Nazarene to completion. Even the snowstorm was merely another test of his resolve.

At Cabillonum, after the galley had pushed out into the current and the men started rowing, they had begun to chant verses in harmony with their oar strokes. Without understanding all of their dialect, Brenos was nevertheless convinced, from the raucous answering refrain of the barge crew, that the words boasted of carnal intercourse with women.

The singing eventually ceased, its words carried off in the howl of the wind.

※

Brenos was dozing when he was startled by Warinar's voice saying, "Abbot, you'll find 'The Queen of Gaul' looking a bit ragged."

He sat and turned around to squint at the red-faced guide. "Queen? Who?"

"Lugdunum." Warinar pointed to the fuzzy outline of buildings materializing on a high ridge in the distance. "After that Dalmatian emperor made Treveri the new prefectural capital, the Queen lost out. They insulted her again a few years ago by moving the mint south to Arelate."

"Where do we go from Lugdunum?" Brenos asked, taking advantage of Warinar's willingness to speak, which he attributed to the guide's anticipation of spending the night in the city's taverns, or even worse, establishments of the flesh.

"The way I came, Cularo to the Genevris pass, then down to Taurinorum in the Padus Valley. We'll pick up the Via Fulvia and—"

"And they'll dig out three stiff corpses in the spring," Liscus interposed with a hoarse chuckle.

"Corpses?" Brenos repeated, alarmed. "What do you mean, Tribune?"

"Word came yesterday, Abbot. Snowstorms have closed both the pass and the mountain roads that lead into Italy."

"But I came through there only a week ago," Warinar recalled.

"Then some god smiled on you," Liscus said. "This time Taranis would bury you in his frozen spit."

"Warinar, what does this mean?" Brenos demanded. "Isn't there another route?"

"A longer one. We could take a barge down the Rhodanus to Massilia. Easy enough—it's with the current. Then pick up a merchant galley to Pisae...*if* we can find a master foolish enough to risk his boat and cargo in winter."

"A sea voyage?" Brenos recalled his short but nauseating sail across the narrow channel from Britannia to Gaul. "Isn't there another land route?"

"The Via Julia Augusta from Arelate, and across to the Mediterranean coastal road."

"Either way you'd be pissing into the wind," Liscus warned.

"That Visigoth king, Theodoric, is making trouble down there, wanting to own the whole Narbonensis coast. The prefect at Arelate is working out a treaty with him, but the city is sealed off. There probably isn't a bargemaster in the region who would risk going downstream now."

Brenos frowned at the prospect of a delay. "Do you have any suggestions, Tribune?"

Liscus blew on fingers numb from the cold, then advised, "Stay in Lugdunum until spring, Abbot, or go back to your monastery while the road is still open."

"No, that's unacceptable. I *must* reach Ravenna."

Liscus shrugged and eyed the snow-covered wharves and a bridge at the lower city, which his galley was rapidly approaching. "Retract oars," he yelled to the crew. "Prepare for docking."

Brenos watched wharf slaves shamble out from the shelter of a warehouse portico and catch ropes tossed to them from the two boats. After passing the coils through holes in stone mooring dogs, they pulled the vessels tight against the dock. When crewmen maneuvered a gangplank into place, Brenos wondered about a place to spend the night.

"Tribune, is there a presbyter's residence nearby?"

"The Basilica of Paul the Apostle is on the Via Bartolomei. The closest residence would be near the church."

"Where?"

"By the Bridge of the Three Gauls. The Bartolomei leads up to the old forum and theaters, but there are inns, Abbot, here along the wharves."

Brenos looked at the warren of streets beyond the warehouses. A few people still bought food at vendors' stalls, but the storm had forced most citizens home. Or to taverns, he surmised from the sounds of loud laughter coming from the curtained doorways of those facing the river.

A young woman in a fur cape, open in front to show a cling-ing red-silk tunic, gestured to him from another entrance alongside the tavern. Brenos turned away quickly. Rented rooms would be above one of the taverns, or worse, situated among the cubicles of the woman's brothel.

"Have one of your men escort us to the presbyter's house," he ordered Liscus. "I'll not spend the night among prostitutes and drunken louts. Warinar, what about the horses?"

"I…got a friend at the…uh…'House of Eros,'" the guide stammered. "I'll shelter our mounts there, and see about getting a barge to Massilia in the morning."

Brenos scowled—the name of the 'house' was description enough—but did not protest the arrangement. "Then meet me here at the galley by the third hour. Tribune, I'm ready. Come along, Fiachra."

At the Via Bartolomei, Brenos squinted to the right, along a straight paved road. The crewman guide said it sloped up to Old Lugdunum, and the remains of its ancient Roman origins, but the driving snow obscured the height in a veil of opaque white.

Brenos and Fiachra were led to a two-story dwelling across from the brick basilican church. The building's doorway was under a porch overhang, still free of snow. The abbot announced himself to the servant who answered the tinkle of the hanging bell. The man took them to a dining room, where a clergyman and his deacon were finishing supper.

"Presbyter Diviciac, you have visitors," the porter announced.

Diviciac glanced up and stood to greet his unexpected guests, but Brenos introduced himself before the man could speak.

"I am Brenos, abbot of the Monastery of Culdees at Autessiodurum. My secretary, Fiachra."

"An abbot? I'm honored"—Diviciac extended a hand—"and you're…Hibernian."

"My accent betrays me, Presbyter?"

"But not unpleasantly, Abbot. I'm Diviciac…this is my deacon, Epagnatos." Brenos studied the thin-faced presbyter, who had intelligent brown eyes and a head that seemed larger than it was, due to a receding hairline, then heard him chuckle. "You look like snow creatures. Servilius, take their coats away to dry, move the brazier closer, and bring two more bowls and fresh bread. Refill the wine jug."

The servant left and Epagnatos took the opportunity to excuse himself as well. Brenos glanced around the room, which was cold despite the glowing charcoal on a portable grate. A faded mural of a pagan river god decorated one wall. A warehouse scene on another was cracked down the center. He guessed that the house might have once belonged to a merchant, and was very old, perhaps even dating from the time of the Nazarene.

Servilius returned with the bread and wine, and an old woman who ladled thick soup from a tureen into the bowls.

"Abbot, Secretary, sit down, please," Diviciac urged. "I hope barley pottage is to your liking. Take bread." He watched Servilius pour wine into the goblets. "Well-watered, I'm afraid. Times are hard for my parishioners."

Brenos murmured his thanks, then reached down with his spoon, scooped up ashes from the brazier and sprinkled them into his bowl, explaining, "Bishop Germanus observes this penance. I can do no less."

"Indeed, Abbot. What…ah…brings you to Lugdunum at the cusp of winter?"

"A churchman's business." Brenos bent low to slurp a spoonful of gritty barley.

"Yes," Diviciac observed, "you Hibernians are beginning to proselytize on the Continent. Do you plan to start an abbey…a monastery, here at Lugdunum?"

"No, but from what I saw in your streets, you could use a monk's discipline."

Diviciac snickered. "What should I do at Rome?" he quoted. "I have not learned the art of falsehoods. A falling tile can brain you—not to mention the contents of all those chamber pots, which people throw out their windows—"

"Make sense, man," Fiachra interrupted.

"Have you not read Juvenal's satire on the evils of Rome? It could just as well apply to our city, and yet Christ, of course, came to save sinners. Isn't that how you understand the Testaments, Secretary?"

"Perhaps."

"Fiachra," Brenos admonished, "remember what we call The Three False Sisters. 'Perhaps,' 'Maybe,' and 'I dare say.'"

"One of your triads I hadn't heard about," Diviciac admitted, "even though I've read some of your literature in translation."

"Indeed? Yet, unlike us you continue to humiliate sinners with public confessions," Brenos taunted. "Still, I would agree in the case of that whorish daughter of Eve who tried to entice me into sin as I came here."

"Christ admonished against throwing the first stone, Abbot."

Brenos reddened; who was this presbyter to counsel him? "The Nazarene consigned fornicators to eternal fire! Females—Eve's descendants—are agents of Satan."

"Come now, Abbot," Diviciac cajoled, "Irenaeus, a bishop martyred here at Lugdunum, maintained that the Virgin Mary's obedience untied the knot of Eve's disobedience. Mary completed the cycle from Sin to Salvation."

Brenos snorted and fell silent. Fiachra's spoon made scraping noises as he scooped barley grains from the sides of his bowl.

"More pottage?" Diviciac asked amiably.

Fiachra pushed his bowl forward, but Brenos shoved it back and stood up. "Enough. Presbyter, have your servant show us our rooms."

Diviciac nodded to Servilius. At the door the abbot turned back. "This bishop Irenaeus. He was martyred along with Saint Blandina?"

"Blandina? You know about her?"

"A young virgin who died witnessing for the Nazarene. Is there a shrine to her?"

"Yes, next to the arena where she was martyred. It's across the river in Condate, an old Gallic community."

"I…I would like to visit the site."

"It's in a hostile neighborhood," Diviciac warned. "The presbyter over there makes little headway in countering holdover pagan superstitions."

"Nevertheless," Brenos insisted, "I shall go."

"I'll send Deacon Epagnatos with you in the morning."

❧

November twenty-second dawned with a brilliant sun that rose into a clear sky the color of a winter lake. The air was colder than the day before, but promised to warm up by afternoon. Diviciac was not there when Brenos and Fiachra came into the triclinium, but Epagnatos had arranged for a breakfast of bread, hard local cheese, and olives.

"You wish to see the shrine of Blandina?" the deacon asked, after the two monks were seated and had begun eating.

Brenos nodded.

"Bishop Eusebius gives an inspiring account of her death—"

"I've read it," Brenos answered curtly. "We Hibernians pride ourselves on our learning."

"Yet, Abbot, the saying is that pride often wears the cloak of humility."

Brenos glanced up sharply. Was this deacon mocking him? "We should go to the galley first. I'm to meet my guide there by the third hour."

Epagnatos stood up. "Finish breakfast and I'll take you to the wharf."

❦

The fronts of Lugdunum's north-facing buildings were glazed with sleet. A handspan of snow coated their rooflines, giving a kind of homogenous white beauty to the decaying stone and stucco structures. Icicles dangled from roof eaves, dripping water as they grew ever-slimmer in the glare of a bright morning sun.

At the Via Bartolomei, the paved road could be seen curving up beyond the city wall toward two semi-circular buildings that were almost invisible in their concealing white mantle.

"The old Roman theaters," Epagnatos explained. "There's a temple complex of Cybele behind them. Diviciac tries to make people understand that the pagan goddess was a precursor to the Virgin Mary, yet sacrifices are still found on her altars."

"Pagan sacrifices," Brenos muttered. "Another manifestation of the evil wood in the Nazarene's vineyard that we have come to prune away."

"Prune away? What do you mean, Abbot?"

"There's my guide over there, beyond the bridge," Brenos said, instead of elaborating. This deacon and his presbyter—all of Lugdunum—would soon find out what was meant.

Warinar stood by the gangplank stamping his feet, surrounded by slaves sweeping snow off the wharf into the river.

"Abbot," he called and hurried to meet Brenos. "I've found a bargemaster who'll take us to Arelate. I already have the horses on board."

"First I wish to visit the shrine of Holy Blandina."

"Impossible. Lothar wants to leave immediately, before the weather turns poor again. And there will be a hunter's moon bright enough so we can stay with the current at night."

Brenos hesitated. Should he risk arriving at Ravenna late in order to pray to a woman who might or might not rid him of his uncontrollable sexual urges?

"Abbot, Lothar is waiting to push off," Warinar insisted.

"Very well. Deacon, I won't need you."

Epagnatos bowed. "Then, Abbot, God be with you on a safe journey."

Brenos gave him a cursory nod and asked Warinar, "Where is this barge?"

"Uh…moored across from the Eros."

⁂

Lothar's boat had a small cabin built into the stern to house his family when they went along on his trading journeys to towns along the Rhodanus River. The Arar merged with its larger, alpine-fed sister, beyond an island opposite Lugdunum's lower city.

The boatman had decided to risk a voyage to Arelate with a load of wine casks, and realized that a traveling churchman had money. Also, his guide seemed desperate. Lothar shrewdly negotiated two gold *solidi* with Warinar—a fifth of a year's earnings—for taking the group aboard, and estimated that the swollen river current would bring them to the southern city in about three days.

Warinar told the abbot he would decide what route to take from there, to reach Ravenna in time.

Brenos was pleased. On Warinar's map Arelate was almost a third of the distance along, and there would be no snow on the southern route to further delay them. Perhaps the storm at Lugdunum had been God's way of preventing an unforeseen accident on the mountain route. Even if they reached the capital a day or two after December sixth, there would still be enough time to contact Smyrna and plan for the revelation of the Nazarene's will at the Nativity Mass.

Ravenna

Chapter eleven

Sigisvult's death had brought the unsettling events of the last few days to a head, and so depressed Getorius that he refused to see patients. Instead, he closed himself off in his study, while Arcadia took care of the clinic. He was not too concerned; since the weather had turned milder, there were fewer patients who came in to be treated for fevers and phlegm imbalances, and he could spend time recovering from his own unbalanced humor.

The palace gave out no details concerning the deaths of Feletheus or Sigisvult. The two men had been on the imperial staff, therefore nothing need be said about them publicly. They were buried in a closed ceremony from the Chapel of the Archangel Michael, which was built in a wing of the imperial apartments.

❦

The day after the funerals a woman came into the clinic complaining of a bloated leg. Arcadia, alarmed by her condition, did not feel competent enough to treat her. She went to her husband's study to ask him to examine the swollen limb.

"Getorius, will you see a patient?"

"What's his problem?" he asked without looking up from a book.

"It's a woman. The wife of Charadric, actually, the guard whose hand you treated."

"What's wrong with her?"

"Her left leg is swollen and as red as cinnabar. Getorius, I know you're upset, but I need your help with this. How long are you going to brood over Sigisvult's death?"

"Call it brooding if you want, but I'm also thinking about what Theokritos said."

"About his tests on the papyri?"

"No, woman!" he snapped, "that two of the witnesses are dead. Three, if you count Feletheus. That leaves you and me—"

"And Galla Placidia, Theokritos, Renatus. What are you getting at?"

"We went to the mausoleum on a…on the whim of Placidia. That manuscript was meant to be disclosed, but not then, and certainly not in that way. It was pure chance that we went on that particular night and Feletheus discovered a hidden niche in the mosaic design. Otherwise, the will papyrus would still be there, ready to be made public when Behan—or someone who hid it there—decided it should be revealed." Getorius slammed his book shut. "That last will and testament of Christ is Behan's prophecy, yet when and where was he going to announce it?"

"I don't want to discuss that now, not with that poor woman in the clinic. Are you coming? Her name is Ingunda."

Getorius sighed, flung the book aside, and stood up and followed Arcadia.

In the clinic he saw a somewhat overweight woman with a youngish face sitting on a chair, her swollen leg elevated on a stool. *Good. Arcadia's done the correct thing*. He wanted to sound cordial, but had forgotten the patient's name.

"Well, Domina…Domina—"

"Ingunda," Arcadia reminded him.

"Yes. Ingunda, I saved your husband's hand once, and now it

seems that one of your legs is trying to have a life of its own. Let me see if I can't make it behave."

Getorius had seen the condition before in heavy women, but they had all been older than Ingunda. He had no idea what caused one leg to suddenly swell up with an imbalance of blood. Soranus of Ephesus wrote in his handbook for midwives that women's tissues were spongier than men's. This was so that they could absorb and store more blood from the process of digestion, and use that stored blood to nourish embryos. This was obvious since excess fluids were purged through the vagina during 'Monthlies' that corresponded with the moon's phases, but the discharge temporarily ceased during pregnancy and lactation. He had also observed that people who had been immobile for a time sometimes exhibited the symptoms.

"This won't hurt, Domina," he said, gently pressing a finger into the swollen tissue. As he knew it might, the impression remained in the leg for a few moments afterward. "Have you stayed in bed for a time recently?"

"My phlegm was out of balance," Ingunda complained. "Antioches told me to rest."

"Antioches?" Getorius frowned. "If you've seen the palace physician, why come to me?"

"He forgets how to cure things. Antioches is old."

"And you remembered that I was younger."

"Getorius," Arcadia muttered through clenched teeth, "you've taken an oath to help whomever comes to you."

"So I have." He tested the tissue again. "This calls for leeching, to drain off surplus blood and restore your balance."

"*Leeches?*" Ingunda shuddered. "Those crawly little insects? I seen them in the marshes."

"Leeches, hirudos, are not insects, not according to Aristotle. And they may be your only hope if you want help for your leg. I don't keep them here, but the palace has a leeching room near the new hospital. My wife will take you there for a treatment."

Taken by surprise, Arcadia stammered, "M...me, Getorius?"

"Part of your training, my dear," he replied in an innocent tone, and with a trace of a smirk.

"Apply several to that leg for the period of about an hour. Perhaps *Antioches* could help you."

Arcadia caught the emphasized sarcasm in his last remark. "Fine. I'll order a litter chair for Ingunda. *My* patient will not be walking even that short distance."

"Good. I'll see if anyone else is waiting."

Arcadia hailed a pair of litter bearers, who were loitering at the corner of the Via Julius Caesar and Via Honorius in hopes of attracting clients. Ingunda climbed slowly into the wicker chair. The carriers started for the palace, with Arcadia walking beside the woman.

"What...what will them slimy creatures do to me?" Ingunda asked in a frightened voice.

"It's quite painless. They'll relieve the excess blood in your leg," Arcadia reassured her, while dreading the thought of dredging around in the vat where the leeches were kept.

"But the furcin' little... Will I lose my leg?"

"Try not to think of that. No, Domina, you'll be walking back home." Arcadia immediately regretted the remark. To give a patient hope was one thing, but predicting the success of a procedure was another. She would have to control her empathy in a more professional manner. "How is your husband?" she asked, to counter her rashness and relax Ingunda.

"Charadric's been promoted to a special palace unit of Frankish guards."

"You must be proud of him." As Arcadia neared the Lauretum Palace's front entrance, she became aware of the two carriers snickering and making strained guttural noises, to mock their passenger's weight. "Let them jest over the small copper they'll get as payment," she murmured.

At the palace entrance Gothic guards were on duty again. Both sentries recognized Ingunda and waved her in. After crossing the atrium and garden, Arcadia dismissed the two bearers, but relented and gave the men a larger *follis* coin than she had intended.

Antioches' office and the clinic where he saw patients were on the second floor, opposite the library. The old physician had stopped training assistants, but beyond his clinic there was a large area recently opened up as a hospital.

Arcadia occasionally helped out in the wards and knew that the idea of a shelter where the poor could be treated was gaining acceptance in the Western Empire. Bishops in the East, like Proclus at Constantinople, had already convinced some wealthy women to fund hospitals in fulfillment of Christ's declaration that if one helped the needy, they also ministered to Him. Aelia Flaccilla, the first wife of the late Emperor Theodosius, had founded a hospital years earlier. Pulcheria, the eastern emperor's wealthy sister, was doing the same.

Bishop Chrysologos had broached the idea to Galla Placidia and urged her to emulate Flaccilla's example. Chrysologos himself had recruited a number of women—'Sisters' he called them—who were willing to renounce the world and live as Brides of Christ and administer the nursing facility. Since Constantine the Great had repealed laws that formerly punished celibates, the unmarried state was now seen as a desirable ideal, and encouraged by bishops. One of the Sisters had told Arcadia that there were some four thousand virgin women in Antioch alone who were devoted to such work.

Antioches was not in his office and the clinic was empty of patients. A corridor led along the western wall, past the hospital and toward storerooms. The leeching room was at the far southwestern corner of the hall, to isolate the unpleasant area. It had been labeled HIRVDORIVM by one of the library scribes.

Arcadia paused in front of the door, feeling her skin pucker in revulsion, yet she forced herself to open it and peer inside, hoping that Antioches was there with a patient.

He was not. The room smelled of mildew and was semi-dark, with the only light coming from a cobwebbed, dirty glass pane covering a high window. While Arcadia waited for her eyes to adjust to the dim light, she fought to keep from gagging at the stench of mold and rotting wood. *I have to set an example for Ingunda.*

She made out two cots next to one wall, and a good-sized wooden vat set on a stand in the center of the room. Its top was at waist level. A hinged door was cut into the removable cover, and a small net hung down on the right side, but she had no idea how difficult it would be to scoop up the slimy creatures.

Arcadia took a deep breath and hoped that one day she would be worthy to swear by Apollo the Healer to keep the Oath that would make her a medica.

"Lie down on that cot, Ingunda," she said gently. "We'll do this slowly, starting with one leech."

After taking the handle of the net off its peg, Arcadia opened the access hatch. The stink of a stagnant swamp rose from the dark water inside. She gingerly brushed off a few leeches that clung to the bottom of the door, and then muttered, "That wasn't very clever. Now I'll have to swish around in the water to net more of the creatures."

Leaning forward and bracing herself mentally for the effort, Arcadia dipped the net into the brackish water. But, instead of sliding into the vat, the bronze ring holding the mesh struck something hard just beneath the surface.

"What the...?" she exclaimed, and bent to look inside for the obstruction. She made out a white form flecked with black oblong leeches, and thought some kind of marble pier had been built into the vat to make it easier to see them. When Arcadia gave the bulky form a harder jab, the shape moved. As it rolled over, a hand came into view. The pale length of arm below the wrist was dark with the creatures. When the body slowly turned past the opening from the inertia of her thrust, a bloated face bobbed to the surface.

Even with the black creatures clinging to the blood-drained white flesh, Arcadia recognized the pudgy features of Archdeacon Surrus Renatus.

She pulled back in horror. Feeling dizzy, Arcadia grasped at the vat's slippery edge for support, but fainted, lost her grip, and crumpled to the tile floor.

Chapter twelve

When Arcadia regained consciousness, she was lying in one of the hospital beds, slowly becoming aware of a young woman wearing a white tunic and veil, who was smiling down at her.

"I am Sister Paulina," the nurse said. "You injured your head when you fell. Are you feeling better?"

Arcadia nodded, then winced after touching a bandage on her forehead. Her skull ached, the inside of her mouth felt dry as the summer sand on Ravenna's beaches, and her stomach was nauseous.

"Ingunda told me who you were," Paulina continued. "I've sent for your husband."

"In that vat," Arcadia croaked through her parched throat.

"I know"—Paulina touched her arm in sympathy—"but be at peace, sister, the lid is closed again. The creatures cannot escape."

Escape? My God, the woman didn't look inside! She thinks I fainted from seeing the leeches.

Paulina tucked another blanket around Arcadia, and she closed her eyes. *Perhaps it's just as well the woman doesn't know about Surrus Renatus until Getorius is told.* Had it really been the archdeacon's body in that black stinking water, or some kind of hallucination brought

165

on by anxiety? No, it had definitely not been an apparition—the rotten smell of the vat's stagnant contents still lingered in her nostrils. Arcadia frantically rubbed at her nose, then her arm, imagining that dark, slimy creatures were clinging to her skin.

She recalled that Getorius had been worried that this very thing would happen. Two of the witnesses to the papyri's discovery were already dead, both within the space of a day, Miniscius the construction worker had probably been murdered too, and now Archdeacon Renatus was obviously a fourth victim—no one could accidentally fall into a vat that size, not even with the cover off. And he had had no reason to be in the room. Bringing the Eucharist to a patient in the wards would be the closest Renatus might come to the Hirudorium, and he would probably have sent one of his sub deacons to perform that simple ministry.

Arcadia opened her eyes, touched the bandage again, and murmured, "When in Hades' name is that husband of mine coming for me?"

⅔

Getorius arrived shortly afterward. He spoke briefly with Paulina, and then came to his wife's bedside.

"Finally," she muttered. "Hades heard my plea."

"Hades? Arcadia, what are you talking about?"

"Nothing."

"Then, how are you feeling? The Sister told me you fell back and injured your head."

"Getorius—"

"Don't talk until I have a look at you." He slipped the bandage off and lightly touched the bruise on Arcadia's forehead, then sniffed the remnants of a glistening poultice on the cloth. "Good, they put camphor ointment on the wound. How badly does your head hurt?"

"Getorius. In that leeching vat—"

"I know. I'm sorry, I shouldn't have sent you to the Hirudorium alone."

"No, no, not that. Where's Paulina?"

166

"At the far end of the ward. Do you want her to bring you something?"

"*NO!* Why won't you listen to me?"

"Is something else wrong?"

"Getorius," she rasped, "the body of Archdeacon Renatus is inside that vat."

"W…what? Renatus? That…that's impossible."

"Don't shout, Husband. I'm telling you, someone drowned the archdeacon in the leech tub. Paulina and the other sisters haven't discovered his body yet."

Getorius slumped down on the edge of her bed. "Then it's just as I feared. Another witness is dead."

"Yes, and it happened inside the palace again. We have to warn Galla Placidia right away. Even she may be in danger, if someone on the staff is involved in this."

"Right. I'll tell Paulina I'm taking you home, then try to schedule a meeting with Placidia."

"I'm going with you when you talk to her."

Getorius knew better than to object to his wife's stubbornness. "Have Paulina help you dress, and ask a sister to walk you home. Meanwhile, I'll find the Gothic Queen's secretary."

❦

In her private reception room Galla Placidia took the news of the archdeacon's murder badly.

"Flavius Aetius is behind this," she screamed, flinging her silver wine cup at the wall. Purple liquid splashed against a mosaic depicting two pigeons on the rim of a fountain, and dribbled down the tiles in streaks. The goblet clanged to the floor, echoing metallic vibrations throughout the room. "He and that Gothic wife of his want to rule the Western Empire."

Arcadia winced. Getorius' slight shake of the head warned her not to react out loud. It was better for the woman to vent her anger without commenting.

"Two of my staff dead," Placidia ranted on, "and now the Archdeacon of Ravenna. Who will be next? The bishop? My son

Placidus? Me? I'm telling you, Aetius wants to be the next Augustus, and quickly at that." She paced the room a moment, and then glared at the couple. "Well? What do you two think?"

"With respect, Regina," Getorius ventured. "Aetius would be more direct."

"Direct?"

"My husband isn't implying that Aetius is plotting something," Arcadia said quickly.

"Oh, what would either of you know about what goes on in this palace?" Placidia scoffed. "You're so immersed in your cures...." She waved out a servant who had heard the clatter and looked in, then picked up the bent cup and set it on a marble table. "Sigisvult dead, now Renatus," she said, her voice a hoarse whisper. "And don't tell me that building master accidentally slipped off a wharf. With all this happening, my son is out hunting again with his two barbarians. Theokritos hasn't given me a report on his tests. Why is he stalling?"

"Your library master wants to be sure," Getorius said to reassure Placidia. "I was impressed by the way he's experimenting in various ways to determine the age of the papyri and writing style."

Placidia slumped down onto a silk-upholstered couch. "This is so important, Surgeon. Have you found out any more about that monk who was found dead?"

"Only that Behan came to the library from time to time, to read."

"These holy men...monastics...have been active in Egypt for years," Placidia went on. "I understand some in the West have also formed communities. Was this Behan trying to proselytize? Why *was* he here?"

"I'm not sure," Getorius replied, "but would you accept a suggestion, Regina?"

"Anything. I'm about at the end of my tether."

"I don't know who he is, but the leader of the Judean community in Ravenna might be told about the will. He could have advice about handling the forgery, or at least give you the Judean reaction to the terms."

Placidia stood and poured herself more wine from a silver

flagon before nodding, "Yes, you have a worthwhile idea, Surgeon. The will may be a forgery, but that didn't stop the so-called letters of Pontius Pilate to Herod and Tiberius from attracting believers. I like your proposal."

"I think the Judeans have a synagogue at the far northeast quarter of the port."

"Yes, Surgeon, I know my city. Come to think of it, I believe the Judeans' leader was a friend of your father's."

"My *father?*" Getorius was startled. "H…how could that be?"

"Nicias once told me the story. I don't recall this Judean's name, but the tax assessors can look it up in their records. The man was a merchant on business in Ravenna or Classis, when the Burgondi raid took place. He heard that his wife had been killed—along with your parents—and never went back to Mogontiacum."

"And now he's what, high priest of the Judeans here?" Getorius was excited at the possibility of talking with someone other than Nicias who had known his parents. "Regina, his connection with me may help in getting him to cooperate."

"Yes, and I'll remind him that my father, Emperor Theodosius, protected Judean rights in his Code. It is worth the risk of telling one other person about the papyri, yet is this man trustworthy?"

"Regina, we must do *something.*"

"You're right, Surgeon. Go to the tax office and find out the man's name. Where he lives. But get an impression of him before you say anything about the will. We don't want some Hebrew fanatic demanding to move into the palace before sundown." Placidia went to her writing desk and took a small square of vellum that had her signet on the front. "This is authorization for getting the information," she said, handing the note to Getorius. "The tax office is near the Scholarian barracks."

"We'll find it. And the Judean."

Placidia walked to the door with the couple. "Surgeon, I want this resolved quickly. If Aetius *is* behind this, I remind you that at least three witnesses are dead."

"How would the commander even find out about the papyri?" Arcadia asked.

"My dear, the man has informants everywhere, probably including some among those who are responsible for forging the will. After the document was released, he would tell us that only his armies could deal with the situation. Meanwhile, he's making sure that none of us who were in my mausoleum that night lives to tell about it."

"With respect, Regina," Getorius countered, "his two Huns could have killed us then, but he sent them to protect you. We may see conspiracies where none exist."

"Like *hypokhondrioi*," Placidia challenged, "patients who come to you with imaginary illnesses? Don't you act as if they are really sick, in order to help them? No, Aetius is undoubtedly as surprised as we are that the papyri were discovered. Go now, but be cautious."

❧

Protasius, the clerk who admitted Getorius, was surly, mistaking him for another citizen coming to argue about a tax assessment. But he ogled Arcadia and asked about her bandaged forehead with exaggerated concern.

Placidia's signet tempered his hostility, but it was the prospect of impressing the chestnut-haired woman that interested Protasius as he led the couple back to the records area. The room resembled a library, with scrolls and bound volumes of deed and property descriptions crowding sagging shelves. The clerk ignored Getorius and explained to Arcadia the intricacies of locating the information *she* wanted.

While Getorius looked on, annoyed, his wife went along with Protasius' flirting in order to expedite matters.

After guiding Arcadia by the arm among the narrow stacks, Protasius pulled down a thick volume, then ruffled through pages interleafed with worn maps. He took her finger in his and rested it on an entry. Rabbi David ben Zadok, he told her, lived in the port city of Classis. It seemed the Judean community of Ravenna did not have a rabbi.

After Arcadia murmured her thanks, Protasius grinned, revealing the stained teeth that caused his bad breath, then said that Placidia's authorization would be valid for lodging at the government *mansio,* an inn for those on imperial business.

Flushed and annoyed, Getorius pulled his wife away by the arm and stalked out, realizing that he had not asked about this David ben Zadok's exact location in the port, yet stubbornly refusing to go back.

༄

Getorius had once considered opening a practice in Classis and remembered a little about the port, two miles south of Ravenna. The naval base for the Roman Adriatic fleet was rundown now, but at one time its docks, berthing facilities, and shipyards could service two hundred and fifty war galleys.

The commercial buildings of Classis spread along the southern curve of its crescent-shaped harbor entrance. Wharves followed this bend, before the waterfront streets straightened out where the Via Armini jogged through the city center and continued south. A wooden bridge spanned a narrow western arm of the harbor and connected an island of shops and warehouses to that end of the port.

In the four hundred years since Augustus Caesar had chosen the site as the Adriatic base for Rome's eastern fleet, the inland arm of the bay had gradually silted up. Alluvial deposits from rivers had added additional soil, which choked up the old galley berths. Classis had also suffered a population decline after barbarians breached the Rhine frontier, thirty-two years earlier. Port authorities had ordered the quadrant nearest the sea abandoned, and a new wall built further in, but the barrier was never completed.

Recently, the vital trade links with North African cities had been cut by the Vandal capture of Carthage, which left the polyglot population of Classis struggling to survive. The port had attracted Asian Pontians, Syrians and Judeans, who competed on the docks with Thracians, Macedonians, Dacians, and even citizens of the northern Pannonian plains. Most of the groups kept to themselves on streets named after their areas of origin. Despite these rivalries, Getorius recalled that the population was fairly tolerant of differences. Tenants of apartment blocks that smelled of regional cooking realized they were bound together by the sea, in a common hope for prosperity.

Discussions among the men often centered on religious

differences between the predominant Arian Christians and a fast-spreading Manichaean faith. Even fanatical Donatists, who had been exiled by imperial decree, still emerged from hiding to argue their justification for excluding sinners from their 'pure' congregations. A few Nestorians, who taught the literal manhood of Christ, as opposed to the dual Natures that even Arians accepted, were endured for a time before they were forced aboard ships and exiled to whatever destination the galleymaster chose. Toleration, it seemed, did have some limits.

For a month now the talk in dockside taverns had been about the capture of Carthage, in October, by the Vandal king Gaiseric. Rome itself, and now the African city; both had fallen to barbarians in the space of a generation. The metropolis of Rome had recovered to an extent, but the topic of many presbyters' sermons was the horror prophesied in the Book of Revelation. Many people accepted that the catastrophic events described were being fulfilled and prepared for the final stage of the world's existence.

Flavius Aetius was not one of them. Instead, he was making sure that what had been a devastating event for the citizens of Carthage would be a revitalizing one for those at Classis. He ordered his fleet prefect to recondition war galleys at the port by stripping older vessels of equipment to outfit newer ones. The commander hoped that the overhauled triremes could repel any Vandal invasion of Italy.

The Western naval commander at Misenum, on the Bay of Neapolis, had been given the same orders, but with a greater sense of urgency. No one knew for certain whether the Carthaginian war galleys had been burned, captured, or been able to escape eastward and find refuge in Egypt. Rumors, to confirm Revelation, tended toward disaster. Misenum was three or four days' summer sailing north of Carthage. Winter would make that a longer, more risky venture, but Sicily was well within reach. Gaiseric and his Vandals were Arians, as was Maximian, the bishop on the island. He was said to have offered his co-religionists hospitality if they invaded.

❦

Getorius ordered Brisios to ready the covered carriage for a journey.

By the fourth morning hour on November twenty-first, the fog was beginning to thin out.

After the gateman slid a leather traveling case into the back, he helped Arcadia onto the seat next to her husband. She felt slightly nauseous from stomach cramps. Her monthlies had begun the night before.

Getorius leaned across his wife. "Brisios, I told Childibert that we're going to Caesena. Your mistress needs to get away for a few days. This miserable rain and taking care of patients have tired her."

Brisios nodded and went to open the courtyard gate. Getorius clucked the mare left, onto the Via Caesar. At the intersection with the Via Honorius, about twenty paces distant, visibility disappeared into a lingering veil of fog.

Arcadia pulled the hood of her coat higher against the damp-ness and turned to her husband. "Why did you tell Brisios that we were going to Caesena? We're going to Classis."

"We don't need everyone knowing that," he answered. "With the Gothic Queen worried about Aetius's spies, the fewer people who know our true destination, the better."

"But, Brisios?"

"I'm sure he has gossiping friends in local taverns."

"Getorius, I'm not sure I appreciate being the excuse for a lie."

He patted her hand. "Sorry, *cara*. We don't know what this is all about and I'd rather be cautious."

"But no one goes to Caesena in the winter, it's a summer resort. Even Brisios could figure that out."

Getorius did not reply, realizing his wife was right and not wanting to antagonize her further by persisting in the discussion.

At the corner of the Via Theodosius the market square teemed with slaves and their mistresses picking out the day's food supplies. Getorius threaded the mare between the carts and pedestrians, then to the right, onto the Theodosius. The carriage passed fragrant smells coming from bakeries and sausage vendors' stalls, and the less pleas-ant tavern stink of stale wine and vomit from the night before. At the Via Armini, where the street had been paved with stones from the ancient walls of Augustus, Getorius guided the mare to the right again. Arcadia recalled walking the road to the old necropolis, when she had searched its tombs, with Veneranda, for examples of clothing that women wore during the Republic.

When the carriage reached the Porta Laurenti, sunlight had broken through the mist and set points of light sparkling on the surface of swamps outside the wall. To the left, the bright blue line of the Adriatic Sea materialized out of the haze.

Getorius steered the mare, carriage wheels clattering, over the boards of the bridge spanning the river. Beyond, the weathered mausoleums and monuments of the necropolis lined both sides of the roadway. A few were decorated with ivy or votive offerings of food, mute testimonials to the fact that crypto-pagans still venerated the dead, despite the ban on their religion.

Arcadia was silent, and Getorius sensed that his wife was still annoyed with him.

"You were right," he said, squeezing her knee, "I should have told Brisios the truth. I was nervous about meeting this David ben Zadok."

"You thought he might be able to tell you more about your parents."

"That's part of it, but we don't really know what Judeans are like. I've never had one as a patient."

"Because they have their own physicians and keep to their own quarter," Arcadia said. "Bishop Chrysologos blames any hostility toward Judeans as being their fault for rejecting Christ."

"Ridiculous! The bishop also condemns Arians, or any other sect that disagrees with the Roman Church."

"Then how do you think Chrysologos would react to the terms of the Secundus Papyrus?"

"That worries me, Arcadia. The will is like a loaded catapult, and it wouldn't take much to trip the trigger. Can you imagine provincial governors, city councils, quietly handing over authority to Judeans? And this Rabbi Zadok may turn out to be a militant Hebrew who'll insist on the testament being made public even before its authenticity is determined."

Getorius fell silent at the prospect. Arcadia gazed off at the stunted trees of a waterlogged scrub forest that was struggling to bracket the highway.

Further on, about halfway to Classis, the road became a raised causeway that was surrounded by a broad swamp and the deposits of sandy soil that were inexorably filling in the port's once magnificent harbor. Squinting to the left of this marshy lake, Getorius saw the dense evergreens of The Pines as a dark line that mimicked the sea's flat horizon. Valentinian was hunting there, far from Behan's abandoned hut, Getorius guessed, which probably now served as an overnight shelter for woodcutters.

The monk's canvas-shrouded body still bobbed in the stream nearby, a grisly captive inside its wicker prison, while it awaited burial.

Classis

Chapter thirteen

Even before the walls of Classis came into view, Getorius commented to his wife on the acrid smell of bitumen drifting inland from the port's shipyards. They arrived at the Ravenna Gate by late morning, greeted by more pleasant odors. Vendors were roasting meat and fish over pinewood coals, selling them to passersby.

The walls and gate towers were lower than those in the capital, but well constructed. Sigisvult had talked about Vitruvius Pollio, the architect who helped design the port for Augustus Caesar, and had read from his treatise on the location of towns. The same cluster of vendors' stalls, idlers and ragged indigents that crowded the entrances to Ravenna were also present here, almost choking off the narrow passage into the city. Getorius strained to guide the carriage through without knocking down a stall, or running a wheel over a beggar's leg. At best that would delay them; at worse, risk a lawsuit in the local magistrate's court.

Once the carriage was beyond the gate and inside an open square, Getorius halted the mare to ask someone where the imperial mansio was located. Two men standing drinking at a wineseller's stall, and armed with swords, looked over, evidently recognizing him as a newcomer. One came over and took hold of the horse's bit. The other, a scarred, beefy man who might have served in the legions at one time, walked around to squint at Arcadia and Getorius.

"Where y'going?" he asked, peering inside the carriage.

"I have business in Classis," Getorius told him.

"Where? Who with?"

"Business," Getorius repeated, not used to being questioned about his movements.

"There's a visitor's tax," the other man added with a snicker. "One gold *solidus.*"

"Show them Galla Placidia's signet," Arcadia muttered under her breath.

"It would mean nothing to these two illiterates, and I'll be with Hades before I pay extortion money. I'm a surgeon," he said more loudly to the man, "here on a personal matter."

"Well, bone-cutter, it'll cost y'gold for that."

By now idlers had gathered around to watch the confrontation. Some joked about the couple while they waited for the gold coin to be handed over—strangers were always frightened into paying.

"A *solidus,*" the man repeated, his face reddening and an edge of anger appearing in his voice.

Getorius ignored him and looked over his head at the nearest vendor to call out, "Where is the imperial mansio?"

The merchant, who saw this scene played out several times a day, grinned and pointed to a villa across the square. "Behind you, Surgeon."

The ruffian glanced around, and pulled on the mare's bridle to keep Getorius from turning the animal's head.

"Let go of my horse," Getorius ordered, as evenly as he could.

Hearing some of the bystanders laughing, the bully hesitated, realizing that the crowd had begun to side with this stranger, who seemed determined to call his bluff. The man spat nervously, released the bridle, and motioned to his companion. "Aw…let's go eat."

After the pair had skulked off into one of the side streets that led to the wharves, Getorius looked at Arcadia. "A bit foolish of me," he admitted, "making enemies even before dismounting. That inn doesn't look like much, but I'm not sure I want to go searching for another one with those two on the loose."

"We'll make it do," Arcadia agreed.

Getorius turned the mare toward the deteriorated front of a two-story building that was set back twenty-five paces from the curb, facing a weed-choked front yard. The fountain positioned in its center was dry. Undoubtedly, Valentinian's inspectors had been bribed to overlook the neglected state of the building.

"You, child," he called to a boy floating a block of wood in a curbside puddle. "Go and bring the manager of this place to me."

The boy returned a few moments later, with a heavy-set middle-aged man wearing a greasy leather vest. Blussus thought he was being paid a surprise visit by someone from the aedile's office in Ravenna until he saw Arcadia. A woman would not be accompanying an inspector.

"You wish lodgings for the night?" he asked, still suspicious. "Or longer perhaps?"

"Protasius at the tax office told us we could stay here."

"Ah"—Blussus raised an eyebrow—"you are an assessor, then?" There were those in town who would pay to know that in advance.

"No, we're just visiting Classis."

The eyebrow curved up again; no one came to the port just to visit. "Your 'visit' involves shipping, perhaps?"

"My husband is a surgeon," Arcadia told him. "We have an authorization from the Emperor's mother to stay here. Show him, Getorius."

"No need, Domina," Blussus fawned, "your word suffices."

"Can you show us a room?"

"Certainly Domina," he replied, bowing. "An honor to host friends of the Gothic...of the Empress Mother. I myself, Julius Blussus, will assure your comfort. Evantius, lead the horse around to our stables."

"Evantius is your son?"

"Both son and 'sun' of my life, Domina."

Blussus chuckled at his pun and led the way to the villa's

entrance, which was on the narrower side of the building, facing a brick drive that went to stables in the rear. Inside, the atrium tile was buckled and cracked. The pool in the center of the atrium was choked with moldering willow leaves, and resembled a mosaic of slim, earth-tone spear shapes. The garden beyond was thick with ragged evergreens that needed pruning and the overgrown stems of dried weeds.

Once beyond the peristyle columns, Arcadia fell back to Getorius' side. "I hope this doesn't reflect the condition of his rooms," she murmured to her husband. "Whatever state stipend Blussus receives obviously doesn't go into the inn's maintenance."

"Don't make a fuss," Getorius hissed back. "We don't need to attract attention to ourselves."

Mercifully, when Blussus pushed open the door to a room in the east wing, Arcadia was pleasantly surprised. The bed was made with what seemed to be reasonably clean linen, and a pitcher on the table actually held water. Although some of the paint had flaked off a mural on the back wall, she could make out a harbor scene; not Classis, but some imagined arcadia from the past, depicting colonnaded warehouses, a bluish mountain range, and a round *Tholos* temple set amid grazing cattle. The mountains and part of a ship merged into the right-hand wall, which had obviously been set up a while ago to divide what was originally a much larger space into two bedrooms.

"I can arrange for a room like this," Blussus offered, sheepishly wiping the chair back with his hand.

"What's wrong with this one?" Arcadia asked him. "I like it. A good dusting is all it would take to make it livable."

"Ah, Domina, unfortunately it's taken. Two merchants have—"

"Then why show it?" she snapped.

"Blussus," Getorius broke in, "whatever room you set up for us will be fine. Where does one have a meal in Classis?"

"I have simple but ample fare. If you would both honor me by dining here?"

"Good. Have your son bring our things in after he stables the mare. We need to go out for awhile."

"I begin serving at the fifth hour."

"We'll be back here by then." Getorius took Arcadia's arm and led her toward the entrance.

"That was the room he shows off," she complained once they were outside. "Ours had better be at least as well kept."

Getorius did not reply. He knew from consultations with midwives that women often became irritable when their menstrual flow began each month. What was the connection? His dissection of several cats had proved that the uterus was fixed in place and did not wander around the body in search of moisture, as was commonly believed. Even if it did, when excess blood was being thrown off the organ should be at rest, and logically, the woman, too. He shook his head and looked east along the Via Armini, toward the old forum. There were more important things to do than humor his wife.

The Via Armini in Classis was similar in length to the one in Ravenna, although about three paces narrower. Various shops catered to customers on the ground level, with balconies or awnings above to protect them from sun or rain. At the harbor area, where a pall of black smoke smudged the horizon, the masts of galleys stabbed a sky that was fast becoming overcast with low rain clouds. The hollow, clunking sound of hammers and a strong smell of pitch betrayed the location of the port's naval shipyards and outfitting docks. Squinting along the road, Getorius recalled that the ruins of the ancient forum were located where the Armini intersected with another broad avenue that led to the waterfront.

"There should be a marble or bronze plaque in the forum with a diagram of Classis," he said, as he guided Arcadia along the sidewalk. "It will help us find the streets, since I didn't think to question Protasius about Zadok's address."

"Why didn't you ask the innkeeper?"

"The fewer who know our reason for coming here, the better." Getorius held her arm to let a cart pass on a cross street. "What's the name cut into that board on the building across the way?"

"Vicus…Syriorum."

"Street of the Syrians. Good, let's keep on."

The forum had been located on the south side of the Armini,

to allow more space for commercial buildings and warehouses in the direction of the harbor. After walking past three blocks of shops and apartments, the couple came upon an area that had been totally cleared, except for two remaining buildings. The nearest was an abandoned temple. Statues of two gods had been brought out from inner shrines and set on the porch, facing the wall.

Arcadia read the inscription's greenish, bronze letters. "The temple was dedicated to Neptune and Mercurius by Tiberius Caesar," she informed her husband.

"Guardians of the sea and commerce." Getorius pointed to an offering of wheat stalks lying on the chipped altar in front. "Pagans still worship here. Whoever is presbyter in Classis hasn't been able to persuade everyone in his flock to throw the old gods into the harbor. That building across the way is probably the Curia, where the plaque with the map should be."

They crossed via a path separating harvested gardens that were planted among the ruins of other structures. As Getorius had guessed, a marble slab was mounted to the right of the doorway.

"This is recent," Getorius noted, after checking the diagram etched on its face. "Valentinian is given credit, but it was put up by Aetius in his second consulship. That was…only two years ago."

"Does it give street names?"

"Yes. Let's see…we're in the forum. That should be the Via Adriatico leading down to the docks."

"It is," Arcadia said. "I can see ships at anchor and a glimpse of the sea. Is there a Street of the Judeans, or something similar?"

Getorius read off the streets going east, "Of the Thracians… Dacians…Macedonians. Here, *Vicus Judaeorum.*"

Arcadia noticed a crude six-pointed star scratched near the street name, two triangles with one reversed and superimposed on the other. "What's that symbol?"

"I think it's the emblem of David, the Hebrew king, but this one is meant as a threat. Some Christians see it as a desecration of the Trinity because the inverted triangle cancels out their symbol. That's not the only disrespect. See that building on the left side?"

Arcadia looked at the diagram labeled ECCLESIA ARIANORVM. "That's across from the inn. I thought it looked like a church."

"Yes, but Arian. Someone has scratched *Hairetikos* over it, 'Heretics' in Greek."

Arcadia shuddered and grasped her husband's arm. "Let's find Rabbi Zadok. I don't think I want to spend much time in Classis."

After walking past the streets he had named, Getorius found the one leading to the Judean quarter, but looking around, he was puzzled. The area was empty of people, with shops shuttered as if no one lived there, and yet the smell of hot food indicated there were inhabitants. He wondered if the place was under a quarantine imposed by port authorities. Seaborne diseases were common where galleys came in from distant countries.

"Wait here," he told Arcadia, then crossed the Armini to ask a lone woman filling a jug at a fountain about the lack of activity. When he came back, he explained, "she says it's the Hebrews' Sabbath. No one is allowed to work, so nothing is open."

"Will the rabbi see us?"

"She said that the synagogue is three blocks down the Judaeo-rum. Look for a building on the right that resembles a temple."

The place of worship was easy to pick out from among the apartments. Situated near the south wall, the synagogue was set back from the street, with an entrance facing southeast, toward Jerusalem. The front resembled that of a Roman temple, with steps that led to a shallow colonnaded porch whose entablature was interrupted by a central semi-circular arch. The building was faced with Tibertine marble, and streaked by black weather stains. A walled, paved fore-court separated the structure from the street.

Several bearded men sat on the synagogue steps. They wore turban-like hats and fringed shawls thrown over dark, skirted jackets that half-covered baggy trousers tucked into felt boots. The group had been engaged in a lively discussion, but fell silent when they noticed the couple walking toward them. It was obvious from their dress that they were not Judeans.

Getorius motioned for Arcadia to stay back, and approached

the men through an ironwork gate. "My pardon for interrupting you," he called out. "I was told I could find David ben Zadok here."

No one replied until one man who looked to be the oldest in the group stood up. "I am Mordecai ben Asher," he said. "Rav Zadok is preparing for the afternoon service. Why do you wish to see him? Who are you?"

"Getorius Asterius, a surgeon from Ravenna. That's my wife back there. She trains with me to be a medica. My…my father knew the rabbi." He unfolded his pass. "I have an authorization from the Augustus."

Mordecai came and studied the parchment without touching it. "This has the signet of his mother. What is your business with the Rav?"

"Confidential, sir, and urgent," he replied. "I didn't realize it was your holy day."

"Is this a matter of life and death?" one of the men called out.

"You could say so," Getorius replied. "Yes, definitely."

He heard the men discuss his reply in a guttural language he assumed was Hebrew.

Mordecai joined in briefly then turned. "The mother of the Augustus would not have given her blessing to you unless the matter was important. I will take you to Rav Zadok. He has a little time before prayers."

Mordecai led the way to an apartment across the narrow street. After Getorius rapped on the door with a bronze knocker in the shape of a lion's head, a youth opened the portal.

Mordecai spoke to him in Greek, but Getorius understood enough to know the servant was told who he was, and that his business was urgent enough for ben Zadok to see a Gentile on the Sabbath.

The building's vestibule was paved in a mosaic design that depicted a candelabrum with seven branches, and other figures Getorius did not recognize. After he and Arcadia were shown into a reception room, Mordecai disappeared down the corridor.

The smell of fish being cooked nearby wafted into the ante-room, but the odor was not strong enough to completely overpower a pleasant scent of incense. While he waited, Getorius thought about his parents. If his father had been about Zadok's age, then the rabbi would be over sixty years old, and a link with a past he had thought forever broken upon Nicias' death. As a friend, Zadok must have known Treverius and Blandina more intimately than Nicias, and might be able to fill in details that the old surgeon had not heard, or had forgotten.

Getorius was beginning to become impatient when the Greek youth entered and motioned him and Arcadia to an office down the hallway.

David ben Zadok stood when the couple entered, but said nothing. Getorius saw a white-bearded, ruddy face that was etched with furrows, like the eroded slopes near Caesena. Watching the rabbi as he studied him for a few moments, Getorius was sure he saw tears glistening in the old man's brown eyes.

"Yes, you…you are his son," Zadok finally said, in a gentle voice that trembled with emotion. "*Barukh k'vod Adonai mi-m'komo.*"

"Sir?"

"'Praised is the Lord's glory throughout the universe.' Zadok smiled. "Young man, you have taken me back thirty years. Please, both of you. Sit down."

"You knew my father, then?"

Zadok nodded. "After the Vandal raid on Mogontiacum, I took Treverius into business with me. You see, there was no longer a need for the maps he made."

"My…mother?"

"Blandina? Beautiful. Intelligent. It was unusual to find a woman in a profession." He smiled at Arcadia. "Am I to understand you are a medica?"

"Sir, I'm only training with my husband."

"Then, young woman, you have some of Blandina's spirit."

She laughed. "So Nicias used to say. I don't know if he always meant it as a compliment."

Zadok nodded in remembrance, then turned to Getorius. "You've come to talk about your parents? Gladly. How did you find out I knew them?"

"From Galla Placidia. But, no, that's not why I came. I do want to know more about them, but I'm here on a…a more important matter."

"Ah. Then perhaps we can talk about your parents afterward," the rabbi replied.

"I would like that, sir. I…I'm here for Placidia."

"The headstrong mother of the Augustus. What is the nature of your mission for her?"

"Rabbi," Getorius warned, "I must swear you to secrecy."

"May he who has not taken an oath deceitfully ascend to the mountain of the Lord," Zadok quoted from a psalm. "If the matter is of such importance, you have my word."

Arcadia noticed her husband hesitate and interposed, "Sir, an important document has been discovered. We're sure it's forged, but there are witnesses. We can't simply destroy it."

"And if there were no witnesses except the Lord?"

Zadok's gentle rebuke flustered her. "Y…you're correct, sir. It still should not be destroyed."

"This…document concerns religion?" Zadok asked, stroking his beard in a nervous gesture. "Ours, perhaps?"

"Very deeply," Getorius said.

"You are Christian," Zadok continued softly. "It relates in your holy book that when your cult was new, Rabban Gamliel cautioned our zealots, who opposed you as apostate Hebrews. He told them that if your cause were not of the Lord it would fail. But if it were a work of His, they would never be able to overthrow it and would, in effect, be fighting against Him. Let us use Gamliel's wisdom in dealing with this document. What, then, is it?"

"Supposedly," Getorius began tactfully, "supposedly a last will of Jesus Christ has been discovered."

Zadok folded his hands, leaned back, and closed his eyes. "Continue, please."

"According to a letter purportedly written by the Apostle Peter, this will was dictated to Pontius Pilate's secretary while the procurator was outside speaking to the crowd."

"Trying to convince them of the condemned man's innocence," the rabbi said.

"Y...yes." Getorius was surprised, expecting the rabbi to be ignorant of the story.

Zadok opened his eyes and sat up, his white brows knitted into an angry frown. "We had no power to put a seditionist to death...is this another attempt to exonerate the Roman authorities? Letters still circulate that accuse our leaders of forcing Pilate...against his wishes...to execute the Galilean."

"It's not that." Getorius hesitated again. Once he told Zadok the terms of the will how would the old man react? He needed to explain further. "The Galilean...Christ...taught that we should love our enemies. Forgive them."

"A compassionate precept, yet difficult to observe."

"Yes, and the ultimate expression of such a love would be to not only forgive your enemies, but to make them your...your inheritors."

"And the greatest enemy of the Galilean?" Zadok asked.

"The Judeans who...who wanted him crucified." Getorius let the rabbi absorb the implications a moment, then continued, "It's a forgery, of course, but suppose Christ did will the world to your people? It would have no meaning at the time, so that's why this letter of Peter states that the document is to be released at a later date."

"There are those," Arcadia added, "who teach that the world will end in sixty years. People who think the final days are almost here will believe any nonsense."

"Your forger has excellent timing," Zadok commented wryly. "Today, you Christians own the world, as it were."

"*Exactly the point*," Getorius emphasized. "Under the will, all of it reverts to you Judeans. Sixtus, the Bishop of Rome, who speaks for Christ, is legally bound to enforce the terms."

Zadok fell silent, toying with an oil lamp whose handle was in the shape of a small menorah, before asking, "You, of course, could not bring this document with you?"

"No, it's at the palace in Ravenna. The librarian is trying to establish its authenticity before it's released."

"Who else knows of this false will's existence?"

"Seven of us were there when it was accidentally discovered."

"Where?"

"Concealed inside a niche in Galla Placidia's new mausoleum. When Theokritos' assistant removed its tile cover, the bolt from a hidden crossbow struck him. And three other witnesses have already been killed."

"Time is short then." Zadok fixed Getorius with brown eyes that expressed both strong resolve and an interior sadness. "You came here to have me predict this document's impact after it is brought to light."

"If you would, sir. Especially on your people."

"For the Hebrews living in the two Roman empires, nothing less than total destruction, the 'abomination of desolation' predicted by our prophet Daniel. Your Galilean quoted him in describing the end of Creation."

"Sir, there are laws to protect you," Getorius objected.

"Laws are the first casualties in war," Zadok scoffed. He stood up, rubbed his eyes and sighed. "This is not the conversation I expected, Getorius, when your name was brought to me. I....I must prepare for the afternoon service."

"Of course, sir. We'll go now."

"At evening prayers tonight, when we say *Havdalah*, the prayer that marks the conclusion of *Shabbat*," Zadok said, choosing his words carefully, "I will pray that the creative work we begin after every *Shabbat* rest will be fruitful in solving this problem. I would like to return to Ravenna with you and examine the document."

"Yes," Arcadia quickly agreed. "Please stay with us at our villa."

Zadok shook his head. "There is a small Judean community there. I will lodge with them." He came around his desk and put an arm around Getorius "You may not know this, but your father and I helped solve a series of murders at Mogontiacum. A treasonable attempt to set up a separatist province."

"I didn't know. Perhaps you could tell us the story on our way back."

"Perhaps. The Augustus…Honorius…awarded us a golden crown." Zadok's smile of recollection faded. "Now we have this new mystery for Treverius' son to solve."

"What time shall I pick you up in the morning, sir? We're staying at the government mansio near the Ravenna Gate."

"By the third hour. We should not delay."

"We'll look forward to the journey with you."

❦

Getorius was silent on the walk back to the inn. His excitement at the possibility of learning more about his father was tempered by Zadok's prediction of civil chaos. Surely the forgers of the will realized that this would happen. Why would they want to create such a catastrophe?

Blussus had set up a room for them on the second story of the east wing. Its single window overlooked the garden and gave a view of the shipyards in the hazy distance. The wind had shifted again, coming in from the east and sending inland blackish smoke from tarring ovens, to merge with the low clouds that threatened rain by evening.

Arcadia was pleased with the room, but hoped the bitumen smell would not overpower the taste of Blussus' food. Cramps in her abdomen had subsided and she felt better. Looking down into the garden, she saw a slave clearing away dead weeds and raking the soil smooth. It seemed Blussus was still convinced that Getorius was there to inspect the mansio and report on its condition. Good. Service should be better.

Blussus served his meals in a large room near the kitchen. The murals on the walls suggested that this might have been the original owner's study. Arcadia identified some of the scenes as the ships embarking for Troy described in the Iliad. The naval theme was consistent with a shipbuilder's interest.

Businessmen who looked wealthy enough to eat wherever they wished occupied nine tables in the room. Blussus evidently spent most of his imperial stipend on food—as his own ample frame testified. The other diners gave Getorius and Arcadia a couple of cursory glances, but none were interested in the couple and they all went back to talking in low tones. One man ate alone, a swarthy, bearded fellow, whom Getorius guessed to be Syrian.

The meal was better than they expected. Grilled sea crayfish preceded a pan omelet of salt fish and cheese, without the cumin seasoning being overpowering. Stewed fruits made up the sweet course.

Despite his harassment at the gate by the two ruffians, Getorius was determined to see the harbor. Arcadia went with him, although she would rather have stayed out of the freshening wind and read a chapter in her volume of Soranus.

The Vicus Porti, across from the mansio, led to the docks. It went past the Arian church, where more graffiti condemning the sect's teaching that Christ was not co-eternal with the Father was charcoaled on its walls. Few people were on the streets in the inclement weather, but Arcadia expected to run into the two thugs in every shop she passed.

At the harbor, a bridge leading to an island was cordoned off and patrolled by guards. Several low-lying war galleys were moored at the curved wharf, being outfitted with new masts. Others in dry-dock ramps across the bay were being equipped with bronze rams salvaged from older vessels. A crew of conscripts sat on benches, straining at long, unfamiliar oars to master the rowing cadences of the hortator's hammer signals. Getorius thought them a pitifully small force to oppose barbarians who had defeated Roman armies in Gaul and Hispania, then crossed the Iberian straits and conquered Carthage.

A misty rain began to fall as the couple strolled along the commercial anchorage, where a few high-sterned merchant galleys bobbed empty at their moorings. With the loss of the African provinces their grain and olive oil supplies would no longer be shipped to Italy, and most of the Egyptian harvests would go to Constantinople.

On a wharf at the end of the Via Adriatico they watched a man in a wagon dole out free loaves of bread to citizens who held out tokens. He seemed to have enough for now, but the interrupted wheat supply could mean famine—and rioting—when the ration was gone.

When Getorius stopped at a tavern to buy cups of hot mulled wine, Arcadia said she thought she saw the Syrian from the inn following them at a distance. Getorius laughed and pointed out that the docks were full of such Eastern types, but she insisted he take her back to their lodgings.

By the time the couple reached the Via Armini again, a chill drizzle that smelled of bitumen and the sea was driving in from the direction of the Adriatic. Sunset came early, so the rainy afternoon was almost dark by the time Getorius and Arcadia went to their room.

Blussus had closed the shutters against the blowing rain, but water had seeped through and trickled down the wall, puddling on the floorboards. Getorius slid Arcadia's bed away from the wet area by pushing it against the north wall.

Aside from that, the room was comfortable. A circular iron stove radiated warmth from a blazing pinewood fire. A stack of the wood lay nearby. Even the gentle drumming of the downpour on the tile roof was soothing. Arcadia hung their wet capes on a peg near the stove before they went down to supper.

Julius Blussus' cook—his wife, he said—had prepared a thick Julian soup of spelt grits, minced pork brain, and rib meat, flavored with lovage and fennel. It was served with fresh bread and a pitcher of Caesena wine.

The meal was filling, and both Getorius and his wife were tired afterward. The early drive from Ravenna, with its unnerving encounter at the gate, the emotional meeting with Rabbi ben Zadok, and the two walks through town had combined to sap their energy.

When Getorius went to bed, the steady, rhythmic patter of rain and the warm room made him fall asleep quickly. Arcadia listened to the rise and fall of his breathing for a moment before wetting her finger and pinching out the lamp wick. Her last drowsy thought was that it would be good to be home again the next day.

Except for a slit of light showing under the door, the room was black when Arcadia was awakened by something brushing her face. Her first reaction was that a roach had crawled onto her, and she lashed out frantically with one hand. The wild fling hit a solid object above her. She heard a muffled curse somewhere near the ceiling, and screamed out her husband's name.

"Getorius!"

Before he could awaken and react, the room's door was smashed off its retaining bolt, and left hanging loosely by one hinge. By the dim light from the hallway, Arcadia recognized the bearded Syrian, and saw the glint on the blade of the sword he held. Getorius was just sitting up as the man lunged toward her. Arcadia covered her face with her arms in a reflexive hug of protection, thinking that now there would be two fewer witnesses to tell of the papyri.

She felt the bed sway from the man's weight, and heard the mattress rip as the ropes holding it in place broke. But she did not feel the expected sword slash. Uncovering an eye, she saw the Syrian thrust his weapon at a leg disappearing up the rungs of a rope ladder dangling from above.

Blussus appeared in the doorway wearing a ridiculously short night tunic. The manager was too stunned to speak as he watched the bearded man, who had eaten a noon meal in his dining room, pull his foot out of the broken bed.

Arcadia's first reaction was to ask the stranger, "You...you followed us this afternoon. Why?"

"My apologies," he replied. "Mordecai, with the Rav's blessing, assigned me to keep a watch on you."

"Keep watch? Who are you?" Getorius demanded, bringing a trembling Arcadia to sit on his bed and putting an arm around her.

"My name is Nathaniel, a student of the Rav."

"Judean? You...you broke your Sabbath for us?"

"The Rav teaches that the Commandments are to help us live, not to allow someone to die because of them." Nathaniel reached up with the tip of his sword and pulled down the frayed end of the ladder until it dangled over Arcadia's bed.

"That's what brushed my face!" she exclaimed.

"Strange that bandits positioned the ceiling opening directly above a bed."

"Nathaniel, my husband moved the bed over there because the floor was wet."

"Then the Lord protected you through that simple act. If the man had reached the floor in silence you might have both been killed." Nathaniel indicated the ceiling and broken door to Blussus. "Manager, you have repairs to make and questions to answer about your accomplices."

"My...my slaves are in charge of this floor," he stammered in protest. "It's the cursed Donatist Circumcellions. They're still everywhere."

"Leave us," Nathaniel ordered. "Find these people a room on the first floor for the rest of the night." Blussus bowed and shuffled off to vent his frustration on the slave staff. Nathaniel propped the door shut and sat on a chair to explain. "I was not told of your reason for visiting the Rav, only that it merited breaking *Shabbat*."

"Who are these Circumcellions that Blussus mentioned?" Getorius asked.

"Fanatics of Donatus, one of your exiled heretic bishops. They prey on strangers and gladly die for their beliefs, but I don't think your attacker was a Donatist. I believe these were common bandits who bribed or coerced Blussus into letting them rob guests of their belongings. His slaves may have made an honest mistake in preparing this particular room for you."

"I see." Getorius was not that sure. Tomorrow he and Arcadia would go back to Ravenna to deal with the deaths of people who had known the papyrus existed. Galla Placidia, Protasius, and possibly Aetius knew about their trip to Classis. The intruder might have been part of a conspiracy, sent to silence them both as witnesses to the will's accidental discovery.

"Nathaniel, we owe our lives to you," Arcadia said.

"The act was a timely *mizvah*, a blessing. I shall accompany you and Rav ben Zadok back to Ravenna."

Getorius grasped his hand. "We appreciate that, Nathaniel. Thank you."

Arcadia also felt better at the news, but her sleep for the rest of the night was disturbed by images of the bandit's hairy legs disappearing up the ladder, and the bloated, leech-encrusted face of Archdeacon Renatus slowly turning toward her inside the grisly vat.

Ravenna

Chapter fourteen

A steady rain that continued all morning slowed the drive back to Ravenna. At the bridge a little more than a quarter of a mile north of Classis, the Via Armini was flooded. Ochre water surged over the paving stones, hampering a detail of sodden legionaries who struggled to clear away tree branches and brushwood. The debris had jammed against the stone arch and was threatening to collapse it.

During the wait Arcadia huddled in her damp cloak, indifferent to the sharp scent of the wet pines. The smell usually invigorated her, but today it had no effect; she was too tired after her restless night. The distant pulse of white-capped surf, the monotonous drumming of rain on the leather carriage top, and the call of jays foraging among the wet trees might have lulled her to sleep, except that the night intruder was yet vivid in her mind. If the man had been sent to silence her and her husband, it meant that the conspiracy extended from the palace all the way to Classis.

Protasius knew they had come to find Rabbi ben Zadok. If the clerk had gossiped to others—or if Galla Placidia was correct in claiming that Flavius Aetius had informants everywhere—it was not surprising that she and Getorius had been found so easily. Aetius even might have guessed that their unusual journey had something to do with the papyri.

Arcadia wanted to dismiss the idea that Placidia was involved, and yet she was the only person to know the actual reason for the trip. And the papyri had been found in her mausoleum. Was the Gothic Queen diverting suspicion from herself by implicating Aetius? No, that made no sense. Why would the mother of the Augustus make public a document that, in effect, gave away the empire of her son in the West, and that of her nephew in the East, at Constantinople? It was not possible that she would be involved in such a conspiracy.

After the arch was cleared and the mucky water washing over the roadway had subsided, Getorius clucked the mare ahead. The four passengers rode in silence until Getorius decided to ask Zadok about the Mogontiacum deaths.

"Rabbi, you said my father and yourself had been involved in solving some murders. Can you tell me about them?"

"A seditious business." After a pause in which Getorius thought Zadok would not continue, the old man wiped his eyes with a linen square. "It was during the winter that the Vandals invaded Gaul," he explained, his voice slightly hoarse from emotion. "The weather was bitter. Citizens…mostly Christians…began dying mysteriously on their namesakes' days. Treverius reasoned out the cause at a *Purim* celebration in my home."

"What is *Purim*?" Arcadia asked.

"One of our Hebrew festivals."

"You must have been very close, to have invited my husband's parents. And, after all that time, to recall this so clearly."

"Young woman, it's as if it all happened within last month's moon," he said. "An ambitious praetorium curator tried to form a rebel province."

"Didn't that kind of treason spring up again when my parents were killed?"

Zadok nodded. "With the usurper Jovinus that time. I was in Ravenna when he was proclaimed Augustus by a Burgond king. My…my wife Penina was a victim of the rebellion, along with your parents. Will the Empress Mother show me the two papyri, or must I be content with hearing them read?"

"No, no, you'll be able to examine both. And we'll ask Theokritos how his tests are coming along."

"Yes, establishing the authenticity of the documents is crucial," Zadok said, and lapsed into silence.

Getorius surmised that the old man was still shaken at the news, perhaps devising plans for his community to deal with the will, if it was released.

※

The downpour continued as the carriage clattered toward Ravenna. Rain-swollen swamps on either side of the causeway took on the look of dull hammered silver, from the spattering raindrop patterns.

※

Ravenna was enduring a less severe repetition of the street flooding that had occurred three weeks earlier. Getorius realized there would also be a flood of patients at the clinic, waiting to be treated.

When he guided the mare through the Lawrence Gate and retraced the previous day's route back to the villa, there were several people huddled in the shelter of the atrium waiting area. Getorius thought he recognized the Gothic fisherman who had lacerated his hand. Since he had not returned as instructed, it could be presumed that rather than healing, the wound had become corrupt with black bile.

At his gate, Getorius told Nathaniel to borrow the carriage and take Rabbi Zadok to the Judean district, where he and the Rabbi would be staying. Getorius knew very little about the area, except that it was bordered on the south by artisans' shops and harbor warehouses, on the west by the Via Armini, and on the remaining sides by the new walls that emperor Valentinian was having constructed.

Getorius began seeing patients that afternoon. As he feared, Varnifrid's hand would be lost. The man had continued working on his boat, and his hand was now a mass of foul-smelling black tissue.

Arcadia scheduled an amputation for early the following morning, yet felt sure the Goth would not come.

The next patient was a stevedore who complained that a lump in his lower abdomen had gotten larger, and that he experienced a leaden feeling after eating. Getorius had seen the condition on dockworkers and farmers, but there was little he could do except fit the man with a padded belt to restrain the bulge, and curse his inability to dissect the area in a corpse to investigate what made the mass suddenly appear.

Most of the patients had been treated when a slave arrived from Senator Maximin, with a message asking Getorius to look in on his mother again. Agatha had developed further ulcers on her withered buttocks, from lying in bed. The note ended with the senator apologizing for the inconvenience and promising to be present at his villa this time.

Maximin stayed in the room while Getorius cleaned Agatha's lesions with a mild vinegar wash, and then applied an olive oil and garlic poultice. He told Fabia to continue the treatment, and saw no harm in the magic amulets the old slave had placed in her mistress' bed.

⁊⁊

Galla Placidia sent word that she would meet with Getorius, Arcadia, and Rabbi ben Zadok on the afternoon of November twenty-sixth. The note also mentioned that Theokritos had succumbed to a feverish phlegm imbalance, but that he would nevertheless be present at the interview.

Placidia chose her private reception room for the meeting. The walls were decorated with paintings that were identical in design to some of the mosaic work in her mausoleum. Spaces between cedar ceiling beams had been painted with floral patterns on a lapis-blue background. Red and lapis border designs repeated the ribbon motif on the arch undersides in the smaller room. Centered in the panels were renderings of fruit baskets, urns and various birds—mallard ducks, doves and a rooster. The mosaic design of two pigeons on the rim of a water basin, against which a frustrated Placidia had flung her wine cup a few days earlier, had been cleaned.

Carpets that had covered the floor and walls of Ataulf's tent when her Visigoth husband was on a campaign, were hung as backdrops for his war trophies. Statuary, part of his loot from the three-day pillage of Rome—in which Placidia herself had been one of the prizes—stood on pedestals along the wall. Other keepsakes from Gaul and Hispania, which had belonged to her second husband, Constantius, were displayed with them. Prominent on the wall behind the throne where Galla Placidia sat to receive important visitors was her monogram in gold tile work, a reminder of her position as the daughter of a former emperor and mother of the ruling Augustus. The effect of the room was intimidating, either by design, or simply because the mementos accumulated over a twenty-year span reflected the Gothic Queen's incredible background and present imperial power.

Rabbi ben Zadok had not yet arrived when Getorius and Arcadia were shown into the room. Theokritos lay on a couch that had been brought in for him. A silver bowl, cup, and linen napkin were arranged on a table next to it. Several oil lamps illuminated the room, but a fire in a circular iron stove had done little to dissipate the damp chill that accompanied the rainy weather.

The old librarian seemed to be asleep. Arcadia thought he looked haggard and thin, with skin that stretched over his facial bones like a sausage casing. This alarmed her, but she assumed that Antioches was treating him. A strong aromatic smell came from a linen bag tied around his neck. Getorius nodded when she looked toward him. He too had recognized the pungent odor of camphor, a medication that was obtained from trees growing at the eastern limits of Roman trading routes, and much too expensive for him to prescribe. Next to the sachet hung the oval Abraxas amulet.

Theokritos coughed and roused himself to spit into the napkin, and Getorius recalled with an inward pang that there were several poisons that mimicked the symptoms of a severe phlegm imbalance.

Galla Placidia also looked exhausted. She had countered a pale complexion by rouging her cheeks almost to the henna shade of her hair, and wearing a white silk tunic. Getorius surmised that the deaths of Sigisvult and Renatus, combined with uncertainty over the papyri and her suspicions of Flavius Aetius, were causing her to awaken after too few hours of sleep. At least for the next month she had one less worry—Aetius was reported to be away at Mediolanum, inspecting the field legions stationed there.

Theokritos coughed again and opened his eyes, but seemed disoriented in the strange room. Arcadia came to him and said, "I'm sorry you're not well. Would you like me...my husband...to examine you?"

Theokritos stared at her with eyes glazed by fever. "Antioches has done that," he rasped.

"At least let the surgeon look at your throat," Placidia suggested. "You sound like a carpenter's scraper."

"Antioches has seen it."

"Antioches hasn't the eyesight he had twenty years ago."

Theokritos waved a hand in a weak gesture of impatience. "You didn't bring me here to discuss my throat, Regina. Where is the Hebrew priest?"

"Ben Zadok was told to be here by the seventh hour."

"Sir, how is your research on the papyrus fibers coming along?" Getorius asked.

"I was taken ill." Theokritos did not elaborate.

"Librarian, we hope this Judean can be of help in evaluating the text itself, not only the material." Placidia turned to Getorius. "I must tell you that Bishop Chrysologos hasn't yet heard from that dead monk's abbot at Autessiodurum."

"The abbot himself wouldn't come," Getorius predicted, "the journey is difficult in winter, even for a courier. We're not even sure that the one who was sent arrived in Gaul safely."

"All this uncertainty," Placidia complained. "The bishop expects instructions in a week or two, but with all this rain he was concerned that the monk's body might be washed downstream to the sea. He ordered it brought to Ravenna."

"Where is it...is Behan now?" Arcadia asked.

"In an ice storage room next to the palace kitchen. The cooking staff objects of course, but the bishop insisted. It will only be for a short time."

"I hope the poor man can be laid to rest soon." When Arcadia saw Theokritos trying to reach for his cup, she went to help him and managed to sniff the pinkish drink. It seemed to be only watered wine. After taking a few sips, Theokritos lay back on the pillows, exhausted by the small effort.

Placidia's steward Magnaric rapped on the door, then entered with David ben Zadok.

Placidia stood to greet the old man out of respect for his position. "We are grateful you came, Rabbi. Is that your title?"

"The word may be translated as 'teacher,'" Zadok replied, bowing slightly. "I hope to be worthy of it, Empress, and of your summons."

"We knew your old acquaintance, Nicias of Alexandria."

"The legion surgeon at Mogontiacum." Zadok indicated Getorius with a hand. "He is responsible for this young man being here."

"Yes, brought to Us in Ravenna." Placidia smiled. "How truly unexplainable are God's ways."

"Indeed, 'Who can know the mind of the Lord, or be His advisor?'" Zadok quoted. "The eternal question of the afflicted Job."

"May I present my librarian, Theokritos," Placidia continued, dropping the formal pronoun. "He is not well, unfortunately."

"May the Lord grant you health again, Librarian." Zadok gently grasped his arm.

Theokritos returned his hold. "We meet as scholars unraveling a mystery. You Hebrews have a reputation for learning."

"A persecuted people must use the pen as a weapon, rather than a sword."

Getorius looked at Placidia to gauge her reaction at the exchange, but she was smiling. He had thought she might have been worried that Theokritos would be hostile, since he considered the Hebrews' unbending insistence on the worship of one God arrogant and irrational.

"This is the mystery," Placidia said, taking two cedar boards off a side table. "Theokritos has flattened the will papyrus onto a wooden panel and held it in place with the golden ribbons you see. The letter of Peter is on this other."

When Magnaric came in with a cup of hot mulled wine, the rabbi declined and explained to Placidia, "My thanks, Empress, but our dietary laws of *kashrut* forbid me."

"Indeed," she replied with a trace of impatience in her voice, "I recall that you Judeans cannot take foods that are unblessed. Another peculiarity of your religion."

"May I sit here, Empress, to study the documents?" Zadok asked her, to avoid continuing the subject.

At Placidia's nod, he took the boards from her and sat on a couch. The silence was broken only by Theokritos' rasping cough as the rabbi read. Zadok went back over the text again and fingered the edges of the fiber sheets before looking up at the librarian.

"The papyrus is of fine quality. What one might expect to find in a procurator's office. I'm told you've conducted tests to determine its age. May I know your conclusions thus far?"

Theokritos shook his head. "That is only for the Regina to see, after I finish. What did you find out from the text, Teacher?"

"Empress"—Zadok looked at Galla Placidia—"I understand there have been several deaths connected to these documents."

"Not directly," Placidia hedged. "Well, one. An assistant to Theokritos."

"Who would do this?" Zadok probed. "For what purpose?"

"I suspect my military commander may be involved. Two of the deaths have been inside the palace."

"The first, you say, was the unfortunate library assistant who discovered the documents' hiding place. Why was the niche equipped with such a trap, do you think?"

"To keep the two papyri from being discovered," Arcadia ventured.

"But, young woman," Zadok chided gently, "one could not think of a more dramatic way to call attention to them."

"My thought also," Theokritos agreed, struggling to sit up, and animated now that a discussion was under way. "The person who accidentally discovered them was meant to be killed."

"One less witness," Getorius said. "And yet hiding the papyri had to be a temporary measure."

"Surgeon, you *do* have skills other than medicine," Theokritos remarked. "Continue your speculation."

"After the verses on Behan's manuscript—the prophecy about the will—were revealed, someone obviously was to remove the documents and make them public."

"Correct," Zadok agreed, "and the timing would be critical. The discovery was premature, yet the actual date could not be far off, or it would risk exactly what did happen." He fingered the papyrus sheet with the will. "Christians have a great festival during our *Kislev*, that is, next month. Near our celebration of *Hanukkah*."

"The Feast of the Nativity is in December," Getorius told him. "The commemoration of Christ's birth."

"Yes, that would be most appropriate for such an earthshaking announcement." Zadok reexamined the letter of Peter. "These Hibernians puzzle me, that this remote people should suddenly be thrust onto the world stage."

"Not unlike you Hebrews," Theokritos commented with a husky chuckle.

Zadok nodded, smiling at the quip. "And that these people should be entrusted with such a document, assuming for our purpose that the will is genuine. An unknown land at the extreme northwest corner of your father's maps, Getorius."

"Ptolemy called the island Ibernia," Theokritos recalled, "but the outline he drew is pure fantasy. It was terra incognita at the time, and still is."

"Then," Placidia suggested, "what better hiding place for four hundred years?"

"An excellent point for the authenticity of the two documents—"

Zadok was interrupted by Theokritos suffering a spasm of coughing. He spat yellow mucus into the bowl, then leaned back on the pillows, his breath coming in short gasps. "What...of the...text, Teacher? What did...you find in it?"

"The language. Is the Latin writing style of Pilate's secretary consistent with the era?"

"Theokritos, save your voice, I could reply," Getorius offered before the librarian answered. He waved a hand in agreement. "Rabbi, Theokritos compared the text with manuscripts by the younger Seneca. Who else, Arcadia?"

"Quintilian. The styles were the same."

"And not difficult for any competent scribe to copy."

"True, Rabbi," Getorius agreed, "which is why Theokritos concentrated his tests on the material. The ink and papyrus fibers themselves."

"Yeshua ben Yoseph spoke Aramaic, the language of Judea at the time," Zadok recalled. "The letter of Simeon...of Peter...is in that language. Our forger is clever."

"The will is in Latin," Theokritos croaked. "Latin would be written by a Roman procurator's secretary."

"*Very clever*," Zadok emphasized. "Empress, have you a copy of the Christian Testament?"

"I do." Placidia went to a cabinet and brought back a richly bound codex containing the writings of the four Evangelists. "A gift from Bishop Chrysologos. What is it you're looking for, Rabbi?"

"I may have detected a contradiction."

"I thought something was out of place, too," Getorius said. "I have no training in these things, but I believe I spotted an error."

"There are *two* contradictions," Theokritos corrected, "as the Teacher also may have noticed. But go on, Surgeon."

"I recalled that the text of Matthew read that Christ said he could ask for the help of several legions of angels. May I, Regina?" At Placidia's nod, Getorius thumbed through the book's pages. "Here. 'Do you think that I cannot appeal to my Father to supply me with twelve legions of angels?'"

Zadok nodded. "We have studied these accounts to determine whether or not our Sanhedrin acted improperly. What is the contradiction?"

"The discrepancy," Theokritos broke in, "is that the papyrus reads, 'The Twelfth Legion of Angels.'"

"So the forger made a glaring mistake?" Arcadia asked.

"Perhaps...not." Theokritos' breathing was labored again. "The writer...was an officer on Pilate's staff. I...checked some ancient records. Legion Twelve Fulminata…was first levied under Julius Caesar…for his Gallic campaigns. But…at the time Pilate was governor…the unit was stationed in Syria."

"Judea was part of the province back then?" Getorius asked.

Theokritos gave a feeble nod. "This Lucius Secundus may have been…in the legion…before being assigned to the pretorium at Jerusalem. A Tribune, perhaps."

Getorius realized, as the librarian already had, that the error actually made sense. "So, roused out of bed, translating and writing in a hurry, with Christ speaking Aramaic, Secundus may have inadvertently copied in the name of his old unit. 'Legion Twelve,' instead of 'twelve legions.'"

Everyone fell silent, stunned at the logic of the error's explanation. Theokritos lay back and closed his eyes, then rasped, "The other contradiction, Teacher?"

"All four Evangelists agree," Zadok replied, "that when Simeon was questioned around the fire, he was in the courtyard of our High Priest, Yoseph Kaiaphas, not that of the pretorium, as the letter says."

"And your conclusion, Teacher?"

"Perhaps a simple one." Zadok held up the board with Peter's letter. "Simeon is writing twenty-three years after the event. If my own failing memory is any indication, his confusion is to be expected."

"Then the errors actually give the documents a measure of believability!" Getorius blurted.

"I stated that our forger was clever," Zadok remarked in a grim tone.

"But how could Peter have sailed the distance to Ibernia?" Arcadia objected. "Some say the Apostle never even reached Rome."

"The man was a fisherman," Getorius countered. "He had to be familiar with boats."

"Fishing on the Gennesaret Lake isn't quite like navigating the Pillars of Hercules," she persisted. "Theokritos, would Peter even have known of the Pillars?" Arcadia noticed that the librarian was in a halfdoze and glanced at Placidia. "Librarian," she called out to him, her voice raised. "Would Peter have known of the western ocean?"

"Ocean?" Theokritos stirred and asked to drink again. Arcadia helped him sip his wine, but he pushed her hand away when she tried to feel the swelling in his throat. "Peter? The western sea?" he repeated in a whisper. "On that we must speculate. The Acts record that he met a centurion at Caesarea, on the Mediterranean coast. Joppa is also mentioned. Traders in those ports would have known of the Pillars, even boasted of having sailed past them as far as Britannia. A common trade route to obtain tin."

"Empress," Zadok said, "again my explanation is simple. If this is the work of the Almighty, as Simeon claims, then the voyage could not fail. He wrote that the boat directed itself, as it were—"

"Nonsense!" Placidia exclaimed in anger and stood up. "The whole document is a stew cooked up from the writings of the Evangelists. Anyone could have concocted it. The letter of Peter, that rambling speech of Christ's—"

"He would have been close to delirium from thirst and loss of blood…" Getorius stopped, regretting the remark. Placidia was upset because the contradictions went against the possibility of the papyri having been forged, and he had added another reason.

Theokritos suddenly leaned over and vomited bile onto the tile floor. Arcadia went to wipe his mouth.

"I'll have him taken to his room." Placidia rang a golden handbell to summon a servant.

"I could help, Regina," Getorius offered, "then examine him there."

"I think not, Surgeon. Theokritos and Antioches are Greeks… and proud men."

After Theokritos was taken out, Getorius turned to Placidia again. "Regina, there are poisons that create the same symptoms as those the librarian is exhibiting."

"Nonsense."

"The unexplained deaths have been in the palace."

Placidia glared at Getorius, then walked around the room, touching her mementos with agitated slaps. "Continue, Surgeon. I did say I mistrusted Aetius."

"Even though I suspect poisoning in Sigisvult's death, allow a doubt that he died of guilt...or shame...or some unknown cause. Archdeacon Renatus certainly did not choose to drown in that leech tub. Someone in the palace has to be involved in his death."

"This archdeacon, what do you know of him?" Zadok asked. "Or the dead Hibernian monk? Begin with him."

"Practically nothing of Behan," Getorius admitted. "I found some writing I thought was a prophecy, but Theokritos dismissed it as a word game."

"Prophets do not have the luxury of playing games," Zadok chided. "These Hibernians are proselytizing on the Continent, bringing some good things from their island. Better agricultural methods...a love of learning. But these 'word games.' Are they connected with the discovery of the Galilean's will?"

"I believe so," Getorius replied. "Behan may not have forged the document himself, but it's clear that he died before he could announce the prophecy about its revelation."

"His drowning prevented that," Arcadia added. "A fortunate accident, if I can characterize the monk's death that way."

"An accident, or the work of the Lord?"

Getorius shrugged—the rabbi saw the hand of God in everything—yet he might have provided a clue to the release of the papyrus. "Sir, you suggested that it might have been intended that the will somehow be revealed at the Nativity."

"It's certain the monk would need accomplices to do so, or was the tool of others."

"Others? Then this may mean something," Arcadia said. "Behan's manuscript had the drawing of a red cockerel on the bottom. We also found the symbol in two other places."

"A cryptic emblem?" Zadok's white eyebrows rose at the information. "We have such symbols in our Kabbalistic literature to identify followers. Where else has this appeared, young woman?"

"Possibly on the Eucharist wine cup from which Sigisvult drank," she told him. "And on a tile from your mausoleum, Regina."

"Then I'm a suspect, too?" Placidia pointed to the wall. "Over there you see a painted rooster."

"No. Of...of course not."

Zadok eased the awkward moment by asking, "Empress, what do you know of this archdeacon who was killed?"

"Renatus arrived here from Gaul. The bishop thought very highly of him. Nothing more, really."

"He came to see us the day before your dinner," Getorius recalled. "Arcadia and I both felt he was overly curious about Behan's manuscripts. And a ring he might have worn."

"As if he knew part of this mystery?" Zadok turned to Placidia. "This churchman was in charge of money that is collected for the poor. A considerable sum, no?"

"I suppose so." She jabbed a finger toward the door. "But Aetius is behind this, just as Stilicho tried to usurp my nephew's throne and make his own son Augustus."

Getorius knew that Stilicho's enemies had leveled the same charge at him. Aetius also had ambitious detractors who would conspire to depose him as army commander. "What then, Rabbi," he asked to distract Placidia, "is your estimate of the will's impact on your people if it were released? Or on Christians, for that matter."

Zadok slumped back on the couch. "First," he replied in a low voice, "your spiritual leader, Sixtus, would be informed. He would call a council to debate the document's authenticity. Yet do you think the citizenry would wait for their decision? Many Christians...too many, I fear...would see to it that no Judean lived long enough to inherit even a single bronze *follis*."

"But this would be a decision of Christ's," Arcadia contended. "Christians are obliged to carry it out peacefully."

"Young woman, who *are* Christians?" Zadok asked curtly. "You Nicenes here? Followers of Arius in the port quarter? Manicheans? Nestorians? There are many divisions in your sect..." He paused, half-smiling at an ironic thought. "This affair might at least unite all of you."

"You're saying the release of the will would result in the destruction of your people?" Placidia asked. "Horrible. Christ would not have wanted that, or Peter. Nor do I."

"Once, when a Christian mob torched a synagogue at Antioch, the bones of our dead were destroyed," Zadok commented wryly. "A magistrate asked why the *living* Hebrews had not also been burned. It was a jest to him."

"Sir, whoever forged the will must realize that chaos would result," Getorius said. "It would somehow serve their purpose."

"Those of the red cockerel."

"I've said all along that it was a conspiracy," Placidia reminded the rabbi.

"But one that goes far beyond usurping the western throne. The destruction of an entire people."

"Then destroy this cursed papyrus!" Placidia cried. "Burn it to ashes!"

Zadok stood up. "Empress, that would not quiet the crow of the cock. Another bird would soon take its place. No, we must expose the authors of this abomination, and quickly."

"Behan was only one man. To root out his accomplices—" Getorius was interrupted by a heavy rapping on the door.

Placidia went to open it. Bleda, the chief of Aetius' Hunnic guard, stood outside with two of his men. The Asiatic looked past her as he held up a parchment sheet.

"Order from Bishop Chrys'lo'gos," Bleda said in heavily accented Latin. "Arrest sur-geon for il-legal di-ssection of a body."

Getorius heard him and felt a spasm wrack his stomach. Marios had been buried for a month now. How could the bishop have found out?

"Ridiculous," Placidia scoffed, pushing aside the indictment. "I'm to appoint him palace physician in January."

"I have bish-op's order," Bleda insisted.

"Whom is Getorius supposed to have cut open?" she demanded.

The Hun held up the parchment sheet he could not read. Placidia squinted at the name. "Behan? Behan from the Abbey of Culdees? Surgeon, that's the dead monk you examined in his forest hut."

"Yes, but I—"

"You dissected his body?"

"No, he didn't!" Arcadia cried, flushing. "We left and told

Optila to have a wicker cage made in which to preserve Behan's body until we heard from his abbot about burial."

"And you've not gone back there?"

"No!"

"Optila is my son's Hunnic bodyguard. I tell you, Aetius will use his band of barbarians to…" Placidia looked back at Bleda. "Very well. But I'll speak to the bishop about clearing this up, Surgeon."

Getorius nodded, grateful for her offer, yet thinking that, meanwhile, he would be confined inside the palace, just as Sigisvult had been—before he was murdered there.

Chapter fifteen

While the bishop's canon law advisers drew up charges and prepared for a trial, Galla Placidia ordered that Getorius be confined in the room of a tribune who had gone to Rome for the winter. His detention was to be as non-restrictive as possible: no guard was to be stationed inside the room, and the surgeon could be escorted to the library to read there whenever he wished.

After Arcadia's initial shock at the charge, she remembered what had happened to Sigisvult and told Brisios to bring her husband meals that had been prepared in her kitchen, until such time as she could visit him herself.

❧

Two evenings after the arrest, Arcadia was surprised when Childibert announced that Publius Maximin had arrived to see her. Her first thought was that the senator's mother, Agatha, had gotten worse, and that he wanted Getorius to accompany him back to his villa to treat the old woman.

Maximin brought in the damp smell of the outdoors as he entered Getorius' study, where Arcadia met him. The senator wore a dalmatic of fine wool, visible under a stylish cloak cut elliptically at the hem. Red calfskin boots showed water stains. His oiled hair, flecked with gray, was combed forward in traditional Roman style, and she thought a faint odor of bay-scented perfume actually enhanced his masculinity. He obviously relished playing the part of an immensely rich and important man.

"Senator." Arcadia held out a hand, hoping her slight frown relayed her disapproval at Maximin's presumption in calling Getorius away to Agatha's whenever he wished.

"Forgive me, Domina," he apologized, gently squeezing her hand. "I fear I may have inconvenienced your husband at times. Only a son's concern for his mother would explain such poor manners."

"He was glad to be of service to her." She was surprised at his admission, but not quite sure of its sincerity. "Senator, my husband isn't here just now."

Maximin released his hold. "Yes, I was appalled to hear of his arrest on such a ridiculous charge. May I offer the services of my personal lawyer for his defense?"

"Th...thank you." Arcadia wondered how he knew of the detention, since Placidia had supposedly told Chrysologos that she wanted to keep the arrest an internal palace matter. "Just how did you find out, Senator?"

Maximin gave a patronizing chortle as he sat down in a wicker chair, and rattled coins in his belt purse. "Ah, Domina, a silver piece to the proper official, even a slave. No, *especially* a slave. Cheaper, and they're hardly noticed, skulking around as they do."

"Who at the palace told you about my husband?"

"A ridiculous charge," Maximin repeated, hedging a direct answer. "I was consul twice, you know. In fact I've been petitioning Valentinian to confer the rank of Patrician on me. Perhaps, my dear, in exchange for the expertise of my lawyer your husband could put in a good word for me?"

"Getorius has no influence with the Augustus."

"With his mother then? I understand Galla Placidia is about to appoint him palace physician."

"It's not been confirmed, Senator." *The man knows everything*, Arcadia thought, as she sat down opposite him.

"The day of your husband's arrest," Maximin digressed, "the Empress Mother talked to a leader of the Judeans?"

The question was another surprise. "Y…yes, Rabbi David ben Zadok."

"There was a document of some nature discussed?"

My God, does he suspect, or perhaps even know that the papyri exist? It's certainly possible with all the palace contacts he's boasting about. "Your… informants didn't tell you what this document was, Senator? You seem to know everything."

"Informants?" Maximin gave an easy laugh and pressed a finger hard against his palm. "Domina, even gold cannot pierce steel. But I'll ask no more. The matter is undoubtedly confidential."

Oh, fine! Now I've told him that a document does exist—

Maximin frowned and reached forward to touch Arcadia's forehead. "That is a nasty bruise, my dear."

"Archdeacon Renatus…" Arcadia stopped. *What am I thinking?* "An…an accident in the clinic, Senator."

He sat back, nodding. "The archdeacon? A pity he died so suddenly in his sleep."

"The bishop reported that?"

"The palace announced his death—"

Arcadia was relieved when Silvia entered the room with a pitcher and poured out two cups of hot mulled wine, ending the conversation about Renatus. When Maximin reached for his, she saw a ring on his finger with the image of a rooster cut into its carnelian stone. She was so shaken at the sight that she knocked over her cup.

"Clumsy," she muttered, standing quickly to brush at the stain on her tunic.

Maximin pulled a linen square from his sleeve and dabbed at the reddish drops. "Did something upset you, my dear?"

"Y…your ring."

"The red cockerel?" Maximin chuckled and reached for Arcadia's hand. He pressed the signet into the underside of her wrist, then held her fingers as the faint impression of a rooster appeared. "It's the emblem of my country place outside Ravenna, *Villa Galli Rubris*, 'The Villa of the Red Rooster.' Fighting cocks are one of my passions, but mainly I raise poultry for the city markets."

Arcadia eased her hand away from his and rubbed at the impression. The Villa of the Red Rooster was a smooth explanation, but could the man be believed? "Did… did you come about your mother?" she asked, still flustered.

"Yes, in part. May I call you Arcadia?" At her nod, Maximin lightly touched her cheek. "Forgive my saying it, but you look tired, understandably so of course, from the strain of seeing patients alone, the unfortunate deaths of your friend and the archdeacon, your husband's detention. Horrible business." He pulled his hand away and twisted the ring a moment before asking, "Arcadia, will you look in on Agatha? Her bedsores are improved, but she needs more of that pain medication."

"Senator, I'm still training with my husband. Wouldn't it be better to call Antioches?"

"The man's old, forgetful." Maximin leaned back and swirled the wine in his cup.

"Actually, Arcadia, I also wanted to invite you to spend a few days at my villa. It's not far, about a mile outside the Theodosius Gate. I think you'd quite like relaxing in the baths…getting away from this abominable sewer smell for a few days. I couldn't be there with you all the time—business concerns—but you would be mistress of the place."

"I'm flattered, Senator, but…what about your wife?" Arcadia recalled the rumors about Valentinian having more than a platonic interest in her.

"Prisca?" He hesitated, then said, "She…she might join you. Yes, by Zeus! I'll tell her to be there."

Arcadia was still wary. Despite his ready explanation, the man was wearing the signet of what Zadok thought might be a far-reaching and deadly conspiracy. "Why invite me like this, Senator?"

"The deed comes back to the doer." Maximin chuckled after

paraphrasing the proverb. "Pure selfishness. As I said, I've heard that your husband will replace Antioches at the New Year. Another friend in the palace…." He winked to let her draw the conclusion.

"And Prisca will be at the villa?"

"Of course. And I believe my wife is…ah…of an age when having a woman physician would please her."

The man's as slick as his hair oil, Arcadia thought, and yet the prospect of a few shamelessly luxurious days was appealing. She would also have unencumbered time to think of ways to help defend Getorius, perhaps find out Maximin's interest in the document he was curious about. Why not go?

"Senator, I'll have to speak to my husband. I'm seeing him tomorrow."

"Understood." Maximin put down his cup, leaned forward, and affected a confidential tone. "I'll speak to the guards' tribune. House arrest can be made quite comfortable. And my lawyer will talk to the bishop about dropping his absurd allegation."

Arcadia knew these were not idle boasts. Maximin's wealth spoke in both the civil and episcopal palaces, even at Rome itself, where the Senate had erected a statue of him in Trajan's forum. *Why not have a powerful friend for a change? Getorius certainly needs one now.*

"Senator, I'll tell my husband I've accepted your offer."

"Splendid." Maximin opened a leather case hanging under his cloak and took out a wax notebook. "A good time would be…yes, the calends of December, three days from now. Will that be convenient for you?"

"Perhaps the first through the fifth?"

"Fine. And you'll look in on mother?"

"Yes, tomorrow before I go to see Getorius."

Maximin stood up and took both of Arcadia's hands in his. "I…my wife…will enjoy your company, my dear. I'll send a carriage for you at the fourth hour on the calends."

"Thank you Senator. I'll see you out."

Arcadia returned to the study, already excited about visiting Getorius the next day, but now there was also the carnelian ring to tell him about. And even though Maximin had not pressed his questions about the papyri, her intuition told her he was aware of more than he had let on. He knew about Sigisvult and Renatus even though Placidia had kept the information about their deaths inside the palace. If there were accomplices to the conspiracy, as Zadok believed, Maximin and his unnamed palace contacts could be crucial.

She was somewhat disturbed at the senator's manner—smooth as the polished marble table on which he had left his empty wine cup. He touched her too often, but his wife would be at the villa, and perhaps she could learn more about Maximin's 'business' dealings there.

⊱

The next day was the beginning of the Advent season, a four-week cycle of rituals that prepared for the commemoration of Christ's birth at Bethlehem over four hundred years ago. Bishop Chrysologos decreed that the time would also mark a transition: including the Lord's Day, the seven days of the week would now be called by the Frankish names already used by the majority of Ravenna's citizens. Some of his presbyters felt this was an unnecessary concession to the language of a largely pagan tribe, but the bishop held firm on the matter as a realistic convenience. Besides, the Roman names commemorated the sun and moon, as well as the old pagan gods Mars, Mercury, Jupiter, Venus and Saturn.

⊱

Arcadia hurried to the palace after treating Agatha, worried that Getorius might take the Eucharist bread and wine if a deacon brought him the Sacrament.

She found him feeling depressed, and about to read from the Advent psalm in a Mass codex he had gotten from the library.

After a long embrace, she said, "Read the psalm to me, Husband. I was thinking of you when I heard it yesterday."

Getorius shrugged. "All right. It starts:

To you, Lord, I raise my very soul.

O my God, in you I have put my trust,
Let me not come to shame.
Do not let my enemies laugh at me.
No one who hopes in you will be put to shame.
Let them be ashamed who are perverse and treacherous."

He looked up. "It couldn't be more apt, could it, Arcadia?"

"Have faith, Getorius," she urged. "Have you found out anything more about the condition of Behan's corpse, or why the bishop is accusing you?"

"I think so, there seem to be no secrets here that can't be bought. Give Charadric a *siliqua* when you leave, and one for his comrade at the episcopal palace."

"All right, but what about Behan?"

"His body was sewn into a shroud before being put inside that cage I ordered."

"By whom?" Arcadia asked.

"I don't know who went out there. But after Behan was brought back to the ice room, two deacons were assigned to dress him in a robe they found in that clothes chest we brought back, then lay him in a coffin. When they cut apart the stitches on the shroud, they found that his abdomen had been pretty well disemboweled."

"What? Could it have been an animal? A ferret or something?"

Getorius shook his head. "The shroud was intact and the body inside the willow-work cage."

"But why are they blaming you? You weren't the last person to see the body."

"The bishop knows of my opposition to his ban on dissection. I've certainly pestered him enough to lift it."

"So? What makes him think you disobeyed his order?"

"Arcadia,"—Getorius brushed at her chestnut hair, then looked into her green eyes. "Arcadia, the deacons evidently found one of my scalpels inside the shroud."

"*Inside?* How could they?" she asked in disbelief. "You didn't examine the body again after we left. And why do they even think it's yours?"

"Do you recall when I had Charadric punch initials on my instruments, like he did on his knife? They say there was a G A in dots on the handle."

"Did you see it?"

"No. It will only be presented at my trial."

"Getorius, how could the scalpel have gotten there? You always have your instruments at the clinic, or with you in your medical case."

"Could I have left one in the hut? No. Hades, I used it on… ah…Pandora."

"That still doesn't explain the dissection. I want to see the body."

"I've already asked and been refused. Behan will be buried by the time of my trial. The only witnesses will be those two deacons…and both are against me."

Both fell silent at the prospect, knowing that under Roman law the accused was generally considered to be guilty, otherwise magistrates felt the charge never would have been brought forward.

Arcadia voiced a thought, "Do you think this might be connected to the papyri? A delaying tactic until after they're revealed?"

"Involving the bishop? *Cara*, that's just too far-fetched."

"I suppose you're right."

"Oh," he recalled, "I also heard some barracks gossip from Charadric. Whoever comes from Behan's monastery should be here by mid-week."

"That would be…Wodnesdag, no? Yesterday, the bishop made the weekday names that Childibert uses official."

"You mean Monandag, Tiwesdag, and so on? How barbaric."

Both laughed at the brief diversion, while Arcadia mentally braced herself to bring up the senator's invitation. "Getorius. Publius Maximin came to see me yesterday."

"About his mother? How is she?"

"A little better. I treated her this morning. What I wanted to tell you is that he wears a carnelian ring with a rooster symbol on it."

"What?"

"He explained that it represented his estate outside Ravenna, where he raises poultry and fighting cocks."

"I believe him. Many of the wealthy have rather sadistic pastimes." Getorius reflected a moment. "What finger was this ring on?"

"Finger?" Arcadia thought back. "On the small digit of his right hand. Is that important?"

"Remember that circle of white you said you noticed on Behan's finger? Maximin is a big man. He could only get the monk's ring on one of his smaller fingers."

"You're saying he's wearing Behan's ring?"

"Not necessarily, Arcadia. I guess I'm looking for anyone who could be one of the accomplices whom ben Zadok suspects might be involved."

"I thought of that, too." Arcadia looked away at a spider exploring the ceiling before saying, "Getorius...the senator has invited me to his villa for a few days next week."

"Oh, fine, *fine*," he snapped, stepping back and sitting down on the bed. "I'm confined here, and you go off to the private estate of a man who may be part of a conspiracy to instigate civil war. Maximin has access to the palace, and he's no stranger to acquiring power. The Gothic Queen may be right...perhaps Aetius is in this with him."

"Getorius—"

"No, hear me out. What better way to declare a crisis, then turn the government into a military dictatorship? Meanwhile, as accidental witnesses to the plot's basis, I die here like Sigisvult, and you're never seen again after going to the villa of the fighting cockerels. Everyone who knew where the papyri were hidden is eliminated."

Arcadia was silent for a moment after her husband's outburst, than said firmly, "Then that's exactly why I'm going. Perhaps I'll find something out." She came to him, knelt down, put her arms around his neck, and nuzzled his cheek with her face. "If Rabbi Zadok is right about the Nativity being the date for the will's release, then there's still a month before we...ah...need to be eliminated. I promise to tell Childibert where I'm going, and I'll take Silvia and Primus with me."

"A woman and a child? I'd feel better if Nathaniel went along."

"I can't risk insulting the senator. Or making him suspicious, if he is involved."

"I'm just tense, *cara*. Worried." Getorius kissed Arcadia's forehead and buried his face in her hair. "Come and tell me about Maximin's place next...Monandag."

She laughed and pulled free. "I promise. And you eat only what Brisios brings you."

※

Arcadia walked back to her villa disturbed at the inexplicable fact that one of her husband's medical instruments had been found inside the dead monk's shroud.

Even Maximin's best lawyer would have trouble defending Getorius on a charge made by two clergymen as witnesses. It's conceivable that a patient could have stolen the scalpel, but I can't think of any who might have a reason to be that vindictive. Who else would go to so much trouble to falsely accuse him?

What could be good news is that someone is coming from Behan's monastery. Perhaps Galla Placidia could question the monk and find out if he knows anything about the hidden documents...or about a plan to release them.

Meanwhile, I'd better select the clothes I'm going to take with me to the senator's villa.

Chapter sixteen

December the first was foggy and drizzling at the fourth hour, when an elegant two-wheeled black carriage with a leather top pulled up to the Via Caesar entrance of Arcadia's home. Arcadia was waiting, yet, despite what she had told Getorius, she had decided not to bring Silvia or her son to the senator's country villa.

Brisios put Arcadia's travel case behind the seats and helped her up to sit alongside the driver. "Agrica is preparing a pan of rissoles," she told her gateman. "Take it to the Surgeon at the sixth hour and remind him he's to eat nothing except what you bring."

"I will, Mistress."

As the carriage pulled away from the curbstones, Arcadia eased the hood of her cloak higher over her head. She had had Silvia draw her hair into a bun in back, a less attractive style Arcadia felt made her look older. She had put on a tunic that was unadorned with embroidery and had not worn earrings.

It's not the time to look attractive, she thought, rubbing at her gold wedding band. On his visit Maximin had groped for her hand at every opportunity; the band would be a reminder for him not to get too interested.

"How far is the senator's villa?" Arcadia asked the driver, after he had guided the mare left, onto the Via Honorius. When he did not reply, she tugged at his sleeve. "How far are we going?"

The man, whose face had been concealed by a leather hood, turned to her, revealing a pudgy, unshaven face.

"How far away is the villa?" Arcadia repeated, a bit frightened at his appearance.

The driver's grin was almost a leer as he pulled aside his cloak and pointed to a silver plaque dangling around his neck. Arcadia saw that it was engraved with the words MVTVS SVRDVS. *Mute and deaf…Maximin doesn't want his driver questioned, and the man can't tell anyone about what he sees. Clever.*

At the intersection with the Via Theodosius the mute guided the horse straight ahead. Arcadia knew that beyond the Porta Aurea, where the Via Popilia angled to meet the Aemilia, an unpaved road led to Forum Livii, some fifteen miles to the southwest. It was probably impassable because of the rain, and Maximin had said that his villa was about a mile from the city.

Arcadia wanted to ask about their route, but realized that even if the driver read lips, he couldn't respond to her question. She felt a moment of helpless panic, recalling Getorius' comment about her never being seen again after going to the Villa of the Red Rooster.

At the end of the Honorius the carriage passed through one of the graceful double arches of the Aurea Gate. Beyond, only a few farmers were on the Via Popilia, hunched over and protecting themselves from the rain with leather cloaks and wide-brimmed straw hats, as they sloshed along next to oxen pulling carts of firewood to town.

An abandoned shrine to Mercurius marked the angle of the Popilia. When the carriage lurched into the ruts of an unpaved road, mud from the wheel spattered Arcadia's cape. After going on about half a mile, the driver turned the horse onto a narrow path to the right. The cobblestone paving was less muddy, but just as bone-jarring.

A short distance beyond the turn, a stone bridge spanned the swollen Bedesis River, whose yellow water churned on to border Ravenna's west and north walls. In the gray light, where the pine forest had been cleared, farms seemed deserted; it was too sodden to work outdoors. After the carriage slowed to cross the boards of another bridge, this one over a creek, a high wall and two-level gatehouse appeared faintly through the misty air. Coming closer, Arcadia saw sentries huddled on its upper porch, a vantage point that gave them a clear view of traffic on the lane. No one could approach the villa unseen.

"The senator's farm is better protected than the legion camp," Arcadia muttered, and was startled when the mute suddenly grabbed her hand, grinning as he held it up to point at the gatehouse roof. Despite the dull light, the sheen of rain made a golden rooster on its top shine brilliantly.

"Yes, the villa of the rooster." Arcadia shook her hand free, and brushed at mud on the driver's sleeve. When he looked at her, she mouthed slowly, "I'm sorry you had to pick me up in this poor weather." Perhaps he could lip-read, and it wouldn't hurt to have a friendly contact at the villa who could drive a carriage.

Guards opened twin wooden doors in the stone wall and waved the mute through with their spears. The main villa was located a few hundred paces beyond the gatehouse. A paved courtyard was surrounded on three sides by a portico that sheltered entrances to the buildings. The center house was built on two levels. A fountain in the middle of the courtyard overflowed, splashing water on paving stones already puddled by rain.

After the mute circled the carriage around the fountain and halted at the portico of the main house, a well-dressed slave materialized from behind a pillar to carry Arcadia's case. As she stepped down, the driver grinned at her again, a look she felt resembled a satyr's leer.

So much for having a friend here. Nevertheless she smiled at him and slipped a silver half-*siliqua* into his hand.

When the slave opened the villa doors, Arcadia caught her breath, overwhelmed by the magnificence of the entrance atrium. Rather than being paved in tile or mosaic, the floor was made of fitted slabs of Tibertine marble. In the center, rainwater sloshed off a roof opening that angled toward a rectangular pool beneath. The rim was bordered by a design of sea creatures, whose open mouths channeled the overflow into an underground cistern. The splashing sound might have been pleasant in summer, but the winter downpour grated on Arcadia's already tender nerves.

She was briefly startled by a life-size bronze statue of the senator that greeted visitors from under a portico. After Arcadia realized it was not the man himself, she guessed it was probably a copy of his statue in Rome. She wrinkled her nose at a pervasive smell. The one incongruous element in the elegant setting was the unmistakable odor of chicken dung that hung on the wet air. *I was warned, Maximin did tell me he raised chickens, but what was that about escaping the stench of Ravenna's sewers?*

The slave took Arcadia's cloak, and divested of the damp garment, she looked up. Publius Maximin stood next to his statue, affecting the same stance. He posed for a moment, then came forward in a swirl of bay scent, both hands extended, smiling.

"My dear. How kind of you to indulge me with your visit."

"Thank you Senator. Your entranceway is … magnificent."

"Yes, isn't it. You must be chilled. We'll go into my reception room before you're shown to where you'll stay. Marpor will take your bag there."

The tablinium floor was warm, and the walls were decorated with paintings depicting scenes from Roman history. Several masks hung in a row beneath the paintings. At a table one of the most handsome men Arcadia had ever seen sat painting a wooden mask. He wore a short tunic that revealed muscular arms and legs. A silver band circled his black curly hair in a style reminiscent of a statue of a Greek athlete that her father owned.

Maximin swept a hand out to indicate the paintings and masks. "The destiny of Rome, another of my passions," he explained. "That's Jason over there. The clever lad carved those masks, which represent famous people in the city's past. The murals begin with Aeneas over here." Maximin slipped a hand around Arcadia's arm and led her to the first painting, where the Trojan hero was shown carrying his blind father Anchises away from the burning citadel. "Do you know the story, my dear?"

"After Troy was destroyed, didn't Aeneas's mother, Venus, guide him to the mouth of the Tiber?"

"Very good, Arcadia. I see that your superior beauty is complemented by superior intelligence." Maximin squeezed her arm and moved on to show her the masks. "The twins, of course, are Romulus and Remus. Next is Tarquin, the last Etruscan king." The senator indicated the next personage. "Ah, here's a hero of mine, Publius Scipio, victor over Hannibal at Carthage. We need a leader like him in Africa now, to drive out the cursed Vandals." He passed several effigies without identifying them, then stopped at one of a glowering man. "Here's another favorite. Lucius Sulla restored senatorial power after the Populares rammed through laws limiting our influence."

The dictator Sulla. Arcadia recalled what her tutor had taught her about the older contemporary of Julius Caesar. After gaining power in a bloody civil war, Sulla had declared a dictatorship and posted lists of his enemies in the forum. More than six thousand of them had been hunted down and killed, including ninety senators who had opposed him. Their confiscated property had been auctioned off. *If this is Maximin's hero, heaven help Ravenna!*

"The next mask is of Julius Caesar," he continued, "but I don't wish to bore you, and you'll surely want to rest before supper. We'll eat sooner because of the early dark."

"Your wife, Senator?" Arcadia prodded him.

"Yes." Maximin twisted his carnelian ring. "Prisca will join us at supper. And I've just had an idea for the entertainment. Jason," he called to the man, "my guest will choose one of these masks and you'll do a pantomime about the person. Who shall it be, Arcadia?"

"I...live on the Via Julius Caesar. How about him?"

"Splendid choice. Did you hear, Jason?"

When the man nodded, Arcadia asked, "What mask is he working on now?"

"Personifications of various cities in the empire. Jason, hold that up."

Arcadia went closer to read the inscription on the turreted

headdress of a female personification. "Smyrna? Senator, isn't that one of the seven cities mentioned in the Revelation of Saint John?"

"I…a…a presbyter could tell you that, I know it as a town in Asia. Now, I'll have Melisias take you to your room."

After he clapped his hands a middle-aged woman appeared at a side door. Maximin nodded to her as if she had already received instructions. Melisias beckoned to Arcadia, and then led the way through a corridor to a small room at the rear of the house.

Arcadia's travel bag was on a stand. Closed window shutters kept out the rain, and an iron stove threw off a pleasant heat. A bed, chair, table, and wardrobe were the only furnishings.

She noticed a silver chamber pot by the bed, but asked Melisias, "Where is the latrine?"

"Dhen milao latina, mono elinika."

"You don't speak Latin, only Greek?" *Well, Melisias, I don't believe you. I'm not letting on that I know some Greek, so let's find out how much you do understand.* "I need to use the latrine quickly," Arcadia repeated, adopting a frantic tone. "Where is it, at the end of the hallway?"

"Use that," Melisias said in Latin, pointing to the chamber pot. Glancing up at Arcadia, she reddened, and hurried out of the room.

"I thought you understood me. Now let's see what's outside this window."

The shutters opened onto the dismal view of a muddy field glittering with puddles, noxious with the stink of chicken dung. The rain had let up, but even though it was around midday the sky was overcast and gloomy. With the shortened winter hours it would be dark in three or four hours. A ground mist rising at the far end of the field obscured several stone buildings, which Arcadia assumed were chicken coops. Maximin had not said at exactly what hour the afternoon meal would be served, but the nauseating smell had already settled in her throat and curbed her appetite.

Arcadia closed the shutters and turned to look inside the wardrobe. Her cloak had been hung up. It felt dry. She unpacked her clothing and hung the items on pegs located around the inside of the cabinet. Afterward she warmed herself at the stove a moment, thinking that at least the room was comfortable, then lay down and closed her eyes. The nervous excitement of coming to Maximin's villa had passed; now it was time to think about the charge against Getorius.

Why would someone excise the inner organs of a corpse, and then try to blame my husband? And how could his scalpel have gotten inside the dead monk's shroud? The bishop will have the mutilated condition of Behan's body, Getorius' scalpel, and two witnesses as evidence. What can Maximin's lawyer do to counter those? Getorius has no witnesses to speak up for him. And if he is right in thinking all this is somehow connected to the papyri, I must find out why Maximin seemed interested in the documents. How much he knows about them.

※

Arcadia was abruptly awakened by a knock on the door and Melisias' voice calling out, "*Kiri, dhipno.*"

"Thank you," she answered back, "I'll be ready in a moment." *Dinner already? I fell asleep.*

When Arcadia came out of her room, Melisias was at the end of the corridor. She led the way to a large dining area on the left of the reception room. Senator Maximin had a reputation for lavish banquets, but on this occasion a section of the space was partitioned off with folding doors, to make a more intimate eating space. Wall paintings depicted Ravenna and its environs, including views of the Apennine foothills and the villas of wealthy citizens, undoubtedly those of his friends. In the west wall, glass-paned windows covered by bronze screens admitted the fading light of a pinkish sunset. Arcadia was pleased that the scented smoke swirling from an incense burner was reasonably effective in masking the pervasive dung smell.

The meal was to be served at a dining table with chairs, not the reclining couches Arcadia had half expected. Maximin stood up when she entered. He was wearing a toga decorated with the twin purple stripes of a senator, a light woolen cloak, and a pair of red boots.

"Arcadia"—he smiled stiffly, fidgeting with his ring—"may I present my wife, Prisca Maximina."

Prisca nodded a greeting without extending her hand.

Rightly suspicious. I'm sure she's wondering exactly what it is I'm doing here. Arcadia guessed that Prisca was about forty, a slim, handsome woman with a simple hairdo that was held in place with a pearl-studded golden diadem. A two-strand pearl necklace circled her throat. She had draped a flowing silk shawl over a full-length tunic that was belted high at her waist.

Maximin sat down again to supervise a slave who was mixing water into a wine flagon. After his steward, Andros, poured pepper and coriander sauce over a platterful of grilled crayfish, the senator asked amiably, "Did the Empress Mother serve this at that dinner she hosted on the ides?"

The question took Arcadia by surprise, even though Maximin had already mentioned that he knew about the meal. "Y…yes. But I'm still not sure why my husband and I were invited."

"Count on the Augustus having a reason." Maximin snickered and glanced at his wife. "A pity Prisca and I were unavailable that afternoon."

Arcadia realized his excuse was a lie. Maximin would not have dared refuse an invitation from the mother of the Augustus, especially when he was petitioning her son for the title of Patrician.

"Is it true that your husband couldn't come here with you?" Prisca asked Arcadia in a voice that was husky, almost masculine in tone.

"Yes, my sweet," Maximin interposed quickly, before Arcadia could answer. "Because of a ridiculous charge that Bishop Chrysologos brought against him. The subject is not dinner conversation."

"No? Then I suppose we *could* talk about your infernal chickens," Prisca retorted, "for we can certainly smell them. Have you shown the surgeon's wife your 'Rooster Coop' yet?"

"Rooster coop?" Arcadia was confused. "The buildings I saw outside?"

"No, 'Rooster coop' is my wife's nickname for my upstairs office," Maximin explained. "It's where I keep my collection of memorabilia. There's also a wonderful water clock that Jason built."

"Ah, Jason." Prisca almost smiled. "Will the Greek Hephaestus be entertaining me tonight?"

Arcadia noticed Maximin flush at her tone of calculated sarcasm. In the Roman myth the crippled craftsman god Vulcan, named Hephaestus by the Greeks, was married to Venus and repeatedly cuckolded by Mars, the god of war.

"My sweet, he and Phoebe will perform a pantomime later on," Maximin replied tersely.

Arcadia leaned aside while Andros used silver tongs to place three crayfish on her plate. When she tasted one, it was excellent, with the coriander seasoning about perfect.

Prisca nibbled at hers for a while, then discarded the shell and looked across at Arcadia. "I understand you study medicine with your husband?"

"She treated Agatha a few days ago," Maximin said. "Very efficiently, too."

"How clever of her." Prisca wiped her fingers on a napkin without looking at him.

"Yes." Maximin cleared his throat. "I was suggesting that you might want Arcadia as a physician."

"How very thoughtful of you, Publius."

Maximin chuckled nervously. "Well, Antioches *is* getting along in years."

"And is not a pretty young woman." Prisca gave Arcadia a wan smile. "Isn't that so, my dear?"

"I....I'd be honored to...to help you," Arcadia stammered. "With my husband's consent, of course." *Your tone may be matter-of-fact, Prisca, but your disposition is as acid as the vinegar I use to treat Felicitas' leg ulcers.*

"Prisca, I told you the rumors," Maximin continued. "Her husband Getorius will be appointed palace physician at the New Year."

Arcadia was grateful that the tense exchange ended when Andros beckoned for a slave to bring in the second course. A silver serving dish shaped like a fluted scallop shell was presented, containing a stew of dried peas cooked with pieces of chicken, thin Lucanian sausages, onion, rissoles of minced pork, and chunks of pork shoulder.

Seasoned with oregano, dill and coriander, it was a simple yet savory meal. She thought Maximin either served more exotic dishes only to his important guests, or perhaps actually practiced the republican austerity at which the Gothic Queen only pretended.

The three ate in silence. Arcadia was unable to think of a way to bring up the subject of the papyri, to see how Maximin might react, but she had more days in which to do so. She realized that she also had to convince the senator's wife that his guest was no threat to her marriage bed.

Andros had just begun the sweet course, frying almond-stuffed dates in salted honey, when there was a stirring at the curtained backdrop of the low stage that was set up against the north wall. Jason stepped onto the platform, followed by a young woman holding a seven-stringed lyre. Both were dressed in short tunics of silver cloth and red sandals laced to the knee. Jason held a mask of Julius Caesar, whose gaunt features and thinning hair had been exaggerated into a frowning, tight-lipped caricature of the Roman dictator.

"Good lad," Maximin applauded. "Andros, light those candles at the front of the stage. What episode from Caesar's career have you chosen to pantomime, Jason?"

"Sir, his capture by Cilician pirates," he replied with a slight bow.

"Good, good. Caesar was quite young then, but he still taught those brigands a lesson." Maximin glanced at Arcadia. "Sorry, my dear. I don't want to give the story away."

Prisca forced a thin smile. "And Phoebe will accompany you on the lyre, Jason?" "Yes, Mistress."

"How charming."

The actor bowed again and arranged the mask over his face. After Andros had finished lighting the candles, Phoebe began a light plucking of the lyre's strings. Jason swayed, picking up the rhythm, then began to recite the verses he had written:

> "Let others praise proud Hercules,
>   and Bacchus of the frenzied maids,

Diana's unerring bow, Neptune's rage at sea,
      or Jupiter, mightiest god of all.
Here, 'tis cunning I will praise.
Young Caesar's mastery of its ways."

Arcadia had not seen a pantomime before. Jason accompanied the music and the sense of the poem's verses with graceful movements of his head and arms as he modulated his voice from frenzy, to rage, to awe.

"Caesar! Through the kings of Alba,
      kin of Aeneas, and love-queen Venus.
Her son Iulus gave the family name.
But Caesar Julius won it fame.
      On wild Pharmacusa, by wilder pirates still,
held for ransom. 'Four thousand, eight hundred
pieces of gold?' Our Caesar laughed!
      Dolts. *Twelve thousand* will they pay,
      But 'til then, in respect, I'll stay.
Practice speeches. Recite my poems to you.
Curb carousing! My mind must concentrate.
But hear me. Ransomed, I'll gain justice yet."

Arcadia was impressed. The man and woman had only had a few hours to compose the piece. The meter was good, and two of the stanzas rhymed, but in different lines.

Jason continued:

"*Return? Justice?* My vulture captors laughed.
Gorged on others' riches, they would threaten
Rome itself, despoil the city, as they had Italia.
Twelve thousand paid. Freed, Caesar gathered
ships. Miletan friends.
Victory gained! Captors, by Caesar's mercy,
first hung, *then* crucified!

'Tis cunning here to you I praise.
Brave Caesar's mastery of its ways."

After Phoebe's final strumming, which echoed the cadence of Jason's closing verses, the actor pulled off the mask and bowed low. When he straightened again, he deftly caught the small purse that Prisca threw to him.

Maximin pretended to ignore the gesture and turned to Arcadia. "Well done, don't you think?"

"Yes, absolutely. I...I didn't remember the story." She thought Maximin might invite the two actors to the table, but they turned and went back through the curtain.

It was totally dark outside now; only a few lights gleamed in the windows of a building on the perimeter of the chicken yard. Maximin picked up a honeyed date with his fingers, ate it, then yawned and stood up.

"Well. I have early business. Arcadia, perhaps you and Prisca will find womanly things to talk about."

"Publius, I have business too," Prisca told him in a cold tone.

"No, no," Arcadia offered quickly, "I'll read in my room. I brought a copy of Soranus on gynecology."

"Fine. Then, may you both sleep well." Maximin left the room without further words.

Prisca pushed back her chair and stood. "I'll have Melisias take you back to your room. She'll call you for breakfast."

"No, I can find it. Ah...Domina?"

"Yes?"

"Nothing." Arcadia blushed. "We...we can talk in the morning. Good night."

When Arcadia returned to her room, she found a twin-spouted oil lamp providing the space with a warm glow. Her travel bag was in the wardrobe, and in its place on the stand were a water pitcher, basin, and towels. The room's door did not have a key lock, but could be secured from the inside by a wooden bar that slid into a bracket.

She changed into a wool night tunic. After washing her face, she tried to arrange her hair into a braid for the night, but gave up quickly.

"I should have brought Silvia for that, at least," she muttered as she rubbed a rose-scented lotion on her face and arms. After crawling under the bedding, Arcadia settled down to read Soranus.

The villa was strangely quiet. Even the distant barking of hounds in farmhouses outside the walls was muffled. Arcadia guessed that watchdogs at the villa might have harassed the chickens, and were not kept there. In any case, Maximin had his own private army guarding the place.

Before she put the book down so she could get some sleep, Arcadia thought she heard the faint crowing of a rooster in a room somewhere, but it sounded unnatural, in some way mechanical, and dawn was still far off.

⁂

At the first early glow of light, a cacophony of live roosters crowing outside the window awakened Arcadia. Groggy from a somewhat restless night in a strange bed, she sat up and looked toward the door. The locking beam was still in place.

"Blessed Cosmas, toward morning I slept like a hibernating bear. Anyone might have…" Arcadia shuddered without finishing the thought aloud. An intruder could have entered, as the bandit at Classis did, and she would not have noticed.

After splashing water on her face and rinsing her mouth, Arcadia dressed in a tan, ankle-length tunic and sat down to comb her hair.

Afterward, she was reading a section in Book iii of Soranus, about conditions peculiar to women, when Melisias called to tell her that breakfast was ready.

A cerulean sky visible through the dining room windows hinted at the possibility of the muddy fields drying out at least partly by afternoon. Prisca was seated alone, watching Andros arrange a basket of bread and dishes of olive oil and honey on the table. She glanced up when Arcadia entered.

"You slept well?"

"Quite well. Doesn't the senator eat breakfast?"

"The senator is probably at the harbor." Prisca selected a roll from the basket Andros offered. "He imports pepper and Macedonian wine…eastern merchandise."

Good, Prisca seems more talkative without her husband here, Arcadia thought, as the steward pulled back a chair for her.

"Publius wanted me to schedule a rooster fight as entertainment," Prisca said with a throaty chuckle. "I declined for you."

"I'm grateful. Domina, I—"

"You may call me Prisca."

"Prisca. Last night I started to tell you—"

"That you had no interest in sharing my husband's bed?"

"Why…yes." The woman's perception and honesty surprised Arcadia.

Prisca pushed the dish of honey toward her. "I know your father. Petronius Valerianus is one of the few honorable men we have left in the cesspool that Ravenna is becoming. His daughter could be no less respectable."

"Thank you. But…you seemed so cold at supper."

"Keeps the senator off balance." The deep chuckle again. "Actually, I would have gone to Caprea in October, but the Vandals made that too dangerous." Prisca sopped up oil with her bread, then asked, "Did the senator seem nervous to you? He kept fussing with that new ring of his."

"New?" A chill rippled down Arcadia's back. Could it have belonged to Behan after all? "Wh…where did he get it?"

"Publius said he commissioned the ring from a Syrian craftsman on the docks. Perhaps he was nervous about bringing you here. Why did he?"

"He thought I needed a diversion while my husband is under arrest. He also came to see me about something."

"Something?" Prisca's eyebrows rose quizzically.

Why did I blurt that out? How much can I tell her? "He asked about two recently discovered papyri," Arcadia replied, and cursed her quick tongue. She had meant to say documents. "Do you know anything about them?"

"Perhaps something to add to his boring library." Prisca looked out the window.

"The weather's cleared. I thought we could relax in the tepidarium after breakfast. Do you ride horseback?"

"Not very well."

"I have a gentle mare for you. We could go out this afternoon—beyond the smell of those infernal fowl—and explore the pinewoods. I love it there—the solitude."

"I'd like that." Arcadia had a brief vision of her bones rotting in the forest of a senatorial estate until the General Resurrection, but agreed, "Yes, a ride in the woods would be very nice."

❦

Arcadia was surprised that during her remaining days at the villa Maximin never appeared again. She came to like Prisca, determining that the woman was alone much of the time when the senator was away on personal or state business. It was obvious that men would be attracted to her, but rumors of a liaison with Valentinian never came up. Prisca did not ask about the papyrus documents again, nor did Arcadia see the senator's mysterious Rooster Coop.

On the day the mute was to take Arcadia back to her house, Prisca gave her a pair of fused glass earrings as a parting gift. She also agreed to come to the clinic after the New Year, for a gynecological examination.

The smell of chicken droppings still clung to Arcadia's clothes as the carriage clattered back through the Porta Aurea. When her house came into view, she realized that she knew no more about conspirators with a red cockerel as a symbol than she had when she left, but she was sure it would be a long time before she would have Agrica serve chicken again!

Chapter seventeen

When Arcadia went to see her husband on the sixth of December, to tell him about her few days at Publius Maximin's estate, she found David ben Zadok in the room with him.

After embracing Getorius, she uncovered a clay pan. "I brought you rabbit rissoles cooked in honey-ginger sauce, the way you like them. Rabbi, may I give you a serving?"

"My thanks, but our religious statutes forbid the eating of such animals."

"I'm relieved you're back, *cara*," Getorius said, as he watched her spoon the meat into his dish. "I was worried about your safety, but evidently without reason, thank God."

"You have been away, young woman?" Zadok asked.

"Senator Maximin invited me to his country villa for a few days."

"He owns a chicken farm outside Ravenna," Getorius explained to Zadok. "I was concerned for my wife because the man sports a signet ring with a rooster symbol. He says it represents his poultry business."

"Yes, we know of the senator in Classis. Enormously wealthy and ambitious, but his influence over the emperor is tempered by Galla Placidia."

"I thought the senator might be connected to the conspiracy because of the ring," Arcadia said.

"But would he boast of it by displaying the sign of the cockerel so boldly?"

"You have a point, Rabbi," Getorius agreed, "that would be too obvious. Arcadia, we were discussing the possibility of examining the case in which the papyri were found."

"Could it tell us anything about the age of the documents, Rabbi?"

"Perhaps. Our goldsmiths would examine the decorations and metal, especially the solder joints." Zadok exhaled and rubbed his eyes. It was obvious that he was tired, and probably not sleeping well over concern about the release of the will. "And yet this might prove nothing," he admitted, "a new container could have been made every generation or so. The leather lining you found could also be recent."

"Then there's no way to really prove that the papyri are not authentic?" Arcadia asked.

"The librarian is taking the correct path, young woman. The fibers will tell us what we wish to know."

Getorius voiced a doubt, "Isn't papyrus subject to quick deterioration? Some of the library manuscripts are in terrible condition."

"The case was sealed?"

"Yes. After Placidia ordered me to open it, I had to use a tile-cutter's chisel to cut through the solder."

"This would have protected the contents."

"Would you be willing to look at the case, sir?" Arcadia asked Zadok.

"Of course, I would like to see it very much," he agreed. "And it is important for us to be doing something, even while the librarian works. How is Theokritos feeling?"

"Still quite ill," Getorius replied, "but he forces himself to continue. I spend my days reading near his office, yet he doesn't let me help."

"He has the case?"

"No, Placidia does."

Zadok shook his head in a gesture of frustration. "I asked the Empress to let our scholars examine the two papyri, but she refused. Will she allow our craftsmen to test their container?"

"I'll ask for an appointment," Arcadia volunteered. "Tell her she might learn more about the documents from an examination of the case that held them."

"I'm grateful, young woman." Zadok stood up to leave. "You'll wish to be alone with your husband now. Our goldsmiths will return the case before the festival of *Hanukkah,* on the twentieth of this month."

"I'll send you word when I have the case," Arcadia told him. "Nathaniel can pick it up."

Zadok nodded agreement and put a hand on Getorius' shoulder. "Have faith, son. In the past the Almighty has seemed to abandon Israelites too, yet a Psalm promises, 'All my enemies shall be confounded and dismayed. They shall turn away in sudden confusion.'"

"I...I'm sure that will happen, sir," Getorius said, more as a comfort to the old man than to himself.

❧

Galla Placidia was receptive to having the golden cylinder examined, but told Arcadia that Rabbi ben Zadok must report whatever his craftsmen found out only to her. She also mentioned that since Bishop Chrysologos had not heard from the dead monk's monastery, he presumed no one had been able to come. Behan would be buried in the cathedral cemetery on December twenty-fourth, the day before the feast of the Nativity.

❧

Nathaniel returned the Celtic case to Arcadia at her villa before sundown on December twentieth, along with a sheet of vellum that

243

explained what little his artisans had been able to discover. The report was discouraging, yet, despite Placidia's warning, Arcadia asked the Judean to come with her and show it to her husband.

❦

"It is difficult to evaluate work that is so unique," Nathaniel admitted to Getorius as he handed him the report. "Our gold workers found no Greek or Roman influence in the design."

"Nothing to date it?"

Nathaniel shook his head. "The material is electrum, a silver and gold alloy that was known even to Egyptian craftsmen in the time of Moses."

"The soldered joints?"

"Nothing to report except that the workmanship is superb. As Rabbi Zadok observed, our forger was clever in his writing, yet even more so in placing the papyri in a container of such authentic design."

"But it could be recent, the style does survive in Gaul," Arcadia said, unwilling to concede failure. "Behan's clothes chest had similar decorations. I have tunics…gowns with Celtic embroidery work…at least one jewelry piece."

"All traditional ancient designs," Nathaniel countered, "which makes dating the case difficult."

Disheartened at what could have been a promising approach, Arcadia rolled up the vellum and slipped it into the container. "Thank your men, Nathaniel. I'll take your report and the case home, and then take them to Galla Placidia in the morning."

❦

After leaving Getorius, Arcadia decided she needed to think out this latest disappointment. Three weeks had passed, her husband was still under arrest, and no lawyer had come to counsel him. Senator Maximin's offer of legal advice seemed to have evaporated like the morning mist on the surface of the Bedesis River.

Instead of going directly home, Arcadia walked along the Via Honorius toward the old forum. It was early evening, when people were indoors eating supper, so she found the area deserted. Looking at the surviving cluster of derelict buildings, which for four centuries had been at the core of civic life in Ravenna, added to her sense of dejection.

Arcadia paused across from a small temple to Fortuna. Because the building had been dedicated to a personification of good luck—especially for married women who wished fertility and a safe delivery of their child—it had been the last one closed by the bishop. Its barred bronze door was visible in the gloom beyond the six porch columns, a mute indication that the goddess, who was once worshipped for bringing good fortune, had been powerless to protect her own shrine.

Arcadia recalled seeing the cult statue as a child. The goddess had been graceful and beautiful, as she imagined her own mother to have been. Fortuna, her father had explained, held a brimming cornucopia in one hand. The other rested on the rudder with which pagans believed the goddess steered the course of their lives. Was Fortuna still inside the temple, neglected, or had her statue been smashed off its pedestal to feed the limekilns? Perhaps thrown into the sea after the bishop's order to close the shrine?

Drawn to the temple, Arcadia crossed the street, then stopped short at the curb.

Mother of God, am I desperate enough to imagine that some connection with the spirit of a pagan goddess who once was honored here might inspire me?

She came closer to the temple steps and saw that someone had placed a pitiful offering of bread and a wooden cup half-full of wine on the lowest stair. The crusts were recent enough not to have attracted pigeons. Perhaps the supplicant was a slave desperate for luck in some way, Arcadia mused, then impulsively pulled the Celtic case out of her cloak and touched it to the temple stair.

Getorius is under arrest on a charge that could have both of us banished from Ravenna. But at least he's still alive. Maximin could be using his chicken farm as a center for a conspiracy that's connected with a forged will. Aetius might be briefing officers loyal to him for a palace take-over this month, when Nativity celebrations will put everyone off guard. Theokritos has been testing the two papyri for almost a month. Is he stalling, involved in the plot? Will he declare the documents genuine, then demand that the will be released?

Arcadia shivered and pulled her cape tighter around her shoulders, fighting a desire to cry. The possibility that Theokritos might be involved had not occurred to her before. *The conspirators don't have the will, yet a duplicate copy might have been made, and be ready to be announced by whoever forged it. Yet I don't know any more about how that might be done than I did on that night of the November ides.*

She wiped her eyes and glanced up at the weathered inscription on the temple architrave, above the columns. "Divine Fortune Smile on Us," she read aloud, then suddenly recalled a comment Getorius had made about someone coming from Gaul. "Fortuna, is there one other hope? My husband said that a person from Behan's abbey should have been here last week. No one came but…but, goddess, give them safe passage. Let them arrive quickly."

A gust of wind blew the crusts of bread off the step. Arcadia tucked the case back under her cape, wondering if anyone had watched her impromptu ritual. She looked down both sides of the street. Except for a man relieving himself against a wall of the baths, no one was nearby.

In the deepening twilight Arcadia grasped the cylinder tightly against her body, then turned and hurried back across the street, to the security of her walled home.

Chapter eighteen

An exhausted Brenos of Slana reined his horse to a halt under a soggy pine tree atop a knoll that was about a mile west of Ravenna. He pushed back his broad-brimmed leather hat, sucked rain off the scraggly moustache on his upper lip, and dismounted to peer at the mist-blurred walls of the capital city.

When a reflexive shiver shuddered through his body, from fever as well as the cold weather, he hunched down, to hoard whatever warmth his wet, mud-spotted robe might still retain. The effort was painful. The raw wound on his side from the leather case chafing against his skin, was now an angry red sore suppurating with yellow pus. Fiachra had tried to heal the inflammation with a solution brewed from dried symphytum leaves, but the medication had not stopped the hot redness from spreading.

The abbot stood again, wiped a damp sleeve across his face, and slipped his pilgrim's staff from its retaining strap, fingering the final notch he had cut into the wood that morning. There were thirty-two marks in all, one for each day of his journey, through what he had come to consider the realm of Satan, toward the Final Judgment. He had lost track of the date, but counting the markings a second time showed that it should be the twenty-first of December; the voyage from Gaul had taken much longer than he had estimated. Brenos imagined that he looked as wet as the otters he had seen in hunters' traps on the Icauna River. It was an apt comparison. He felt just as furious at both his weak secretary and the treacherous guide as the caged animals had at their sudden captivity.

Warinar had disappeared that morning. When Brenos had awakened in the woodcutters' hut on the slopes above Faventia where the two had sheltered, he had found Warinar missing, along with the packhorse. The abbot assumed that when Warinar realized he had forfeited the bonus of a gold piece by arriving at Ravenna later than he had promised, the sullen guide had stolen the animal as payment and slipped away.

Fiachra had disappeared eight days earlier, at Florentia, just before the final climb to the Apennine summits. Brenos imagined that his brother monk had convinced himself that he had undergone enough penances to rectify all the transgressions he might incur in his lifetime. Whatever the reason, Fiachra was not there in the morning when the horses were readied. Satan had put Fiachra to the test, just as the angel had warned the Church of Smyrna, and the man had failed. Had not the Nazarene predicted that some seed would fall by the wayside? Fiachra had already protested at Lugdunum that he was ready to return to Culdees. At that point, in deference to his oath of obedience, he had gone on with his abbot, yet he had not stayed the course.

Brenos leaned against the tree to rest, and recalled his incredible journey. Everything had gone well until Lugdunum, where Warinar had been told that crossing the Genevris Pass into Italy would be impossible. Heavy snow and continuing poor weather had closed the alpine road, so he was advised to remain in Lugdunum until spring, or return home immediately.

Brenos had insisted on going on. By the grace of the Nazarene, Warinar found a bargemaster making a journey south to Arelate on the Rhodanus River, with a cargo of wine casks. From there the man said the three travelers could take the Via Julia Augusta to where it ended on the Mediterranean coast. At Forum Julii, the abbot could board a boat to Pisae—if he could find a galleymaster foolish enough to risk a winter sea voyage. Otherwise, the bargeman suggested following the coastal road to Genua, where it would connect with the Via Aemilia Scauri to Pisae. From that city they would take the Arnus and Sieve River roads until the rise to the Apennine crests began. Once over the pass at the summit, the descent to the Adriatic coast would be relatively easy.

The trio had found conditions in the Viennensis Province unstable, particularly at Arelate. Despite having signed a treaty with Ravenna, Theodoric the Visigoth king had never abandoned his ambition to control the entire Mediterranean coast. Theodoric's most recent attack on Narbo had failed, and he had been taken prisoner. A new treaty was being worked out, but Arelate was closed off and patrol galleys blocked downstream barge traffic to the mouth of the Rhodanus River.

While his horse nibbled at dead grass under the pine, Brenos unslung a wineskin and swigged the dregs of a cheap vintage bought from the civic guard at Faventia. It did little to slake his feverish thirst, and every movement pained his raw wound. Beeswax waterproofing on his leather food case had long weathered off; the last chunks of bread were damp and moldy; and yet the poor fare was a small inconvenience, he thought, as he eyed what was left of the route he would take. "The Road of the Golden Gate," Warinar had called it, an apt name for the highway on which the head of the Gallican League would arrive to carry out the Nazarene's mandate.

In searing pain from the raw wound on his side, Brenos remounted and clucked his horse forward, glad now of his decision at Lugdunum to go on despite the hardships. At Arelate he had been able to enter the city by appealing to the bishop and citing his rank as abbot. From there the Via Julia Augusta had crossed rich vineyards, olive groves, and grain fields that were relatively unplundered despite the recent barbarian wars. Contingents of mercenaries hired by each community made sure that the countryside remained free of bandits.

As head of a monastery, Brenos used the prestige of his church office, and Warinar had shown the signet of Valentinian III on his travel authorization to pass them through without much harassment.

At Forum Julii, on the coast, Warinar had advised taking the road, rather than a galley, as much to avoid certain seasickness as a potential sinking in a winter storm. The former reason was the most likely, so Brenos agreed.

The new monastery of Lerinum was on an island a short distance beyond Forum Julii. Brenos recalled that he had been tempted to rest in the company of a fellow abbot for a few days and have his wound treated, but he did not know the churchman and was unwilling to face questions about what forced him to travel such a distance before spring brought better weather.

Once inside the province of Italy, Warinar had said they would be more secure. Yet, at an ambush near Albinganum, only a timely showing of the emperor's authorization and a bribe of silver coins saved the three men from being murdered and their bodies thrown into the sea.

Warinar had bought fresh horses at Genua and turned south along the Via Aemilia Scauri to Pisae. The road was more crowded with traffic, yet also safer because of it. The Arnus River segment from Pisae to Florentia went relatively well, but it was at the latter town that Fiachra decided he had done enough penance and would go no further. From Florentia, a dirt road that twisted back upon itself in sharp, rising turns led up to the Apennine pass. There the weather turned miserable again, with morning fog and daily rains that washed out sections of the mountain road and threatened the horses' footing.

Now, despite his exhaustion and pain, Brenos felt growing excitement. He was finally here! The Nazarene had guided him safely to Ravenna. Behan would have already announced his prophecy about an imminent event of earthshaking significance, and everyone in the Western capital—from emperor to slave—must be in a state of expectancy, wondering what it was that would be revealed.

❧

They would soon find out. It remained only to be contacted by Smyrna and whatever other Gallican League associates were in the city, then prepare for the exact method of revealing the Nazarene's will at the Mass of the Nativity Vigil.

Chapter nineteen

Bishop Peter Chrysologos was surprised to learn of the Hibernian abbot's arrival. In an interview, he told Brenos it was commendable that he, as head of a monastery, had been willing to suffer the discomforts of a winter journey to attend the funeral of one of his monks. The bishop insisted that the abbot stay in the episcopal residence, and also deliver the eulogy at the Mass for Behan on December twenty-fourth.

Brenos' lingering anger at Fiachra and Warinar metamorphosed into panic when he realized that he was more than two weeks later than he had planned in arriving at Ravenna. There were only three days left to be contacted by Smyrna, remove the papyrus with the will from wherever it was concealed, and arrange for its revelation at the Nativity service. He had assumed that the prophecy Behan would announce to prepare for the discovery had been made public, and became very uneasy when the bishop did not mention it.

His anxiety subsided a bit when Chrysologos told him he would be introduced to the congregation at the morning Mass, which commemorated three martyrs who had been victims of persecution by the apostate emperor Julian II. Even if Smyrna were not at the service, word of an abbot who had just arrived from Gaul would get out quickly. He had not met the League's contact, but had written to him through Behan. Smyrna, after sending the note that "the cockerel was ready to crow," must be as anxious that Brenos had not appeared on schedule, as the abbot was about being delayed.

What would Smyrna be like? Behan had been clever in saying that he would use his access to the library to make contacts within the palace. Clerks gossiped. It would not be too difficult for a simple monk to learn who was disgruntled and ambitious, a person, perhaps, who had lost prestige and who could be persuaded to be part of an effort to replace a corrupt government with a true Christian state that would be administered by an Order of holy monks. And Smyrna must be ruthless enough to condone the civil war that would inevitably result.

❧

Galla Placidia arranged for a private meeting with the abbot. It was a courtesy to a churchman who held a rank equivalent to that of a bishop, but she also wanted to find out—discreetly—how much he knew about the manuscripts found in Behan's hut, especially the papyri that Theokritos was testing.

Brenos was overawed after seeing the number of buildings in Ravenna and their size. Bishop Chrysologos showed him his Ursiana basilica, with its five aisles, and said it rivaled the one that the great Constantine had built in Rome. Except for the glimpse of the white buildings Brenos had caught on the hill at Lugdunum, he had not been able to visualize any structure larger than his Collegium at Culdees.

❧

When a deacon escorted Brenos to the Lauretum Palace, the abbot could only gape at the magnificence of this residence of the Western Augustus. The construction and size of the building, the magnificence of its mosaic floors, the colorful clothing on the guards, a glimpse of an indoor garden as large as the docks at Autessiodurum; all made him forget the pain in his side for a time.

The deacon left the abbot alone in Galla Placidia's reception room. Even though he had been told that she was the mother of the emperor, Brenos was astonished at the richness of the room's furnishings. Even the governor's office at Autessiodurum, a room with expensive furniture compared to a monk's cell, did not approach the wealth and luxury displayed inside this woman's reception area.

As Brenos sat nervously waiting for the arrival of the emperor's mother he was tormented again by the excruciating pain of his suppurating wound. He blamed a feeling of weakness on fatigue from his journey, and a lingering nausea on the contrast between the bishop's rich meal and the sparse travel rations he had endured for so long.

To distract himself from his discomfort, Brenos stood and walked around the room, looking at the silver and gold statuettes set on stands. Behind some of them, along the wall, pagan goddesses, harlots frozen in stone, stood alongside bearded idols and portrayals of smirking men and women wearing outlandish hairstyles. On the area behind what he assumed was Placidia's throne, an elaborate monogram in gold tiles displayed the letters AGP.

Brightly colored coverings hung on walls, and lay beneath his mud-stained travel boots. Some partially hid tile designs of long-eared demons with brutish faces and erect penises, who tried to copulate with equally shameless nude Daughters of Eve.

Half delirious from fever and fatigue, Brenos felt his initial awe at the display of riches—the mosaics, tapestries, carpets and sculptures—turn into a nascent rage and fear. In a sudden revelation, like a bright light pulsing behind his eyes, the abbot recalled John's apocalyptic vision of a woman seated upon a scarlet beast. The name of Babylon, the great mother of harlots, was written on her forehead. An inner voice surfaced to reveal to him that *here in Ravenna*, not in Rome, was the lair of the Harlot about whom the Apostle John had written!

What was it John had been commanded to write to the Angel of the church in Smyrna? "I know how hard pressed and poor you are—and yet you are rich." Now, by the Grace of the Nazarene, he, Brenos of Slana, Abbot of the Monastery of Culdees, stood inside the temple where the Beast was worshipped amid fiery red, azure blue, and sulfur-yellow colors, in the company of idols made of gold, silver, bronze, stone and wood. He was in the den of the Beast, and the golden monogram of Placidia-Babylon on the wall was its mark. Yes, not the City of Rome, but *Ravenna*, the lair of the Western Emperor, was the haunt of unclean spirits, a place where kings and nations of the earth were made drunk on the wine of fornication, and the merchants that John had mentioned grew rich on bloated wealth.

Brenos squinted from pain and held his head. The brilliant light inside his skull hurt his eyes like flashes of miniature lightning bolts. With a hoarse laugh, he steadied himself against a marble table. The Gallican League had been formed just in time, for the sickle was ready to gather in the earth's grape harvest. This very room would soon become the winepress of God's wrath that John had foreseen. Blood would flow from the press to the height of a horse's bridle. *Let the Harlot come clothed in purple and scarlet, adorned with gold and jewels… pearls…holding a golden cup….*

The abbot's eyes lost focus. Objects in the room blurred, as if seen reflected in a pool of water. After a month spent in cold outdoor air, the heat and smell of incense was overpowering. An acrid bile rose to Brenos' throat. He was about to turn toward the door and run out, when he heard a female voice speaking to him.

"Our greetings to you, Abbot."

Brenos squinted, trying to make out the nature of the woman who approached him. She seemed to be dressed in a purple tunic with red trim, and wore a golden tiara and necklace of glittering jewels. Was it a golden cup that the Harlot held out to him in her outstretched hand? He shivered in horror and staggered back, away from the unclean apparition.

"Are you well, Abbot?" Galla Placidia asked. "You seem ill, but We imagine your journey was incredibly tiring."

"No…no…" He continued moving away, confused, frightened, unable to think of a rational response.

The abbot's appearance startled Placidia. She had caught glimpses of Behan when he came to the palace library, an unkempt man in a soiled gray robe, yet that might be expected in a holy one unconcerned with the world. This abbot, however, resembled a wild Hyperborean rather than a churchman living in civilized Gaul. His cheeks bristled with several weeks' growth of dark beard, and his strange tonsure was half-grown in. The homespun robe he wore was flecked with mud and smelled rancid as a result of his journey, she realized, yet she had expected the abbot to groom himself more carefully for the interview.

"I am Galla Placidia, mother of the Augustus," she continued, dropping the formal pronoun, "and in my own right, Queen of the Goths."

After Brenos realized who the woman was, he recovered from his momentary hallucination, and yet was still unsure of how to address her. Hibernia had kings and queens. "Queen" might be proper, and she had called herself by that title.

"Queen, I…I am Brenos, Abbot of Culdees," he told her, regaining a measure of firmness in his voice.

"Yes, the bishop told me." Placidia smiled and handed him the golden cup. "My steward prepared this hot wine to warm you after the alpine snows. I find it commendable that you came from Gaul just to bury one of your brothers."

"Queen, the Nazarene commanded us to bury the dead. I am his servant."

"Nazarene?" Placidia repeated in surprise. "Christ has not been referred to by that name in decades. Indeed, you do come from the furthest limits of the world." She indicated a cushioned chair, "Please, Abbot, sit there. I noticed that your right side seems painful."

"A bruise from the journey." Brenos sat and brushed a hand over the silk material. It felt smooth and sensuous compared to his rough woolen robe, but he would not let it, or the room, or especially this Harlot-Queen, distract him.

"A pity about your monk Behan's death," Placidia sympathized when Brenos said nothing further. "Tell me of your Order. I know something of Egyptian holy men, yet little of those who come from Hibernia."

"We follow the rule of Ciallanus," Brenos replied, more at ease now that the queen's questions had turned to a familiar subject. "I see my task as one charged with the pruning of the Nazarene's vineyard, casting unfruitful and dead wood into eternal fires."

"Indeed, abbot," Placidia retorted, "but would you not agree that in pruning a vine an inept vintner may destroy it?"

"Queen, the Nazarene has commanded that I do this."

"Commanded *you*, abbot?"

"A humble instrument of Ciallanus."

"Why do your Hibernian liturgies differ from those of our Roman Church, which are founded on the Rock of Peter?"

The Harlot is clever. Brenos flushed and shifted in his chair to ease the pain in his side. *She seeks to trap me with silken questions, like a spider's web ensnares an unwary fly.*

"Abbot?"

"Queen, your liturgies have been corrupted," Brenos lashed out in rising anger. "We, 'The Friends of God,' call for self-denial, penances. Discipline—"

"All are virtues that even our pagan ancestors practiced," Placidia replied. "Yet already the asceticism of some Egyptian monks has become fanaticism. Cruel penances replace rational judgment about the offenses and discipline becomes tyranny. Our Roman civilization is based on laws passed to moderate those extremes."

"The Nazarene said he would vomit out those who were lukewarm."

"Abbot, do you not confuse conscientiousness with blind certitude?"

"Behan died in the arms of the Nazarene," Brenos said, returning to the subject of the dead monk. He had to find out how well his prophecy had been received in Ravenna, and the sense of expectation it had aroused in the citizenry. Why hadn't the bishop mentioned it? Brenos gulped a swallow of the Wine of Fornication, but the unfamiliar spicy taste made him gag. He wiped his mouth on a soiled sleeve. "Fortunately, Queen, before his death Behan had completed his mission of preaching the prophecy about the Nazarene's revelation."

"Prophecy? Revelation? What are you speaking about, Abbot? I've not heard of a prophecy. Nor has Bishop Chrysologos told me of one."

"Not…heard?"

Brenos spilled wine from his cup when he set it down too quickly. Could the monk have died *before* he was able to announce the imminent disclosure of the Nazarene's last testament?

"You *are* ill, Abbot," Placidia observed. "I'll summon my physician."

"No, no. Wh…what exactly happened to Behan?"

"I thought you knew that he drowned. When my surgeon examined your monk's body, he found manuscripts on his desk. When you speak of prophecies, are you referring to those manuscripts?"

"Manuscripts?" *What does the Harlot mean? Perhaps one of them is the prophecy, and I can confirm it to the bishop.* "Y…you have them here?"

"No, in the palace library. On another matter, Abbot, a…document…that had been hidden was uncovered by accident. Could it be connected to this prophecy you mention?"

"Document?" Brenos's stomach spasmed at her question, and he fought to keep from retching. Was it possible that the Nazarene's will had been prematurely discovered? He choked back bile and forced himself to keep from trembling. "What kind of document?"

"A forgery, undoubtedly, but—"

"Where is this document?" he demanded, under control again. "I must see it."

"I was about to say that my librarian, Theokritos, has been trying to determine its authenticity. He has been ill, but told me I could have his results this afternoon."

Brenos fought for the discipline he had learned in performing his harsh penances. "This librarian, where is he?" he asked, more calmly. "May I see him?"

"Theokritos is in his room, but I've told you that he is not at all well."

"Our Hibernian rite of private confession often promotes healing in those who are…ah…perhaps reluctant to reveal their sins in public."

"Sins, Abbot?" Placidia suppressed a smirk by taking a sip of her wine. *Theokritos might be a Gnostic, or even crypto-pagan, but he would never undergo the humiliation of confessing to a monk. On the other hand, my librarian might be able to draw information from the abbot that I could not. What harm could there be in allowing Brenos to see him?* "Very well, I'll have my steward escort you to Theokritos' room, but the results of his experiments are to be given to me alone."

"Of course, Queen."

Placidia rang her golden bell to summon Magnaric. When the steward came in, she told him to take the abbot to Theokritos' room near the library.

As Brenos followed the man, he felt drained of energy, yet, despite that, the unsettling news had given him the strength to find out what had happened, and the Harlot Queen an opportunity for him to do so.

After Magnaric left, Brenos rapped on the door. There was no answer, but he found the portal unlocked. He pushed it open slowly and peered in. The stale air in the sickroom smelled of camphor. Theokritos lay on his bed, propped up by pillows, his eyes closed.

"Librarian, I am Brenos of Slana," he called out. "Abbot of the Monastery of Culdees."

Theokritos slowly opened his eyes and turned to see who was speaking. "Slana? Culdees?" he croaked. "The names mean nothing to me."

"I am Behan of Clonard's abbot," Brenos elaborated, coming closer to the bed. "I came as soon as I heard news of his blessed death."

"Why *blessed*?" Theokritos scoffed.

"I understand our brother died in a penance while praising the Nazarene. I consider that blessed."

"Nazarene? That term is used only among a few fanatical Christian sects. Abbot, why did you travel this far in winter just to bury an obscure monk?" Theokritos asked suspiciously. "If there was uncertainty over burial jurisdiction a courier could have brought an answer. Why are *you* here?"

"Did you know our brother?" Brenos asked in an attempt to counter the old man's obvious mistrust.

"He came to my library to read."

"Behan would." Brenos forced a chuckle. "It is said that Hibernians are wedded to their books and, indeed, I would like to see your palace collection. Our own Bishop Germanus has a number of rare volumes in his library. Culdees has a modest selection, but most are written in Celtic."

"Your monk had some manuscripts in that language."

"Yes, our brother was...was always writing." Brenos felt his heart beat faster and sat down on a wicker chair near the bed. "I...I understand you're trying to determine the authenticity of those manuscripts."

"Not the ones the surgeon brought me," Theokritos replied hoarsely. "They were mostly gibberish, at least the part written in your barbarian tongue."

What is he referring to? The prophecy is written in Latin. "Tell me what Behan wrote, Librarian. One person's gibberish may be another's vision."

"Vision, Abbot? Even worshippers of Dionysus see visions, only to awaken in the morning with a swollen head."

Brenos forced a laugh to cover his impatience. "And the Latin manuscript. Did you also think that one to be nonsense?"

"Latin manuscript?" Theokritos rasped. "How could you know that one of the manuscripts was written in that language?"

Brenos realized his error and tried to distract the sick man from it. "May I help you drink, Librarian? Your throat seems dry."

Theokritos waved a hand toward a cup on the table. "A little of Antioches' poison."

Brenos sniffed the drink. "Mint crushed in wine. Our monks would succumb to many illnesses to...to drink this," he quipped, but his voice faltered. As he held the cup while Theokritos sipped the medication, the thought that the will might have been discovered clogged Brenos' mind. He had to find out exactly what the old man was testing, and deflect his attention away from his slip about the Latin manuscript. "You have many ancient volumes in your library?" he asked as he put down the cup.

Theokritos nodded and lay back. "Some were brought from Mediolanum when Honorius made Ravenna his capital. Homer, Plato. Herodotus…" His voice trailed off in a spasm of coughing, and he closed his eyes.

Brenos felt new alarm. He had to find out which manuscript the librarian had found without further arousing his suspicion, yet could not risk tiring the old man and be forced to leave. "I ask about your library because the Queen told me you were testing the age of a document that was recently discovered." Theokritos only responded with a dry cough. "Librarian," Brenos insisted, his voice rising, "*where is this papyrus?*"

"Papyrus?" Theokritos opened his eyes and eased himself to a sitting position. "How did you know the manuscript was made of papyrus? The material has been out of general use for decades."

"Th…the Queen mentioned it," Brenos lied, realizing he would have to be more cautious. For a sick old man, the librarian was alert. "Have you come to a decision about the document's authenticity?" When Theokritos did not reply, Brenos pushed in another direction. "Is it a new letter of Pilate? The others are forgeries, but many good people are deceived."

"It is not that."

"No? But you have come to a conclusion?"

Theokritos nodded slowly, but said nothing. Brenos waited a moment, then demanded, "Well? Do you believe the papyrus to be a forgery or authentic?"

"That is written only for the Regina's eyes to see."

"Of course." *Old fool. Would he have stored the papyrus in his library? No.*

If it is the Nazarene's will and Theokritos has discovered it to be a forgery, he would keep it near him. In this room. He wouldn't have expected a stranger to visit. At the least his conclusion is here somewhere. Brenos glanced around at the sparse furnishings. Besides the bed there was the wicker chair, a single wardrobe, and a shelf of books above a writing desk that was much like the ones in the scriptorium at Culdees. Cabinet doors closed off storage space under the slanting top. *That's where the papyrus would be placed! So would the damning results of his tests.* Brenos looked back at Theokritos. The librarian was slumped against the pillows, his eyes closed again. He seemed asleep.

Even though Brenos stood up carefully, the wicker chair creaked. His hands felt clammy as he began to ease himself toward the desk with as little noise as possible. He was halfway to it, when he heard the rustle of bedclothes and looked around. Theokritos was sitting up, his glance darting from the abbot to the cabinet doors and back again.

"It's in there, isn't it?" Brenos asked in a husky whisper. "The papyrus is in the cabinet. Let me see your test results. The Queen won't have to know."

"What? No, get away from there!" Theokritos ordered. "How did you know the documents were written on papyrus, or that there was a Latin scroll? You…you're part of the conspiracy to release the will. That's why you came."

The will! It is *the Nazarene's testament!* As Theokritos struggled to get up from the bed, Brenos strode back and snatched up a pillow from behind the old man's back. Before Theokritos could cry out, the abbot had stuffed the soft bag over his face and pushed him back onto the mattress.

Suffocating the librarian was more difficult than Brenos expected—he had been weakened by exhaustion, from the rigors of his winter journey, and by the fever. As he struggled to keep Theokritos' face pressed hard against the pillow, Brenos winced at the agonizing pain stabbing out from the rawness on his side. The librarian's arms flailed around, trying to tear away the deadly covering, and his legs kicked out to push his assailant away.

One of Theokritos's feet caught Brenos in the groin and threw him off-balance for an instant and the old man managed to work his head free. The abbot glimpsed his terror-filled eyes, before frantically stuffing the pillow hard over the librarian's face again. His effort must not fail. The success of the Gallicans' plan depended on finding the Nazarene's will, and this stubborn librarian had it.

"*Brandub!*" With the spat-out Celtic curse, Brenos stiffened his arms and pushed against the pillow with all his remaining strength.

Theokritos' struggle ended moments afterward.

Breathing in gasps from his exertion, Brenos propped the librarian's body up against the pillows, arranged the rumpled bed-clothes to look normal again, then went to the desk and opened the cabinet doors.

Theokritos had made no effort to conceal the vellum on which he had penned the results of his experiments. Brenos found it in a cedar box, on the lower shelf. His hands shook as he unrolled the white sheet. He glanced past the record of the experiments, to the librarian's conclusion, making sure it was the Nazarene's will that the man had been testing, then turned as pale as the white vellum page.

Brenos mumbled the conclusion to himself. "Theokritos of Athens, Library Master to Flavius Placidus Valentinianus III, at the court of Ravenna, through the results documented above, declare that the papyri of the Apostle Petros, and the Last Testament of Jesus, the said Christos, are authentic and genuine."

Brenos was stunned. *Th…the old fool thought…thought it was real! Theokritos declared the will to be authentic!* As his shock ebbed, the abbot replaced the vellum in the box, then rummaged through other scrolls stored on the shelves to find the will itself. All were blank. *Brandub,* he cursed again, silently. The two papyri were elsewhere in the palace. How had they been discovered, and who else knew of their existence? *Perhaps now, with the librarian dead, only the Queen, the emperor's mother, knows.*

He slumped back down into the chair to think. If the documents were in the palace, Smyrna could help locate them, but why hadn't the man contacted him? Had the Gallican plot been discovered, or had Theokritos been recruited as one of the conspirators and agreed to declare the will genuine? That would have been clever.

A rap at the door startled Brenos, sending a shiver of alarm through his body. The portal opened and the Queen's steward, who had brought him, looked in.

"Pardon, Abbot," Magnaric apologized. "The Empress Mother was worried at your absence."

"I…I was about to come to her with poor news. I was praying with Theokritos for renewed health…for both of us. After we said a

Confiteor together, her librarian slipped into eternal sleep, just…just moments ago."

Magnaric glanced over at the figure on the bed, signed himself with a cross, and murmured in Gothic, "*Atta, wairthai wilja theins*…Father, thy will be done."

"Steward"—Brenos slipped a silver coin from his belt purse— "tell the Queen about the librarian's death for me. I…I must get back to the bishop's residence immediately."

⁂

In his room, as Brenos' feelings of tension eased gradually, he laughed aloud. It was a manifestation of nervousness, yet, strangely, also of relief, when he realized that the premature discovery of the Nazarene's will might actually work to the advantage of the Gallican League.

The second phase of the plot—determining the authenticity of the two papyri—was well under way, accomplished, in fact. A respected Greek scholar, the librarian to the Western Augustus, had studied and tested the documents and pronounced them authentic. There would be further debate, of course. Sixtus III, the Bishop of Rome, would call together secret councils in the Lateran Palace, but the weight of evidence was on their side and the endorsement of the emperor was already in. Brenos was confident that the pontiff could not delay making the will public any longer than the start of the forty-day penitential season in late winter—exactly as the League had anticipated.

A rap at the door interrupted Brenos' musings. When he opened it, one of the bishop's servants handed him a note. He told the man to wait, then went back in, standing at the far side of the room, near a window. He tore at the red wax seal, destroying some of the signet image in his eagerness to anticipate the contents.

After reading a moment he murmured, "Praise the Nazarene, the message *is* from Smyrna. I'm to be in the narthex of the Basilica of the Holy Cross, next to Galla Placidia's mausoleum, at the tenth hour this afternoon. A carriage will meet me and drive me to an estate outside Ravenna called the Villa of the Red Rooster." Brenos chuckled at the apt name, then pieced enough of the crumbling wax back together to make out the symbol of a cockerel.

The abbot had no response for the servant to take back, but before dismissing him, ordered the man to bring him an armful of fresh yew branches.

Chapter twenty

On the same afternoon that the death of Theokritos was reported to Galla Placidia, Getorius, confined in the room assigned to him, heard the clack of hob-nailed boots in the corridor outside. He sat up from the bed, where he had been reading what the ancient Greek historian Herodotus said about embalming methods, wondering if there had been some new development in his case. Would he be freed? He heard the bolt slide through its retaining brackets, then Charadric swung open the door. A ruddy-faced Flavius Aetius stood at the jamb, in a swirl of cold air from the garden.

"Commander..." Getorius set his book aside and stood up. "I...I'm honored."

Aetius dismissed the compliment with a wave of his hand, then turned and spoke in Hunnic to a man with oriental features who accompanied him. The guard sheathed his curved sword and took a position by the open door.

"My bodyguard, Kursich, is my left hand," Aetius explained. "I remembered you, Surgeon, from that unfortunate dinner where I made a fool of myself. Thought I'd ask you a few questions about why you're here."

"I'm grateful. Please sit down, although I must apologize—my borrowed furnishings are somewhat spartan."

Aetius grunted his thanks, and dropped heavily into the room's only chair. He rubbed his eyes with a thumb and forefinger. "I do feel tired, like an old pack mule after a season's campaign."

Getorius guessed that the commander must be aged around forty, but sixteen years of fighting against barbarians and potential usurpers in Africa, Gaul and Italy had aged him; he looked at least a decade older. Aetius wore a new pair of heavy field boots, but had set aside his worn campaign uniform for a tunic of fine wool that was belted at the waist with a silver-inlaid leather belt. A curved dagger of Hunnic design hung from it. The enameled gold pendant around his neck portrayed one of the mounted Asiatic warriors, a not-so-subtle reminder to Galla Placidia that fourteen years earlier, he had enlisted sixty thousand loyal Huns as allies to depose the usurper John. The army had arrived too late, but the warriors had frightened Placidia enough for her to bribe them to return home, and to reluctantly accept Aetius into her service.

All Ravenna knew that the commander had been appointed consul twice, and that Valentinian had recently awarded him the rank of Patrician. Even though he was Supreme Army Commander, citizens had begun to refer to him as "The Emperor's Patrician."

"You're just back from inspecting your field legions?" Getorius asked.

Aetius nodded. "Between here and Mediolanum. Rain the whole time, but with Carthage in Vandal hands our men needed a boost in morale. I convinced the Augustus to distribute his New Year bonus to them early."

"That should help."

"Hopefully. I'm also trying to mitigate some of the bad feeling against our Goths that still exists in the area."

"Ever since Flavius Stilicho was murdered and the families of his allies slaughtered afterward?"

"You do know your history, Surgeon, that was over thirty years ago." Aetius bent to brush away dried mud on the toe of one boot, then looked up at Getorius. "I have a better understanding of barbarians than anyone since that unfortunate commander. As a child I lived among Huns as their hostage. Stilicho was betrayed and murdered after being promised asylum."

"Lured outside of a church here in Ravenna and killed." Getorius understood why Aetius had not forgotten the man who had held the same post as supreme army commander—their positions were similar.

"The most stupid thing Emperor Honorius ever did," Aetius went on. "It's probably human nature that Stilicho would have liked to see his son made Augustus, as his enemies claimed, but his truly unforgivable offense was failing to maintain the Rhine and Danube frontiers intact. Citizens even hailed him as 'Savior of the West' at one point, for all the good that did him in the end."

Getorius knew that Stilicho had allowed himself to be executed rather than provoke civil war. Galla Placidia did not like or trust Aetius. She resented the fact that her regency guardianship over Valentinian was now over, yet she needed the commander's military expertise. Aetius, in turn, depended on the continuation of his victories to maintain his position and avoid Stilicho's fate.

"Well,"—Aetius glanced around the room—"I see they gave you Cassian's quarters, but the tribune seems to have taken almost everything with him to Rome."

"I'm comfortable enough."

"I was told of the charge against you, Surgeon, so I'll aim directly for the target. *Did* you dissect that monk's body?"

"No, sir."

"I'm inclined to believe you, but...well...my men report that about three weeks ago you went out in the direction of the stream where the corpse was kept."

So Aetius was informed about our journey to Classis. What else does he know? Perhaps he's not that sure of the target, or how many others might be involved in this.

"Surgeon?" Aetius asked.

Getorius tried not to sound defensive when he replied, "I had business in Classis."

"Mind telling me what kind of business?" After Getorius

hesitated, Aetius came over and put a hand on his shoulder. "I said I believed you, but the charge was brought by the bishop. The Augustus wouldn't interfere even if he felt like doing so. Do you know why someone would want to implicate...to dishonor you this way?"

"I don't." Getorius did not elaborate. If Placidia was correct and Aetius was involved in a palace plot involving the will, the worst he could do would be to tell the commander that he knew about the existence of the two papyri. "I have no idea, I only know I wasn't involved."

"All right." Aetius rubbed his eyes and sat back down. "There's something going on, but it's well hidden. My men have heard only a word here and there...not enough for me to make any sense of anything. But perhaps my comment at dinner that night about a secret document wasn't a total jest. Has someone 'discovered' a testament of Constantine that wills the Western Empire to the Bishop of Rome? Shall I put the Scholarian Guards on alert?"

"I...I couldn't say, sir." *Now Aetius is mentioning a will. Is the man toying with me about what he already knows, like a cat with a wounded bird? Does he hope I'll drop my guard and then tell him something?*

"In the name of Hades, Surgeon, talk to me!" Aetius burst out. "Do you want to be exiled with your wife to some gull-dung-spotted rock off the Dalmatian coast? What were you supposed to have done? What part of the monk's body were you charged with...mutilating...as the indictment reads?"

"Arcadia told me the deacons said it was the abdominal area."

"Neither of you has seen the corpse?"

"No. Bishop Chrysologos wouldn't allow it."

Aetius ran the fingers of one hand along his dagger sheath a moment. "The bishop's tribunal won't hold your trial until after the new year," he predicted. "Chrysologos has decided that the monk will be buried on the twenty-fourth of December. In three days."

"Literally covering up the evidence. That won't help me, but I suppose the bishop will be glad to have the matter laid to rest, as it were, even though nothing has been heard so far from Behan's monastery."

"You don't know? The monk's abbot arrived here from Gaul yesterday."

"His *abbot*?"

"Yes, a churchman named Brenos. I'm just as astonished as you that he would make that long a journey in winter. I had enough trouble getting back over a much shorter distance."

Getorius barely heard the comment. The arrival of the head of the monastery to which Behan belonged had to be connected to the revelation of the will. He wondered how much it was safe to tell Aetius, but the commander was still talking.

"…And not a single galley from the Egyptian grain fleet would risk a winter voyage, despite the fact that we offered the captains a handsome bonus in order to help avoid a food crisis."

"Egypt? I've been reading about the country in Euterpé, the second book of Herodotus…" As Getorius reached over the bed to show the volume, a sudden thought came to his mind. "Of course, Egyptian priests! Sigisvult had mentioned something about embalming Behan's corpse."

"What are you talking about, Surgeon?"

Getorius held up the old historian's book and waved it at Aetius. "Commander, don't we have an Egyptian colony in Ravenna?"

"Yes, a small one, in the port area…commercial offices, a temple to Isis, little else. Why do you ask?"

"I've been reading about embalming. This may be an impossibly long throw of the javelin, but if I could tell you exactly what organs had been excised from Behan's corpse, would that help my case?"

"Hardly, Surgeon," Aetius replied softly. "If you were responsible, of course you'd know what parts had been removed."

"If I told you where to find the organs, in a place where I couldn't possibly have had access?"

"Then there probably wouldn't be a case." Aetius chortled. "Except, perhaps, a new one for practicing sorcery!"

Aetius seems pretty honest. If I want to find out if my hunch is correct, I don't have much choice but to trust him. "You owe me nothing, Commander," Getorius said, retrieving a wax note tablet and stylus from the table, "but if you think I'm innocent, take a few men and, well, 'raid' is probably the wrong word, but if you could go and inspect the sanctuary of Isis in that Egyptian temple…"

"What are you getting at?"

"Not only does Herodotus mention embalming rites," Getorius explained as he wrote in the wax, "but I found a Latin translation of a Coptic manuscript in the library about ancient funerary rites for someone named…I think, Nes-Nekht."

"And?"

"Have your men try to locate four small jars, probably made of alabaster. They would have the heads of a man, a dog, a jackal, and a…a falcon carved on the lids. This is what you'll find inside."

Aetius took the tablet. "Liver and gallbladder in one," he read. "Lungs and heart. Stomach. Large and small intestines." He looked up with a frown of disgust.

"What is this butcher's list you've given me?"

"Commander, show it to the deacons who were in charge of the body. I think that word got out in the port area about Behan dying in that isolated location, and his body might have been used to practice embalming rites. Secretly. Apprentice priests are no more anxious to be arrested than I am."

"I don't know—looking inside that temple could be touchy," Aetius warned. "With African grain no longer available, the Augustus wants to be certain that nothing alienates local Egyptian interests. Reports of an intrusion into a religious rite of Isis would be certain to enrage him."

"Then what will I need to take with me when I'm exiled to that Dalmatian rock?"

Aetius smiled at Getorius's jest as he slapped the tablet covers together. "Fine, Surgeon, I'll do what you ask…but I was also told that one of your surgical instruments was found inside the dead man's shroud."

"I know." Getorius' elation at his guesswork faded. "I can't explain that, except to say that it didn't get there through sorcery."

"No. All right, I'll take two guards to the temple…pretext of a tax inspection or something like that."

"I'm grateful, Commander."

Aetius stood and grasped Getorius' arm. "That pretty wife of yours must be frantic at your arrest."

"Arcadia's strong, sir. I'll tell her what you're doing to help when she brings my supper."

"Let's hope you're right about the embalmed organs. I'll let you know what we discover…if anything."

Once Aetius and his bodyguard were gone, Getorius' doubts surfaced again. Based on speculation about the dissection that might be groundless, he was asking a possible conspirator to help him. The commander—without actually going to the temple—could come back and say he had found nothing. Getorius slumped back down on the bed and picked up the history book.

"I don't even know if Egyptians still practice the embalming you describe," he muttered to Herodotus, "especially in a damp climate like Ravenna's. Once Behan is buried my trial will only have the two deacons as witnesses. They'll say they found his body mutilated and my scalpel inside the shroud. All I'll be asked to do is identify the instrument. Any magistrate would draw the same conclusion of guilt."

What's the penalty for mutilating a corpse? Probably close to that for desecrating a tomb. At best I'd be forbidden to practice medicine, and at worst, as Aetius suggested, I could be exiled to some desolate island in the Mediterranean Sea.

Getorius was aware of the irony in the thought. His immediate fate would be of small consequence if whatever conspiracy was underfoot succeeded. By the date of the trial, controversy over Christ's intentions would have begun to pit Christian against Judean communities in the major cities of both empires. Through the resulting slaughter, the apocalyptic horrors that John had described would be fulfilled in his and Arcadia's lifetime. Indeed, an isolated island might be a temporary haven.

Aetius said that an abbot from Behan's monastery had arrived. He has to be connected with the papyri. The first thing the man would do is to contact those who know about the will. Hades! Here I am, helpless in this room, while he and his fellow conspirators are in the city finalizing their plans to institute a theocracy.

Chapter twenty-one

Hunched over in his tattered cloak, and with wet boots making a squishing sound on the paving stones of the Vicus Galla Placidia, Brenos of Slana saw the queen's mausoleum up ahead. He glanced to the west. A faded red sky held the dark etched silhouettes of ragged clouds; the light rain would soon stop. The cold drops felt good on Brenos' feverish face, but he was forced to walk with an awkward lope to keep his robe from rubbing the painful ulcer on his side. Perhaps he should have consulted the queen's physician, but there had not been time.

By that final glow of rosy light, the abbot noticed that Smyrna's carriage was already waiting next to the first narthex arch. The two-wheeled rig was painted black, almost invisible in the twilight, and had a leather top to keep off the rain while it took him to the Villa of the Red Rooster. There, Smyrna would sort out what had happened after the confusion caused by Behan's untimely death, and the accidental discovery of the two papyri.

In his letter Smyrna had boasted of his access to the palace of the Augustus, so it should not be too hard for him to locate the documents in time for the vigil service, although that was only two days away.

When Brenos reached the carriage he looked up at the driver, who motioned him to climb alongside. Once his passenger was seated, the man pulled back his hood and pointed to a silver plaque hanging around his neck. The abbot squinted at the letters, making out the words MVTVS SVRDVS, and nodded that he understood. *Clever of Smyrna to send a deaf-mute to pick me up. Nameless. No questions and no answers either.*

The mute directed the mare along a narrow street that paralleled the Honorian wall. At the Theodosius Gate, guards chuckled and exchanged mocking comments with each other about Mutus, before waving the carriage through with a sweep of their spears.

About a quarter mile beyond the gate, the silent driver guided the horse to the left, off the main stone-paved road and onto a muddy pathway that was scarcely wider than the carriage. The rain had stopped. Since the pinkish tinge of twilight on the horizon was barely enough to light their way, Mutus slackened the reins, letting the mare instinctively follow the rutted path.

Brenos heard the carriage wheels sound a hollow clatter as they passed over the boards of a bridge spanning a river. From the persistent sound of rushing water beneath it was clear that the stream was swollen almost to the point of breaking its banks.

A small distance beyond, the far eastern boundary of the *Villa Galli Rubris* was fenced by a low stone wall. An opening in the barrier was lit by torches and blocked by a large wooden sawhorse, rather than a gate. The mute rang a handbell until two men came out of a cottage alongside and moved the obstruction aside.

It was almost totally dark as the carriage lurched on, with just enough twilight left to make out the black outline of the villa buildings in the near distance, which were set behind a higher wall. Torches blazed in holders on the gatehouse, their smoky light reflecting off the underside of a bronze rooster that surmounted the roof. Brenos half smiled. Behan had chosen his accomplice well. The very openness of the cockerel images would allay suspicion, should an outsider see and question the Gallican League symbol.

Several guards armed with lances patrolled the gate. After being admitted, Mutus drove the carriage past a two-level barn structure and another barracks-like building. To their left was the gateway to the villa compound. The driver stopped at the near end of a courtyard, which led into the main villa buildings. Smoking torches on a three-sided portico revealed a fountain in the center, but it was turned off. Brenos frowned, aware of an unpleasant smell of chicken dung that hung on the damp air.

When Mutus turned toward the abbot, Brenos saw the dancing flicker of torch flames animating the driver's face. A shiver ran down his neck; the man's coarse features resembled the blank grin of a Culdees monk who had gone mad after being possessed by demons. He jumped from the carriage. A guard materialized from the portico shadows, motioning for the abbot to come with him. As Brenos followed, he felt reassured at the presence of so many sentries. Smyrna had his own army. That would be useful in controlling the turmoil that would be sure to follow the disclosure of the will.

The guard led the way across the courtyard, toward the portico of the villa's central building. After opening the door to a darkened atrium, he motioned the abbot inside. Brenos could hear the splash of water falling into a pool from a roof opening, and through the gloom he thought he could see a figure standing by one of the columns. The guard indicated the door of a room immediately to the right, then walked away and was lost in the portico shadows.

Brenos entered a small reception area that was illuminated by a single oil lamp set on a bronze stand. Three chairs and a round table were the only furnishings. A curtained doorway was on the right. The walls were undecorated except for six masks that hung on the side opposite the door. Drawn to them, Brenos studied the effigies and realized that each carved and painted female face was the personification of a city, with her headdress forming a wall and gate.

As he read their names, cut over the gate entrances, he was surprised to recognize the code names of the Gallican League affiliate cities: EPHESVS, PERGAMVM, THIATIRA, SARDIS, PHILADELPHIA, and LAODICIA. Yet there should have been seven masks. The second peg, where the SMYRNA mask should have hung, was empty.

As Brenos waited, trying to control his nervousness, he again wondered how Behan had found his accomplice. The monk would have gone to the library not only to read, but to glean information from palace gossipers, both freemen and slaves. He would also have visited the bishop's residence and churches, where presbyters and deacons might voice their complaints to a simple monk, a "holy fool for Christ."

Behan undoubtedly must have heard about Smyrna in this way. The man would be someone disaffected with his status in government or business, perhaps even the army. Once Behan had been convinced the man had resources and position, could be trusted, and would cooperate, he would describe the mission of the Gallican League and the unimaginable power that would come from being part of the conspiracy. There was rivalry even among bishops and abbots—how much more so in an ambitious layman? Smyrna's letter had implied that he was familiar with palace government. Good, he would have the administrative skills for implementing the League's plan to set up a theocracy—God's kingdom on the earth.

A century ago the Emperor Constantine had had such a vision, but his sons squandered his legacy in deadly squabbles over territory. Then, an apostate emperor tried to revive the worship of pagan idols again. Two subsequent dynasties had failed to stem the tide of barbarians and heretics inundating the empires, and the present weak emperor and his mother had turned Ravenna into the lair of the Harlot, of whom John had warned in his Revelation.

A rustling of the curtain that closed off the door opening interrupted the abbot's thoughts. He turned away from the masks. A tall, bizarre figure wearing a black robe with the outline of a skeleton embroidered on the front swept in through one side of the curtains. The Smyrna mask concealed its human face, and the two bony hands held wooden paddles with the Greek letters A and Ω painted on them.

Alpha and Omega? Brenos felt his skin pucker at the unexpected entrance of this supernatural apparition before he made the connection. John's vision to the Angel for the church at Smyrna was of

Alpha and Omega, Christ the First and Last, He who had died and come back from the grave again. *Clever I suppose, yet I had expected to meet a sophisticated accomplice, not some theatrical phantom in a satanic costume.*

The figure posed a moment, holding up the two paddles, then asked in a voice that was muffled by the hollow headpiece, "Brenos of Slana, Abbot of the monastery of Culdees?"

"Yes...yes, that is who I am," he stammered, recovering from his surprise. "And you are Smyrna?"

"Sit down, Abbot," the figure commanded.

Brenos wanted to remain standing, the better to bolt from the room if need be, but did as he was asked and sat, choosing the chair nearest the lamp, where he could see the specter more clearly. Smyrna had towered over him by at least a head when standing; now that he was seated, the costumed figure still loomed like some overpowering courier of evil.

"Our plan, Abbot, seems to have gone wrong," the voice intoned through the Smyrna mask, "just as an unexpected storm at sea may destroy a galley."

Brenos' scalp tightened at the confirmation of what he feared. "So...so it's been hinted to me. I was delayed by such a storm and came later than I expected."

"An unfortunate circumstance, Abbot. It may be yet a further whim of Fortune, but the testament of the Nazarene seems to have been unearthed by those who are not Gallicans."

"I've just learned that, but only one other person may be aware of it, the Emperor's mother. We need only find where the will is now. I believe it to be in the palace."

"And you were the building's architect?" Smyrna mocked. "Go, then, find the document."

"I...I meant that the papyri must be near the librarian's room. Wherever he was testing the manuscripts." Brenos was sweating now, intimidated by the apparition in a way he had not been since his novice days at Clonard. He needed to impress this Smyrna, and so he blurted out, "Did you know that Theokritos declared the will to be authentic?"

"Authentic? Who told you this?" Smyrna demanded, his sarcasm replaced by a tone of angry surprise.

"I…" Brenos hesitated. No one knew he had looked inside the librarian's cabinet after suffocating him. "Th…the old man told me before he died."

"And you told whom?"

"No one. Nobody. On my oath to Ciallanus, no one," Brenos babbled. "Now, only you. But we *must* locate the Nazarene's will in time for the Nativity Mass."

"You sound desperate, Abbot, and you should be. The fate of our Gallican League depends on finding the document in time."

"Yes, yes. I discovered only the librarian's result…" Brenos stopped. He had almost slipped again, after saying he had been *told* the results of the tests, but Smyrna either did not catch the error or ignored it.

"You mentioned the librarian's room," the muffled voice said, "but the will could be with the Empress Mother. I will try to locate it."

"Wh…what of the prophecy?" Brenos asked nervously. "Behan evidently failed to announce it."

"The fool drowned beforehand, in one of his penances."

"I received word of his death at Culdees, and the note—your note—about the cockerel being ready to crow. We agreed Behan's murder was the signal for me to come, but you mentioned no accidental death, nor that the prophecy had not been revealed. How were the two papyri discovered?"

"All you need know, Abbot, is that the witnesses were…are… being silenced."

Brenos felt resentment surface at the man's arrogant and patronizing attitude. He had called it "our" Gallican League. This Smyrna was meant to be a mere instrument for bringing about a theocracy that was his, Brenos', idea.

"Abbot? Your mind has wandered."

Smyrna's voice brought Brenos back. "Yes. There…there isn't much time for you to find the Nazarene's will."

An eerie chuckle sounded from behind the mask. "Only until the cock crows twice more."

"Twice more?" There were two dawns until the Nativity, but was the comment intended as a taunt about Peter's betrayal of the Nazarene? *Does this... this satanic apparition think he is being deceived, that I have betrayed my own Gallicans?* The pain in Brenos' side was excruciating. He realized that he had to get out of the oppressive room, try to sleep, but first he must arrange another meeting. "When will you contact me again?"

"Tomorrow, at the monk's funeral, I will tell you what I have found out. Now, Mutus will take you back to Ravenna."

When Brenos stepped up into the black carriage again he was trembling. A blinding white light behind his eyes pulsed regularly, mimicking each beat of his heart. Nauseous, it was all he could do to keep from vomiting. There was no choice but to trust Smyrna, yet there were only two days left in which to locate the papyri. If the prophecy had to be announced after the disclosure of the Nazarene's will, Behan's accidental drowning would be a suitable excuse, but once the terms of the will were made public, no one would really care any longer.

No, wait, Brenos thought. *I could announce the prophecy at my eulogy for Behan. It's not the way I had planned it, but the will itself is the crucial document. Smyrna must locate that papyrus.*

As the carriage rattled back across the bridge Brenos rankled at his humiliation. Smyrna had questioned him as if he were a novice monk and only a small part of the conspiracy, not an abbot and head of the Gallican League. Yet he would be patient. Once the Nazarene's testament was made public and the League triumphant, an arrogant associate like Smyrna would be humbled—destroyed in the winepress of God's wrath!

Chapter twenty-two

Late on the afternoon of December twenty-third, Getorius was pleasantly surprised when Charadric admitted both Arcadia and Silvia to his room.

Arcadia called the guard back as he turned to leave, "A moment, Charadric. How is your wife Ingunda's leg? The Surgeon treated her after I…I—"

"Yes, I leeched her," Getorius broke in to cover his wife's embarrassment.

"She's better, Domina," Charadric replied. "The redness has gone away."

"Good."

"Full use of your hand again?" Getorius asked. "That was a nasty wound I stitched up." In answer the guard grinned and rapidly flexed the fingers of his left hand. "Fine. I heard you've been promoted to lead one of the elite Germanic units that Aetius is forming from some of the palace guards."

"After the new year," Charadric replied. "I'll go now…let you visit with your wife."

"Good fortune to you."

"We brought your supper instead of having Brisios come," Arcadia said after the guard left. "Put the basket on the chair, Silvia, then you may go back to the villa."

"Appreciated," Getorius remarked, "but I'm almost too excited to eat. Flavius Aetius was just here with good news."

Arcadia grasped his arm. "The charge against you has been dropped?"

"Not quite, *cara*…" Before explaining, Getorius waited for Silvia to leave, and checked the hallway for anyone who might overhear, then took hold of Arcadia's hands. "I had an idea when the commander last came to see me. During the course of our conversation he reminded me of an Egyptian colony in Ravenna—"

"Idea about what?"

"I'd been reading Herodotus on ancient embalming methods. It was admittedly a long shot, but I thought some of their Isis priests might have found out about Behan's death."

"And excised the organs?" Arcadia pulled her hands away. "Husband, it's hard to believe they'd be that bold."

"I *said* it was a long shot. I asked Aetius to look for canopic jars in their temple. He found all four of them."

"Then you're exonerated!" she cried. "That's wonderful."

"There's still the matter of the scalpel. But Placidia did say she would talk to the bishop about having me released."

"When would you be freed?"

"Bishop Chrysologos is preoccupied with the Nativity celebration this week. Probably not until the new year."

"Getorius, that's too late. If a duplicate will exists it would be brought out in place of the original at the Nativity. At least Rabbi Zadok thought it might happen then, but we still don't know how that might be done."

"Woman, what do you want me to do?" he snapped, then regretted his outburst. "Sorry, Arcadia. I've been frustrated just sitting in here, but you're right. Aetius' discovery doesn't change the threat posed by the Secundus Papyrus." He kissed his wife's forehead and held her close, burying his face in her hair.

"I understand." Arcadia pulled free after a moment. "Now eat what I brought."

"Smells good." He picked at the corner of the cloth covering the basket. "What did Agrica cook?"

"Pork and lentils," she told him, taking a bronze pan from inside the basket. "Put that dish and knife on the table, I'll spoon your food out." Getorius laid the hamper back on the bed and sat on the chair. "It was clever of you to remember that Egyptian rite," Arcadia commented as she watched her husband slice into the meat.

"A chance remark of Sigisvult's made me curious enough to read Herodotus. And you had mentioned the historian yourself in the clinic once."

"When we talked about Pandora," she recalled.

Getorius noticed that Arcadia's brows had tightened into a scowl. "*Cara,* don't look so worried. I can stand a few more days of this."

"But there's still the problem of your scalpel. Finding the jars doesn't explain why someone tried to implicate you in a crime."

"True, and I've had a lot of time to think about that. If my being detained here is connected to having discovered the papyri, I've been—in a sense—eliminated as a witness. Placidia intervened and insisted that I be kept here, rather than in an underground cell, but the person responsible couldn't have foreseen that she would do that."

"That was fortunate—anything could have happened in that cell. You're safer in this room."

"But what about you? You were also a witness."

"Childibert and Brisios are at the house," she said. "I'll be fine."

"I want Brisios to come with you when you visit."

"It's only around the corner—"

"In Hades's name, woman, *listen* to me! Do what I say until I can be with you."

Arcadia shrugged agreement. "All right, Getorius. Perhaps Senator Maximin would let us get away to his villa for a few days after the

New Year. You might look in on his mother when you're released, even though he seemed pleased when he saw the way I treated her."

"Maximin actually remained in the room with you? He only watched me once while I treated Agatha." Getorius was spooning up lentils, when he abruptly paused to exclaim, "Zeus' beard, that could explain it!"

"Explain what?"

"Publius Maximin. On the last occasion that I went to see Agatha, he stayed in the room. I didn't think anything of it, but the senator could easily have taken the scalpel from my case."

"But that makes him part of all this. What would he gain from it?"

"Arcadia, you're the one who saw the cockerel ring. That abbot, or whoever is at the head of the conspiracy, needed accomplices. During the time Behan was in Ravenna, the monk must have recruited Maximin."

"I don't know. You thought I'd never come back from visiting his farm."

"*Cara*, I just was making sure you were careful while you were there."

"I can't believe the senator would be involved in this kind of horrendous conspiracy."

"The man's experienced the headiness of having power, and he has none right now," Getorius reasoned. "It must rankle him to be forced to appeal to a person like Valentinian for Patrician status."

"But Placidia suspects that Flavius Aetius is involved."

"Maximin would need his army. And it wouldn't be the first time a commander has betrayed his emperor."

"Both in it together?" Arcadia was silent for a moment, then said, "If you're right, neither one of us will survive. Even Galla Placidia is in danger."

"This is December twenty-third. There's little more than a day to stop them, and I'm still confined in here."

"Getorius, I...do you remember when we were falling in love?" Arcadia reached into the basket to pull out a slim volume she had packed with the food. "We read Ovid's *Ars Amatoria* together and laughed over the part where…here, I've brought it."

"With all this happening, woman, we're going to read love poetry?"

"Just this part. It begins, 'If you are wise, cheat women only and avoid trouble. Keep faith except for this deceitfulness.'"

Getorius chuckled in remembrance. "You almost threw the book at me when I showed it to you."

"It's the next verse. You read it."

Getorius took the book and found the place. "Deceive the deceivers, they are mostly a profane sort. Let them fall into the snare they have made." He looked up, puzzled. "So?"

"I have to set that snare, Getorius. There's not much time and you'll have to trust me."

"No!" he objected. "I mean, what are you going to do?"

"Where are the papyri now? Would Theokritos still have them?"

"Theokritos? You haven't heard, have you? Placidia is keeping it quiet, but he died yesterday."

"What? How? He succumbed to the fever?"

"Charadric told me palace gossip says it happened after that Hibernian abbot heard his confession."

"Confession?" Arcadia scoffed, "with that Gnostic amulet Theokritos wore?" She stood and came over to hug her husband for a long moment, then looked at him and brushed at the gray strands in his black hair. "Getorius, we two and the Gothic Queen may be the only witnesses left. I must have the Secundus Papyrus and Peter's letter today, by the time it gets dark outside. Can we pay Charadric to let me stay here tonight? We haven't made love in…in too long a time. Tell him we don't want to be disturbed."

"I like that last part, but not the other. Why do you want the documents? We don't even know where they are."

"Theokritos stored them somewhere in his office or room." Arcadia smoothed the lines in her husband's forehead with her fingers, then looked directly into his eyes. "I said you'd have to trust me." She reached into the basket and took out the golden case that Nathaniel had returned. "I've had this locked in your study. I…I want to put the two papyri inside the case again. As Rabbi Zadok pointed out, if this is of the Lord, then it will succeed no matter what I, nor anyone does."

"I don't believe God is involved."

"Nor do I," she agreed, "but I don't want us to end up murdered like Sigisvult and Renatus. And if that abbot is part of this conspiracy, Theokritos may have been another victim. Will you do what I ask?"

"But we don't know where the documents are. And to steal them from under the noses of—"

Arcadia shushed him with a finger against his lips. "Would there be any copyists working in the library now?"

"I don't think so. They told me they were let off early because of the Nativity vigil tomorrow."

"Then the library shouldn't have anyone in it."

"True."

"Theokritos was working on the experiments in his office," she recalled, "but after he became ill he stayed in his room. The will could be in either place. I'm sorry to say this, but the confusion right now may help us. Placidia is probably occupied with bonuses for the Scholarians and Nativity gifts for the palace staff—to say nothing of her concern over Aetius' intentions."

"So…what are you suggesting?"

"Charadric lives in one of the barracks rooms like this one, with his wife. He can move around the palace without arousing suspicion."

"And you want him to search for the papyri? Hades, woman…" Getorius took a deep breath and exhaled, resigned to not arguing with his wife any longer. "All right. Charadric is indebted to me for saving his hand, and probably his wife's leg. I'll tell him to look in Theokritos' room first, then his library office."

"Can Charadric read?"

Getorius shook his head. "I'll describe what he's to look for."

Arcadia took a small piece of vellum from her purse. "There's one more thing…that snare I mentioned. Have him leave this where he finds the documents."

Getorius looked at a sketch on the vellum. "A red cockerel? All right, but we don't know that the conspirators haven't already found the papyri. Or that Theokritos wasn't in on the plot and gave the documents to this abbot."

"And, Getorius, we could speculate until the General Resurrection. I need to act *now*."

"I'll go find Charadric."

※

Charadric had already heard the latest barracks talk about Getorius being released, and saw no problem in letting Arcadia stay the night. A gold *tremissis* persuaded him to search for the documents that Getorius described. Palace security was lax at this time of year. Guards were in a festive mood, anticipating the Nativity and New Year celebrations, where they would reaffirm their oath of loyalty to the emperor and receive gifts of equipment and money.

※

Using his guard's passkey, Charadric entered Theokritos' room. Because of the palace confusion that Arcadia had anticipated, no orders had been given about the librarian's funeral, and he was still laid out on the bed. His shrunken jaw had dropped grotesquely, and his thin body barely made a bulge under the bedclothes.

Charadric assumed that the desk cabinet was the only place in the room where documents could be stored. Inside, in a cedar box, he found only one sheet with writing on it, but it did not match Getorius' description. He left it in place.

The library was not deserted, as Charadric had been told it would be. A copyist working on the text of Valentinian's New Year address to his Scholarian guards nodded to him in recognition—the guard had taken Getorius through the copy room to read every day for three weeks. Charadric told him that Getorius wanted writing materials from Theokritos' office.

Behind the curtain the old librarian's worktable was still littered with the dishes and jars he had used in his experiments. Getorius had described the two papyri as being flattened out on cedar boards and held in place with golden ribbons. They were not on the table, or on Theokritos' desk, but there was a wall cabinet above it. Charadric silently forced its lock with his dagger blade.

Inside, among manuscript scrolls, the glint of gold caught the guard's eye. Theokritos evidently had taken the documents off the boards, rolled them up again, and held them in place with the golden bands. This had to be what the surgeon wanted.

With the papyri concealed under his cloak, Charadric had reached the book stacks before he remembered Arcadia's scrap of vellum. He went back and placed the red rooster drawing inside the wall cabinet.

It was almost dark by the time Charadric headed back to Getorius' room. In the garden he passed Heraclius, who was headed for the slave quarters, and guessed that Valentinian had returned from hunting and ordered the eunuch to bring him a young girl for the evening. Eudoxia, sulking at her husband's prolonged absence, had no doubt locked him out of her bedroom.

※

When Charadric took the papyri from under his cloak and gave them to Arcadia, she breathed a prayer of thanks to Blessed Cosmas, a patron saint of physicians. She could think of no other appropriate holy person and had, in fact, not really expected the guard to find the documents.

Later that evening Getorius and Arcadia made love with an intensity they had never reached before. It was as if the end of an age was at hand, and they were not sure that they would survive the resulting chaos. Afterward, Getorius fell into a deep sleep—the type of sleep that had eluded him for weeks because of worries over the forged will and the false accusation against him.

Arcadia lay in a half-doze, but awakened fully when she heard the sixth hour guards talking as they came off duty. It was the mid-point between night and day and, perhaps, she mused, for the life that she and her husband had known—as well as for everyone in the Western and Eastern Roman Empires—if her plan failed.

Rising quietly, Arcadia slipped on her tunic and cloak, then pulled its hood over her head. She eased the twin papyri back into their golden case, concealed the cylinder in the folds of her cape, and stepped out into the winter night. Icy air had followed the earlier rain. Now, frost glistened on the paving stones of the walk leading to the garden. She turned left, toward the kitchen area and its ice storage room.

"You brought this with you, Behan," she murmured, patting the hard bulge next to her tunic. "Tomorrow you can take it back to wherever you're going."

Chapter twenty-three

Arcadia walked quietly, hugging the walls of the imperial apartments. A few sputtering torches threw orange, smoky light on the poplar and black yew trees in the garden. She had once asked the palace cooks to reheat food brought for Getorius and, near the kitchen, saw the ice blocks that had been cut from mountain lakes and stored in a room close to where staff meals were prepared.

Behan's corpse would be there.

She kept to the shadows and hurried past the wells of flickering torchlight, worried about being seen, and also about having to pass the area where Valentinian kept his menagerie of animals. Fortunately, all the apartment windows were dark, except for a warm glow in two near the end. In a dark area between the torches, Arcadia paused to listen for any noises—footsteps, voices, or the jingle of a patrolling guard's equipment—that might betray someone's approach. Waiting, she glanced up. Far above her head the velour blackness of the sky was dotted with the glimmering points of Capricorn, as the Ram constellation swung around to replace the Archer of the past month. Ironic, she mused, Sagittarius had been an appropriate sign for the November deaths, which had begun with the bow bolt that killed

Feletheus. And it was fortunate that the winter moon, almost in its full phase, would not rise for more than two hours.

Patting the bulge of the case under her cloak for reassurance again, Arcadia neared the palace chapel dedicated to the Archangel Michael. Sigisvult and Surrus Renatus had been buried from there in hasty, private services.

She had just passed the entrance when a peacock unexpectedly voiced its unearthly, piercing cry from the zoo area across the way. The sudden sound sent a shiver through Arcadia, even as a leopard growled a rumbling warning in response. She froze in her steps and held her breath, silently praying to Cosmas that she had not set off a cacophony of animal calls which would alert the sentries and send them out to investigate the cause.

While Arcadia waited, the smell of offal from the animal cages reminded her of the week she had spent at Maximin's farm. *What role does the senator have in all this? Getorius thinks it might be a bid for power, but Maximin would have to be very desperate to ally himself with an order of monks no one seems to know anything about. Or perhaps he knew Behan from visiting the palace library?*

The zoo creatures settled back into quiet. Arcadia thanked Cosmas and slowly exhaled, her breath a cloud of spectral vapor melting into the cold darkness of the garden.

Once she had reached the kitchens in the north wing of the Lauretum, Arcadia recalled that the ice storage room was in an alcove immediately to the right of the kitchen. It had its own door so that the frozen blocks could be brought directly in from outside, without going through the kitchen itself. A lamp hung in the recess, throwing enough light to show that the portal was bolted shut.

My Furcing luck!—Arcadia gave a muffled laugh at her impulsive mental vulgarity—*I thought it would be unlocked because there's no need for ice in the winter. And the presence of a dead body in the room should be enough to frighten slaves away from entering to steal supplies.*

After examining the locking wards Arcadia saw that they were a standard design resembling the ones used to secure the outer clinic door. She searched her purse and found the key, eight wards that pushed up their corresponding pegs to release the bolt bar. After working the projections into their slots, she breathed another prayer of thanks to Cosmas. They matched. The bolt rasped through its brackets with a screech she felt could be heard in every room of the palace. Arcadia quickly entered and pulled the door shut after her.

The air inside the small room was damp, and as cold as that of outdoors, but it smelled of mold and rotting food, instead of the pungent evergreens and frost-speckled earth of the garden. Arcadia's leather boots were instantly saturated with icy water that soaked a layer of pine needles, which had been laid down to absorb the wetness. A high window admitted a feeble light from a torch set outside on the opposite wall. The glow reminded her that she had forgotten to bring a lamp. *You fool...totally unprepared for this.* As her eyes adjusted to the dimness, a flicker of lights on the left became apparent, above an oblong box. Deacons had left small vigil candles burning on the storage shelf behind the wooden coffin in which the monk's body lay.

After she came closer, Arcadia detected a faint odor of spices coming from the bier, instead of the stronger smell of putrefaction she had braced herself to expect. She thought that might help ease the grisly task ahead.

"Behan," she whispered, taking the golden case out from under her cloak, "as I said, you brought this with you and now you'll take it back."

After loosening the cylinder's cover, Arcadia placed the tube on the back shelf, then moved the vigil candles closer to the edge, so she could see better. The oak coffin was set on two barrels, bringing its top up to the height of her waist. She was relieved to see that the lid was pegged down only part way, probably because the bishop would ask the abbot to identify Behan before his burial. She blew on her cold fingers to restore circulation, and thought back to the night she had helped her husband dissect the corpse of Marios.

Getorius had begun to feel sick at what he was doing. Will I really be able to go through with this? What must Behan look like after being in the water so long?

Arcadia sucked in a breath and pulled up on the nearest peg. The squarish dowel held fast. Damp air had swollen the wood and expanded it in its retaining hole.

Blessed Cosmas. Please.

It took Arcadia half an hour, broken fingernails, and the sides of her thumbs and index fingers scraped raw before she was able to coax the six stubborn pegs loose. By then she was shaking, both from the exertion, and from the dread of realizing that the most horrifying part of her task still lay ahead.

The oak lid was heavy. After struggling to slide the cover off, Arcadia managed to lean it against the coffin's side. The smell of putrefaction was stronger now, almost strong enough to overpower the sweetness of the powdered spikenard, myrrh, and cassia bark that had been sprinkled on the corpse. Balsam branches covered the body. She slowly removed the evergreens, laid them on the wet floor, took a candle off the shelf, brought it closer and forced herself to look at the dead monk.

The deacons had dressed Behan in a new tunic of undyed gray wool and covered his face with a linen cloth.

"Mercifully so for us, Cosmas," Arcadia murmured, hoping that a whispered conversation with the patron of physicians would bolster her courage. "Bloated features that have been soaking in river water for almost seven weeks would not be a pleasant sight, would they?"

Arcadia set the candle down, clenched her jaw, and lifted the monk's robe. Above a loincloth, the dark cavity from which the organs had been excised by the embalmers yawned open. She wished she had taken a more active part in the animal dissections Getorius performed, rather than relying on him to tell her only as much as he felt she should know. Now she was faced with an abdominal cavity that was exposed down to the posterior tissues.

The deacons had sprinkled the three fragrant spices inside the cavity to help control the stench of decay, but in any case Arcadia's sense of revulsion was tempered by admiration for the clean way the Egyptian priests had taken out the organs. Herodotus described how embalmers cut along a body's flank with a sharpened Ethiopian stone. If the Isis priests followed tradition she thought they might have used a blade of black volcanic glass—the *obsius* mentioned by the Elder Pliny.

Struggling to stem a rising sense of nausea in her throat, Arcadia took the Celtic case and worked it lengthwise into the cavity, then angled it up until it pushed against a collarbone and the base rested on the pelvic wall.

"Cosmas, our cylinder fits! Now all we need do is sew the opening together, replace the lid, and get out of this charnel house without being seen."

With stiff, cold fingers, Arcadia fumbled in her purse and found the suturing needle she had already threaded with silk. Her raw bruises stung and her hands were numb from handling the chill metal case. She made an attempt to warm her fingers by passing them over the candle flames, but, nervous at being discovered, decided she could not delay any longer.

Tears blurred her vision as she strained to pull together the cold, shrunken flaps of abdominal skin. They finally joined, but although she began suturing the tissues using the technique Getorius had shown her, she became impatient to close the gap, and finished with a stitch she had learned as a girl in working with cloth.

By the time Arcadia completed the closure her fingers were as hard and white as marble. The sour taste of bile coated her throat. She smoothed down Behan's tunic without rechecking the sutures, then clasped her frigid hands a moment in the relative warmth of her armpits.

Levering the heavy coffin lid back into position further drained Arcadia's strength. She began shivering uncontrollably. Her feet were deadened from standing in the icy water. Half-limping to the door, she opened it and stepped outside to gulp in the clean night air. After pushing the portal shut, she turned to lean against a porch column, retching in painful heaves, and blew on her bruised fingers.

"Cosmas, we've still got to get back to Getorius' room," she murmured, after wiping her mouth on a sleeve. "Help me."

At the end of the portico, Arcadia turned onto the garden path, and was shocked when she bumped into someone in the dim torchlight. She gave a reflexive gasp of fright, and was stunned when she recognized Heraclius. A disheveled, ascetic-looking man with him held a lantern higher so the eunuch could see who had collided with him. Heraclius squinted at Arcadia, and his soft, fleshy features hardened into a scowl.

"Ah, the woman 'surgeon'," he said without concealing the sneer in his tone. "What are you doing here at night?"

"I…I was given permission to stay with my husband."

Heraclius glanced around in mock surprise. "Your husband has strange bedroom arrangements. No, woman. Look at your wet shoes. Why were you in the ice storage room?"

Arcadia could think of nothing except to tell the truth. "I…I couldn't let that poor monk be buried without…without suturing his wound closed."

"You, a woman?" the eunuch's companion snarled. "I am Brenos, abbot at Culdees. You dared touch the flesh of one of my holy men?"

"I… had already examined Behan with my husband, after he drowned."

"And how did you enter tonight, to perform this charity?"

Heraclius' question reminded Arcadia that she had not relocked the door. Under the circumstances a lie might be acceptable to Cosmas. "The door was unbolted," she replied as evenly as possible. "Perhaps a…a slave was careless."

"Perhaps, also, you will show the abbot and me the example of your brilliant needlework?" The eunuch's voice had lost none of its sarcasm.

"Of…of course."

At the ice room door, Heraclius grunted after he saw the bolt pushed to one side. Once inside, he pulled out the wooden pegs and eased aside the coffin lid.

One last favor, Cosmas, Arcadia silently prayed. *Don't let his light reveal a bulge in Behan's abdomen.*

While Heraclius held the lantern, Brenos moved aside the evergreen branches, then lifted the monk's robe and peered underneath. He eyed the sewn-up wound a moment, gave a snort, and flipped down the material in a gesture of irritated frustration.

After forming a mental thanks to Cosmas, Arcadia exhaled quietly. As the abbot turned and stalked out of the room, she heard his sandals make an absurd squishing sound on the soggy pine needles and choked back a nervous laugh. Heraclius glared at her, then followed Brenos outside.

At the door Arcadia watched the two men disappear in the direction of the palace's second story, where the library and hospital were located.

They're looking for the papyri. If Heraclius is a partner in the conspiracy and is searching the palace, Behan made a poor choice in recruiting him. Placidia loathes the man and would never allow him in her private rooms, where he might expect the documents to be found. How ironic that a plan which probably took years to devise might fail by a matter of fractions of an hour.

⁊

When Arcadia eased herself into Getorius' room, the twin-spouted oil lamp was burning, but Getorius was still asleep. She desperately wanted to call a servant and have hot water brought in—a bath was out of the question—but contented herself with rinsing her hands and bruised fingers in the icy water of the room's bronze washbasin. She wiped them over and over again on a hand towel until their greasy feel was lessened, if not gone completely. The dank feel of the ice room and its smell of decay would take longer to leave her. Trembling from the strain of her ordeal, Arcadia lay down on the bed, pulling her cloak over herself. The movement woke her husband.

"Arcadia? Where have you been?" he demanded, sitting up and looking at her. "You're dressed again and…and your shoes are soaking wet."

"I went outside to look at the December stars," she hedged, slipping her injured fingers under her cloak. "I met Heraclius with that abbot in the garden."

"Heraclius? How would Heraclius know…what did I hear his name was, Brenos?"

"Yes, the abbot told me."

"How would a holy man like Brenos know Valentinian's castrated procurer?"

"Getorius. Don't talk like that."

"I don't trust the man. Or what there is left of a man in him."

Arcadia let the comment pass, but sat up on the edge of the bed, laid aside her cloak and removed the wet boots. "We guessed that there had to be accomplices in the palace, Getorius. Who better than Heraclius, who must have a passkey to every room? Both were headed toward the library."

"They probably ransacked Theokritos' room and his office. We are fortunate that Charadric got there first." Getorius looked over at the tabletop. "Arcadia, where is the case…the two papyri?"

"Y…you said you'd trust me, Getorius."

"They aren't here? Arcadia, what have you done? You can't just destroy them."

"I've promised not to," she snapped and slipped down under the blanket. "I'm tired. May I get some sleep now?"

Getorius shrugged. The smell of their lovemaking was still in the bed, but was now augmented by an inexplicable scent of spices. *Why destroy that pleasant memory with an argument?* He lay down beside his wife and slipped an arm over her shoulder.

⁂

Just before the dawn watch, Charadric rapped at the door. Arcadia would have to leave until the order for Getorius' release came through.

She combed her hair before going outside. Behan's funeral was only a few hours away. Would anyone have occasion to open the coffin again before that?

"I'll let you know what happens at Behan's funeral," she told her husband, then hurried out before he could notice the bruises on her fingers.

Chapter twenty-four

At the second hour after sunrise on December twenty-fourth, Getorius answered a knock on the door of the room where he was confined. Heraclius stood outside, together with a gaunt man who looked seriously ill.

"Surgeon," the eunuch said in his high-pitched, womanish voice, "this is Brenos, from the monastery of Culdees. The abbot is ill from his winter journey. His right side is especially tender."

"Then he should see Antioches. I have no medical supplies here."

"Surgeon, you must examine him," Heraclius insisted, pushing his way into the room. "Brenos is to give the eulogy for his dead monk, Behan, this morning. Prescribe a potion for the abbot's fever."

"Very well. Abbot, sit down on the bed." *So this is the man who may be responsible for the forged will. Arcadia said she saw him with Heraclius last night. Brenos is obviously ill, but perhaps both men are here to see how much I know about the papyri.* "I can probably get you arctium for the fever," Getorius told him after feeling his face and forehead, "but what happened to your side?"

"Chafed from carrying a case with…that held my valuables for the journey."

"An incredible accomplishment. You came all that distance from Gaul just to bury your monk."

"As the Nazarene commanded us."

Nazarene. Both the letter of Peter and the will papyrus used that archaic title in referring to Christ. That's a definite connection with this man. "Abbot, you'll have to lift your robe so I can examine the wound." After Brenos complied, Getorius removed a dirty linen rag that was tied around the raw area. An inflamed area the size of his palm suppurated pus. "A very nasty wound, Abbot, the main source of your fever, but both your hot-cold and wet-dry humors are also seriously out of balance. I'm ordering an immediate warm bath, then the hospital sisters can apply a boiled symphytum root poultice to this wound—"

"Impossible," Brenos objected, standing and tugging down his robe. "I'm to be at Behan's funeral in two hours."

"I advise against it, Abbot, you need medical treatment immediately. Can't you write down something for the bishop to say?"

"No."

"Perhaps the abbot could return immediately after the funeral," Heraclius suggested.

"If it's that important."

"I assure you it is, Surgeon," Brenos insisted. "Behan, unfortunately, died before he could preach a p—"

"Preach penitence," Heraclius quickly interposed. "Come, Abbot, we must make you more presentable for the funeral."

Strange birds, to flock together, Getorius thought, as he watched the two turn the corner into the atrium corridor. How had this Brenos connected with the emperor's eunuch so quickly? The abbot had arrived in time for the Nativity, and Heraclius would be a powerful ally in a conspiracy. Arcadia had suspected as much, but Getorius couldn't talk to her about it yet. She would be away all morning attending the last rites for Behan.

❦

Because the Basilica Ursiana was being prepared for Nativity services, Behan's funeral had been scheduled to take place in the church of Saint John the Evangelist. Galla Placidia had commissioned the smaller basilica as a votive offering to fulfill a vow she had made to the Apostle sixteen years earlier, after returning to Ravenna from Constantinople for the funeral of her half-brother Honorius. During a storm on the Adriatic, between Aquileia and the capital, she had prayed to John for her survival and that of her small son and daughter. "...*Galla Placidia cum filio suo Placido Valentiniano et filia sua Iusta Grata Honoria Augusta liberationis periculorum maris votum solverunt*," read her dedicatory inscription. It definitively told everyone that her offering of the basilica to the Apostle had dissolved her debt to him for being rescued from the dangers of the sea. To make the votive more graphic, Placidia had ordered the miraculous rescue to be depicted among the mosaics in the apse.

Bishop Chrysologos, who had dedicated the basilica, was disturbed that it had since become the only island of Nicene orthodoxy in Ravenna's port quarter, an area that was known as a refuge for Arian heretics. Three blocks north was the sect's Church of the Resurrection, administered by a woman presbytera named Thecla.

※

Arcadia stood in the nave of the Basilica of John the Evangelist, behind the first scattered row of citizens who had come for Behan's funeral. None had known the reclusive monk, so most came out of curiosity to hear a eulogy by the Hibernian abbot from far-off Gaul.

Beyond Behan's oak coffin, sunlight filtered through alabaster windowpanes, illuminating the nave and apse mosaics with a soft glow. On the central arch, two scenes of Placidia's rescue at sea flanked a picture of Christ giving the Book of Revelation to John the Evangelist. Below her apse votive inscription, members of the imperial family—Arcadius, Eudocia with Theodosius II and their daughter Licinia Eudoxia, now the wife of Valentinian III—were shown in mosaics, on each side of Bishop Chrysologos, as he celebrated the dedicatory Mass in the company of an angel.

Arcadia felt good despite her ordeal in the icehouse. A deacon had arrived earlier that morning with the message that Getorius would be released after the midday watch, in a Nativity amnesty granted by the bishop.

She looked up again at the mosaics. Despite the troubled times, the elegant, formalized portraits were reassuring symbols of *Roma Aeterna*, Eternal Rome, a state and government, but also an attitude of mind that had endured for twelve hundred years. Neither disastrous defeats in war, civil anarchy, bloody dictatorships, mutinous legions, nor recurring barbarian invasions had destroyed the concept of *Romanitas,* a semi-mystical "Roman-ness" that survived and rose again, phoenix-like, after each calamity.

Constantine had hoped that the growing influence of Christians would act as a unifying force to institute a *Pax Christiana,* which would rival the Golden Age of Augustus as both a temporal and spiritual empire. It was ironic, Arcadia thought, that Christian fanatics like those who destroyed pagan temples and libraries and had murdered the Alexandrian woman philosopher Hypatia, went against Constantine's vision of peace. And now this Hibernian abbot was attempting to bring about the horrifying apocalyptic vision in John's book.

Arcadia stroked her bruised fingers, where fragile scabs were forming, and glanced at Bishop Chrysologos sitting on a cedar wood throne behind the altar table. The golden light coming in through seven apse windows silhouetted the bishop, his presbyters, and deacons in a heavenly radiance.

Arcadia turned with the others when the echo of the front doors opening sounded through the three aisles of the nave. Brenos limped in, the thump of his pilgrim's staff accompanying the slap of his worn sandals on the mosaic floor. She noticed that he had cleaned himself, and had his beard and tonsure trimmed. The abbot's stained robe had been replaced with a plain tunic of homespun wool.

When Brenos took his place next to the coffin, he looked flushed and exhausted.

Arcadia noted that he seemed startled, and that he glanced around nervously, after he saw the funeral pallium covering the oak box. The linen cloth was embroidered with a Christogram, X P, set in the center of a palm wreath and flanked by the Greek letters A Ω—alpha and omega. Why did the common funerary symbols upset him? Perhaps Hibernians did not know the Greek language.

Brenos scrutinized the people in front of him for a moment, as if expecting to recognize someone, then he held up his pilgrim's staff.

"Brothers," he announced in a hoarse voice, ignoring any women in the gathering, "I show you thirty-two notches, one for each of the days I spent traveling here from Gaul to bury a holy one. My brother, Behan, was sent among you in Ravenna to preach a prophecy, but was called by the Nazarene before he could do so."

A prophecy? Arcadia thought, excited now. *And he uses the archaic term, "Nazarene."*

"A prophecy," the abbot continued, "that will be fulfilled before the cock crows again."

By morning! Rabbi Zadok was right. Is there a duplicate will, or does the abbot expect his accomplices to find the original by then? Arcadia half-expected Brenos to produce another golden case from under his robe and pull out a papyrus for all to see, but he went on.

"What is this prophecy? I tell you, brothers, that the vineyard of the Nazarene has gone unpruned for too long. Unruly shoots choke out the fruits. Weeds grow among the good seed that must be harvested and burned. Agents of Satan destroy the good seed. A harvest is at hand for the winepress of God, which John saw in his vision, and yet the faithful mill about like sheep unsure of their shepherd."

The man isn't making much sense, Arcadia thought. *His metaphors are from the Testaments, but garbled…grapes and weeds with sheep. The abbot supposedly came here to eulogize Behan, yet has barely mentioned his monk.*

Arcadia noticed Bishop Chrysologos shift on his throne and whisper to Tranquillus, his presbyter at the Basilica of the Holy Cross. She thought the bishop was probably as mystified as she was at the abbot's erratic diatribe.

Even though the basilica was cold, Brenos wiped perspiration from his face with a sleeve before continuing. "Rav…Ravenna, is the dwelling p…place of the Harlot revealed to John in his vis…vision."

He was stuttering now, in a spray of spit droplets that were backlit by the apse windows. "I...I saw this in a vision of my own. Riches, scarlet and purple cloth. Gold, pearls...a golden cup...idols drunk on the wine of fornication.

"Only the holy ones, those who have renounced these things... we disciples of Ciallanus...will be saved after the Nazarene comes to judge the world. The Slaughtered will become the Slaughterer. We monks, 'holy fools' to some, will rule like kings over the earth. Who *then* will be the fool?"

Arcadia was stunned at the implication of the abbot's words. *The man is advocating a theocratic government run by his order, yet Christ insisted that his Kingdom was not of this world. And even Theodosius hadn't dared to advance such a concept.* This Behan was threatening to do no less than the Egyptian Christian fanatics, but this time his wrath would be directed against entire Judean communities.

Arcadia saw Chrysologos tug at Tranquillus' sleeve and nod toward the abbot. The presbyter came down the apse stairs to stop him, but Brenos shrugged off his hold. "The Nativity vigil!" he shouted. "That is when the Gallican League mandate will be revealed! The fulfillment of my prophecy."

Tranquillus whispered to Brenos and gestured toward the people. Arcadia turned to see some of them hurrying back to the entrance, either confused or frightened at the man's incoherent words. What was this Gallican League he had mentioned?

When Arcadia looked around again she was surprised to see Publius Maximin peering out of a door that led to the Diaconicon, a storage and vesting room to the left of the altar.

Maximin? Why would the senator bother coming to Behan's funeral? And what is he doing in an area reserved for the clergy?

After Maximin slipped out of the room and made his way along the side aisle to the front entrance, Arcadia looked back at the apse. Tranquillus was guiding the abbot around the coffin; Brenos evidently had agreed to end his eulogy and proceed with the interment.

❦

At the burial ground alongside the basilica, Arcadia watched in relief as the first clods of earth were thrown onto the oak lid of Behan's coffin. The Greek word *koimeterioi* came to mind. Her tutor in that language had said Christian Greeks called their burial places "dormitories," where the elect would sleep until the vision of John was fulfilled, and Death and Hades gave up the dead who had been in their keeping. Death would be no more. The Risen Saints would enter the New Jerusalem in a Glorified Body, where God would live with them, and wipe away every tear from their eyes.

Behan, Arcadia mused, would awaken and stagger in with a golden, but frigid, surprise in his belly.

❧

Brenos was taking off the funerary stole he had borrowed when he found the folded note under his volume of penitentials. It said that Smyrna would have him picked up at Galla Placidia's mausoleum, and he would be taken to the villa again.

The time, during the second night hour, was later than he would have liked. It would be totally dark then, and the Nativity vigil readings would take place only five hours later. Yet, on reflection, Brenos thought the lateness might be reassuring. Smyrna had undoubtedly located the papyri and wanted to turn them over to him. As a co-celebrant of the Mass, he could easily find an opportunity beforehand to conceal the documents in the proper section of the codex. Then the last testament of Christ would be revealed by an abbot of the Hibernian Order, to which it had been entrusted!

Chapter twenty-five

The sunny day had clouded up by evening, as a winter storm came in from the southwest. After flashes of lightning were seen and the rumble of thunder heard, most citizens stayed indoors to avoid being affected by the unseasonable omens.

A thick, wet snow was falling by the time Brenos stood waiting in the shelter of the narthex arches and heard the clomping of a horse's hooves. He watched the black carriage turn into the Vicus Galla Placidia, shook off the white flakes accumulating on his cloak, and eyed the snowflakes swirling down from the sky. He did not like snow; there was enough of it in Gallic winters. Fortunately, these flakes were melting as soon as they touched the paving stones.

The abbot had gotten there a half-hour early, about the time his stomach began to bother him. The Vigil of the Nativity was a day of fasting, yet he had taken a little fish before leaving the bishop's residence. It was an oily species from the sea, not the delicate Icauna trout he was used to eating. He suspected that it was spoiled as well, the bad taste hidden under a cumin sauce.

As the carriage stopped a short distance away—perhaps the mute had not seen him—the storm bred a flash of lightning that whitened the black vehicle with a chalky wash. The effect lasted only an instant before the white-spotted darkness closed in again. Brenos thought the flash and distant rumble of thunder were good omens, indicating that even the elements were combining to announce the dramatic end of an age. He ran out and climbed onto the seat next to the driver, this time silently cursing Mutus for not being able to tell him more about his master. Smyrna probably had not been among the assembly at the funeral that morning—the people had all looked like freemen laborers or slaves. And yet Smyrna had been close by, able to hide the note during the service. Was he possibly a churchman?

Brenos eased himself back against the leather seats. Despite the fiery wound in his side, the pain in his stomach, and a dull ache in his head, he felt relatively calm. He expected that at the villa Smyrna would give him the papyri. In a few hours the Gallican League would be recognized as the legal executors of the Nazarene's will.

The eulogy had gone well that morning until an imbecile presbyter had forced a stop. Even so, he had made his point. There had been only a few people at the funeral, yet word would get out quickly that the Hibernian abbot had preached about a prophecy that would be fulfilled at the Nativity vigil service. The bishop's cathedral would be packed with citizens attending the night Mass.

Mutus repeated the route he had taken before, flinching at the intermittent lightning flashes, and struggling to control the frightened mare.

Wet snow was coming down heavily when the carriage was waved through the gatehouse. The same guard as the day before appeared in the courtyard and escorted the abbot to the reception room. As the moments passed, the pain in Brenos's head and abdomen increased. He became aware of the dung smell again, which added to his rising sense of nausea.

Nervous, staring at the six masks on the wall, Brenos felt a hatred for Smyrna slowly surface. Flickering shadows caused by the lamp flame gave the painted faces an animation that resembled a kind of leer, as if they were mocking him. Was Smyrna doing the same from behind the curtain, humiliating an abbot by keeping him waiting as if he were a penitent novice seeking absolution?

What if Smyrna did not have the documents after all? The Alpha-Omega figure had insisted that he did not, yet could the bizarre apparition be believed?

The emperor's mother knew about them, and Smyrna had boasted of his contacts in the palace. Perhaps Behan had been murdered before he could announce the prophecy, so that Smyrna and his Harlot Queen could use the will for their own purposes. Were they planning to betray the Gallicans? Without proof of the miraculous discovery of Peter's letter and the will, the League members in the six other cities would be laughed out of the churches when they predicted the discovery.

Brenos doubled over, rocking to relieve the cramps in his stomach and feeling a sense of rising panic at the realization that his life was in danger if Smyrna planned to betray him.

The curtain moved. Brenos looked up. Smyrna, dressed in the Robe of Death, but holding only the apocalyptic Omega symbol of the End, appeared at the same instant as a flash of lightning. It was hard for Brenos to believe that the dramatic coincidence had not been staged, but almost as quickly as the flash, the abbot's suspicion was replaced by anticipation.

"You have found the Nazarene's will? Let me have it. There is little time left."

Instead of showing the papyrus, Smyrna pointed an empty skeletal hand at Brenos. "Who thinks to deceive me, Abbot, deceives himself."

"Wh…what do you mean? Give me the testament, you fool."

A muffled sneer sounded from behind the mask. "A drawing of your league's pet cockerel was in a wall cabinet above the librarian's work table. Is that where *you* found the documents, Abbot?"

"Cockerel?" Brenos protested. "What cockerel? The eunuch and I searched the librarian's office and found nothing. The cabinet was already open."

"I ask you again, Abbot," the voice demanded. "What do you intend to do with the will that you have not told me?"

"Nothing. *Nothing!*" Brenos screamed in frustration. "I don't have it!"

Smyrna pulled a vellum sheet from his sleeve and held it up. "At least you were truthful in saying Theokritos declared the will to be genuine. I found his results."

"Good, you brought them," Brenos croaked. "They will be useful in proving authenticity." He reached for the sheet, but Smyrna pulled back, and then held one end in the lamp's flame. "No! What are you doing?" Brenos screamed. "You're destroying the proof! It…it is you who betrays me…betrays the Gallicans." The abbot surged forward at the man, but Smyrna flung a last scrap of flaming vellum at him.

Brenos paused to beat at the sparks on his robe, then glared at Smyrna's mask. Its feminine features seemed to metamorphose into those of the caulker's daughter who had humiliated him long ago. He rubbed his eyes. What kind of sorcery were the Harlot and Alpha-Omega practicing on him? John wrote to the city of Smyrna that Satan would put some to the test. Was the Harlot testing him, like the Hibernian girl? Would this fornicator with kings mock him, just as the caulker's slut had? No. This time *he* would be victorious, just as John had promised to the faithful.

"*Brandub*…Black Raven!" Brenos cursed, then leaped at Smyrna to tear off his mask.

When the apparition deftly stepped aside, the momentum of the abbot's thrust carried him through the curtain and into a hallway. His wet sandals slipped on the tiles and he sprawled to the floor with an involuntary scream at the pain in his side. Ahead, he saw stairway leading to a second level. *Smyrna has hidden the papyri upstairs.* Brenos crawled to the steps and clambered halfway up on his knees, but when he tried to stand, tripped on the hem his robe. Smyrna, close behind, grasped at his foot. Brenos wrenched free, leaving a sandal in his enemy's hand, and clawed his way to the top stair.

Orange light spilled from a doorway at the end of a hall. Brenos stood and limped to the room. Breathing hard, he leaned against the doorframe and looked around. Several oil lamps with wick spouts in the shape of cockerel heads illuminated the chamber. By the flickering light, he gradually made out cases and shelves that displayed every conceivable type of rooster figure. Life-sized sculptures of the fowl stood in rows on the shelves. Some were molded in unglazed terracotta, others brightly painted or finished in the blue-green patina of faience work. Almost as many were fashioned of bronze or silver. Several glittered with the luster of gold. Among the statuary lay ceramic and silver platters, also decorated with rooster motifs.

Brenos picked up one of the golden figures. *What sorcerer made these images to mock my Gallican symbol?* he thought, then heard the sound of trickling water coming from a device in one corner of the room. Curious, he walked closer. A tall column inscribed with lines and numerals from I to XII was fastened above a circular tank. The brass statue of a rooster, with a pointer in its beak, indicated one of the numbers.

As the abbot circled the device, trying to understand its use, the sound of running water increased and a clicking noise came from inside the tank. The rooster slowly turned toward the column, which began to rotate. It stopped when the brass bird's pointer indicated the numeral III.

Fascinated, Brenos waited for something further to happen, aware that the smell of chicken dung seemed stronger. He heard the clucking of poultry outside the shuttered window. Half mad with pain and frustration, he flipped the retaining hooks off the shutters and pushed them open. When he leaned out to look around, a spattering of rain wet his face and a streak of lightning whitened the muddy yard below. In the instant of brightness he was able to make out an enclosed arena that reminded him of a cock-fighting area the guards at Autessiodurum used for their sport. Smyrna—someone—trained fighting birds here. Brenos looked around, searching for the cocks, and noticed a stone shed across the yard. They were probably inside, he thought, huddled together against the storm and cackling aimlessly from fright. Yes, he could hear them.

Holding the golden rooster, Brenos wiped rain from his eyes with one hand and stared at the stone building. Suddenly, the white light flooding his mind also seemed to illuminate the place where he would find the Nazarene's last will.

Of course! That rooster coop is where the papyri are hidden! It makes sense.. its guardians are the cockerels at the Villa of the Red Rooster. They will give me the Nazarene's will. Are they not the birds the Gallicans chose for their symbol? In gratitude, they will reject this Smyrna, this Satan, and restore the will to its proper owner, so the prophecy can be fulfilled. I…I must get down to that shed.

Brenos turned away from the window. He was face to face with Smyrna.

"You daemon, I will see what human form you have!" The abbot lunged forward to tear away the mask, but the apparition pushed hard at his chest. Brenos lost his balance. Still clutching the golden figurine, he felt himself somersault backward through the wet air and slam down on his back into the muck of the yard, with an impact that left him gasping for breath.

Dazed, he lay still a moment, struggling to regain his breath by sucking wet air into his lungs. When Brenos looked up, blinking at a cold rain that washed his face clean, he saw Smyrna gazing down at him from the window. He had taken off the mask and was holding it in one hand. The man's features were blurred, but his mocking laugh sounded like the cackle of a hen.

Brenos spat mud out of his mouth and struggled to get up. He could not move his legs. In panic now, he recalled seeing the same paralysis in a worker who had fallen off a scaffold at Autessiodurum. The man had never walked again.

Brenos of Slana, Abbot of Culdees, closed his eyes and licked moisture from his lips. It was gritty and tasted of chicken dung. When he looked up again, the heads of several roosters blocked out his view of Smyrna. The birds were eyeing him with cold stares that seemed more sinister than curious.

Then the seventh angel poured his bowl upon the air; and out of the sanctuary came a loud voice…which said, 'It is over!' And there followed flashes of lightning, loud voices and peals of thunder. And God made Babylon drain the cup which was filled with the fierce wine of his vengeance.

The nearest rooster, bolder than his mates, pecked at one of the shiny orbs below it, in a cautious probe for danger. Brenos's scream of terror was drowned out by a cacophony of savage clucking, as the vision of Alpha and Omega disappeared from his consciousness in a final burst of pain, and a dazzling white light.

Chapter twenty-six

Getorius had been released shortly after the first evening watch began. As well as authorizing his release, Bishop Chrysologos had granted him a dispensation from fasting, so around the fourth hour after sunset he was eating a late supper, while Arcadia watched.

"If this abbot is up to something, we should get over to the Ursiana well before the service," he told her, pushing aside his plate.

"In case he has a duplicate will?"

"Right. But how he intends to make it public is—"

"Master," Childibert interrupted as he pushed aside the curtain and looked into the dining room. "Master, the young Judean has come to see you."

"Nathaniel? Bring him in."

"That's strange," Arcadia commented, "I thought Nathaniel told us he would be celebrating a week-long Hebrew festival."

"Welcome," Getorius said after Nathaniel came through the curtain. "Take off your wet cape. Have you eaten supper?"

"Yes."

"Then join me in drinking a cup of wine. I'm celebrating my freedom."

"That is not why I came…" Nathanial hesitated, then said, "My thanks, but I…I cannot accept the wine."

"Your dietary laws," Arcadia recalled.

"Yes. Although it is still our Festival of Lights, not all of us are celebrating, but I congratulate you on your freedom, Surgeon."

"What does your festival celebrate?"

"*Hanukkah* recalls one of our more successful attempts to shake off an oppressor at the time of Antiochus Epiphanes."

Getorius held up his cup. "Then, Nathaniel, I'll drink *for* you to a quick end of this forged papyrus business. We're going to confront that Hibernian abbot tonight at the cathedral. Ask him what he knows about the papyri."

"That is why I came." Nathaniel sat at the table and asked, "Have you heard more about the false will? We are only hours from its possible release."

"I can assure you, Nathaniel, that the matter is at rest," Arcadia told him.

"How is that? Do you have it here?"

"No. Not…not exactly," she said.

Nathaniel shifted uneasily in his chair. "I must warn you. In the weeks since you showed us the documents we have sent word for Judeans in city garrisons to be alert tonight, also to those in army units along the Padus River. If this abomination comes to pass, no Judean soldier will be caught with his sword sheathed, or his shield down."

"Your people have nothing to fear," Arcadia assured him, "but, in any case, they would be protected by the law."

Nathaniel shook his head. "Rabbi Zadok doubts that. Last year the new Code of Theodosius at Constantinople—which was ratified here by Valentinian—has statutes that prohibit Hebrews from holding public office, or building new synagogues. You can see that the release of this will, genuine or not, would ultimately result in that even the two emperors dared not include in the law."

"Genocide?" Arcadia exclaimed. "But that's terrible. We…we never heard."

"You Christians weren't affected. The new statutes simplify additions to the laws since Constantine compiled the original codes a century ago. Good overall, I suppose, if you're not Judean."

"I would think…what is it this time?" Getorius asked, seeing Childibert by the curtain again.

"Master, the Senator is here to see you."

"Publius Maximin?"

"Yes, Master."

"Why would he come at such a late hour?" Arcadia wondered aloud. She went with Childibert through the adjacent reception room and peered around a corner of the curtain, into the atrium. Maximin seemed upset, pacing the floor and slapping a mud-stained leather tube against his thigh. "Thank you, Childibert. I'll bring the senator in."

When Arcadia escorted Maximin into the dining room, Getorius extended a hand. "Senator, we're honored. This is Nathaniel, a pupil of Rabbi ben Zadok in Classis."

Maximin nodded to the man, but turned to Getorius. "The reason I am here is not a pleasant one. May we go into your study? I have an urgent matter to discuss."

"Of course…but…Nathaniel?"

"The Judean may come. This also concerns his people."

Puzzled, Getorius led the way around to the room. Maximin refused the wine Arcadia offered him, but dropped heavily into a chair, cradling the leather tube close to his body as if he expected someone to snatch it away.

"This is not a social call," Maximin began. "I…I went from the port to my country villa a short while ago. Prisca was with me. We planned on going to the vigil service from there, but my steward, Andros, told me guards had found that abbot who came from Autessiodurum dead in my rooster yard."

"Brenos at your villa? Dead?" Getorius repeated, shaken at the news. "How… how can that be, Senator?"

"I was not there, Surgeon," Maximin responded curtly. "I have no idea how he got into my house."

"Did Andros say what happened?" Arcadia asked.

"An accident, evidently. The man fell out of my study window and broke his neck."

"How did he get in past your guards?" she persisted. "Why was he there in the first place?"

The wicker chair creaked as Maximin leaned back and fondled the case. "One of my rooster figurines—you saw them, Arcadia—one of the golden ones was found clutched in his hand."

"You're saying the abbot is a thief?"

"My dear, there is undoubtedly some evil in all of us," Maximin hedged, "yet what he was doing in that room is beyond my comprehension. I've never even met the man."

Arcadia felt that was probably untrue. She had seen him look out of the vesting room during the abbot's erratic eulogy at Behan's funeral, so he may have met with Brenos afterward. She recalled the many guards she had seen at the farm. Ulysses himself, much less the abbot, could not have entered unobserved. "Senator, did you question Jason and Phoebe?"

"That's another strange thing. Their quarters are next to my main reception room. Everything of value has been moved out."

"You're saying Jason and Phoebe are gone?"

"So it would seem, Arcadia. And after all I've done for those two—"

"Senator," Nathaniel broke in, "what is it you have that involves Judeans?"

"This." Maximin held up the mud-encrusted tube. "I found the case strapped to the abbot's body. There was a horrible wound on his side where the leather had chafed his skin raw."

"Yes, he came to me about it," Getorius recalled, "but...what's inside the case?"

"In light of the events that have happened since that monk was found dead, in November, I thought you should see it." Maximin glanced at Nathaniel. "Whether you tell the Judean community is your affair. I would not." He pulled white vellum sheets from the cylinder, unrolled the first and held it up to show the title and a red cockerel drawn above it in red ink.

"The Gallican League," Arcadia read aloud. "That's the name the abbot mentioned at Behan's funeral. What is it, Senator?"

Maximin cleared his throat. "The document seems to be some kind of declaration by the organization."

Getorius joined his wife in reading. "They call themselves 'The Vigilant Ones.' That helps explain the cockerel drawings we found. I said they were symbols of vigilance."

"Cockerels?" Maximian repeated as a question. "You have seen this charter before?"

"No, just images of the bird."

"The symbol is not important now," Nathaniel said, "but you may have found the key to this mystery. Quick, continue reading. This abbot undoubtedly has accomplices who are not dead."

The others listened in silence as Getorius repeated aloud the rationalization of the Gallicans for unleashing their apocalyptic plan.

Arcadia was the first to comment. "War, famine, murders… unimaginable horrors. Nathaniel, Rabbi Zadok predicted that these would result if the papyrus was released."

"And I see now that they would not only affect my people, but also any Christians who opposed these fanatics in their attempt to impose a theocracy."

"Fanatics?" Maximin scoffed. "These are traitors to Rome, with that Hibernian abbot as their leader."

"This may not be over yet," Getorius warned. "That charter lists accomplices in the empire's major cities. Let me…yes…the code name of the League's contact here in Ravenna is Smyrna."

"So when Brenos contacted this Smyrna," Arcadia reasoned, "he found out that the man didn't have the papyrus, that it had accidentally been discovered." She pointed to a section of the text. "This Clause Four shows Zadok was correct. The Nativity Vigil Mass tonight was the occasion set to make the will public and fulfill the prophecy."

"You keep talking about a papyrus, and now a will," Maximin said. "The charter only speaks of a scroll, and you've mentioned a papyrus twice now. Was it some kind of testament?"

Arcadia glanced at her husband.

"Theokritos called it the Secundus Papyrus, Senator," Getorius told him.

"Ah. There was palace gossip about the librarian finding an ancient document. He believed it to be authentic."

"Authentic? That's impossible," Getorius told him, "yet if Theokritos reported that it was to Galla Placidia, she may have thought it true. We must get this Gallican charter to her immediately. It confirms the conspiracy she suspected, if not all of the actual persons involved."

"It is still of concern," Nathaniel said. "The librarian was mistaken in his conclusion—or chose not to tell the truth. Even though the abbot is dead, this Smyrna could yet reveal the false will."

"Nathaniel"—Arcadia touched his sleeve and looked into his eyes—"I think not. Remember when Rabbi Zadok predicted that if this were not of God it would fail? It's too evil to be His work."

Nathaniel shook his head, unconvinced. "I need proof that the document will not be revealed."

Getorius recalled his wife's cryptic assurances of the night before. She still hadn't explained how, just by looking at winter stars, her boots had become soaked and her fingers bruised. What had she done to help God?

"Arcadia, if Placidia thinks the will is authentic," Getorius said, "she'll be frantic to find it. If she even suspects we're involved in disposing of the papyrus, there'll be more than house arrest in both our futures. Can we afford to wait and find out if this is from God or not?"

"Until the General Resurrection, husband."

"Resurrection?" *My God! After Arcadia went out, did she somehow slip the golden case into Behan's coffin? Hid it under his robe?* Getorius blanched at a third possibility. "Y…you didn't—"

"Senator," she interrupted quickly, looking past her husband, "will you see to it that Placidia gets this Gallican charter?"

"Of course." Maximin snickered softly. "Those other cities. When the prophecy about the discovery of Christ's will is found to be baseless, those who announced it will be seen as fools."

Christ's will? Arcadia glanced back at Getorius. *Maximin said he was unaware of the nature of the papyrus, and Nathaniel only mentioned a will in a general way. Since its details are not specifically mentioned in the charter, how could the senator know what was to be revealed?*

"Over-ambitiousness," Maximin continued, sneering. "That was the flaw in this abbot's plan. I doubt he could have gotten accomplices to act in all the cities he named. Hibernian monasticism is in its infancy on the Continent."

"Looking back, Senator, what do you think were the roles of Sigisvult and Renatus in all this?" Arcadia probed, to ascertain how much Maximin knew. "Was Theokritos one of the Gallicans?"

"It…it's possible, I suppose."

Getorius picked up his wife's speculation. "Theokritos could have been going through the motions of testing the papyri, even though he planned to declare them both authentic all along."

"His tests were pretty convincing to me," Arcadia said, "but I can't believe Sigisvult was involved. It was his workmaster who was found dead in the harbor."

"It's clear now that was no accident," Getorius added. "After the chance discovery of the papyri, it was necessary for this Smyrna to eliminate the witnesses."

"Yet the impact of this false will would be so great," Nathaniel added, "that Behan needed to recruit only a few accomplices."

"But how, in such a short time?" Arcadia asked.

"There are those who would gladly join him, to use the false will for their own purposes."

"The monk was in the library many times," Getorius recalled. "That also gave him access to palace staff."

"Then Theokritos was obviously involved," Maximin said. "He and the monk conspired together in the library."

"Senator, would the librarian sacrifice Feletheus?" When Maximin shrugged without answering, Getorius went on, "If Theokritos knew where the papyri were hidden he would have had to do so, or give himself away. That bow trap was meant to be triggered by a lone intruder. Miniscius—the workmaster—would be the first person on the site in the morning. He would have found the body and disposed of it. Remember, it was only on a whim of Placidia's that we were in the mausoleum that night and made the discovery. Now I'm concerned about whom else Behan might have recruited in the palace."

"Heraclius?" Arcadia suggested. "I told you I saw him with Brenos in the garden last night."

"Last night?" Maximin raised an eyebrow. "What were they doing?"

"Just walking."

"Walking to where?"

Getorius rescued his wife with a question, "Why would Renatus have been killed if he was part of the conspiracy?"

"I've been puzzled by that, too," Nathaniel admitted, "yet, as archdeacon he controlled a substantial amount of money. The Gallicans needed funds. He might not have known the exact details of the plan, so when he unexpectedly became one of the witnesses, this Smyrna may have been afraid the man would change his mind, or worse, expose the conspiracy."

"Then he didn't intentionally poison Sigisvult," Getorius realized. "Someone must have been able to put the atropa in the wine. That rooster you found on the broken glass, Arcadia, was just a coincidence...a Christian symbol."

"Renatus was also deceived."

"Right. And it's obvious now that the abbot was supposed to arrive much earlier. The report of Behan's death must have been the signal for Brenos to come to Ravenna."

"Then Behan was murdered, like I thought!"

"Except, Arcadia, that wouldn't have served the abbot very well. He needed Behan here to introduce his contacts."

"But the courier who went to Autessiodurum must have brought Brenos a message from Smyrna that everything was ready," Arcadia speculated. "He made Behan's death the excuse for going to Gaul in the winter."

"Your murder theory does begin to make sense," Getorius admitted. "The abbot may have been the only one to know the will was a forgery, yet even if he didn't know who Smyrna was, he had to have been in touch with him, probably through Behan. Smyrna wanted the most important witness to the conspiracy eliminated."

"Brenos arrived late," Arcadia continued, "then found—to his horror—that Behan had drowned before he could announce the prophecy. Even worse, that the two papyri had been discovered."

"The abbot came to Ravenna a sick man, then had, what, three days to contact Smyrna and locate the will before the Nativity vigil? That accounts for the irrational sermon you heard at the funeral, Arcadia. The man was frantic to find the papyrus."

"Oh Lord, you have destroyed the wicked," Nathaniel murmured, paraphrasing a psalm.

"I hesitate to say this," Maximin ventured, "but Aetius could be involved. He might even be Smyrna, the abbot's accomplice."

"The last thing the commander needs, Senator, is civil unrest."

"Surgeon, Aetius could use the riots as an excuse for demanding the powers of a dictator. Later on, like Sulla, or Julius Caesar—more recently Constantine—he might find it difficult to give up supreme command."

"With respect, Senator," Getorius went on, "what is frightening is that these Gallicans were willing to destroy communities to institute a rule where people would be forced to believe as they did. Admittedly, Rome hasn't been much of a republic for centuries, but we're talking about a group willing to sacrifice our laws—a civilization built up over a thousand years—to their own warped religious ends."

Maximin tapped the charter against his knee, but did not comment.

"We discovered a rule book in Behan's hut that suggested these Hibernians are disciples of a leader named Ciallanus," Arcadia recalled. "Is he part of this?"

"I doubt it, or he would have come here himself," Getorius replied. "Brenos must have led a few like-minded monks within his order, who then found laymen to recruit. It was risky, yet even Ciallanus would have had to accept the will's provisions."

"When religious fanaticism is considered a virtue, it becomes a dangerous one," Nathaniel observed.

Maximin abruptly stood up and slid the Gallican charter sheets back into their case. "We may never know all those involved. I'll take this to the Empress Mother. It should convince her that Theokritos was mistaken."

"She'll want a magistrate to look into Brenos' death," Getorius said.

Maximin looked at him, startled. "Why would she? My guards, who found the abbot's body, will swear he suffered an unfortunate accident in the commission of a crime." The senator paused when he reached the door and stabbed at the air with the muddy case. "Brenos was not authorized to be there and laws on trespass and theft are quite clear. You needn't show me out, Surgeon. I wish you a joyous celebration of the Savior's birth, my dear. And of the end of your festival, Judean."

After Maximin was gone, Arcadia commented, "As I've said, he's smooth as that marble table top. I don't want to believe the senator is involved, but he walked out of here wanting us to think that a visiting abbot from Gaul—a complete stranger to him—somehow sneaked into his well-guarded villa just to steal a statue of a chicken! Of his two missing actors, Jason, at least, had to have a part in this."

"Who were Jason and the woman he mentioned?" Getorius asked.

"Phoebe. She performed a pantomime with him after supper. My God!" Arcadia gasped, "Jason was painting a mask labeled Smyrna when I saw him. After luring Brenos to the villa, and with Maximin away, *he* could have impersonated the man—thrown the abbot off guard."

"Actors mimic conspiracies, they don't initiate them," Getorius objected. "If Maximin is involved he may have had doubts of the plot's success by early December, when no one had yet come from Autessiodurum. But even so, who's going to file charges against the most powerful man in Ravenna? Besides, as he pointed out, trespass and theft laws favor the victim."

"But you thought he was responsible for your being blamed for the dissection."

"Arcadia, he's undoubtedly much more conniving than I gave

him credit for. Under confinement, I would have been eliminated at the will's revelation. After that, no one would care."

"Yet, if something went wrong, you'd still be alive. Maximin has said he wanted you to help him get Patrician rank." Arcadia shuddered. "Placidia was to be killed."

"So were you, *cara,*" Getorius reminded her softly. "We narrowly escaped anarchy."

"What will other accomplices do when there's no revelation?"

"The plot is exposed," Nathaniel said to Arcadia, "but that the senator exposed it is a puzzle. Your theory, Getorius, may be correct. There's no truth in his story of this abbot's death, other than the man was at the senator's villa, for some reason."

"With the Gallican League plan unraveling because the documents had been discovered, Maximin lost his nerve and decided to abort the conspiracy."

"And tried to blame both Theokritos and Aetius."

"Arcadia, Maximin certainly had enough time to look for the papyri inside the palace," Getorius said. "That 'gossip' among palace staff is nonsense…he *saw* Theokritos' results. Christ! The senator had Behan strangled and planned to seize power with the abbot. When the plot looked like it would fail, he had Brenos killed."

"The most important thing is that this is ended." Arcadia turned to Nathaniel. "And you needn't worry about the forgeries, they'll not see the light of day. Tell Rabbi Zadok to inform your men that there's no danger to them."

The words were still a woman's riddle, but Nathaniel nodded and stood up to go back to the Judean quarter.

After he left, Arcadia said, "I…I feel so drained by what we just heard, but I suppose we'd better get ready to attend the vigil service."

"I understand, *cara*." Getorius pulled his wife into an embrace and kissed away the glistening tears at the corner of her eyes. "Have Silvia help you. It isn't too cold out, but wear a woolen tunic and fairly heavy cape."

As Getorius put on wool hose and a clean tunic, he decided to leave things as they were and not question his wife any further about what she had done with the golden case and the two papyri. What he had guessed about her actions was an ironic end to the entire affair. However incomplete the details might be, the evening's events had exposed the Gallican conspiracy. Maximin was undoubtedly involved with Smyrna as the abbot's contact, might even be the conspirator himself, yet there was no way to prove it. As he pointed out, his guards would testify that the abbot must have accidentally fallen in the act of manifest theft, while trespassing on a senatorial estate. They would cite the golden rooster clutched in his hand. *It's a ridiculous charge, but the law is on the senator's side. And after Bishop Chrysologos has read the Gallican charter, he'll also condemn the fanatical abbot who wanted to implement his twisted interpretation of John's apocalyptic vision. Chrysologos won't inquire too closely into Brenos' death and will probably leave out the details in his report to Bishop Germanus at Autessiodurum.*

Chapter twenty-seven

When Getorius and Arcadia left their villa to walk to the Basilica Ursiana for the Nativity service, the snowy drizzle had stopped. A southwest breeze ruffled the surface of the remaining street puddles, and the night air smelled of smoke from bonfires burning throughout Ravenna to celebrate the birth of the man who had called himself the Light of the World.

The low, scudding clouds and rippling sheets of water were tinted a pale orange hue by the celebration flames. In the countryside, beyond the city walls, Getorius imagined that a few pagan worshippers tended their own blazes in secret, to lure back the sun god Helios—or Belenos as the Celts called him, or Tiwaz, the Germani—from his southward wandering.

Brisios saw himself as a self-declared guard and walked ahead of his master and mistress on the way to the cathedral. Childibert and Agrica followed a few steps behind, with Silvia and young Primus lagging further back. Most citizens went on foot, but a few oldsters were being carried in litter chairs. Maximin's black carriage clattered past on the Via Honorius, along with a few other rigs that belonged to senators and palace officials. Bishop Chrysologos had urged that people walk to the basilica, in imitation of the shepherds who had journeyed to see the newborn child in Bethlehem, four hundred and thirty-nine years earlier.

At the basilica, Arcadia spotted Publius Maximin's carriage on the torch-lit front plaza, with a shadowy form hunched on the seat.

"It's too dark to recognize the driver," she said, "but it's probably that mute."

"I'd like to be sure that the senator actually did show the Gallican charter to Galla Placidia. Let's go inside. Perhaps we can ask him."

The vast interior of the Ursiana was dimly lit. The altar was illuminated solely with four tall candles on stands, although many more unlighted lamps and candles were clustered nearby. The five-aisled cathedral had been dedicated to the Resurrection of Christ, as had, coincidentally, Ravenna's older Arian church. To distinguish between the two, Nicene Christians referred to their church by the name of its late founder, Archbishop Ursicinus.

Inside the nave, men and women mingled freely and chatted with each other, unlike churches in the east, where the congregation was separated by an iron railing—men on the right and women on the left. Yet even here not everyone was treated with the equality the Apostle Paul had envisioned: members of the imperial retinue stood apart, with chairs being available only for that family. A pregnant Eudoxia was already seated, with a nursemaid standing next to the Augusta, rocking her first baby. Valentinian was in whispered conversation with his steward Heraclius. The emperor's bodyguards, Optila and Thraustila, lurked nearby in the shadows of the nave arcade.

Galla Placidia, dressed in the magnificent tunic she had worn at her republican dinner, but with a silk veil replacing the Visigoth crown, knelt in prayer on the bottom step of the altar platform.

To one side, away from everyone, Flavius Aetius talked with a blonde woman, whom Getorius assumed was Pelagia, his Germanic wife.

Toga-clad senators and palace officials also conversed in separate groups, but Maximin was not among them.

"The only one I recognize is Protasius," Getorius said to Arcadia, "that records clerk we dealt with before going to Classis."

"Where?"

"Over to the right. The man is talking to someone who looks like he might be his assistant."

"He's not a clerk," Senator Maximin remarked, appearing from behind a marble column. He grasped Arcadia's shoulders in a light embrace. "*Pax Christi*, my dear. Surgeon, I must thank you. Mother is here, sitting up front in that wheeled chair you suggested she have made. You've given her new hope."

"I'm pleased, Senator."

"That man you see with Protasius is Leudovald. He's an interrogator in the judicial magistrate's office. He would have questioned you if the…ah…if what you had been accused of had been a civil concern, not the bishop's."

"Senator, what was Placidia's response to the Gallican charter?" Getorius asked.

"The Empress Mother took the abbot's case."

"And?"

"I'm not privy to what she does… Oh, Senator Justin just came in. I must talk to him about his visit to Constantinople."

After Maximin hurried away, Getorius turned to his wife. "As you said, Arcadia, the man is smooth. He stayed long enough to tell us that the Gothic Queen has the charter, but nothing about her reaction or intention."

"She wanted the papyrus burned. She might—" Arcadia stopped when she saw a procession of churchmen filing out from the vesting room. "There's Bishop Chrysologos. He's ready to start the service."

Ravenna's seven senior deacons, holding lighted candles, preceded the bishop. Five presbyters followed Tranquillus, who walked ahead holding aloft a codex of Jerome's Latin Testaments.

The clergymen began to sing an antiphonal psalm, whose words were gradually picked up by some members of the congregation.

"The Lord is my light and my salvation;
   whom should I fear?

The Lord is the refuge of my life;
of whom should I go in dread?
When evildoers close in on me to devour me,
it is my enemies, my assailants,
who stumble and fall."

"Not a very celebratory hymn," Getorius whispered to Arcadia, "but then the Vandal capture of Carthage has dampened everyone's morale."

"What could have happened if we hadn't discovered the papyri would have been much worse." Arcadia shuddered and grasped his arm tightly. "I'm so nervous, Getorius. My stomach is totally out of balance."

"Everything will be fine, *cara*," Getorius reassured her, not entirely convinced. The procession wound its way to the apse, as the final verse of the psalm echoed in throughout the nave.

"Wait for the Lord, be strong, take courage
and wait for the Lord."

Deacons and presbyters seated themselves on marble benches set around the altar. Bishop Chrysologos moved behind the table, raised his hands to a prayer position, and intoned a greeting to the congregation.

"*Dominus vobiscum*. The Lord be with you."

"And with your spirit," the people responded.

Tranquillus knelt before the altar platform and chanted, "*Introibo ad altare Dei*...I will go unto the altar of God."

The rite continued with the bishop asking God's blessings on the catechumens, and then with petitions for the sick, the imprisoned, slaves condemned to penal labor, and finally for deliverance from further depredations by the Vandals.

A deacon went to the marble pulpit to read from the prophet Isaiah.

"The people who walked in darkness have seen a great light.
Upon those who dwelt in the land of gloom a light has shone."

One by one the other deacons arose and held their flaming wicks down to light the oil lamps and other candles until, by the end of the reading, the apse area was ablaze with light.

"I've been imagining Brenos here if we hadn't discovered the papyrus," Arcadia leaned over to whisper to Getorius. "I wonder at what point in the readings he intended to reveal the will?"

"The prophecy had to do with a gospel of John. It would make sense if the first reading were taken from an epistle of Peter's, since the letter was forged to look like it came from the Apostle. Brenos probably would have selected the texts to reinforce his revelation of the will, then, in a homily, explained the role of his Gallicans as its protectors and executors."

The deacon at the pulpit announced a reading from a part of Peter's second letter, which he said dealt with both prophecy and the Hebrew people.

Getorius felt uneasy and whispered to Arcadia, "If Brenos recruited clergy other than Archdeacon Renatus to his Gallicans..." His thought was too disturbing to finish.

"But first note this," the deacon read from the letter, "no one can interpret any prophecy of Scripture by himself. For it was not through any human whim that men prophesied of old. Men indeed they were, yet impelled by the Holy Spirit, they spoke the words of God.

"But the Hebrews had false prophets as well as true, and you likewise will have false teachers among you. They will import dissenters, disowning the very Master who brought them, and bringing swift disaster on their own heads."

"That can't be the reading the abbot would have chosen," Getorius whispered. "It refutes his own case for believing his prophecy. Who could have...?" He glanced toward Galla Placidia. She had been looking at him, and now turned away. Was it a trick of the light, or was her mouth curved in the trace of a smile? "The Gothic Queen..."

Arcadia pulled at his sleeve. "Getorius, what are you muttering about? Sing the response."

"A holy day has dawned upon us.
 Come you nations, and adore the Lord,
 Today a great light has come upon the earth.'"

Tranquillus came to the pulpit to announce that the Nativity reading would be taken from the Testament of John, which explained the mystery of the Father's love as revealed in Jesus.

"In the beginning the Logos, the Word, was, and the Word was with God…"

The text was familiar; both Getorius and his wife had read and heard it many times. Now both could anticipate the point at which Brenos would have suddenly held up the Secundus Papyrus and announced that the prophecy of Christ's immeasurable love had been fulfilled: "So the Word became flesh and resided among us, and we had a view of his glory, a glory such as belongs to an only-begotten son from a Father; and he was full of undeserved kindness and love."

The abbot would then have read the terms of the Nazarene's will as 'proof' of the love John mentioned. In the pandemonium that would have followed the first stunned silence, it was conceivable that Ravenna's Judean quarter would have been attacked that same night by angry protesters.

⁂

The service ended with Bishop Chrysologos escorting the imperial family out through a side entrance. Maximin was lost in the crowd of officials. When Getorius and Arcadia came out the front entrance with the other people, the senator's carriage was gone.

The couple walked in silence to the corner of the Via Basilicae and the Honorius, and Arcadia took her husband's arm. "Is the nightmare over, Getorius?"

He shrugged. "You were probably right in thinking that Galla Placidia has burned the Gallican charter, and Theokritos' test results."

"That still bothers me."

"What?"

"Theokritos. Do you think he truly believed the will was genuine? I...I'd come to like him."

"I didn't read his conclusions, but for the tests he used papyrus scraps that were the same age. A monastic forger would have access to similar manuscript pages. While I was detained, I did some research on that Gnostic amulet Theokritos wore. Abraxas was the name of an armed rooster figure, with serpents for legs...some kind of protective pagan daemon. The cock was sacred to the sun god because he greeted dawn and banished the evil forces of the night."

"Theokritos was too intelligent to believe all that," Arcadia retorted. "I think the amulet was just a pagan curiosity for him."

"I guess I'd like to believe that he was impartial in judging the authenticity of what he called his Secundus Papyrus."

"A church council would have eventually ruled against it, wouldn't it?"

"Probably, but these Gallicans might have consolidated their power by then...even convinced enough believers on the council to overrule the truth."

Arcadia shuddered at the possibility, and drew her cape closer around her body. "I'm frightened that there might have been so many involved. Will they—or someone—try something like this again?"

"You might as well ask if there'll be sick people at the clinic tomorrow. Some people's need for power is as unexplainable as...as why some wounds heal and other don't."

After walking along the Honorius toward their villa for a time, Arcadia asked, "Will we see Rabbi Zadok again?"

"I'm not sure. He'll have to deal with the anti-Judean laws Nathaniel mentioned. I just wish he had told me more about the murders he and my father solved."

"His mind was on dealing with the effects the forged will would have on his people if it were released."

"I suppose."

When Getorius guided Arcadia around street puddles across from the old forum, she looked over at the temple of Fortuna. The pagan building was dark in contrast to the Ursiana, which had been brightly lit with lamps and candles, but nearby bonfires brought a golden glint to the bronze letters of the inscription.

"Divine Fortune, you—and Saint Cosmas—did smile on me," Arcadia murmured.

"What did you say, *cara*?"

She squeezed her husband's arm more tightly. "Nothing, really."

At the corner of the Via Theodosius, Getorius had paused to watch children playing around fires in the marketplace, when he heard a distant but familiar sound.

"Did you hear that?" he asked Arcadia.

"What, Getorius?"

"I'd swear on Aesculapius that I just heard a rooster announcing the dawn. It must be the reflection from all the fires on the low clouds making it mistake the time of day."

"The false dawn of another deceiver." Arcadia laughed and pulled Getorius across the street, toward their villa. "It may be late, but I'm going to get that copy of Ovid out again so we can read parts of it together."

"In the bathhouse pool?"

"Maybe not there, at least not tonight. But I do feel safe inside that warm little octagonal universe," Arcadia admitted. "That day we examined Behan—after we came home and made love in the pool—I had this uneasy feeling, a kind of premonition that Ravenna was not as secure as it seemed behind its walls and swamps. They might keep barbarians out, but that night I imagined enemies inside the city who could destroy our world."

"You were right, *cara*. Those Gallicans weren't imaginary foes."

"That's what's so frightening."

Getorius guided his wife around the corner of their street. "Senator Maximin's mother admitted to me that she worried because he had become too ambitious. If the senator was part of the Gallican League, he was clever enough not to go down with them. Yet he may try something else. "

"Getorius, there's our house. Let's forget all this and give

Childibert, Silvia and Brisios the Nativity gifts I have ready for them and their families. We—and Ravenna—actually have much to be thankful for on this festival night."

THE END

About the Author

Albert Noyer

With degrees in art, art education and the humanities, Albert Noyer's career includes working in commercial and fine art, teaching in the Detroit Public Schools and at private colleges. He lives in New Mexico, and has previously published another historical mystery, *The Saint's Day Deaths*.